VICIOUS
CIRCLE

VICIOUS CIRCLE

A NOVEL OF COMPLICITY

ROBERT LITTELL

THE OVERLOOK PRESS
WOODSTOCK & NEW YORK

First published in paperback in 2006 by
The Overlook Press, Peter Mayer Publishers, Inc.
Woodstock & New York

WOODSTOCK:
One Overlook Drive
Woodstock, NY 12498
www.overlookpress.com
[for individual orders, bulk and special sales, contact our Woodstock office]

NEW YORK:
141 Wooster Street
New York, NY 10012

LONDON:
Gerald Duckworth & Co. Ltd.
90-93 Cowcross Street, London EC1M 6BF
inquiries@duckworth-publishers.co.uk
www.ducknet.co.uk

Cataloging-in-Publication Data is available from the Library of Congress.

Book design and type formatting by Bernard Schleifer
Manufactured in the United States of America
ISBN-10 1-58567-926-7/ISBN-13 978-1-58567-926-3
10 9 8 7 6 5 4 3 2 1

For Emir and Alma

*In hope that when they are old enough
to read this book the Israelis and the Palestinians
will be living in peace*

Behold, thou shalt bear a son, and shalt call his
name Ishmael . . . And he will be a wild man;
his hand will be against every man, and every
man's hand against him . . . And Hagar bare
Abram a son.

Genesis 16

And God said, Sarah thy wife shall bear thee a
son and thou shalt call his name Isaac. And as
for Ishmael, I have blessed him and will mul-
tiply him exceedingly . . . But my covenant
will I establish with Isaac.

Genesis 17

VICIOUS CIRCLE

SOMETIME IN THE RECENT PAST

THE SETTING SUN SCORED THE NAVIGATOR'S LINE BETWEEN SKY and sea, drawing blood, flinging long shadows inland on the flat Levantine coast. Flecks of last light chipped off the gold leaf of the Dome of the Rock on the Temple Mount. Not far away, a panel truck with the hand painted logo "Kosher Pizza" and "We Deliver" written in Hebrew on both sides crawled along a street on the French Hill, a small Jewish neighborhood built on the north-eastern slope of Jerusalem after the Six Day War. The driver, a young woman with short cropped hair and wrap-around sunglasses that masked her eyes but drew attention to the smallpox scars that disfigured an otherwise handsome face, pulled up next to a bus stop. Rolling down the window, checking an address on her clipboard, she asked a teenage girl waiting for a number four bus for directions to the apartment building on Etzel Street where students from Hebrew University on Mount Scopus rented rooms. "You're on Etzel Street," the girl told her in Hebrew. "The numbers are hard to make out after sunset. The building you want is the second one down from the top of the hill on your right." The girl, who was wearing a short skirt and a body hugging turtleneck sweater, snickered. "What makes kosher pizza kosher?" she demanded. With a shrill laugh, she supplied the answer to her own question. "I suppose it means some Orthodox Rabbi who won't touch a female of the species when she's menstruating blessed the bacon."

The young woman driving the panel truck gnawed on her lower lip. "I only deliver," she said. "I don't justify."

"You speak Hebrew with an accent," remarked the girl waiting for the bus. "Where are you from?"

"I'm a Yemenite Jew."

"Where in Yemen?" the girl asked but the young woman had already thrown the panel truck into gear and started up the hill. Two apartment buildings from the top she swung into the driveway that led to the front door of tarnished brass and rain-stained glass and cut the motor. She rapped twice against the partition behind her shoulder and said softly, in Arabic, "God is great, Yussuf. We are arrived."

A young man dressed in a zippered yellow jumpsuit with "Kosher Pizza" embroidered over the breast pocket emerged from the rear of the panel truck carrying a boxed pizza and a delivery ticket. At the front door he pushed the buzzer to an apartment on the second floor known to be rented to half a dozen students from Hebrew University. "Pizza delivery," Yussuf said in Hebrew when a female voice responded. The student assumed one of her roommates had ordered pizza and dispatched an electric current to the lock on the front door, which instantly clicked open. Yussuf held the door for the nearly blind doctor who had been in the back of the panel truck with him. The doctor, wearing windowpane-thick eyeglasses with wire frames and tapping a long thin bamboo cane on the pavement before him, followed Yussuf through the shabby lobby and up the stairs, careful to stay half a floor behind him.

At the fourth floor Yussuf pushed open the fire door; the doctor, a heavy-set man, on the short side with short-cropped hair, remained out of sight on the landing. At the far end of the long and narrow corridor a burly Israeli wearing aviator's sunglasses and an open necked sport shirt outside his slacks tipped his folding metal chair off the wall onto its four legs. Yussuf stopped under one of the corridor lights to consult the delivery ticket. "Which door is four-sixteen?" he called in Hebrew to the Israeli.

"This is four-sixteen," the Israeli replied, "but nobody told me about a pizza delivery."

Yussuf started toward the Israeli, who rose to his feet and reached behind his back to grip the butt of the revolver wedged into his belt. Holding the pizza in his left hand, Yussuf said amiably, "Somebody

owes me thirty-eight shekels," and he offered the delivery ticket to
the Israeli, who towered over him by a good head.

The Israeli, with his giant right fist wrapped around the butt of
the revolver, accepted the delivery ticket with his left hand. He made
the mistake of taking his eyes off the delivery man for a moment. He
noticed "Apt 416" written in ink immediately under the address on
Etzel Street. He saw the name of the young American woman who
rented the apartment, Goodman, on the top of the delivery ticket.
And then his eyes went sightless as the thin dagger with the tapered
blade that Arab farmers used to kill fowl plunged between the second
and third rib into his heart, severing the pulmonary valve, drawing
blood, cutting off life.

Catching the bodyguard under an armpit, Yussuf lowered him
back onto the folding chair, then patted the pockets of his slacks in
search of the key to the apartment. He found it as the doctor, his
bamboo cane scraping the surface of the linoleum along the wall,
came up behind him. Holding the bodyguard's revolver in his left
hand, Yussuf slipped the key into the lock and noiselessly opened the
door to four-sixteen. He quickly dragged the corpse through the door
and propped it up in a sitting position against the Syrian camel sad-
dle in the entranceway. The doctor rested one hand on Yussuf's
shoulder and followed him down the hallway to the bedroom.
Grunts of exertion came from behind the door, as if it led to a gym-
nasium. Yussuf turned the knob and opened the door and stepped
into the room, which was lighted by Palestinian rush candles and
perfumed with incense. Except for the large mattress on the floor, the
room was unfurnished. Two naked figures appeared to be wrestling
on the mattress. The former general, now Minister without portfolio
in the coalition government, was flat on his back, his skin glistening
with perspiration as the American woman, his mistress for the past
seven months, worked her lean body up and back, then down and
forward, above him. The Minister must have caught a glimpse of
shadows flickering on the wall because he tried to push the woman
off just as Yussuf, reaching over her shoulder, slit her throat. She collapsed onto her lover's body. The sticky rivulet of blood spurting
from her neck soaked into the sweaty tangle of gray hair on his chest.

Yussuf, leaning over the mattress, punched the dagger through the man's right palm, impaling his hand to the mattress, then aimed the revolver at his right eye. The Minister, whose courage in combat was legendary in Israel, managed a hoarse whisper. "Fuck you, whoever you are," he muttered, breathing hard from the pain. The doctor, kneeling on the carpet, began to probe the Minister's skull behind the ear, searching with the tips of delicate fingers for the distinctive knob of bone. When he found it he produced a pearl-handled Beretta from the inside breast pocket of the double-breasted suit jacket he wore over his white robe. Knowing the Minister understood Arabic, he recited a passage from the Holy Qur'an. "*Whoso judges not according to what God has sent down—they are the unbelievers. And therein We proscribed for them: A life for a life, an eye for an eye, a nose for a nose, an ear for an ear, a tooth for a tooth, and for wounds retaliation.*"

He worked the slide on the pistol, chambering the first round, then pressed the tip of the barrel to the spot immediately under the knob of bone and pulled the trigger. The Beretta, chosen by the doctor because of its small caliber, barely made a sound as it dispatched a bullet into the Minister's skull. There was a reflexive muscular spasm from the brain-dead man, then the utter stillness that suggested the absence of life.

Rising to his feet, retrieving his bamboo cane, the doctor made his way to the window and tugged aside the cheap curtain thumb tacked to the sash. He could make out the blur of the full moon rising over the Judean hills. "Shadows are all I can see," he whispered as Yussuf joined him at the window.

Yussuf said, "At this hour shadows are all anyone can see."

"Look into the shadows with your youthful eyes and tell me what you see."

"In the near distance I see the shadows of the Judean desert."

"And beyond?"

"Beyond the Judean desert I see the surface of the Dead Sea silvery with the pale light of the full moon."

"Look further."

"Beyond the Dead Sea I see the deep shadows of the hills of Moab in Jordan."

The doctor nodded. "In the Jewish bible, it is said the descendants of the Prophet Ibrahim's nephew, who was called Lot, inhabited the kingdom of Moab."

Yussuf seemed taken aback. "You have read the Jewish bible?"

"Clearly, the Prophet himself, who was the Messenger of God, was familiar with the Jewish bible through his contacts with the Jewish tribes in Yathrib, the oasis that became known as Medinat an-Nabi, or more simply, Medina." The doctor turned away from the window. "Clearly," he murmured, following another thought as he moved like a phantom through the rushlight toward the door, "God is most great who permits His blind servant to smite the enemies of Islam."

The predawn raid on the apartment in the city the Arabs called Nablus and the Jews called Schrem was to be Elihu's swansong—the elite Mossad commando team that he'd led for more years than he cared to remember had already held a raucous dinner in a seaside restaurant in Jaffa to celebrate his promotion to *katsa*. From now on Elihu, a veteran of twenty-thee raids—including the famous one led by Ariel Barak into the heart of Beirut—would run agents from a secret Mossad bureau in Jaffa as opposed to personally leading them into combat.

The five soldiers, dressed, like Elihu, in frayed Arab robes with *kafias* wrapped loosely around their heads, were superstitious—last missions were notoriously jinxed for the individual who was retiring from active service. To a man the team wanted Elihu to stay with the Mercedes-Benz taxi and survey the deserted street, but he wasn't buying into that; he had led his raids from the usual position of the commanding officer in an Israeli military unit, which is to say from the front. His last mission would be no exception.

The team parked the taxi in the alley next to a closed petrol station. Elihu motioned for the driver to stay with the car; if there was any activity in the street, he would alert the others. Each member of the team had a tiny speaker in one ear and a small microphone attached to the cuff of his robe at the wrist. Now they heard Elihu's tinny whisper in their ear. "In the Torah there is a formula that instructs Jews how to deal with the assassination of our Minister and the murder of the American girl twelve days ago. *And thine eye shall not pity, but life shall go for life, eye for eye, tooth for tooth, hand for hand.*"

The men checked their weapons—three carried Uzis with folding metal stocks and clips taped back to back for fast changing; Elihu and his second in command, Dovid Dror, were armed with Russian Makarov pistols fitted with silencers—and set off down the deserted Street of the Prophet. Walking soundlessly on their Adidas basketball sneakers, they passed the entrance to the apartment building and the shuttered windows of the mini-market and turned down an alleyway reeking from the overflowing metal garbage bins. At the back of the apartment building they scaled a wooden fence and jumped into a well-tended garden filled with bougainvillea clinging to an arched steel trellis. One of the men picked the lock on the coal chute and pulled open the slanting wooden doors. Signaling for the others to put on their night vision goggles, Elihu dropped into the coal bin and led the way through several vaulted brick-walled basement rooms to a narrow staircase.

The team's specialist on locks tried half a dozen skeleton keys before he found one that worked in the old lock. Motioning for his men to wait, Elihu stopped on the first step and listened intently. Satisfied with the quality of the silence, he pointed at the fifth member of the team, who immediately crouched next to the door as Elihu led the others up the staircase. At the third floor the team's locksmith came up with a skeleton key that fitted into the hallway door. In the airless corridor filled with the odor of fresh paint, the raiding party took up positions on either side of the steel door that led to the apartment of the local head of the Al Aksa Martyrs Brigades.

Studying the door through his goggles, Elihu identified the two dead bolts mentioned in the Mossad pre-mission briefing, then glanced at his men, all of whom nodded. Raising his Makarov, he shot out the two locks and shouldered through the door. One member of the team crouched at the door of the apartment to cover the hallway. Elihu's second in command and the other raider swept into the apartment behind their leader. The sound of a woman calling in Arabic, "Mustafah, is that you going to the toilet?" came from one room. With Dror covering his back, Elihu kicked open the door with the poster of the Al Aksa mosque taped to it and burst into a bedroom. A fleshy woman sleeping on the four-poster bed crushed a pillow to the bosom of her nightdress hoping it would protect her from a terror she could hear but not see. The bald, rail-thin middle-aged man in gaudy pajamas lying next to her groped wildly for the pistol on the night table with his only hand; he'd lost the other years before when a letter bomb he was preparing exploded prematurely. Elihu stepped up to the bed and shot him once behind the ear, then fired a second shot through the palm of his hand so there would be no doubt about who had delivered retribution. The woman screamed. The scream seemed to echo through the apartment, then the building, then the neighborhood, which started to come to life.

"Lights visible all over the Street of the Prophet," the team member at the taxi calmly reported into Elihu's ear.

"We're finished here," Elihu said into his microphone as he backed out of the bedroom. Two women servants, with blankets pulled tightly around their bodies, stood at the entrance to the kitchen staring into the Uzi of one of the raiders.

"Go, go, go," Elihu cried into his microphone.

The commandos retreated from the apartment in the order they had decided on when they rehearsed the raid in a hangar on their base. Elihu brought up the rear. Heads appeared in windows above them as the Israeli commandos raced under the bougainvillea in the garden. Angry voices shouted in Arabic into the night. Elihu detonated a smoke grenade to cover the retreat as his men scaled the wooden fence. In the alley he barked another order into the microphone. "Car to the mini-market."

From the Street of the Prophet came the screech of brakes. The raiders flung themselves into the taxi, which began to move before the doors slammed shut. The Mercedes, running without headlights, careened around a corner as shots rang out behind them. The three men in the back seat ducked as a bullet shattered the car's rear window, showering them with shards of glass. At the end of the narrow street the driver spun the wheel, spilling the car down a slope onto a dirt track that ran through a garbage dump dubbed "Gehenna" on the Israeli battle map. "Headlights," Elihu snapped. The driver flicked on the low beams in time to slalom around the goats grazing in the next field, their front legs tethered to prevent them from wandering away during the night.

Elihu looked over his shoulder. All of Nablus seemed to be lit up. From the minaret of a mosque on the edge of the city a hand-cranked siren began to wail. A swirl of dust, rising like a sandstorm toward the waning sliver of moon, trailed behind the taxi as it raced between the two Army jeeps stationed along the route of the exfiltration. They were almost home free. The taxi bounced up an embankment and turned onto a paved road. Only when they had driven past the two tanks, with sergeants saluting them from the open turrets, did Elihu order the driver to slow down. He switched on the two-way radio to check in with the base as the men, mentally exhausted, slumped in their seats. From the radio came the low growl of the Mossad operations commander. "Congratulations on the successful conclusion of your last combat mission," he said after Elihu had sent the coded signal indicating the target had been killed and the raiders had escaped unhurt.

"Looks like you broke the jinx, Elihu," Dror, the second in command, called nervously from the back of the car.

But Elihu, watching the lights of Jerusalem glimmer in the darkness ahead, was lost in thought. "We must never forget," he said softly. He was barely aware of talking aloud.

The men in the back seat exchanged looks. "What must we never forget?" Dror asked quietly.

Elihu could have been speaking to himself. "That we live in a corner of the planet where absolutely no one, least of all the hundred million Arabs around us, respects weakness. Which is why, when the last verse of the Pentateuch is read, we chant: *Hazak, hazak, ve-nit'-hazak—Be strong, be strong, and we shall be strengthened.*"

SOMETIME IN THE NEAR FUTURE

An Excerpt from the Harvard "Running History" Project:

Testing, three, two, one. *If you don't know where you're going, any road will take you there. (This particular travel tip is from Lewis Carroll.) The voice level work for you? Okay, here goes nothing. My name—*

Excuse me a moment. Who? Have him get back to me. I'm going to be tied up until lunchtime. With the exception of the President, don't put anyone through until I'm finished here.

Sorry. Where was I?

My name is Zachary Taylor Sawyer, Zack to my friends, Old Rough and Ready to the people who associate me with my illustrious ancestor, the twelfth President of the United States, Zachary Taylor, and think that, like him, I ride rough-shod over anyone who gets in my way. I'm pushing fifty-five from the right side; will be for a few more months. I taught history and political science at Harvard until eleven months ago, which is when I was invited to come to Washington as the Special Assistant to the President for Middle Eastern Affairs. For the record, this morning I'm participating in Harvard's "Running History" Project, under which senior government officials agree to record history as it's being made on the condition that these tapes will not be released to the public for twenty-five years. The object of the project, as I understand it, is to give future historians access to the raw material behind the decision making process—the endless battles over turf, the position papers that take no position, the brain storming sessions where original ideas are shot down by time servers who have no alternatives to offer, the furious disagreements that are shoved under the carpet to give the impression that the highest level of government speaks with one voice.

You really think I'm being cynical? I thought I was being accurate. Speaking as a historian, I suspect that history tells us more about ourselves than the past—it tells us how we distorted what we chose to remember. But that's another story.

Where to begin? I s'pose the best thing would be to describe where we're at, and then tell you how we got there. Where we're at is nine days from the signing of the peace treaty between the Israelis and the Palestinians, and the creation of a viable Palestinian state within mutually agreed frontiers. The person who was on his way out when you came in was the White House protocol chief, Manny Krisher. We were ironing out the last wrinkles in the signing ceremony. Manny was generous enough to say that he didn't know how I'd convinced the Israelis and Palestinians to sit down around the same table, much less sign a treaty of peace.

I told Manny what I usually tell people who ask me how I did it. It was a matter of timing. I came on the scene long enough after 11 September for the world to become weary of Bush's endless war on terror and the so-called clash of civilizations—the materialistic and secular West crusading against a spiritual and fundamentalist Islam—that was alienating Muslims around the globe. I came on the scene when Wahabi fundamentalists posed a credible threat to the Saudi monarchy and the price of oil out of Arabia hit one hundred dollars a barrel, driving up inflation and driving down economic growth in every industrialized country. I came on the scene when European leaders—as his Excellency, the British Prime Minister, bluntly told Bush's successor in my presence— were ready to reassess their historic ties to America if Washington didn't rein in the Israelis and get them to agree to the existence of a viable Palestinian state, which, in the British view, would pull the rug out from under the Wahabis and stabilize Saudi Arabia and bring down the price of oil.

No, that part of the meeting didn't make it onto the pages of the New York Times *or the* Washington Post, *and for good reason—it would have scared the bejesus out of voters across Europe. The British PM, the German Chancellor, the French President, all over here for that U.N. summit, sounded like Delphic oracles who had coordinated their message, which essentially was that, unlike the U.S.A., their countries had enormous Muslim populations that might erupt like Mount Vesuvius if the Palestinians didn't get their homeland, and soon.*

Good question. Were they exaggerating? You know, even exaggerated perceptions have a way of shaping reality, which was the case here. In essence the European leaders had swallowed the jihadist's bait; without admitting it in so many words, they were blaming Israel for the existence of Islamic fundamentalism in the world. The fact of the matter is that the Islamic fundamentalists were around before the sovereign state of Israel was created in 1948 and they'll be around after the sovereign state of Palestine comes into existence. The fact of the matter is that the impoverishment of the Arab masses and their lack of hope that things will get better before they get worse—which is the stuff off of which Islamic fundamentalism feeds—will still be around when the struggle over this sliver of Holy Land winds down.

Yes, yes, I have to agree: they will certainly come up with another festering issue to rally their troops if we manage to solve the hundred-year Israeli-Palestinian conflict. But here's the beauty of it all—here's what I convinced the President of: Just because the European analysis was driven by an imperfect grasp of Islam and the historical forces at work in the world doesn't mean we shouldn't take them at their word, or look as if we are. In pressuring the Israelis, Washington would be seen to be responding to Europe's legitimate concerns. And solving the Israeli-Palestinian conflict—even if it's not the antidote to Islamic fundamentalism's drive to restore the seventh century caliphate and what the Koran calls Hakimiyyat Allah or God's rule—could only serve America's long-term interests in the sense that it will become more difficult, if not impossible, to blame us for Palestinian tribulations.

I'm laughing because you're right. As the President was kind enough to point out at her most recent press conference, a good deal more than luck was involved in getting the two sides to the negotiating table. Let's start at the start. It's no state secret that I was summoned to Washington by a President who'd been intrigued by my book Breaking Vicious

Circles. *She seemed as much impressed by the tone of the book as its contents. As she told me the first time we met, she didn't come across many Middle East mavens, her husband included, who were as detached as I was.*

Along with my reputation for deadpan detachment, I brought to the job the hard-nosed heresy that the way out was to raise the stakes. Even before the European leaders drove the point home with their Delphic chant, the political climate was ripe for heresy. The rash of terrorist attacks on Israeli cities and Israel's tit-for-tat retaliatory raids on the Palestinian territories were still fresh in everyone's memory. When another terrorist attack struck the continental United States a month after the new President was sworn in—I'm talking about that crop-dusting plane that attempted to spray Indianapolis with anthrax spores; deaths would have been in the thousands instead of the dozens if the winds hadn't carried off most of the anthrax—anti-Israel sentiment, never far beneath the surface, turned up in the public discourse. We all heard it—on the TV talk shows, at cocktail parties, in elevators. The sentence usually began with some variant of the phrase, "If it weren't for the Jews . . ." Taking advantage of the fact that the general public was fed up with America getting blamed for the Israeli problem, Congress passed and the President signed into law—despite intense opposition from the Jewish lobby and its allies on the evangelical Christian right—a measure doing away with tax deductions for contributions to organizations that distributed money to foreign governments or entities. Overnight donations to the United Jewish Appeal dried up. When the Israelis orchestrated a not-very-subtle campaign against the sitting President, the other shoe dropped: acting on my advice, the United States suspended the delivery of arms to the two leading recipients of foreign aid, Israel and Egypt.

You remember what happened as well as I do. The move, which would have been unthinkable only a few months before, caused a Richter-scale quake in Middle East politics. The Israeli Air Force flies American jets. Without spare parts, they would have to begin cannibalizing planes in order to keep others in the air. The Israeli government spumed for several days and then imploded, elections were held and a coalition of the more moderate secular and religious parties cobbled together a slim majority in the Knesset. Which is when I began shuttling between Jerusalem and Cairo and Riyadh and what was left of the Palestinian Authority's headquarters in Ramallah after repeated Israeli air strikes. Brandishing the usual carrots and sticks, I persuaded the two sides to grudgingly agree to cease fire. The Palestinian Authority, under intense pressure from the Egyptians and the Saudis, who were under intense pressure from European capitals, finally got serious about jailing Hamas and Islamic Jihad and Fatah and Al Aksa activists and shutting down the suicide bombings; Israel, fearful of losing American support for the first time since the creation of the Jewish state, pulled its Army out of the Palestinian cities on the West Bank it had occupied, ordered its soldiers to stop shooting rubber bullets at children throwing stones and gradually opened the borders to Palestinians who held permits to work in Israel; within weeks twenty thousand Palestinians were crossing into Israel daily, and returning home at night with pay envelopes in their pockets. When the cease fire held, the belligerents were dragged—kicking and screaming, according to the Washington Post—to the negotiating table at the Mt. Washington Hotel in New Hampshire, the scene of the Bretton Woods Conference after World War II.

Which pretty much brings us to where we're at this morning. If the cease fire holds long enough for us to get this damned treaty signed, the hope is that the silent majorities on both sides will come out of the woodwork—

Hold on a sec, CNN's put a map of Israel on the screen. Can you turn up the volume? Thanks.

". . . we'll go live to our correspondent in Jerusalem. Joel?"

"When the two sides initialed the Mt. Washington peace treaty, forty-one days ago, everyone in Israel took a deep breath and held it. Now, with nine days to go until the actual signing, the silence is deafening. People tend to jump when a car backfires or a door slams or an ambulance siren wails in some distant part of this ancient city. As a senior American diplomat put it to one of my colleagues in Washington: 'If a shot is fired, you can bet your bottom dollar it's going be heard 'round the world.' Joel Plummer, reporting from an eerily quiet Jerusalem."

Okay, you can turn it down.

For the record, the senior American diplomat is none other than yours truly, Zachary Taylor Sawyer.

ONE

THE *khamsin*, A BLISTERING WIND FROM THE FURNACE OF HELL, swept up from the endless reaches of the Sahara. It was the earliest *khamsin* in memory and the most brutal in years, and was taken by some as a portent of plagues to come. Like a tidal wave, the bone-dry gusts seemed to pick up speed and mass as they spilled across the Suez rut into the Sinai and the tangled *wadis* of the Israeli Negev beyond, scalding the desert, stirring the sand into storms that disfigured the face of the late afternoon sun. Its force spent, the *khamsin* curled westward to break against the wedge of land on the shore of the Mediterranean that the Israelis call *Aza*, the Palestinians call *Ghazeh* and the world knows as Gaza.

Their windows closed and caked with sand, two civilian automobiles—a dirty yellow 1950s Chevrolet with tail fins and a baby-blue Nissan station wagon—barreled down the buckling asphalt road from Yad Mordechai, an Israeli kibbutz founded just outside Gaza after World War Two by survivors of the Warsaw Ghetto uprising. In the distance an Army jeep, its needle-like machine gun sweeping the orange groves inside Gaza, could be seen patrolling the dirt track that ran along the Israeli side of the chain link fence separating Israel from the Gaza Strip. "To live by the Torah isn't enough," the Rabbi was telling the journalist in the back seat of the station wagon. His voice was hoarse from giving interviews and saying the same thing over and over—though each time he managed to come at the material with an ardent freshness, which left his audience with the impression that the Rabbi was inventing himself as he went along. "Stop me if I'm talk-

ing too fast for you to take notes. We must follow God's commandment to the Jewish people and settle every square inch of the land of
the Torah. Without the lava of the land burning through the soles of
our shoes, we are spiritual cripples. The land is a means to an end;
the end is redemption of the Jewish people and the coming of the
Messiah."

The journalist, a lanky American in his late thirties named Max
Sweeney, sat hunched over the coffee-stained pages of a child's copy
book, scratching notes as the Fiddler on the Roof (as he had nicknamed the Rabbi the moment he spotted his bulging eyes and dancing side curls) rambled on. "You were one of the founders of the
Jewish settlement Beit Avram, in the hills above Hebron—"

The Rabbi cut him off. "Hebron is where it all began," he said.
He removed his perfectly round steel-rimmed eyeglasses, dragged
an enormous handkerchief from the breast pocket of his double-
breasted jacket and started to clean the thick lenses. "Read the
twenty-third chapter of Genesis," he plunged on, his cataract-
scarred eyes agleam with maniacal energy. "It's where Abraham purchased the first dunams of holy land; where David, commanding
Israel's hosts, set up his capital before moving his act to Jerusalem;
where our patriarchs Abraham and Isaac and Jacob are buried." The
Rabbi carefully hooked the eyeglasses over one oversized ear and
then the other and watched the point of Sweeney's pen scratching
across the page; even with eyeglasses, the Rabbi's vision was so poor
that the handwriting looked like the hills and valleys made by a
stylus on a polygraph. It occurred to him that he hadn't verified
Sweeney's credentials; for all he knew, the American journalist
could be working for the CIA. Not that it mattered; he'd take whatever press coverage he could get. "Anyone who thinks we should
abandon Hebron," the Rabbi continued, his voice a strained rasp,
"is defying God. That's the bulletin I came to deliver to the Jews
meeting in Yad Mordechai today."

"If the Israelis and the Palestinians wind up signing this Mt.
Washington peace treaty that the Americans rammed down their
throats," Sweeney ventured, "you'll be obliged to leave Hebron, along
with a hundred other settlements in the West Bank."

"There's still nine days to go before the ceremony," the Rabbi noted. "Anything could happen between now and then."

"The cease fire has held up for three months."

The Rabbi snickered. "Arafat's successor turns out to have more brain matter between his ears than Arafat. He'll keep his people in line and get as much as he can through negotiations, then he'll take a deep breath and come back for more, count on it."

"It's no secret that you're dead set against the peace process," Sweeney persisted. "How far would you be willing to go to derail it?"

The Rabbi coughed up a ruthless laugh that struck Sweeney as being just shy of maniacal. "I'd convert to Islam if I thought it would put an end to this asinine government policy of trading holy land for profane peace."

The driver, a Russian-Jewish Zionist with a loaded Uzi submachine gun resting across his thighs, snorted in satisfaction. "Hell will freeze over before our Rabbi converts to Islam!"

In the front of the station wagon, Efrayim Blumenfeld, the young rabbinical student who served as the Rabbi's secretary, twisted around in his seat. "We're almost at the Ashqelon interchange," he announced.

The convoy sped past a corpulent Israeli Arab in a long gray robe riding an emaciated donkey and flailing away at the animal's flank with an olive branch. From the minaret of a dilapidated mosque in an Arab village set back from the road, the high-pitched voice of a *muezzin* calling the faithful to prayer boomed out from a loudspeaker. *"Allahu Akbar, Allahu Akbar."* The Rabbi, who had taught himself Arabic on the theory you were better armed if you spoke the language of your enemies, translated for the journalist. "He is saying that God is most great. He is saying, 'I witness that there is no god but Allah; I witness that Muhammad is His messenger.'" Gazing through the sand-stained window, the Rabbi didn't bother to mask his contempt. "Some messenger! Some message! But then what can you expect from the incoherent ranting of an illiterate camel driver?"

The journalist glanced at the Fiddler, who was kneading a purplish bruise on the pale skin of his forehead. "I've been meaning to ask you all day," Sweeney said, "how you hurt your head?"

"Praying at the Wailing Wall."

"You're making a joke."

"He beats his head against the Wall when he talks to God," the secretary explained over his shoulder. "It's the only time our Rabbi has ever come face to face with someone as stubborn as he is. In a manner of speaking, it drives him up the Wall."

The journalist, who was gathering material for a profile on West Bank Jewish militants in general and the Fiddler on the Roof in particular, waited for the laughter. When none came he understood the answer was serious and jotted it down. "It's a matter of record that the Jewish fundamentalist who assassinated Prime Minister Rabin in 1995 had been an early student of yours at Beit Avram," he said. "He was said to have been reading your book *One Torah, One Land* the night before he committed the crime."

"Hundreds of students have studied Torah at Beit Avram. Tens of thousands have read my book, which is about the unbreakable bond between *ha-aretz,* the land of Israel, and the Torah. What my students and readers do with this information is their business. It's not my fault if one of them decided to excarnate the Prime Minister."

"Excarnate?"

Efrayim turned in his seat belt. "Our Rabbi takes the Torah's injunction '*Thou shalt not kill'* to its logical conclusion—he won't even let the word *kill* pass his lips."

"Okay. Let's come at the question from another direction. There are rumors that your settlement, Beit Avram, is the home of the Jewish underground movement Keshet Yonatan, the Bow of Jonathan; that you are the spiritual leader of the movement and the guru to its mysterious leader who signs himself by the name of Ya'ir."

"'*From the blood of the slain, from the fat of the mighty, the bow of Jonathan turned not back.*'" The Rabbi, an amateur poker fanatic famous for playing his cards close to his vest, managed to produce a smile that transmitted no information; he could have been betting a straight flush or a pair of threes. "Two Samuel, chapter one, verse twenty-two. I would have thought a serious reporter for a serious newspaper had better things to do than check out cockamamie rumors."

The journalist absently brought his middle finger up to the small plastic device in his left ear; his drum had been ruptured when a mortar shell exploded next to his car in Beirut several wars back. His right ear had not been affected but his colleagues understood that he could only distinguish sound in his left ear with the help of the small plastic aid. "Are you denying there's a Jewish underground?" he asked. "Or are you denying you are its spiritual leader?"

The Rabbi, whose name was Isaac Apfulbaum, shrugged his gaunt shoulders. "Either. Or."

Up front the driver worked the windshield wipers and the sprinkler to clear sand from the window. The Ashqelon interchange with its transparent bus shelters on both sides and a swarm of hitchhiking soldiers loomed ahead. The driver pulled the station wagon onto the dirt shoulder and cut the motor. The Rabbi climbed out of the car and, with the American journalist trailing after him, walked over to a group of soldiers to shake the hand of each of them; to Sweeney's eye, the Rabbi looked like an American politician wading into a crowd of constituents to spread the gospel of his reelection. When the Rabbi offered his hand to a young Israeli officer, the soldier thrust his fists deep into his pockets. "I know who you are," he declared in Hebrew. He noticed someone he took for a journalist behind the Rabbi scribbling furiously in a copy book and switched to English. "You stand for everything I despise."

The Rabbi took the insult in stride; in the years since he had immigrated to Israel from the Crown Heights section of Brooklyn and, along with fourteen families from his Brooklyn congregation, founded Beit Avram, he had developed a thick skin. "I stand for the people of Israel on the land of Israel," he remarked tiredly. "I stand for God."

He turned away to accompany the journalist to his car, which he had parked across the road when they met that morning. "I am told you have a chip on your shoulder against the Jewish state," the Rabbi said. He angled his head, causing his thick eyeglasses to catch the light and turn opaque. He shifted his weight from one scuffed black shoe to the other. "I am told you write stories that are invariably anti-Israeli."

"If you think I slant my articles, why did you let me tag along with you today?"

The Rabbi studied Sweeney in the fading twilight. "As long as you spell my name correctly—it's I for Isaac Ap*ful*baum, with an f after the p—and quote me accurately, my arguments will resist your efforts to distort them. In a nutshell, I'm a religious Zionist. I have bad teeth because I'm too busy studying Torah to go to a dentist. I wear a hand-knitted *kippah* on the back of my head and would carry a gun if I could see well enough to shoot my enemies and not my friends. I am absolutely convinced that the creation of the State of Israel in 1948 was a religious event. I believe our victory in 1967, which reunited what you call the West Bank and we call the biblical provinces of Judea and Samaria with the rest of Israel, was the handiwork of God. For me, Genesis 17:8—where God gives Abraham and his seed *all* of the land of Canaan for an everlasting possession—is the heart of the heart of the Torah. For too long Jews were a people without a land, and Palestine was a land without a people. Now the people and the land have come together and nobody—not our crazy Israeli politicians, not the conscience-stricken Diaspora Jews, not the lunatic Islamic fundamentalists, not even a *goy* journalist with a chip on his shoulder—is going to separate them again."

The word *goy* struck Sweeney like a slap in the face. He snapped shut the copy book and slipped it into a pocket of his worn safari jacket. "There are good-thinking people, Jews as well as *goys*, who would argue that Palestine was never a land without a people. When the British counted noses in 1918, they found 700,000 Arabs and 56,000 Jews—"

"In the history of the world there has never been a Palestinian people," the Rabbi said flatly. "Jews have lived on this land for the last three thousand years, long before Islam's hooligans swept down from the Arabian desert to plunder Palestine." Squinting, he studied the bloated sun, which appeared to be snared in the barbed wire atop the chain link fence ringing an electricity station. "We could continue this discussion for hours, but I have to get back to Beit Avram for a meeting."

Neither man offered to shake hands. "Another time, perhaps," Sweeney said.

"Fax your article to my office. Then we'll see about a second interview."

The Rabbi turned on his heel and, splashing through an oil slick, crossed the road to the station wagon. The three young religious Jews serving as body guards flicked away their cigarettes, checked their weapons and climbed back into the Chevrolet. The driver, a reserve lieutenant in a reconnaissance unit when he wasn't studying Torah at Beit Avram, rolled down his window and called to the Russian-Jewish Zionist behind the wheel of the Rabbi's Nissan, "Stay close. Whatever happens, don't stop." Then, with the Chevrolet in the lead, the two cars sped off toward Beit Avram, a Jewish settlement of three hundred souls planted like a *yarmulke* atop a windswept Judean hill in the spine of mountains between the Mediterranean and the Dead Sea.

Both cars switched on their headlights as the twilight thickened into night. The Rabbi, worn out from the long day on the road, tried to cat nap in the station wagon's back seat but the headlights of oncoming cars kept him awake. "How long?" he called to the driver.

"Three quarters of an hour, an hour if we run into traffic."

Efrayim said, "It's not sure we'll get there in time for the meeting."

"My getting there," the Rabbi observed dryly, "will be the signal for the meeting to begin."

After a while Efrayim looked over his shoulder and whispered into the shadows of the back seat, "Rabbi, are you sleeping?"

"If I were sleeping I wouldn't have heard you ask if I were sleeping."

"Excuse me, Rabbi, but what did you mean this morning when you said prayer was a waste of time?"

"To pray is not the worst thing you can do with your time, but it's a waste of time in the sense that there are better things you can do."

"For instance?" Efrayim persisted.

A sixteen-wheel trailer truck roared past in the opposite direction. Apfulbaum waited until the noise subsided, and said, "My Rabbi in Brooklyn used to teach us that if the Torah didn't instruct Jews to pray, he wouldn't pray—he'd study Torah."

"So studying Torah is the best thing a Jew can do with his time?"

"Studying Torah and obeying God's commandment to settle all the land of the Torah, these are the best things a Jew can do."

"What if someone is already occupying the land of the Torah?"

"Do you remember what happened to the Amalek nation when it rose up against the Israelites fleeing Egypt?"

Efrayim, who had been studying Torah since he was a child, smiled brightly. "God instructed Moses to blot out their memory."

"And who has heard of an Amalek Liberation Organization today?" the Rabbi asked. He laughed under his breath at his own little joke.

Efrayim thought about this. "Rabbi?"

"What is it now?"

"If our demented Prime Minister goes ahead and signs that peace treaty in Washington, we'll have to give an awful lot of the land of the Torah back to the Palestinians. If we give back the land, how will we be able to obey God's commandment to settle all of the land of the Torah?"

"God will surely stay the Prime Minister's hand at the last moment."

"The way he stayed Abraham's hand when he was about to sacrifice his son Isaac?"

"Something along those lines."

Rounding a curve near the Zohar Reservoir, the headlights of the lead car swept over a white Volkswagen camping car parked up ahead at the side of the road. A tall religious Jew with side curls, wearing a black ankle-length coat and a black fedora, waved his arms over his head to flag them down. A young woman, also a religious Jew judging from her shawl and pill box hat and the long skirt that plunged to her ankles, stood nearby with her eyes downcast.

"*Haredim*," muttered the driver in the point car, using the Hebrew word for the ultra Orthodox Jews.

"Keep going," the young man sitting next to him ordered, but the driver of the Rabbi's station wagon was already honking his horn and slowing down, so they pulled up, too. The three young body-guards, their side curls and the ritual fringes of the *tallith katan* fly-ing in the dry gusts coming off the desert, cocked their Uzis as they stepped out of the Chevrolet.

The Rabbi's station wagon had come to a stop next to the camp-ing car. The Rabbi's Russian driver, his finger curled around the trig-ger of the Uzi concealed along the seam of his trousers, opened his door and stepped out onto the road. The Rabbi rolled down his win-dow. "What's the trouble?" he called in Yiddish to the religious Jew standing next to the parked Volkswagen.

"We ran out of benzene," the young woman, her face disfigured by smallpox scars, replied in Hebrew.

The tall young man in the ankle-length coat approached the Rabbi's car. "We are on our way back to Ashqelon," he explained, speaking Hebrew with an accent Apfulbaum couldn't immediately place. "Do you have a jerry can you could lend us? We will reimburse you for the benzene."

The driver of the Chevrolet came running back along the road. "Something's not right," he shouted. "They're speaking Hebrew instead of Yiddish—"

The warning—*Haredim* only spoke Hebrew when studying Torah or talking to God—came too late.

From the folds of her shawl the young woman whipped out an automatic pistol and, gripping it in both her hands, sent a hail of bullets plunging into the driver's chest. Gun shots erupted from the darkness at the side of the road, cutting down the two body guards standing next to the Chevrolet before they could squeeze off a round. The driver of the Rabbi's Nissan dove onto the asphalt and fired his Uzi in short bursts at the flashes at the side of the road until the clip ran out. He was trying to jam in a second clip taped back to back to the first when a grenade rolled across the road and exploded near his feet.

In the darkness and the confusion, one of the bodyguards from the Chevrolet, wounded in the head and stomach, managed to drag himself across the road into a tangle of underbrush at the shoulder.

Wiping the blood from his eyes with a forearm, he looked through the bushes. Two Mercedes-Benzes materialized out of the dunes at the side of the highway and screeched to a stop near the Volkswagen bus. In the glare of their headlights, figures in jeans and black turtleneck sweaters, their faces masked by black-and-white *kiffiyehs*, could be seen wrenching open the doors of the Rabbi's station wagon. Several Arabs dragged the Rabbi and his secretary from the Nissan and prodded them into the back seat of the first Mercedes. A heavy-set man, on the short side with short-cropped hair, came around in front of the Rabbi's station wagon. He was wearing a double-breasted suit jacket over a flowing white robe. The Nissan's headlights spilled his shadow down the road and onto the rear of the Chevrolet. The Arab dropped to one knee next to the body of the Russian driver, who was twitching in agony from the grenade explosion. When the twitching suddenly stopped, the Arab felt for the driver's pulse and, bending over, put his ear against the wounded man's mouth. He must have decided that the driver was still alive, because he seemed to probe with the tips of his fingers behind the Jew's ear as he drew a small pistol from the inside breast pocket of his suit jacket. He pressed the barrel of the pistol to a spot on the driver's skull. The hollow *phffffft* of a small-caliber weapon reached the ears of the wounded bodyguard hiding in the thicket. Close by, voices called out in Arabic. The beams of powerful flashlights danced on the road. One of the attackers opened a large pocket knife; the wounded bodyguard watching from the thicket could see light glinting off the blade as the Arab leaned over the body sprawled next to the Chevrolet. The other attackers started searching for the missing bodyguard. One of them came across a trail of blood on the asphalt and trained his flashlight on the thicket across the road. As he started toward the thicket, the headlights of a vehicle topped a rise a kilometer away.

The heavy-set Arab in the robe and suit jacket shouted orders. Two of the men in turtleneck sweaters lifted a wounded Arab into the back seat of the second Mercedes. Doors slammed. Low beamed yellow headlights flicked on as the two Mercedes careened off in the direction of Gaza.

TWO

THE TWO MERCEDES SPED ALONG A DIRT ROAD, FORDED A shallow stream at a spot marked by two logs driven into the bank and pulled up in an apple orchard. The lights strung along the top of a security fence around a kibbutz flickered in the distance; from the orchard, with a little imagination, it was easy to take the kibbutz for a cruise ship and the sea of impenetrable blackness around it for the Mediterranean. In the back seat of the first Mercedes, the Rabbi and his secretary, their wrists bound in front of them, their heads covered with leather hoods, waited in the darkness. Both men stiffened when they heard footsteps approaching. The heavy-set Arab with short cropped hair came up behind the car and nodded at one of the young men in turtleneck sweaters. "Cut open their sleeves," he ordered in Arabic.

The young man, whose name was Yussuf Abu Saleh, pulled out his pocket knife for the second time that night and, leaning into the back of the car, slit open the jacket and shirt sleeve on the left arm of each prisoner. The Rabbi's secretary, Efrayim, gasped. When his turn came, the Rabbi filled his lungs with air but said nothing.

From a small metal container, the Arab with the short-cropped hair, whom the others knew as "the Doctor," removed the two syringes he had prepared that afternoon. The Rabbi gritted his teeth and breathed heavily through his nostrils when he felt the needle prick his skin. As he slumped against his secretary, Efrayim cried out through his hood, "Oh God, you have executed him." When he felt the Doctor's fingers searching for a vein in his forearm, he started to tremble uncontrollably. As the needle pierced his skin he began to intone the Shema from the book of Deuteronomy: "*Shema yisra'el, adonai eloheynu . . . adonai—*" Then his head slumped forward onto his chest.

Four members of the raiding party carried the drugged prisoners over to the small delivery van parked next to a beat-up silver Suzuki with Israeli license plates. The van bore the logo "Fine Bedouin Robes and Carpets" printed in English on its sides. Each prisoner was crammed into a large straw hamper and covered with layers of robes and carpets. Then the hampers were loaded into the van and other hampers packed with robes and carpets were piled on top of them. Yussuf locked the back door of the van and handed the keys through the window to the driver, a pock-marked Bedouin smoking a foul-smelling hand-rolled cigarette and listening to a cassette of a popular Egyptian singer on the car's tape deck. The young woman who had passed for a *Haredi* when the Rabbi's car was being flagged down sat next to him. Her name was Khloud but everyone knew her by the nickname Petra, after the ruined Nabataean city in the Moab Mountains where she was born. For the ride back to Jerusalem she had changed into the long dress and the off-white head scarf of a religious Muslim. "Drive slowly," Yussuf instructed them. "Use the dirt tracks into the West Bank to avoid Israeli checkpoints, come at Jerusalem from the Jericho side, when you arrive in the Old City pull into the alleyway next to your shop and flash your lights twice. Our people will take care of the rest."

Yussuf grinned at Petra and he and the Bedouin exchanged high-fives through the open window. The motor coughed into life. The van, driving without headlights, edged onto the dirt road that skirted the nearby kibbutz before cutting across the fields in the direction of the West Bank and Jerusalem.

Yussuf joined the Doctor at the second Mercedes. The Palestinian who had been wounded by the Rabbi's driver firing his Uzi from the asphalt lay slumped across the back seat. An older Arab who had been trying to stem the bleeding climbed out of the car. "He's spitting up blood," he announced.

"That means he was shot in the lungs," the Doctor said.

"He cannot be allowed to fall alive into the hands of the Jews," Yussuf warned. "He knows too much."

"We must get the two Mercedes into Ghazeh before dawn," one of the Palestinians called nervously.

The Doctor could feel the hot breath of the *khamsin* on his cheek. He said, "Two minutes," and climbed into the back seat alongside the wounded man. He cradled the boy's head in his arms. "Anwar," he whispered. "It is me, the Doctor."

Anwar, who was in his early twenties, opened his eyes. He coughed up blood, then gasped for air. With infinite gentleness, the Doctor's fingers worked their way under the boy's turtleneck and probed his chest until they found the entry wound. It was immediately above the latissimus dorsi and angled up toward the left lung. There was no exit wound, which probably meant the bullet had struck a rib and caused massive trauma inside the body.

An ugly gurgling sound came from the back of the boy's throat. "I am going to pull out of this, right?" he whispered.

The Doctor leaned over him until his lips were touching the boy's ear. "Even better. Tonight you will enjoy the company of seventy-two virgin brides; tonight you will talk with the Prophet." In the darkness he brought a hand up to the boy's skull, which was damp with perspiration, and began to search with the tips of his fingers for the distinctive knob of bone behind the ear. "'*Whosoever fights in the way of God and is slain,*'" he murmured, quoting one of his favorite passages in the Qur'an, "'*we shall bring him a mighty wage.*'" He slipped the pearl-handled Beretta from his breast pocket and pulled back the slide on the top of the barrel to chamber the first round, then warmed the tip of the barrel in the palm of his hand before pressing it to the spot immediately under the knob of bone. Holding the boy's head against the car's arm rest, he pulled the trigger. There was a hollow report, something like a husky cough, as the pistol sent the bullet drilling into the skull. The boy's body jerked once before collapsing back into the seat.

Moments later the two Mercedes, with the still warm body of the martyr on the floor in the back of the second car, were speeding west along Bedouin tracks toward the Gaza Strip. The Suzuki with Israeli license plates and its two passengers, both carrying forged papers identifying them as Arabs from Abu Tor, a half Palestinian, half Jewish village outside of Jerusalem, headed north toward the main coastal highway. The Doctor planned to go to ground in Abu Tor. When things quieted down, he would make his way, tapping a long thin bamboo cane on the pavement before him, past the Israeli checkpoints to the safe house perched above the maze of streets in the Christian Quarter of the Old City of Jerusalem and, God willing, begin the interrogation of the Rabbi.

THREE

CROUCHING BEHIND A PILE OF CINDER BLOCKS, YUSSUF ABU Saleh waited until the Israeli patrol completed its sweep along the road that separated the Jewish half of Abu Tor from the Palestinian half. From the Old City of Jerusalem beyond the Hinnom Valley—the *Gehenna* where people burned garbage in the time of the Islamic Messenger Jesus—a bell atop the Church of the Holy Sepulcher tolled the half hour. As the echo faded, Yussuf scaled the wall and dropped into the garden behind his father-in-law's villa. A dog in one of the Jewish houses on the top of the hill bayed at the moon hanging over Mount Scopus. Several dogs in the Arab houses below barked back. The ancient saluki tied to a tree in the garden stood up and sniffed at the air, but sank back onto the grass when she recognized the intruder. Making his way across the garden to a trellis, Yussuf climbed through an old rose bush to the small balcony on the second floor. Inside the villa everything was dark. He scratched at the window. In the room a match flared, and then the wick of a candle burned brightly. An instant later the window was flung open and Yussuf found himself in the arms of his wife.

"*Ahlan wa sahlan*," Maali murmured into his neck, her lips pressed to his skin. "My house is your house."

"This is not the sentiment of your father," Yussuf noted.

"My father is a lawyer," she whispered back. "He sees only the legal aspects of what you do. He has lost sight of who is right and who is wrong." She discovered blood in the palm of his hand where a thorn had nicked the skin and kissed it away. Shrugging the thin straps of her night dress off her shoulders, she drew the turtleneck over his head and pressed herself against his body. "My heart, my husband, welcome home to your bridal chamber, welcome to your marriage bed."

"You are wonderfully beautiful," Yussuf declared. "Two weeks is a long time for lovers,"

Maali led him to the brass bed and pulled him down on top of her. "It has been sixteen days and sixteen nights, my love, my heart. Where have you been to?"

Yussuf ran his fingers through her jet black hair and looked down to see if the fire was still smoldering in the eyes he loved. "There are questions a wife does not ask," he instructed her. He kissed her shoulder and her breast and her mouth. Then he sat up. "We have been married six months tonight. I have an anniversary gift for you."

"You are my gift," she insisted, but she smiled with delight.

He produced a ring from his pocket. She raised the candle to inspect it. She could make out the words "Erasmus Hall" and the date 1998 inscribed on the inside of the ring, and some sort of crest on the stone in its center. "Never before have I seen such a ring," Maali said. "Where did you get it?"

"From a Jew named Erasmus Hall."

"You would have me wear a ring bought from a Jew?"

Yussuf smiled. "I took it from him. He did not object because he was dead."

"Who made the Jew Erasmus Hall dead?"

"I and my friends did. I noticed the ring on his small finger. When I could not remove it, I took out my pocket knife and cut off his finger."

Yussuf tried to put the ring on the fourth finger of her left hand, which was believed to be directly connected to the heart. When it wouldn't fit, he took her finger into his mouth and sucked it. He removed her wedding band and worked the Jew's ring over the joint and onto her finger, and then replaced the gold wedding band. "The ring of the late Erasmus Hall is so tight you would not be able to remove it even if you wanted to."

Maali held up her hand and inspected the ring. "You actually took it from a dead Jew!" she whispered.

"I hate them. Killing them is not enough after what they did to me, to my family, to my people, to my religion." He tightened his grip on her shoulders. "I cut off the finger and threw it to a dog in Abu Tor."

Maali declared with emotion, "I will wear this trophy of your victory over the Jews with pride."

Yussuf stripped and stood on a small Bedouin carpet as Maali sponged his body, and the healed bullet wound in the flesh of his shoulder, with orange blossom water from an enamel bowl. She fed him dates and wedges of apple to break the Ramadan fast. Then she took his hand and led him to the brass bed to break the marriage fast.

FOUR

JUST AFTER MIDNIGHT, A TALL, LEAN MAN DRESSED IN A pinstriped suit hovered over the wounded boy on the gurney as he was being rushed toward surgery through the scrubbed, harshly lit corridors of Hadassah Hospital. A male nurse trotted along on the other side holding high a plastic container of glucose, which dripped through a tube into the boy's forearm. The hair on the boy's head was matted with blood; a piece of his scalp hung loose like a flap, exposing a section of skull the color of sidewalk. On the stretcher, the boy's jaw worked, as if he were chewing on words but having trouble swallowing them. ". . . short . . . heavy-set . . . short cropped hair . . ." The man in the pinstriped suit leaned closer to catch the rest. A orderly materialized at the double door of the surgical theater. "The police are not permitted past this point," he announced.

Straightening, the tall, lean man backed away and turned to watch through a window as half a dozen doctors in pale green smocks and surgical masks, moving with the languid grace of people underwater, bent over the wounded man. Then a nurse inside the operating theater tugged closed the curtains, blocking the view into the room.

FIVE

AS THE FIRST STREAKS OF DAWN STAINED THE SKY IN THE EAST, Maali came awake with a start to discover the candle sizzling at the end of its wick and Yussuf's dark eyes fixed on her as if he never expected to see his wife again; as if the memory of her was all he could take with him. "You must be gone before it grows light," she warned with a shudder. "The Jews come around every day or two asking about you."

"What do you tell them?"

"My father says you are an outlaw and not welcome under his roof. I say that I am the bride of a holy warrior fighting a holy war."

Yussuf grinned at the spectacle of his wife facing down both her father and the Jews. "How do the Jews react when you tell them this?"

"The one with eyeglasses and the insignia of an officer on his shoulders laughs. The tall one who wears a ring in his ear like a woman calls me a whore. He says they will kill you and have sexual intercourse with me. He uses a vulgar expression for sexual intercourse." Maali drew her husband closer and lowered her voice. "I do not tell the Jews, I do not permit the thought to pass my lips when I talk to my father, I barely whisper it to myself: I am the wife of a servant of the *mujaddid.*"

"The Doctor does not say this in so many words."

"He does not deny it."

"He acknowledges it as a possibility." Yussuf pressed his lips against Maali's ear. "He bears the mark of Allah on his forehead—a permanent bruise that comes from pounding his head against the floor when he prays. The Doctor is a holy man who talks to God."

"Repeat to me the *mujaddid*'s message."

Yussuf focused on the flame dancing at the end of the candle; the light was suddenly so intense it caused his eyes to smart and he had to turn away. "He believes in a universal Islam that rises above Sunni-Shii differences. He teaches that Islam has not failed Muslims; we have failed Islam. He teaches that you are either a true believer or a *kafir*, an infidel who rejects the message of Islam and the Messenger. There is no middle ground. He teaches that Islam united the tribes under the Prophet Muhammad; that the tribes, acting in the name of Allah, the Merciful and Compassionate who is closer than the jugular, routed the Byzantine and Persian armies, conquered Iraq and Syria and Palestine and Persia and Egypt and Morocco and Libya and Spain. He teaches that the lessons of history are clear for those who wish to learn them: Muslim victory depends on faithfulness to the word of God and the example of the Prophet. When we suffer defeat, it is to be interpreted as the price we must pay for our infidelity."

Maali clung to her husband. "I worry about you—I dream terrible dreams in which you are being tortured to death. I am terrified you will be betrayed—"

Yussuf kissed his wife's neck. "That is out of the realm of possibility." He reached over to retrieve his wallet from a shirt pocket, and pulled a small folded piece of paper from it. "Take a look. All the members of the Abu Bakr Brigade carry this in their wallets—it serves as a secret identity card. The copies are numbered. Mine is number seven. The paper is a kind of coded organizational chart. The Doctor has patterned his Abu Bakr Brigade along the lines of the human nervous system. Each cell is completely independent from every other cell. Orders originate in the heart of the Doctor's cell. *Dendrites* branch out from the cell body to carry out these orders. Instructions to other cells are passed along something called the *axon*, which snakes out from the main cell but never actually makes contact with the other cells. The messages from one cell to another are transmitted at a gap called the *synapse*, where the cells approach each other but do not touch."

Maali became aware that she could make out the color of Yussuf's eyes. She moistened her thumb and first finger and snuffed out the flame of the candle between them. Sighing, she leaped from the bed and began to throw on clothing. "Where are you off to this time?" she wanted to know.

"I told you there are questions—" He shook his head; the Maali who defied both her father and the Israelis could be trusted. "To Jerusalem. To the Old City."

She wound a cotton scarf over her head, covering all of her face except her eyes. "You will attract less attention if you are accompanied by a woman."

"There is no question of your going with me."

Her eyes burned brightly in the folds of the scarf. "There is no question of my not going with you. Besides which, it is too great a distance to go on foot."

Yussuf gave in with a grin. "I permit you to accompany me, but only as far as the Damascus Gate."

"And I," Maali said with a shrewd laugh, "permit you to permit me."

She wheeled her scooter out of the tool shed in the back of the garden and walked it downhill until she could no longer see her father's villa. Yussuf appeared from an alley, climbed onto the scooter and kicked over the motor. Maali rode sidesaddle behind him, one hand on his shoulder, the other around his waist, as the scooter bounced down Siloam Road under what the Christians call the Mount of Olives and onto Jericho Road. Pickup trucks brimming with crates of vegetables and jugs of olive oil and bamboo cages filled with live chickens converged on the Sultan Suleiman Road heading toward the Damascus Gate, the main Arab entrance into the old walled city.

At the side of the road in front of the Damascus Gate, Maali took leave of her husband. "We will lay again in the marriage bed," she declared fiercely. "It is written."

"*Inshallah*," he said. "God willing." He touched the back of her hand with the back of his hand. On the spur of the moment, he whispered, "If you need me, leave a message for Tayzir the florist with the lame shoemaker across from the El Khanqa Mosque in the Christian Quarter. He is our *synapse*, where the cells approach each other but do not touch."

"For Tayzir the florist," she repeated, proud to be trusted with this information, "with the lame shoemaker across from the El Khanqa Mosque in the Christian Quarter."

Yussuf started toward the gate. When Maali saw him looking over his shoulder, she pulled off her scarf and shook loose her long black hair and raised the hand with the Jew's ring on the fourth finger in proud salute. Her husband waved back. Then, tucking the end of his *kaffiyeh* under the headband so that the lower half of his face was hidden, he ambled past the Israeli paratroopers lounging under the archway. One of the soldiers, with a whip antenna jutting from his backpack, spoke into a telephone. "Mobile unit four," he said, "at the Damascus Gate, seven thirty, nothing unusual to report."

In a stairwell near the Israelis, Mr. Hajji, the stooped Palestinian who as far back as anyone could remember had been guarding valises and changing money for tourists, was chalking up the day's exchange rates on a black board. "Sorry, sorry," he told a Bedouin woman clutching two live chickens by their legs. Narrowing his eyes, he looked past her at the young woman outside the gate whose features looked vaguely familiar. "I do not deal in rubles," he mumbled, his mind elsewhere.

SIX

Across the Levant, Muslims were sitting down to the evening "break-fast." Off the Israeli coast, the running lights of a tanker clawing like a crab toward Haifa flickered in the dusk. Eight minutes later the ship's bow wave lapped against the Jaffa shore and trickled up the beach to the terrace of the seafood restaurant run by a retired general who free-lanced for the Mossad's *Paha*, the department that tracked the daily movements of Palestinian terrorist groups. A billboard on the roof of the restaurant, illuminated by two spotlights, announced the establishment's name in Hebrew, and added in English: "One whale of a meal." The billboard wasn't only there for publicity purposes; hidden behind it was a bank of short and medium wave antennas that would have revealed, to anyone who spotted them, that fish weren't the only thing being fried on the premises. The parking lot at the side of the restaurant was filled to capacity, but not all of the cars belonged to clients. In the restaurant itself, waiters in white aprons scurried between the kitchen and the crowded tables carrying trays filled with fresh mackerel, sea bass and the day's special, shark. Off the kitchen, a creaky wooden staircase led to a thick curtain that concealed a steel door surveyed by a hidden security camera. In the narrow hallway beyond the steel door sat a burly former paratrooper armed with a sawed-off pump-action shot-gun. In a dimly lit room off the narrow hallway, half a dozen men in civilian clothing were gathered around a large Sony television set. The image on the screen, grainy and slightly out of focus, showed Rabbi Apfulbaum, his wrists handcuffed before him, sitting on a heavy wooden chair in front of a bricked-in window. He looked pale as death, but those who had seen him in person or on television talk shows knew that he always looked pale as death. Curiously, he didn't appear to be frightened; what could have passed for a faint smile of satisfaction played on his thin lips, as if what had happened to him proved that he had been right all along. The left sleeves of his shirt and jacket were slit to the elbow; the loose cloth flapped around his wrist when he moved his hand to brush away a fly. The Rabbi's eyes, pressed into a permanent squint, stared out at the camera; stared out at the men studying the image on the television screen.

"He's squinting," noted a voice in the darkened room, growling in slightly slurred Hebrew, "because he is unable to focus without his eyeglasses, which were found at the scene of the kidnapping. Without glasses he is virtually blind; he can only make out shapes and shadows. As for the sleeve, our people assume that the terrorists anesthetized him with an injection after the kidnapping."

"Notice the bruise on his forehead," remarked Baruch, the detective from Mishteret Yisra'el, the national police force. He combed his fingers through a mane of prematurely white hair; each hair, he would say on the rare occasions he talked about it, represented a tear he had not shed. "In religious circles, it's known that it comes from drumming his head against the stone when he prays at the Wailing Wall."

On the screen the camera panned past a terrorist to the Rabbi's secretary, Efrayim, sitting stiffly on another wooden chair, his wrists also in handcuffs, his eyes tightly closed, his lips and Adam's apple working. The camera returned to the terrorist standing behind the two chairs immediately in front of a Palestinian flag tacked to the wall. A tight-fitting black hood with slits for the eyes covered his head. A Russian AK-47 with a folding stock hung from a sling across his chest. He tugged a slip of paper from the pocket of his short-sleeved shirt and, rolling his R's, began to read in accented English. "In the name of God, the Merciful and Compassionate: the Islamic Abu Bakr Brigade has celebrated the holy month of Ramadan by capturing two Jewish prisoners of war. In exchange for E. Blumenfeld, we require the release of El Sayyid Nosair, a Palestinian patriot serving a life sentence for the 1990 killing of the Jewish terrorist Rabbi Meir Kahane. In exchange for I. Apfulbaum, we require the release of the one hundred and four patriots now being held hostage in the Jewish prison south of Beersheba. The Isra'ili government has five days to release El Sayyid Nosair, and until the Feast of the Breaking of the Fast, *Id al-Fitr*, to arrange for the release of the hundred and four patriots. There will be no negotiations, and no further contact between us. Failure to meet our legitimate demands will result in the execution of the sentence of death on I. Apfulbaum and his secretary, E. Blumenfeld."

"*Id al-Fitr* marks the end of the month of Ramadan," explained Wozzeck, an Arabist on loan from a Shin Bet–financed think tank.

"The first deadline doesn't give us much time to find the hostages and free them," observed Dovid Dror, a young lieutenant colonel on detached duty from the almost mythical General Staff commando unit.

"What are we dealing with here?" asked Baruch as the retired general, whose name was Uri Almog, ran the cassette from the beginning. "The Abu Bakr Brigade is a new blip on our radar screen."

Altmann, a Shin Bet specialist on Palestinian terrorist groups, ticked off the various possibilities. "It could be a splinter group of frustrated Fatah Hawks, the armed wing of Arafat's Fatah movement. Or some itchy warriors from the Ikhwan, the fundamentalist Muslim Brotherhood operating in Egypt; it wouldn't be the first time the local fundamentalists got their Islamic brothers in Cairo to do their dirty work for them. It could be the Islamic Jihad or the Shiite Hezbollah militia working out of the Lebanon, or even some al Qaida survivors from Afghanistan. Or a new incarnation of Hamas's Qassam Brigades, for that matter; according to intelligence reports the Qassam activists have been chaffing at the bit for weeks."

"Whoever they are," Baruch, always the plodding cop, noted, "they're not amateurs. Without negotiations, it's going to be almost impossible to track them down. We've never caught kidnappers without some kind of contact between us and them."

"Freeze the image there," ordered the man presiding over the inter-agency Working Group set up to deal with the kidnapping of Rabbi Apfulbaum. Know by the *nom de guerre* Elihu, he was a *katsa*, or handler, on temporary assignment from *ha-Mossad le-Modiin ule-Tafkidim Meyuhadim*, the institute for intelligence and special missions, better known as the Mossad. The *katsa* directed the Mossad's *Metsada*, a top secret section that ran Israeli spies operating under deep cover in Arab countries. A living legend to the few who were aware of his existence—before becoming a *katsa* he had participated in some two dozen Mossad commando missions to neutralize Palestinian terrorists—he favored pinstripe suits and shirts with cuff links, which made him look more like a London City banker than a native *sabra* born and raised in the wilds of the Israeli Negev. He was lean and tall and ramrod straight, and wore the mantle of authority with the instinctive sureness of someone who usually exercised more of it than was written into his job description. Now, gazing at the television screen, he sucked on the stem of an unlit pipe as he spoke, which had the effect of slurring some of his words. "There's a Palestinian flag on the wall behind the terrorist," he said. "Can you give us a closer look at the lower right-hand corner, Uri?"

The retired general who owned the restaurant and leased the second floor to the Working Group—none of the parent organizations were willing to let the *katsa's* Group meet on the terrain of a rival organization; the general's safe house was considered neutral turf—ran the tape back. He froze the image and toyed with some dials on the console. The camera zoomed in until the corner of the flag filled the screen. "There's something on the wall next to the flag," Elihu said.

On the screen, what appeared to be the edge of a handbill or leaflet came into focus. "Looks like a poster," said Altmann.

"Hold on," Wozzeck said. He knelt in front of the television screen. "Look here—the paper has been divided into squares. You can just make out the left-hand row."

"What we're looking at is a calendar," Uri Almog said from the console.

"There's writing down the side of the margin," Elihu said. "Can you blow it up?" he asked the general.

The screen filled with the blurred strokes of a typewriter, which suddenly spilled into focus. The six men in the room craned their necks to read the vertical writing down the side of the calendar. "It's in Arabic," Wozzeck said. He touched the screen with his finger tips as he read out the words. "'The Ghazeh Central Import-Export Bank.'"

Elihu nodded toward the general, who switched off the television set and turned on the naked bulb in the overhead fixture. The six men, blinded by the sudden light, settled into chairs around an oval table filled with ash trays and wine glasses from the restaurant, and bottles of mineral water.

For a long while everyone stared at the table. Finally Dror, a combat veteran who had been Elihu's second in command on the *katsa*'s swansong raid into Nablus, broke the ice. "The *mechabel* in the black hood is wearing a short sleeved shirt," he said. "He's dressed for Aza, which, remember, was sweltering from the freak *khamsin* that, for once, didn't hit Jerusalem or the West Bank. If he were somewhere in the hills around Jerusalem or the Judean mountains, he'd be wearing a long-sleeved shirt, maybe even a sweater."

"The Rabbi *is* in Aza," Wozzeck decided, "but not for the reasons you think." He glanced around the table at the others. "In the end, it's a very straightforward business: they obviously planted the calendar and the short sleeves, so it begins to look as if they want us to think the Rabbi is in Aza. But they're not stupid; they know we'll figure out they want us to think he is in Aza. Which means we're going to take it for granted that he's somewhere else. Which means the Rabbi must be in Aza."

"What we're really discussing here," suggested Baruch, a big man who looked people in the eye and said exactly what was going through his head, "is how smart we think the Palestinians are." Baruch's gaze settled on Wozzeck. "Somehow we always wind up thinking we're smarter than they are. I agree that we must start with the assumption that they're deliberately dropping hints that the Rabbi is in Aza, but I give them more credit for brains than you. I think they're hinting at Aza because they're one jump ahead of you, Wozzeck—they expect us to conclude he is in Aza for the reasons you explained. Which means the Rabbi must be somewhere else."

Wozzeck splashed mineral water into a wine glass and, holding it by the long stem, studied the liquid as if it were vintage wine. "Palestinians are not that subtle," he decided.

Almog shook his head. "You're both being too cerebral. The tape we just looked at was mailed from Aza's central post office."

Baruch, something of an amateur archeologist who specialized in tracing missing peoples of antiquity, tapped a forefinger against the side of his nose. "I could deliver an envelope to Tel Aviv tonight with stamps cancelled in Atlantis, which sank into the sea three thousand five hundred years ago."

From under the floorboards came the faint clatter of dishes and the distinct sound of someone shouting in Hebrew, "Two cognacs and a bill for table fourteen." Elihu sucked loudly on the stem of his pipe.

"Do you ever light that thing?" Altmann asked irritably.

Elihu mumbled something about having given up smoking for his forty-fifth birthday in order to have a fiftieth. After a moment he said, "I have to agree with Uri—we're complicating things unnecessarily. Even if you dismiss the calendar and the short sleeves and the postmark on the tape, you still are left with the cars. The bodyguard who survived told the truck driver who arrived on the scene that the Rabbi and the secretary had been taken away in two Mercedes. We found tire tracks in the dunes at the side of the road where the Rabbi was kidnapped, so we know the bodyguard wasn't dreaming up the two cars. We spotted the tracks again going cross country into Aza where the security fence was cut between two Israeli check points. The Palestinian police found the two Mercedes abandoned in a fruit warehouse near Aza City at a quarter to seven this morning." Elihu tapped the bowl of the pipe in the palm of his hand. "Unless we come across evidence to the contrary, I think we have to assume the Rabbi and his secretary are in Aza."

Baruch, who was odd man out in the sense that he was the only one in the room who wasn't an Arabist of some sort, came back to the question of the cars. "The Palestinian Authority let two of our people in to take a look at the cars. I happened to be one of them.

The steering wheels and door handles had been wiped clean of fingerprints. The body of one of the terrorists, apparently wounded in the kidnapping, was still in the back of the second Mercedes. The autopsy report that came through late this afternoon confirmed what any idiot could have figured out. The *mechabel*'s left lung had been perforated, there was internal bleeding, but the immediate cause of death was a low-caliber bullet fired into his brain behind the ear."

There was a loud knock on the door. One of the young women working the night shift in the communications alcove came in carrying a plastic tray filled with coffee mugs. She wore a mini skirt and walked barefoot because of a blister on her heel. "Eat your hearts out," she announced, noisily depositing the tray on the table. "We forgot to buy diet cream." At the door she tossed her head to get the stray strands of henna-tinted hair out of her eyes. "Nobody's perfect," she said. Before anyone could agree, the door clicked closed.

"We were talking about the low-caliber bullet behind the ear," Almog reminded everyone.

Elihu actually sighed. "We had to tackle this sooner or later." He produced a small pad from the pocket of his suit jacket and flipped through the pages until he came to the notes he had made that morning. "I managed to speak with the surviving bodyguard as he was being wheeled into surgery at Hadassah Hospital. I was the last person to talk to him before he died. He caught a glimpse of the Arab leading the attack. He described him as being on the short side, heavy set, with short cropped hair, wearing a long white caftan under a suit jacket. The Arab knelt in the headlights of the Rabbi's Nissan to examine the body of the driver who was wounded by a grenade. He appeared to feel for his pulse, then bent over him and put his ear to his mouth—"

"To see if he was breathing," guessed Almog. "Under battle conditions we do the same with our wounded."

"What you're describing," Baruch, always the cop who dotted the i's and crossed the t's, remarked, "could be the professional gestures of a medic or a male nurse."

"The Arab must have discovered signs of life," Elihu went on, "because he drew a small pistol from a pocket of his jacket, felt with the tips of his fingers behind the wounded man's ear, then placed the muzzle to the spot behind the ear and pulled the trigger. According to the autopsy reports, both the Rabbi's driver and the Palestinian terrorist whose body was found in the abandoned Mercedes died in precisely the same way—from a single .22-caliber bullet fired with surgical accuracy into the medulla, the lowest part of the brain stem, which controls the heart beat and breathing. Death in both cases was instantaneous."

"He murdered the driver because he was Jewish," Wozzeck said, his slight Polish accent thickening as his voice turned nasty. "He murdered his own *mechabel* because he didn't want a wounded man to fall into our hands and identify his leader."

Baruch put into words what everyone was thinking. "The method of execution—the single .22-caliber bullet fired directly into the medulla—matches the *modus operandi* of the killer who first came to our attention when he assassinated our minister without portfolio several years back. Over the years of the *intifada*, the same killer has executed eighteen Palestinians accused of collaborating with us. We had a psychological profile drawn up on the murderer. It suggested he had a personal grudge against collaborators that goes far beyond any ideological rejection of those who aid his enemy; it raises the possibility that the killer was once betrayed by a collaborator and may have spent years in our prisons."

"Any point of winding up the brothers Karamazov and pointing them in the right direction?" Altmann asked. He was referring to the two defrocked Russian rabbis, known in house as Absalom and Azazel, who presided over several basements filled with the old national police archives that, for lack of funding, hadn't been scanned and put onto a computer.

Baruch posed a rhetorical question. "What would they look for? A short, heavy Arab who spent an unknown amount of time in one of our Negev country clubs after being fingered by a collaborator? Come on! Absalom would laugh us out of town. That description could fit thousands of Palestinians."

Elihu closed his pad. "With the abduction of the Rabbi and his secretary, we must deal with a worst case scenario: the killer and his accomplices, who call themselves the Islamic Abu Bakr Brigade, are targeting Jews in order to shatter the cease fire and prevent the Mt. Washington peace treaty from being signed."

"Did they waylay the first car to come along?" Altmann asked, thinking out loud. "Or were they gunning for Rabbi Apfulbaum?"

Baruch brushed the question away impatiently. "If they were going to kidnap the first Jew who came along they wouldn't have attacked two cars, one filled with young men armed with Uzis. No, no, we have to assume they were targeting Apfulbaum."

"They knew he'd been invited to Yad Mordechai—the reunion there of Jews who'd been expelled from their Aza settlements in 2005 was announced in the newspapers," Dror agreed. "They knew he would be returning home to Beit Avram at nightfall."

"Why Apfulbaum?" Altmann persisted.

Elihu pushed back his chair and, tapping the bowl of his pipe in the palm of his hand, strolled over to the window. One floor below three couples, the women's arms linked through the men's, were emerging from the restaurant. All six were tipsy and singing Hatikva, a gloomy national anthem even when performed well. Smiling to himself, Elihu turned back to the room. "The answer is to be found in the settlement Beit Avram, which is populated with religious extremists furious at the government for trading holy land for a precarious peace. The answer is to be found in the rumors about the Jewish underground cell that was created in Beit Avram. The terrorists kidnapped Apfulbaum because they think what we think—that for the Jewish extremists, he is the keeper of the flame; that he must know the identity of the mysterious Ya'ir, the leader of the Jewish underground who signs manifestos boasting about the assassination of local Palestinian leaders; that if Apfulbaum can be made to talk, what he reveals could hurt the State of Israel more than any Hamas terrorist bomb."

"For Ya'ir's sake," Baruch drawled from the table, "I hope Apfulbaum doesn't know the answers to their questions."

"For Apfulbaum's sake," Wozzeck said with a twisted grin, "I hope he does know the answer to their questions."

"Have we touched all the bases?" Elihu asked.

"You left out the curious business of the missing finger," Baruch said. Born and raised on a kibbutz in the northern Galilee directly under Syrian mortars, he was the only one in the room not in awe of Elihu. "The coroner noticed something that our people on the scene missed—the small finger on the left hand of one of the bodyguards, a Brooklyn boy named Ronni Goldman who immigrated four years ago, was missing. At first they assumed it had been shot off during the attack. Then one of the more experienced coroners took a closer look and decided it had been crudely amputated under the knuckle." Baruch shook his large head. "Don't ask me what this means—I haven't the foggiest idea."

Dror, who had lived in America when his father was posted to the Israeli embassy and had earned a degree in literature from George Washington University, joined Elihu at the window. They listened for a moment to the soft lapping of the surf against the shore. Dror, a combat veteran with a livid shrapnel scar across his right cheek, said in English, "'The heart can think of no devotion greater than being shore to ocean.'" He added quickly, "That's a line from the American poet Frost."

Jamming the dead pipe back into his mouth, gnawing on the stem, slurring his words, the legendary Mossad *katsa* shot back, "This heart can think of a devotion greater than being shore to ocean. It's the preservation of Jewish lives in the Jewish state." Embarrassed at the outburst, Elihu turned abruptly toward the others in the room. "Here's where we get to earn our pay checks," he said. "We have to find the Rabbi and his secretary before this short, heavy-set killer fires .22-caliber bullets into their brain stems."

Baruch said, "Without negotiations, without contacts, it's difficult to know where to start."

Elihu said, "I may have something up my sleeve. It's a long shot . . ."

An Excerpt from the Harvard "Running History" Project:

F or obvious reasons I can't give you much time today—the you-know-what has hit the fan here. How did I hear about it? As usual I had one eye on CNN and saw the map of Israel come up on the screen. They had footage of the three bodies sprawled on the road, the fourth bodyguard being rushed into the hospital on a gurney, the Prime Minister waving off the camera and calling "No comment" in his accented English, the Palestinian leader condemning the breaking of the truce in English, as usual, as opposed to Arabic. CNN had barely cut away from Israel when the telephone on my desk started ringing. It was the President's press secretary—he was a bit rattled and wanted guidance. I told him to say there would be no statement of any kind from me or anybody else in the White House until the smoke cleared. I told him I would speak to the Israeli Prime Minister and the Chairman of the Palestinian Authority, after which I would brief the President. Once the President and I had spoken, I told him I'd get back to him to see how we were going to handle the press.

Yes, that's what you do if you want to stay alive in this town: you "handle" the press.

I put in calls to both the Palestinian and the Israeli leaders. Their keepers tried to palm me off on deputies so I went into my "Old Rough-and-Ready" act—I let them know I wouldn't settle for deputies, I didn't want spokesmen or spokeswomen, I wanted principals, I wanted the horse's mouth. If for some reason they couldn't come to the phone to speak to the representative of the President of the United States, I suggested it might be in their best interests if someone brought the phone to them.

Needless to say, I was put through to both of them but I got the impression that, like me, they were getting their information from CNN. I received assurances from both that they would say nothing and do nothing to make matters worse for twenty-four hours. Which is to say, everyone was going to take a deep breath. I briefed the President, then I put a call through to the Director, CIA, and asked him to have his people supply me with updates every half hour—I didn't come right out and say it in so many words but I was asking him if he could tell me more than CNN. I instructed my secretary to assemble the usual suspects in the operations center. We were going to hunker down and go into a damage control mode. Then I settled back into my chair and shut my eyes and took a deep breath myself.

As a matter of fact, I did see the piece on the Mt. Washington negotiations in the New York Review. *He asked for an interview but I politely declined—I subscribe to the theory that the best Presidential advisers are the ones who are neither seen nor heard. Yes, some of what he wrote was accurate, though by no means all of it. The business about our getting off to a slow start misrepresented what actually happened. The opening sessions at Mt. Washington weren't slow, they were excruciating. At the first meeting the two sides wrangled over everything under the sun: the shape of the negotiating table, the level of representation, whether the Americans should be seated at the table or standing by in the next room to break stalemates, whose maps would be used when it came to discussing actual frontiers, whether the United Nations ought to be involved, how contacts with the press would be handled. It took five days of intense negotiations just to fix the number and composition of subcommittees that would work out compromises on which settlements would be dismantled and what the status would be of those that remained inside the new Palestinian state, water rights, Palestinian access to Israeli ports, control of the air space over the Palestinian state, the size of its militia and what arms would be permitted, how many Palestinian refugees would be allowed back into Israel, what compensation would be offered to the others. When, after three weeks, the negotiations stalled, the President personally intervened. Everyone today remembers the speech in which she declared the day was long past when America would permit lunatic fringes on both sides to drive policy; and she went on to lay out, for the first time, the general guidelines of an American-sponsored plan for peace—a seismic departure from the previous American position, which supported only a process designed to produce just such a plan.*

It's true that I wrote the chunks of the speech dealing with America's support for a peace plan instead of a peace process, but the President deserves the credit for delivering it.

Behind the scenes, we upped the ante: we let it be known that unless the Israelis and the Palestinians agreed to our plan, the United States would suspend economic as well as military aid to the Middle East and refuse to veto UN Security Council resolutions calling for interposing United Nations peacekeepers between the two sides. One by one the differences between the negotiating teams where whittled down until they fitted into the President's "General Guidelines." The work in the final inch, to use Solzhenitsyn's memorable phrase, was agonizing for both sides, not to mention for us. The Authority reluctantly abandoned its insistence on the right of return of millions of Palestinian refugees to Israel and the Israelis, in turn, promised to provide compensation for those who had been obliged to flee their homes in 1948. The Israelis also agreed to evacuate most of the Jewish settlements on the West Bank, and cede Arab east Jerusalem and half of the Old City to the new Palestinian state in return for a solemn declaration from all Arab states in the region acknowledging Israel's right to exist within internationally recognized borders. A last hurdle—Israel's insistence on keeping a security zone along the Jordan River—was cleared when I convinced the Pentagon to agree to guarantee Israel access to real-time US satellite surveillance of the entire Middle East.

Fair question. Where I'm at now is I'm shrugging off a persuasive despair. I have the sinking feeling this is going to be the last moment of grace before a terrible khamsin *rouses the Levantine demons to fire and fury because a quirky Jewish rabbi managed to get himself kidnapped.*

SEVEN

LOCKING HIS CAR IN THE SPRAWLING PARKING LOT, SWEENEY MADE his way on foot to the festering wound known as Erez, the main crossing point between Israel and the Gaza Strip. Since the kidnapping of the Fiddler on the Roof, security had become tighter than ever. The edgy Israeli frontier guards kept loaded clips in their assault rifles and their fingers on the triggers as long lines of sullen Palestinian men wound past on their way to work in the fields and factories up the Israeli coast. From a low tower, an Israeli officer bellowed through a battery-powered bullhorn, in Arabic, for a Palestinian truck to stop before it came to the first cement-and-sandbag strong point in the wide Erez alley. Behind one of the sandbags, a pudgy sergeant wearing a net-covered helmet and high-collared flak jacket swiveled his machine gun and sighted on the truck's tires, ready to shoot them out if the driver didn't instantly obey.

The spectacle at Erez never failed to dazzle Sweeney: one hour and ten minutes down the road from the creature comforts of Jerusalem—the roof-top terrace of his apartment in Yemin Moshe with its spectacular view of the Old City walls, the ice cubes rattling in the driest martinis this side of the river Jordan, his hand resting lightly on the sexiest female thigh in the holy land—and he was knocking on the gate of D. Alighieri's inferno.

Not that there was any problem getting in. Getting out of Gaza, for a Palestinian, was an ordeal; you had to have a spanking clean charge sheet and no known relatives in any fundamentalist organization and a special magnetic identity card that the Israelis swapped for new ones whenever they wanted to give the Palestinians a hard time. Entering Gaza, on the other hand, was a piece of cake. Barely glancing at Sweeney's American passport and his government-issued press card, a baby-faced border guard who looked as if he had never shaved in his life waved him through the indoor border post. Sweeney appeared to be a consenting adult, the cranky gesture seemed to say. If he was dumb enough to walk into this hell on earth, the Israelis weren't going to stop him.

A hundred yards up the Erez alley, past endless coils of tangled concertina wire and more strong points protected by steel spikes set in the road, Sweeney reached the local Palestinians, come to pick up their clients in ancient automobiles that billowed clouds of dense brown smoke when the drivers kicked over the motors. For a hundred dollars a day, cash on the barrel head, you got ferried to your rendezvous in Gaza or one of the swarming refugee camps; for another hundred the driver would organize a demonstration for or against anyone or anything you named; for an additional sawbuck, he would translate the slogans scrawled on every naked wall in the Strip. Two Christian Arabs Sweeney recognized as reporters from a Gaza news agency were loading television cameras into the back of a battered Buick station wagon. A prime-time newscaster Sweeney remembered from his Beirut days— the newscaster used to pick his brain for the price of a three-course meal in the St. George Hotel—was passing out American cigarettes to the scrawny Palestinian kids hawking tiny cups of thick sweetened coffee. "My man Sweeney, how you doing?" Prime Time called.

"I'm hanging in there," Sweeney answered. "What do you have lined up?"

"I've got a noon interview with the head honcho. I promised him six minutes, no commercial breaks, as long as he wears a checkered kerchief—shit, what do you call those damn things?"

Sweeney, who had not managed to arrange an interview with anyone higher than dog catcher in his eight months as Jerusalem bureau chief, said, "*Kiffiyehs.*"

"Yeah. That's it. *Kiffiyehs.* I knew that. I just couldn't remember how to pronounce it. Hey, Sweeney, there are three problems with growing old. The first is you start to lose your memory. Awh, shit! I can't remember the second and third." Prime Time cackled at his own joke until he was short of breath.

Sweeney's driver, universally known as Roger because the Palestinian had picked up the habit from American war movies of acknowledging orders with the word "Roger," had parked his beat-up Lada at the end of the line. It occurred to Sweeney that only God knew how a car constructed in Russia wound up in the Gaza Strip. On the other hand, all cars finished in a junk yard, so there was probably a logic to it after all. Roger, wearing his habitual Indian shirt buttoned up to the neck, a brown suit and sandals, squeezed his overweight body in behind the wheel. "Where we off to today, Mr. Max?" he asked as Sweeney settled onto the seat next to him.

"I want to see the wake," Sweeney said.

"Roger, Mr. Max," Roger said, an eager smile spreading across his round face, the gold crowns glittering in his lower jaw. "The wake it is."

There was a grinding of gears and a violent shudder under the hood as the Lada, with a backfire that sent several men ducking for cover, started up the road. A hundred yards further along they came to the Palestinian Authority check point. Another baby-faced policeman, this one wearing a crisp blue uniform and a blue beret and carrying what looked like a brand new Chinese-manufactured Kalashnikov tucked under his arm, took Sweeney's passport and passed it to a short mustached man wearing goggle-like sunglasses and a green belted raincoat.

The Green Hornet, as Sweeney dubbed him, looked up from the passport. "Max could be a Jewish name," he announced in perfect English, scrutinizing Sweeney through the open window.

"Jesus could be a Jewish name, too," Sweeney shot back.

"Jesus was not a Zionist," Green Hornet said.

"There's a lot of things Jesus wasn't," Sweeney retorted. "A Christian is one of them."

"Westerners cannot resist giving lessons to Palestinians," observed the Green Hornet. "One day you will understand that there are also things to be learned from us."

Sweeney smiled uncomfortably. He didn't see himself getting into a theological discussion with the boss of a Palestinian policeman who had one finger on the trigger of a Kalashnikov. "Look, I'm not Jewish," he said. "Sweeney is an Irish Catholic name."

Roger leaned across the seat. "Sweeney is a friend of the Palestinian people," he said in English. (Sweeney always came across with a generous tip at the end of the day, a charitable action Roger liked to encourage.)

The Green Hornet handed the passport back through the open window and turned toward the next car. Struggling with the gear box, Roger jammed the stick shift into first and, with a series of jerks, managed to get the Lada rolling in the direction of Gaza City.

A Mercedes taxi filled with Arab women and valises piled high on the roof rack overtook the Lada, kicking up a cloud of chalk dust that obliged Sweeney to cover his nose and mouth with a handkerchief. Laughing at the discomfort of his passenger, Roger swung around a Bedouin boy, a goat slung around his neck, leading a string of camels, and a donkey pulling a cart sagging on its axles under a load of oranges, then splashed through a swamp of sewage onto a side road that took them, within minutes, into the heart of Gaza City.

With the abduction of the Fiddler, who was believed to be somewhere in Gaza, security was high on this side of the border, too; Palestinian police armed with submachine guns stood in front of their jeeps surveying traffic at every crossroad. The streets, dust-clogged and reeking from garbage, teemed with barefoot children and women in long robes lugging baskets of vegetables. Clustered around small tables in bleak cafes, bearded men smoked hand-rolled cigarettes and played backgammon. At every corner claxons shrieked; there were very few stop lights in Gaza and each intersection had become a test of manhood as drivers tried to bluff their way through. The Lada swung past the sprawling office complex in central Gaza known as Al Saraya, where the Palestinian Authority held court; workmen on bamboo scaffolds were rebuilding the wing that had been bombed into rubble by Israeli helicopters before the cease fire went into effect. Leaning on the horn, Roger inched the car through a horde of people waiting for the bride and groom to emerge from a wedding hall, and turned into the Gaza neighborhood of Shajaiyah. "The martyr lived in his family's house down the narrow street there," Roger said, pulling onto the sidewalk and cutting the engine. Carefully locking the car, he led the way to a portal in a whitewashed stucco wall. He pointed to the Arabic writing over the door. "This is the word *Shahid,* which Westerners translate as *martyr* but really means *witness,* meaning that the dead boy, whose name was Anwar, bore witness to God and the Prophet."

The driver rapped his knuckles on the door. A teenage boy wearing a sweatshirt with a Palestinian flag on the chest opened it. Roger spoke to him in Arabic. The boy, gesturing with the grace of a ballet dancer, motioned with his palm for the two visitors to enter.

Sweeney stepped onto the concrete of the bare open courtyard filled with rows of white plastic chairs. Thirty or so men in polyester trousers and sandals sat silently around an open grate on which coffee was being brewed. A giant framed photograph of the late Anwar hung from one wall; it had been taken in a Gaza studio but made to look as if the boy was posing in front of the great Dome of the Rock Mosque in Jerusalem. There was Arabic writing on the wall under the photograph, which Roger, leaning toward Sweeney, translated. "It is what we call the *shahada,* the single most important verse from the sacred Qur'an, which an infidel recites when converting to Islam and a Muslim recites at the time of his death. '*Ash'hadu an la illahu ila Allah wa'ash'hadu anna Muhammadan rasulu Allah.*' '*I bear witness that there is no God but Allah, I bear witness that Muhammad is the messenger of Allah.*'"

The boy in the sweatshirt, who turned out to be Anwar's kid brother, made his way down the rows of mourners holding a tarnished brass tray filled with almond biscuits and small porcelain cups of brackish coffee. Roger handed a cup to Sweeney and took one himself. "It is polite to drink," he whispered. "The coffee is bitter even though at the home of a martyr it is usually sweet. This is because the boy's father is bitter at the death of his son at such a young age."

"I heard he threw garbage at the feet of a local Imam who came to pay his respects," Sweeney said.

"This may be true," Roger said with artful vagueness.

"Which one is the father?"

"The older gentleman with patent leather shoes and his head bowed onto his chest."

"I'd like to ask him some questions."

Roger turned to the gaunt Palestinian sitting next to him and said something. The Palestinian got up and walked over to Anwar's father. Bending, he mumbled something in his ear. The father lifted his eyes and studied Sweeney, then nodded his head once.

"The father of Anwar accepts to reply to your questions," Roger said.

Sweeney looked across at the father. "Please accept my condolences on the death of your son."

Roger translated. The father, his features drawn, the lids of his eyes heavy with grief, nodded again.

"Is the coffee you serve bitter because the bullet that killed your son was fired by a Palestinian?"

When Roger hesitated, Sweeney said, in a tone that left him no room to maneuver, "Translate."

"Roger." Sweeney's driver turned back to the father and repeated the question in Arabic. Sweeney knew he had translated correctly when several of the men sitting around the room gasped.

The dead boy's father thought a moment before responding. Then, measuring his words and speaking with great dignity, he launched into a lengthy reply. Sweeney turned to Roger. "He tells," the driver said, whispering a running translation as Sweeney scribbled notes on the back of the page containing the interview with Rabbi Apfulbaum, "that he would find no comfort if an Isra'ili bullet had killed his son. He tells that he himself is for the treaty of peace even if it leaves the Jews in possession of Arab lands. He tells that he bitterly regrets the death of his son, but understands the frustration that drove Anwar to join the armed struggle against the Jews." The Palestinians around the courtyard rocked back and forth on their chairs in solemn agreement. "He tells that his son's wrist was broken by the Jews during the *intifada* when he was caught throwing stones at an Isra'ili patrol. He tells that the broken bones mended, but not the broken pride in Anwar's head. He tells that he himself works for the Palestinian Authority tax assessment office, so he knows that more than a million Arabs, half of them under the age of sixteen, are crowded into this forty-kilometer-long open-air concentration camp. He tells that the lucky ones get permits to work in Isra'il; that the wage one man earns supports the twenty others who sit around cafes playing *sheshbesh* and thinking up schemes to hurt the Jews."

From somewhere in the city came the shrill sob of a police siren. Roger's translation trailed off as Anwar's father cleared his throat and shook his head and said something else. "He asks you to reply to *his* question," Roger said. "'What hope can we offer to our children under these circumstances?'"

Sweeney looked up from the notebook into the eyes of the father of the boy who had been shot dead, so the Israeli press was reporting, to prevent him from falling alive into the hands of the Shin Bet. "Say to him I am only equipped with questions, not answers. Say to him again I feel only sympathy for his family's loss."

Roger translated, listened to the father's reply and said, very quietly, "He tells that everyone he talks to is equipped with questions, not answers. He thanks you from his heart for coming to this house of mourning."

Returning to Roger's Lada, Sweeney was surprised to discover a beautiful young man with round blue sunglasses and a pointed beard leaning against one of the fenders. Obviously a cleric of some sort, he was wearing a white skullcap and a long white *galabiya*, and looked like the male equivalent of a vestal virgin. Sweeney immediately pinned the nickname on him. Vestal Virgin swatted flies from his face as he said, in elaborate English, "Good day to you, Mr. journalist Sweeney."

"Hello to you," Sweeney said. He caught a glimpse of Roger eyeing the bearded man suspiciously.

"So: there is an Islamic tradition that goes back to the time before the Prophet when the secular concept *islam* meant defying death while fighting for the honor of your tribe," the man said. "From that day to this, when a martyr falls in battle, another martyr immediately comes forward to take his place."

"Good for Islam," Sweeney said with a straight face.

"Would it interest you to meet the warrior who will join our ranks in the place of the fallen martyr Anwar? It will surely provide you with what I believe journalists in America call a scoop."

Sweeney glanced at Roger, who shrugged his fat shoulders imperceptibly. "Sweeney is a friend of the Palestinian—" the driver started to say, but the Vestal Virgin cut him off with a burst of Arabic before turning to Sweeney. "I told him that if you weren't known to us as a friend of the Palestinian people, I would not be inviting you to meet the martyr of the *mujaddid*." He backed off a few paces and spread his palms wide. "If I intended to kidnap you, I would not invite you to follow me. I would produce a weapon and leave you no choice in the matter. Come. As the American President Roosevelt once said, you have nothing to fear but fear itself." The cleric looked past Sweeney. "You," he instructed Roger in English so the American journalist would understand, "will wait here for him."

Sweeney remembered an old Talullah Bankhead line. "If I'm not back in an hour," he told Roger, "start without me."

"Start what?" the driver called plaintively, but Sweeney had already stalked off after the cleric.

Walking at a brisk pace, never looking back to see if the American was still behind him, Vestal Virgin led Sweeney through the maze of side streets and alleyways of the Gaza souk. They strode past stalls brimming with apples and cucumbers and branches of dates and cheap plastic blonde-haired dolls. They stepped over suitcases filled with kerchiefs or small Japanese transistor radios or wind-up razors. One unshaven man with crutches under his armpits peddled bottles of aftershave out of a knapsack strapped to the back of a young woman. Sweeney noticed that knots of men seemed to magically part when one among them spotted the cleric approaching. Cutting diagonally across a field filled with rusting parts of cars and tractors, he followed his guide into Jabaliya, Gaza's largest refugee camp. "What does it mean, the martyr of the *mujaddid*?" he called, but Vestal Virgin, flying past a warren of open sewers and corrugated tin-roofed houses, didn't bother responding. They skirted goats grazing in the ruins of a demolished house. Stench from open sewers and burnt tires and rubbish piling up in drifts against walls mixed with the odors of fresh bread and anise seeds. Dogs with ribs pressing against their flesh and tails curled between their hind legs skulked in the shadows of tumbledown mosques. Through an open window Sweeney caught a glimpse of women in shawls watching an Egyptian soap opera on an enormous color television set.

The cleric ducked down a narrow alley and entered a store with bare shelves and paint peeling from the walls. Sitting on woven mats in a back room, three bearded Palestinians looked up when the American journalist entered. Without waiting for an invitation, Sweeney settled cross legged onto a mat. One of the bearded men offered him a plate filled with wedges of orange and green grapes. At the rear of the room the door to an alleyway opened and a young man with slicked back hair—he didn't look a day over sixteen—slipped in and took his place on a woven mat. Sweeney's guide said, "You are free to ask him any question you wish except his name."

Sweeney popped an orange sliver into his mouth and studied the boy, who was dressed in a long white robe and sandals. His feet were very dirty and he was chewing gum. "How old are you?" the American asked.

"Twenty-two," the young man said.

"What year were you born?" When the boy didn't respond immediately, Sweeney looked Vestal Virgin in the eye. "Here's the deal: This interview is only useful to me if I am convinced he is telling the truth."

"He is seventeen. Like all boys he exaggerates his age."

Sweeney turned to the boy. "Aren't you afraid?"

The bearded cleric translated the question. The young martyr-to-be carefully removed the chewing gum from his mouth and helped himself to a grape. He spit the seeds into the palm of his hand before replying. "He answers your question with a question," the cleric said. "'Why should I be afraid? Holy warriors will be rewarded in this life with victory and the spoils of war. Those who fall in battle will be rewarded with eternal life as martyrs. Life is beautiful, but the death of a martyr is more beautiful. On the day of reckoning, I will stand before the throne of God to be judged according to the record found in the Book of Deeds. The martyr will sit at the feet of the Prophet, who sits at the right hand of God.'"

"Describe the life after death that awaits a martyr."

"The Qur'an teaches that the Garden of Paradise is a heavenly mansion of perpetual bliss with flowing rivers and beautiful gardens where the tears of my mother are transformed into roses and jasmine."

"Can you describe God?"

"I cannot. The Qur'an does not reveal God, but God's will for all creation." The young man wiggled his toes in his sandals, then raised his eyes and quoted in the high-pitched voice of a choir boy, "'*No vision can grasp Him. He is above all comprehension.*'"

Sweeney had the distinct impression he was listening to a recorded announcement. On the other hand, even if the clerics had trotted out a theology student, as opposed to an aspiring terrorist, the replies made good copy. And there was something in the boy's eyes, an ember of fanaticism . . . Perhaps he *was* capable of blowing himself up on an Israeli bus or gunning down Jews from a roadside ambush; perhaps Sweeney *was* talking to the next victim of a low-caliber bullet fired with surgical accuracy (as the Israeli newspapers gleefully put it) behind the ear into the brain. Sweeney decided to try another tack. "Now that a peace treaty is to be signed in Washington, the Palestinian Authority has been throwing people like you in prison. Does it bother you that you are an outlaw in your own country?"

"The Palestinian Authority is making a terrible mistake," the boy said. "The politicians who pretend to be our leaders have been tricked into signing the treaty, tricked into arresting those of us who dedicate our lives to the liberation of Palestine. Between us and the Jews there can be no peace until they have returned the land they stole."

"Militarily speaking, the Israelis are much stronger than the Palestinians. How can you hope to make them return the land?"

"We cannot lose. The reason for this is that the Jews value life while we value death." The young man smiled self-consciously as he added: "The Qur'an teaches that as long as I follow the straight path, the way of God, to whom belongs all things that are in the heavens and all things that are on earth, victory is inevitable. If the Jews have up to now won the battles, it is not because they have more tanks and planes; it is because we Muslims have failed Islam. Thus teaches the *mujaddid,* Abu Bakr."

Sweeney turned to Vestal Virgin. "That's the second time I've heard that word. What does it mean, *mujaddid*?"

"The *mujaddid,*" the cleric replied with a quiet intensity that made the apprentice martyr catch his breath even though he didn't understand what was being said, "is the *Renewer* sent by God in the first years of each century to restore Islam. There are amongst us some who think that Abu Bakr may be the long-awaited *mujaddid.*"

"I would give my right arm to interview Abu Bakr," Sweeney said. He brought a forefinger up to his hearing aid. "That would really give me what the Americans call a scoop."

Vestal Virgin noticed the hearing device for the first time. Reaching over, he plucked it out of Sweeney's ear and held it to his own ear.

With his good ear, Sweeney heard him bark, "Say something."

"Yassar Arafat was a closet Jew and secretly ate kosher food until the day of his death."

The cleric grinned as he returned the hearing aid. "What is wrong with your ear?"

"I heard things I shouldn't. In Beirut."

"Like what?"

"A shell from a mortar exploding next to my car."

From somewhere over the roof tops came the recorded voice of the *muezzin* summoning the faithful to the second prayer of the day. "The interview is completed," the cleric announced. He motioned to the boy, who popped the gum back into his mouth as he sprang to his feet and let himself out the door. "One of my colleagues will guide you back to your automobile."

"How do I get in touch with you again?" Sweeney asked from the door.

"You don't." Vestal Virgin managed a devious smile. "When there is a scoop worthy of a friend of the Palestinian people, *we* will contact *you*, Mr. journalist Sweeney."

Twenty minutes later Sweeney found Roger tinkering with the motor of his Lada. "Did you get your interview, Mr. Max?" the driver asked cheerfully.

"What do you know about someone called the *mujaddid*?"

The cheerfulness drained from Roger's face. "There is no such person," he declared vehemently. "This *mujaddid* is a figment of Islamic imagination. If there really is a Renewer, it would be healthier for me not to answer your questions, and healthier for you not to ask them." Clamming up, Roger gunned the engine and concentrated on steering the old car through the torn streets of Gaza toward the Erez checkpoint.

EIGHT

ELIHU WAS GOING OVER SITUATION REPORTS AND INITIALING decrypted messages when Baruch finally got through to him on the phone. "Let's scramble," he said. Both men flicked switches on their consoles. "Anything coming out of Aza?" Baruch asked.

"Not a peep," Elihu said. "The Palestinian police are combing the Strip. Our own people are touching antennas with the handful of local agents we have left. So far the result is a big blank. It's almost as if Rabbi Apfulbaum and his secretary have dropped into a sink hole."

"I'm calling from Jerusalem," Baruch said. "I was going over a sheaf of informer sightings when I spotted something that made my nose twitch. Do you remember the Nablus bomb factory the Palestinian cops uncovered last summer? They found enough chemical fertilizer and detonators to make dozens of bombs, along with two local *mechablim*, but the guy who ran the factory, a twenty-seven-year-old Islamic fundamentalist named Yussuf Abu Saleh, slipped through their fingers."

"Abu Saleh. The name rings a bell. Isn't he the Hamas organizer whose two brothers were killed in a shootout some years ago in Jenin?"

"Yussuf was wounded in the shootout and sent to prison, but he eventually escaped from the Negev detention camp," Baruch said. "After that he disappeared from the radar screen. There was a report he'd been spotted at one of the secret al Qaida training camps in the tribal area between Afghanistan and Pakistan. When the Americans attacked Afghanistan after 11 September, Yussuf vanished into Pakistan. About a year ago we picked up rumors that Abu Saleh had surfaced in Nablus and antagonized the local Hamas folks by joining a new fundamentalist splinter group. He apparently took half the Nablus Hamas cell with him, along with a lot of their weapons. Hamas was furious enough to put a price on Abu Saleh's head; like the Mafia, Hamas is not an organization that takes defections lightly. Soon after that we heard rumors that Abu Saleh was recruiting for a kidnapping that was being organized to derail the signing of the Mt. Washington peace treaty. When I heard about this, I nosed around and came up with an intriguing detail: it turned out that Yussuf was married. We assumed he would stay away from his wife, but you never know, do you? I mean, dogs in heat have been known to scramble over electrified fences. So we gently leaned on the bride."

"Why gently?" Elihu demanded; he belonged to the school that argued that all force should be applied forcefully.

"She's the daughter of a rich Abu Tor lawyer," Baruch explained.

"So what did *gently* get you?"

"*Gently* didn't get us the time of day. She made no bones about being proud of him. But she swore she hadn't set eyes on Yussuf since the wedding night and didn't know where he was. We bought both these stories."

"Money down the drain," guessed Elihu.

"There may be a break in the case," Baruch went on. "That's what I'm phoning about. When Abu Saleh disappeared from Nablus, our people distributed photos of his wife to informers. According to the sighting file, one of them may have spotted her at the Damascus gate early in the morning. The young woman in question pulled off the scarf covering her face and waved to someone."

"How come the nuts and bolts boys didn't jump on the sighting while it was still fresh?"

"They thought she could have been waving to anybody—a girl friend, someone she does volunteer work with. But I remembered that Abu Saleh's wife had taken the veil. A devout Muslim wouldn't remove her scarf and reveal her face to anyone but her father or her brothers or her husband. The father and brothers were still in bed at that hour of the morning. So I figure the person she was waving to could have been the dog in heat."

"Lean on her again," Elihu advised. "This time don't wear kid gloves. As the British say, maybe she can help us with our inquiries."

NINE

MAALI, WHO DID TWELVE HOURS OF VOLUNTEER WORK A WEEK in a neighborhood Red Crescent clinic, checked with the woman behind the reception desk to see when her next stint was scheduled. Still wearing the white ankle-length apron over her long robe, she covered her head with a shawl and, pushing through the heavy door of the building in East Jerusalem, made her way to the back of the lot where her scooter was chained to a fence post. Standing on the starter, she kicked over the motor and pulled out into the traffic choking Nablus Road. She had blackmailed her father into buying her the Italian scooter four years before by threatening to run off with a Syrian, something she never had the slightest intention of doing, but then all was fair when it came to wrangling things out of her father. Since then she had met and married Yussuf and, inspired by her husband's example, turned deeply religious. She was ashamed of many of her teenage escapades—she had played the role of the spoiled princess to the hilt—but she never regretted the scooter, which allowed her to move freely about the city she loved, studying the Qur'an in a mosque one day, doing volunteer work for the Red Crescent the next, from time to time meeting Yussuf in the homes of trusted friends.

Halfway down Nablus road the traffic slowed to a crawl because of an accident, so Maali turned onto Amer Ibn El-Atz, which was being repaved and was closed to automobiles. Riding on the sidewalk, she could make out the fire-ball reflection of the midday sun in a high window up ahead; for a moment she thought the building was actually on fire. Near the corner where Amer Ibn El-Atz crossed Salah El Din, a BMW motorcycle with two men on it overtook the scooter and, veering sharply, forced it into a narrow driveway. Furious, Maali was about to shout an insult she had picked up from her younger brother, something impugning the driver's masculinity, when a bear of a man wearing a leather motorcycle helmet and goggles leaped on her. Before she could cry out he pinned her to the ground and, tugging free her shawl, pressed a sweet-smelling handkerchief over her mouth and nose.

Maali came to in the back of a small delivery van filled with burlap sacks of pistachio nuts. In the dirty light filtering through the two small windows in the back doors, she could see the man with the leather helmet and goggles sitting across from her, his legs stretched straight out, his spine against the side of the truck, calmly breaking open nuts and popping them in his mouth. She couldn't make out whether he was a Palestinian or a Jew. When he offered her a fist full of pistachios she turned her head away. "Your mother is a whore," she muttered in Arabic, hoping to identify her abductor from his response, but he only laughed under his breath.

Suddenly she remembered the ring Yussuf had taken from the dead Jew named Erasmus Hall. Wriggling into a sitting position, she hid her hands behind her back and tried to work it off, but she couldn't force it past the joint.

She was still struggling to remove the ring when, twenty minutes later, the delivery van bounced over what felt like railroad tracks, climbed a ramp and reversed up to a loading port. The engine was cut. The man in the motorcycle helmet held out a blindfold and motioned for Maali to put it on and knot it. "I categorically refuse," she said, raising her chin as she twisted the ring around so that the stone was on the palm side of her hand.

Speaking perfect Arabic, the man said so quietly that she shivered: "If you don't do it, I will."

Maali knotted the blindfold. The man reached over and adjusted it, then rapped twice on the side of the van. Maali could hear the back doors being thrown open. Strong hands reached in and pulled her from the van. With someone gripping each elbow, she was led up stone steps and through a door, then up a long flight of metal steps and into a warm room, where she was shoved up against a wall. "Remove the blindfold," a voice ordered in Arabic.

She tugged the blindfold down around her neck and immediately understood why the room seemed so warm; she was almost blinded by a bank of blazing spot lights trained directly on her. She could hear the soft buzz of whispering coming from shadowy figures in the back of the room. Then a man said, again in Arabic, "Yes, I'm absolutely sure she is the one I saw."

Two muscular women in blue jeans and turtleneck sweaters started to push Maali toward the door. As she was being led away, someone carelessly turned off the spotlights before she was out of the room. A man cursed in Hebrew and one of the women jerked the blindfold up over her eyes, but it was too late; over her shoulder Maali had caught a glimpse of a stooped Arab hastily pulling his *kif-fiyeh* up to cover his face. She could have sworn the man looked familiar—and then it came to her. Of course! It was Mr. Hajji, who had changed her Egyptian pounds into Israeli shekels at the Damascus Gate after her trip to Cairo.

Maali was hustled down a long corridor. She could hear metal doors clanging shut behind her and the voices of women whispering encouragement in Arabic from cells along the way. She was pushed through a door and instructed to remove the blindfold. Blinking, she found herself in a small, whitewashed room with a stainless steel table against a wall. One of the guards issued instructions in Hebrew, a language Maali understood but refused to speak. The prisoner was to strip to the skin. When Maali didn't move, the woman arched her penciled brows. "What are you ashamed of?" she asked.

Maali had heard stories of how the Isra'ili police systematically humiliated their prisoners before they questioned them. She was determined to remain calm. "Am I arrested?" she asked, but instead of answering, her jailers once again gestured for her to disrobe.

A fat woman wearing white trousers and the white jacket of a medical worker entered the room. "You must do as they tell you," she said in Arabic. "If you don't take off your clothing, they will summon the men and instruct them to do it for you."

Moving deliberately, Maali removed her garments and folded them one by one on the metal table until she finally stood naked in the middle of the room, with her right hand covering the ring on her left hand and her left hand covering her pubic hair. The woman pulled on a rubber glove and dipped her forefinger into a small jar filled with Vaseline. Then she motioned for the prisoner to bend over and grip her ankles. Tears spilled from Maali's eyes as the two women jailers folded her over like a sheaf of paper. She sucked in air as the medical worker roughly probed her vagina and then her anus. Straightening, she snatched a formless gray shift flung at her by one of the guards and hastily pulled it over her head. The medical worker came around with a small cardboard box and pointed at the prisoner's silver earrings. Maali took them off and dropped them into the box. The woman nodded at the gold locket around the girl's neck and the rings on her hands. Maali's heart sank as she worked her engagement ring, and then her wedding band, off her fingers and added them to the box. The woman pointed at the gold-colored ring on Maali's fourth finger. Maali made a half-hearted attempt to remove it, and then shrugged. "It's too tight," she said.

"Rules are rules," the woman said. She spread some Vaseline on the finger and worked the ring back and forth until it came free. She was about to drop it into the box when she noticed writing on the inside. Holding the ring up to the light, she sounded out the word. "E-ras-mus Hall." She looked at Maali. "This is a strange ring for an Arab woman to be wearing. Where did you get it?"

TEN

AS THE SUN BURNED ITS WAY THROUGH LOW CLOUDS INTO THE Judean Hills, the recorded sing-song message summoning the faithful to the fourth prayer of the day echoed from the minaret of the El Omariye Mosque in the Old City of Jerusalem. "*Allahu Akbar, Allahu Akbar,*" cried the *muezzin.* "Come to prayer, come to prayer. Come to prosperity, come to prosperity. God is most great, God is most great. There is no god but Allah." In the safe-house off Christian Quarter Road, only accessible by a maze of alleys and stair-cases and rooftop passageways, the Doctor prostrated himself before the *mihrab,* the niche cut into the wall to indicate the direction of the Kaaba built by the Messenger Ibrahim at the heart of the holy city of Mecca. Drumming his bruised forehead against the cracked Moorish floor tiles, savoring the pain, he recited the opening verse of the Qur'an: "In the Name of God, the Merciful, the Compassionate. Praise belongs to God, Lord of all Being, the All-merciful, the All-compassionate, the Master of the Day of Doom. Thee only we serve; to Thee alone we pray for succor. Guide us in the straight path, the path of those whom Thou hast blessed."

Next to the door reinforced with steel plating, the young Bedouin woman known as Petra sat before a green Israeli field radio, moni-toring military and police wavelengths through headphones. She was wearing blue jeans under her embroidered Bedouin robe. A kerchief was thrown loosely over her short hair. Two AK-47s, along with several gas masks and a carton filled with loaded clips and hand grenades, were within arm's reach. Across the room, a large British

Mandate map of Palestine, with place names in Arabic, was taped to the wall over a bricked-in window. On the kitchen table that doubled as a desk, glass paperweights with snow scenes from Switzerland weighed down stacks of newspaper clippings and messages.

Seeing that the Doctor had almost finished his prayers, Petra, who spoke Hebrew like a native Israeli and had been disguised as a *Haredi* when the Rabbi's convoy was flagged down near the Zohar Reservoir, removed the headset, which pinched her ears, and set out a pot of sweet tea and honey cakes on a low table to mark the end of the day's Ramadan fast. Settling cross-legged onto a Bedouin cushion before the low table, the Doctor poured himself a steaming cup of tea and blew noisily across the surface to cool it. Leaning over the table, cupping his hand to collect the crumbs, he nibbled on one of the cakes and swallowed an amphetamine capsule with his first gulp of tea. Across the room, in front of the *mihrab*, Yussuf Abu Saleh sank to his knees and began the evening's recitation of the Qur'an; each night of Ramadan he read aloud a thirtieth of the holy book in order to finish on the Feast of the Breaking of the Fast that marked the end of the holy month. "*God knows well your enemies*," he intoned.

> *Some of the Jews pervert words from their meaning . . . twisting with their tongues and traducing religion. If they had said, "We have heard and obey" . . . it would have been better for them, and more upright; but God has cursed them for their unbelief . . .*

Finishing his break-fast, the Doctor walked over to the laundry sink in the corner. Letting the water run, he removed his jacket and rolled up the sleeves of his robe and carefully scrubbed both of his hands and wrists and forearms to the elbows with soap and a brush, then raised his hands above his head and shook them dry. Slipping back into his jacket, he nodded to Petra, who came over and turned the faucet off for him.

Pushing open the thick reinforced door with the soft toe of his shoe, leaving the door ajar behind him, the Doctor made his way into a rectangular room illuminated day and night by a single 150-watt bulb suspended from a braided electric cord. The two armed guards, the el-Tel brothers, Azziz and Aown—one lounged on an Army cot under a bricked-in window while the other straddled a kitchen chair back-to-front and surveyed the prisoners—saluted the Doctor with grins; the youngest of the two, Azziz, leaped to his feet and spun the chair around so that the Doctor could sit on it in the normal way.

Picking at a crumb lodged between two teeth, the Doctor sat down on the kitchen chair, removed his thick wire-rimmed spectacles and meticulously cleaned the lenses with the hem of his long robe. His eyes, as usual, were bloodshot and swollen from fatigue. For the Doctor, there were not enough hours in the day, or days in a lifetime, which is why he kept himself awake with amphetamines. Replacing his spectacles, squinting through them to bring objects into focus, he studied the two prisoners, their heads covered with thick leather hoods, sleeping in the heavy wooden chairs set away from the wall with the Palestinian flag and the Ghazeh Central Import-Export Bank calendar. The short-sleeved shirt, the calendar had been Yussuf's bright idea: if you dropped enough hints that the Rabbi was being held prisoner in Ghazeh, so he had reasoned, the Jews would eventually conclude that we were trying to convince them he *wasn't* in Ghazeh and decide that he was. Yussuf's ruse seemed to have thrown the Isra'ilis off the scent; the public declarations on Isra'ili television and radio, as well as private intelligence reports reaching the Doctor from Ghazeh, indicated that the Jews were convinced the missing men were somewhere in the Strip. And Petra, monitoring the Isra'ili wavelengths, could detect no unusual police or Army activity in the Jerusalem area.

The ankles of both prisoners were lashed to the thick legs of the chairs, their wrists handcuffed in front of them. The younger of the two Jews slumped in his seat, his breath coming in frightened rasps. Rabbi Apfulbaum sat erect, his chin nodding onto his chest and jerking back up under the hood.

The Doctor leaned forward and pulled the hood from the Rabbi's head. Then, striking a wooden match, he held the flame to the tip of a rough Palestinian Farid and dragged on the cigarette in short, agitated puffs, as if he was smoking for the first time in his life.

Defying gravity, the ash grew longer than the cigarette until it finally broke off and drifted down onto the lapels of his double-breasted suit jacket. The Doctor, staring intently at his prisoner, didn't appear to notice the ashes. The foul-smelling smoke must have irritated the Rabbi, because he leaned away and, raising his manacled wrists, waved the back of one hand to dispel it. "In America," he remarked in Arabic, his eyes straining to make out his captor, "they print on the packs that cigarette smoking is hazardous for your health."

The Doctor grunted. "Being an Islamist in a Zionist-occupied country is hazardous for your health," he said in Hebrew. "Being right when everyone around you is wrong is hazardous for your health." He summoned a cheerless laugh from the depths of his gut. "In any case the question is academic because, as the holy Qur'an tells us, nobody lives a fraction of a second longer than God gives him to live." He reached out and grasped the Rabbi's bony wrist and felt for his pulse. After a moment, still talking in Hebrew, he commented, "All things considered, you appear to be in satisfactory health. How old are you?"

"Fifty-three," the Rabbi responded in Arabic.

"Do you have a family history of high or low blood pressure? Fainting? Heart trouble?"

"*Min fadlikoum*," the Rabbi said testily in Arabic. "*Please.* Stop this farce of inquiring about the health of someone you are going to put to death."

Switching to English, the Doctor said, "It is awkward, your talking Arabic, my talking Hebrew. I propose, *ya'ani*, that we meet on the no-man's land of English."

Apfulbaum's tongue flicked nervously over his parched lips. He sensed he had won the first skirmish. "We will talk in English if it suits you. But let's not delude ourselves—between us there can be no such thing as a no-man's land. We both want the same splinter of Holy Land, and I mean to have it."

The doctor smiled coldly. "You are what the Isra'ili newspapers call a maximalist, *ya'ani*. For you, there is no question of compromise. All or nothing is your creed. I myself am ready to negotiate an equitable settlement. I am ready to permit the Jews born in Palestine before 1948 to remain in the Islamic state I mean to create on the condition they convert to Islam."

"And the others?"

"They can go to hell, *ya'ani*."

The Rabbi's riotous brows danced above his bulging eyes. "Here, at last, is a charter member of the Amalek Liberation Organization," he cried excitedly to his secretary. He spun back to his interrogator. "Okay, okay, cards on the table. God promised Abraham and his descendants, me among them, all the land from the brook of Egypt, which we call the Nile, to the great river Euphrates. Contrary to published reports I consider myself a minimalist, inasmuch as I am prepared to settle for less than God offered Abraham; I, too, am willing to negotiate an equitable settlement, one giving the Jews everything between the Mediterranean and the River Jordan. When we've digested that, say in thirty or fifty years, we'll phone you up and make an appointment and raise the subject of the Euphrates."

The Doctor played the game. "What do you propose to do with the Palestinians who already live between the Mediterranean and the Jordan?"

Apfulbaum snorted contemptuously. "They can emigrate to Syria, which is worse than hell, *ya'ani*. The Jewish people occupy one sixth of one per cent of all Arab land, what Lord Balfour called 'a small notch' when he set it aside in 1917 for a Jewish state. I tell you frankly, the angels will abandon heaven to sell used Egyptian cars in Tel Aviv; God—blessed be His name—will turn up as a television anchor man before anyone takes a thimbleful of this sacred soil away from us."

Leaning against a wall, Azziz watched the two nearly blind men eyeing each other with a wordless fury. He wondered how long the prisoners would remain alive; he wondered how long he and his brother would remain alive. He had once confided to his brother that he could feel the temperature of the air rise the instant the Doctor entered a room; his almost sightless eyes seemed to burn with a fierce anger, which he kept bottled up inside him. He rarely lost his temper, though it would have been better if he let some of the anger seep out from time to time. Even those, like Azziz, who considered them-

selves disciples of the Doctor and suspected he was the long-awaited
Renewer were secretly terrified of his anger. They knew from experience that it could erupt into savage violence at any moment; they
knew they as well as the Jews could become its victims if the Doctor
decided their deaths would serve his cause.

In the strained silence, the soft voice of Yussuf reading from the
Qur'an could be heard.

> *Whosoever obeys God, and the Messenger—they are*
> *with those whom God has blessed, Prophets, just men,*
> *martyrs, the righteous.*

Petra slipped into the room with a cup of green tea and offered
it to the Rabbi. Wrapping both hands around the cup, Apfulbaum
brought the tea to his lips, all the while squinting over it at his interrogator. "I seem to have misplaced my eyeglasses. It probably happened in the excitement of the attack on my car."

"When I was a student at the American University of Beirut a
lifetime ago," the Doctor said, "I picked up some colloquial Arabic.
When a Lebanese Arab conquers an enemy he says, 'I broke his eye.'"
The Doctor felt the cigarette singe his lips and quickly dropped it on
the floor. "I broke your eye, *ya'ani*." His long fingers played with a
loose button on his jacket. "I see now that I am going to enjoy our
conversations. I will admit something that will surprise you: I have
never before spoken seriously with a Jew I wasn't afraid of, which is
understandable since the great majority of the Jews I talked to were
my interrogators or my torturers or my judges or my jailers. I spent
twelve years in Jewish prisons. *Twelve years, ya'ani!* Every conversation with a Jew was an ordeal. I was afraid they would take away my
spectacles, without which I, too, am virtually blind; I was afraid they
would take away my books or my cigarette ration or my right to one
visitor a month. I was afraid they would kick the chair out from
under me and then smile politely and ask me if I had slept well the
night before. There were times, I tell you openly, when I was afraid
they would kill me; there were others when I feared they would not."

The Rabbi couldn't restrain himself. "One confidence deserves another. I have never before had a serious conversation with an Arab who wasn't afraid of me; who wasn't eager to assist me, to ingratiate himself with me, to guide me, to agree with me."

The Doctor pushed himself to his feet. "For too long you Jews have seen every Palestinian, every Muslim, as a terrorist. Now you have the good fortune to be confronted with a real flesh-and-blood terrorist, someone come to life from your nightmares to wage holy war for Allah and for Islam. Even without eyeglasses, *ya'ani*, even without *sight*, you can learn from the experience. If you look with your broken eyes you will see something deeper than terrorism: a yearning to serve God and do His will."

Apfulbaum had a sudden vision of himself as a *bar mitzva* boy, sitting at the enormous table in the Brooklyn *yeshiva*, his feet barely reaching the floor, delivering outrageous answers to his Rabbi's Talmudic questions. "Who does he think he is," the old Rabbi had complained on more than one occasion, "the Messiah?" Now, face to face with a Muslim terrorist, Apfulbaum couldn't resist the urge to shock him. "With my broken eyes I see a crazy follower of a crazy religion."

Efrayim wheezed for air under his leather hood. Thinking that the young man was suffocating, the Doctor reached over and snatched the hood off his head. Gasping, the secretary stared in terror at his jailer. Turning back toward Apfulbaum, the Doctor's fingers stole toward his breast pocket and settled on the pearl handle of his pistol; he contemplated shooting the Rabbi out of hand for his blasphemy, but the admonition in the Qur'an came as if by magic into his head. "*Act you according to your station . . . watch and wait.*" He withdrew his hand. "All religions, even yours, *ya'ani*, appear at first glance to be crazy. Explain how Yahweh could give Moses His instructions at the burning bush one minute, and then try to murder him for no reason under the sun the next. Explain why your God punishes Adam and Eve for a single transgression and drowns mankind in a great flood for some vague offense, and then commends the generosity of Joseph for forgiving his brothers who sold him into slavery. It is this craziness, or put another way, this larger-than-life-ness, this irreducibility to man-measured logic, that gives to

Islam its intrinsic beauty. We shall talk again tomorrow night after
my colleagues and I have broken the Ramadan fast. We shall talk
every night. I will ask you about your community of Beit Avram. I
will ask you about the Jewish underground movement, of which you
are said to be the spiritual leader. I will ask you about the Jewish terrorist who signs himself by the name of Ya'ir when he takes credit for
the assassinations of Palestinians."

"Ask, ask," Apfulbaum cooed like an owl. "I will play the cards
God has dealt me as long as I am able to. I understand that when you
grow bored, you will pull this stinking hood over my head. I understand that when you become fed up with my failure to provide
answers, you will kill me."

Yussuf's voice drifted through the partially open door:

> Wherever you may be, death will overtake you, though
> you should be in raised-up towers.

"You misunderstand the game, ya'ani," the Doctor said, slipping
the leather hood back over the Rabbi's head. "You have reached what
the followers of the Messenger Jesus would call the last station of
your cross. I am not offering to exchange answers to my questions f
or your life; I am offering to exchange them for your dignity. You and
your friend here will live or die depending on whether your government meets my demands. You will live or die with or without dignity
depending on whether you meet *my* demands."

Returning to the outer room, the Doctor went immediately to
the laundry sink and scrubbed his hands again to purify himself after
the contact with the infidel. Petra, who did the shopping and
brought back newspapers every morning, prepared the evening meal
on the electric hot plate and served it on porcelain dishes: there were
zucchini stuffed with meat and covered with a milky sauce, soft
cheese and pitta bread, tea and almond biscuits. Yussuf finished his
reading of the Qur'an and joined the Doctor at the low table. "How
did it go?" he asked. "Do you think he will talk before the deadline
comes and we are obliged to kill him?"

"I locate his center in an invincible arrogance," the Doctor said, thinking out loud, "and his arrogance in the seemingly unshakable conviction that Jews are superior to Muslims, Israelis are superior to Palestinians and he is superior to me. If, with God's help, I can shake this conviction—if I can bring him to respect me, to love me even—his arrogance will abandon him and his center will fall apart, at which point he will tell us what we want to know; he will rack his brain for details to convince us that he is not inventing answers." The Doctor smiled to himself as he recalled some lines from the holy Qur'an. "'*We will draw them on little by little whence they know not,*'" he murmured. "'*My guile is sure.*'"

In the back room, it was Azziz's turn to stretch out on the cot. Yawning, Aown pulled the hood over Efrayim's head, then shuffled in his open-backed slippers to the Turkish toilet in the corner, dropped his trousers and squatted above the hole in the floor.

Rocking back and forth in his chair, choking on the foul smells emanating from the leather of the hood, Efrayim moaned to himself. "Ah, I am condemned to death."

"Stop sniveling and pull yourself together," Apfulbaum whispered harshly. "We are all condemned to death. Our friend was right: Nobody lives a second longer than God gives him to live."

Efrayim was horrified. "You're quoting from the Koran, Rabbi."

"The Koran stole from the Torah, Muhammad plagiarized Moses. Abraham, a patriarch to the Jews, is reincarnated as one of several Messengers for the Islamists."

Efrayim barely heard him. Wracking his brain for omens, he found one that caused him to catch his breath. "He permitted me to *see* him, which means he doesn't expect me to leave here alive."

"What does he look like?"

"His face looks as if a smile has never crossed his lips. He is smug, and cock-sure of himself. He thinks that God is on his side."

"I could hear that much in his voice. I meant physically."

"He is a short man with short cropped hair and the delicate fingers of a concert pianist. He wears small round spectacles which are so thick they magnify the pupils of his eyes."

"He suffers from tunnel vision," the Rabbi guessed. He snickered. "God's metaphor."

"There is an injury on his forehead, not unlike yours. His skin is bruised, the bone of his skull bulges as if he's been butting his head against a wall."

"You are describing a frustrated Palestinian."

Efrayim asked, "What does it mean, this word *ya'ani* that he repeats over and over?"

"It is a nervous tic, the equivalent of *well* or *you know*, not a term of endearment."

"He means to kill us," the secretary repeated. "It is against government policy to trade Jewish hostages for Arab prisoners."

"When the time comes to die," the Rabbi told his young secretary, "we must do so with such dignity that the one who slays us will understand the Jews are the chosen of God." And he added: "If the game is dignity, I will be an apt player."

An Excerpt from the Harvard "Running History" Project:

I have to hand it to you, you're asking all the right questions. You need to understand that in the best of times the Middle East portfolio is a can of worms. The President's Special Assistant for Middle Eastern Affairs walks a tight rope between the Jewish lobby in America and the Arab reality in the field; between the Defense Department and the CIA; between the White House and the State Department; between the Congressional hawks, who are ready to fight to the last drop of Israeli blood, and the doves, who haven't learned anything from history about appeasement. Inside any administration the long knives are always sharpened and out when it comes to Israel and the Arabs. Which explains why you noticed my secretary fitting on the headset and taking down the conversation I had with the President in shorthand. Henry Kissinger used to do the same thing when he was sitting in the basement of the White House working for Richard Nixon. Like Kissinger, I want to have a record of the conversation in case things go from bad to worse and the White House Praetorians decide someone has to fall on his sword.

You guessed it, that someone won't be me.

As for the conversation with the President: after what seemed like an eternity she finally came on the line. There were no apologies for keeping me waiting, no small talk. "What do you make of this kidnapping, Zack?" she said, her voice as curt and crabby as ever. I don't think I'll ever cease being awed by the woman's ability to turn on the charm in public and yet be so graceless in private. I once saw her, her photo-op smile pasted on her lips for the benefit of the cameras recording the moment, tell an Undersecretary of State, sotto voce, "I don't give a damn what you think. Just do it."

You're right, I am straying from the subject.

The subject is Israel. The subject is the kidnapping of this crazy Rabbi what's-his-name. That's it. Apfulbaum. I reported to the President that we had gone into a damage control mode, our object being to keep the lid on long enough to get this peace treaty signed in Washington. I told the President I'd talked to both sides again this morning. The bottom line is the Israelis won't wear sackcloth and ashes if Apfulbaum winds up dead. From the Prime Minister's point of view, that'll be one less critic of the peace process to deal with. On the other side of the fence, the Palestinians won't light memorial candles for the Abu Bakr Brigade for much the same reasons.

"So I'm off the hook," the President said. (Her use of the first person singular wasn't lost on me; seen from the Oval Office, it's the President's opportunity to win a Nobel Prize, as well as America's security and regional stability, that's at stake.) Yes, "I'm off the hook" were her exact words; I can have my secretary show you her shorthand notes if you'd care to see them. After which the President added, "Even if this ends in a shootout, they'll still turn up in Washington for the signing, right?"

At which point I said something like, "Wrong, Madam President. For the record, the signing is still on the agenda; neither side wants to be seen to be the first to back away from the peace agreement. Off the record, both sides are saying the same thing: they're afraid of getting sucked back into a vicious circle. It's the principle that plagues them: if an Israeli politician is to survive politically, Jews who get murdered by Palestinians must be avenged, and vice versa."

I got the feeling that the President's patience was being sorely tested. "Listen, Zack," she said; I'm quoting her from memory again. "I want you to read them the riot act. Lean on them—the President of the United States expects this to be treated as an isolated incident. Let them let the police deal with it. The President of the United States won't permit the tail to wag the dog; she won't put up with a return to the status quo ante, where the lunatic fundamentalist fringe on both sides drove policy. You remind the Israelis that my get-tough-on-Israel policy plays surprisingly well in the streets. You remind the Palestinians that you can count the Palestinian voters in the U.S. on the fingers of one hand. God damn it, Zack, I haven't come this far to let the peace thing slip through my fingers."

That's correct. That's what she said. "Peace thing."

No, there was no goodbye, only the shrill peal of the severed connection ringing in my ear.

ELEVEN

THE SHIN BET MANDARINS DIDN'T BEAT AROUND THE BUSH. "We appreciate your coming over on such short notice," said the bald man presiding over the morning session in the Tel Aviv conference room. He introduced himself and the others around the table using first names. "I'm David. This is Zev. This is Itamar."

"I wouldn't pass up an invitation from Israel's illustrious FBI," Sweeney said sweetly. He nodded toward the portly man in sunglasses sitting on the sill of the window. "Who's he? J. Edgar Hoover?"

"He's from Amnesty International," David said with a straight face. "He's here to make sure we don't tickle you to death."

"You guys are a laugh a minute," Sweeney said. "Do any of you have last names, or do you go through life using only first names?"

The men around the table avoided each other's eyes. At the window sill, J. Edgar, as Sweeney now thought of him, actually cracked a languid smile. David said, "Our press people got hold of the story you wrote on the Aza wake. It was very moving. Our hearts bleed for poor Anwar, who had the bad luck to be wounded while murdering four Jews and abducting two others, and was then shot in the brain by his own side so he wouldn't fall into our clutches."

"War is hell," remarked Sweeney.

The man called Itamar said, "You've been in Israel long enough to know that the Shin Bet is in the life and death business of defending Jews from terrorist attacks. You could make our work easier if you told us more about the *mujaddid*, or Renewer, you mentioned in your article."

"Does this Abu Bakr, whoever he is, actually claim to be the Renewer," David wanted to know, "or are some Islamic fundamentalists claiming it on his behalf? What is the relationship between the individual who goes by the name Abu Bakr, and the Abu Bakr Brigade which claimed responsibility for the kidnapping of Rabbi Apfulbaum and his secretary? Is Abu Bakr the active leader of the brigade, or just its spiritual leader?"

"Did Jesus claim to be the Messiah," Sweeney shot back, "or did the disciples hang the label around his neck? Was there any connection between this Messiah and the uprising against the Romans organized by Barabbas?" He stretched his lanky body in the chair. "Whichever, everything I know about the Renewer is in my article."

The agent called Zev tapped a stack of loose-leaf books filled with photographs of Palestinians. "We have pictures of thousands of people who took part in *intifada* demonstrations. You would be rendering a service to Israel if you could identify the cleric who guided you to the store, as well as the kid who was served up as the next martyr."

Sweeney said, "Don't tell me, let me guess; if I cooperate, you'll plant a tree for me on a barren hillside and hang a plaque on it identifying someone named Max—no last names, please—as a righteous gentile."

Itamar flattened a map of the Jabaliya refugee camp on the table with the palm of his hand. "It would be useful if you could tell us where the cleric took you—even if you only have a rough idea."

"There were too many twists and turns for me to pick out the route even if I had a sense of direction, which I don't. Look, it's obvious to me even if it isn't obvious to you that the cleric and the kid were the B team engaged in public relations for the Islamic fundamentalist folks. I know you guys think Palestinians are dumb, but even they aren't dumb enough to trot out the A team for an American journalist who's bound to be questioned by Israelis with only first names. The whole thing—the talk of a Renewer, the cleric, the kid— was a PR job."

David observed coldly, "That's not what you said in your article."

"I wrote it the way it happened. The reader is free to put any spin on the story he wants."

Itamar said, "You didn't write about the Rabbi's kidnapping the way it happened. You barely mentioned the four dead Jews. You left out the business about the finger being cut off."

Sweeney shrugged. "You guys are trying to make me feel guilty for going into Gaza and talking to a father who was mourning the death of his son."

From the window sill, J. Edgar said quietly, "The four dead Jews have fathers who are mourning the deaths of sons. You didn't knock on their doors."

"Look," Sweeney said, "as long as I don't jeopardize Israeli security by spilling state secrets, whom I interview and what I write about is my business."

David tried one more time. "You were taken to meet the martyr who is supposed to step into the shoes of the dead Anwar. That makes it Shin Bet business. You may be right—the cleric with the pointed beard who took you into Jabaliya, the fresh-faced kid you met there may come under the heading of public relations. But we have to act on the assumption that the kid you interviewed could walk into a crowded Tel Aviv movie theater tomorrow carrying a knapsack crammed with explosives—unless you pick out his photograph and we can convince the Palestinian Authority's cops to incarcerate him first."

Sweeney swallowed a yawn. "The least you guys could do is serve coffee and doughnuts at this hour of the morning."

"How about it, Mr. Sweeney?" David said pleasantly. "Do us a favor and take a look at our loose-leaf books."

"What's in it for me?"

Itamar lost his temper. "What do you want, a medal or money?"

Sweeney scraped back his chair and stood up. "I work for a respectable leftwing publication, not the Shin Bet. The moment I become an agent for the Shin Bet, I lose my credibility as a journalist."

David said quickly, "I guarantee nobody is going to know you helped us."

"Why didn't you spell that out before? The kid you're looking for is seventeen years old, has dirty feet and the angelic smile of a choir boy. Ah, yes, and he chews gum." Sweeney had to laugh. "Listen, I can personally name three reporters who cooperated with you. If I know who they are, you can bet the Palestinians know who they are. And if the Palestinians know, everyone in the Middle East knows. Which is why two of the three are afraid to set foot outside Jewish Jerusalem. The third still goes into the West Bank on assignment, but he's suicidal."

Itamar angrily folded the map. "We're wasting our breath. This is the guy who wrote the article about the reservist complaining he was ordered to break the arms of Palestinians."

"You fellows tried to get me kicked out of Israel over that one," Sweeney noted. "You backed down when it turned out the reservist did complain, and arms were broken."

David pushed a small button on the telephone console. A uniformed guard opened the door. "He'll show you out," David said.

"I'm a big boy," Sweeney said. "I can find my own way."

"That's what you think," Itamar mumbled.

J. Edgar came off the window sill. "It goes without saying, this meeting, what was said during it, is off the record."

Sweeney turned back at the door. "Hey, it doesn't go without saying. Here's the deal: everything is on the record until someone says it isn't. I promise not to quote anything you say from here on out." Sweeney looked from one to the other. "Don't get nervous, I'll only use your first names when I write about how the Shin Bet tried to recruit an American journalist."

"Anti-Semitic prick!" Itamar muttered under his breath.

"I heard that," Sweeney said. "Too bad it's off the record. It'd make a perfect kicker to my story."

TWELVE

I T WAS BARUCH, WITH HIS DETECTIVE'S MANIA FOR DETAIL, WHO fitted the first two pieces of the puzzle together. He had phoned his wife from his Jerusalem office to say he would be late for supper. "So what's new?" she had asked with a faint laugh in her voice. Baruch never talked shop at home but knowing him, she took it for granted he would be burning midnight oil after the kidnapping of Rabbi Apfulbaum. "Only once, call to say you'll be home early," she had quipped, "I'll die of a heart attack."

"Thanks," Baruch had said.

"For what?"

"For being there. For having a sense of humor. For keeping the food warm." He had added quietly, "For keeping the flame alive."

"Are you all right, Baruch?"

His answer had almost been lost in a low growl. "I'll never be all right."

"Me neither. I miss her so." She had caught her breath. "Sorry. We weren't supposed to . . . Sorry."

Hanging up, Baruch turned on the desk lamp and picked up the silver-framed photograph of his daughter. He had snapped the picture the day she finished officer's school. The back of her hand covered her mouth, trying to stifle a smile of pride, but her eyes gave her away. She was nineteen years old and freckled and lean and beautiful in her short khaki Army skirt and khaki sweater. "Do me a favor, phone up when you get back to the base," Baruch had said when he dropped her off at the bus station after her leave. "Oh, *aba*, I'm an officer in the Israeli Army, not a school girl." She had pulled a face. "If it will make you happier, I'll call."

She never called. The radio had interrupted its program for a bulletin. A bomb had exploded at the Beit Lid junction. Twenty-one soldiers, three of them girls, had been killed, dozens more had been wounded. His daughter had been identified from her dog tags. At the funeral the next day Baruch's wife had collapsed when a personal message from the Prime Minister had been read aloud. "Jews have died for Israel in the past," he wrote, "they will die for Israel in the future. I have no consolation to offer, only an unshakable conviction to hang on to: this land, this people, would not exist if it weren't for the girls and boys, our daughters and our sons, whom we bury today." As for Baruch, his hair had started to turn white the morning of the funeral; within three weeks it was the color of chalk.

Baruch set the silver frame down on the desk and glanced again at the photograph of Rabbi Apfulbaum, snapped in the Jewish kibbutz of Yad Mordechai hours before he was kidnapped. Picking up a magnifying glass, he took a closer look at his face. Was it his imagination or could he actually see the Rabbi's eyes burning with biblical zeal? Baruch didn't know whom he feared most or liked less, the crazy Jews or the crazy Muslims, each armed with fundamentalist versions of ancient myths that took every biblical or Koranic injunction literally; each flaunting an arrogance that came from having a hot-line to God; each confusing his subjective world view for an objective orthodoxy. Shaking his head, Baruch began reading the official account of the conversation between a Jerusalem police brigade commander and Attorney Nabil Abad al-Chir, the father of the prisoner Maali.

> Q. You are positive there is no trace of her in the Jewish hospitals?
>
> A. Nothing. I can say for sure that she was not in an accident.
>
> Q. And your jails? The Jewish jails—
>
> A. I had a search made when you phoned me yester-

day. There is no Maali al-Chir Abu Saleh in Israeli
hands.

Q. What about the Italian scooter?

A. There is nothing on the scooter either. Look, it's
no secret your daughter is married to the Abu
Saleh who is high on our most wanted list. So if he
couldn't come to her, maybe she went to him.

Q. She would have left a note—

A. Girls. I have two myself. When it comes to chas-
ing after boys, they sometimes forget they have parents. I'll call you if we hear anything . . .

Baruch flipped to the next page and started reading the transcript
of the interrogation of the wife of Yussuf Abu Saleh. He had conducted enough interrogations in his career to read between the lines.
The prisoner Maali would have been brought into a room with
padded walls and no heating, and seated on a stool whose front legs
were slightly shorter than its rear legs to be sure she was uncomfort-
able. All four legs of the stool would be bolted to the floorboards.
Strong spotlights would be trained on her; saturated in light, angling
her head to escape it, shielding her eyes with a forearm, she would
look like a deer caught in the headlights of a car: frightened, con-
fused, ready to bolt at the sound of a twig snapping if there had been
some place to bolt to. From the darkness beyond the lights, the tone-
less voice of the interrogator would pitch questions at her.

Q: When was the last time you saw your husband?

A: I answered that yesterday. I answered it this
morning.

Q: Answer it again.

A: I have not set eyes on Yussuf since the night of my
wedding, six months ago.

Q: Then why were you waving to him at the
Damascus Gate?

A: I wasn't [unintelligible].

Q: If you weren't waving to Yussuf, whom were you waving to?

A: I don't remember waving to anyone.

Q: You were seen waving to someone. You uncovered your face and waved. Which means you were waving to your father or one of your brothers or your husband, Yussuf.

A: Maybe it was my younger brother, Sami. Yes. I [unintelligible]. It must have been [unintelligible].

Q: Speak louder. It was seven thirty in the morning. Sami was sound asleep in the home of your father in Abu Tor.

Baruch skimmed the transcript to the end, then reread the last page.

A: I haven't been permitted to sleep since you arrested me. I must sleep.

Q: You haven't been arrested. You have been detained for questioning. You will be permitted to sleep when you have told us what we want to know. Whom were you waving to at the Damascus Gate?

A: I want to see my mother.

Q: Whom were you waving to?

A: [unintelligible].

Q: Whom were you waving to?

A: The light stings my eyes.

Q: Where did you get this ring?

A: What ring? Oh, *that* ring. I bought it from a Bedouin who sells jewelry in the souk.

Q: What is the name of the Bedouin? What street is his shop on?

A: I don't remember.

Q: How long ago did you buy it?

A: A month, maybe [unintelligible].

Q: Take her back to the cell.

A: I vomited on my dress. I [unintelligible] the smell. You must give me another dress—

This was the first time Baruch had seen a ring mentioned in the Maali interrogation. He wondered why the interrogator had bothered raising the subject. Had something caught his eye? Baruch flipped through the dossier to the official interrogation center description of the detainee's possessions, with Maali's almost illegible signature on the bottom of the page.

One leather wallet containing forty-five shekels and twenty agora in notes and coins, along with an Israeli identity card and a motor scooter registration card.

One key, believed to be the front door key of her father's villa in Abu Tor.

One 14-carat gold chain and locket containing a lock of hair and a black-and-white photograph of a man we've identified as Yussuf Abu Saleh.

One pair of silver clover-leaf earrings.

One 14-carat gold engagement ring with a slightly scratched garnet stone.

One 18-carat gold wedding band.

One gold-colored ring with an unidentified crest on an unidentified stone and a man's name, "Erasmus Hall," and the date 1998 engraved on the inside.

"Who is Erasmus Hall?" Baruch asked aloud. He swiveled in his chair and gazed through the window at Jewish Jerusalem, stretching to the horizon and turning mauve in the musky twilight. Baruch, a namesake of the scribe who recorded the doomsday declarations of the prophet Jeremiah six hundred years before Jesus, had been a cop here for all of his professional life. Jerusalem, for him, was a city of sediments, a dozen Jerusalems piled one on top of the ruins of the other. If you strip-mined it, brushing away layer after layer, you just might one day reach something that looked suspiciously like bedrock: King David's Jerusalem. He wondered if there had been cops in David's capital. There surely had been crime and where there was crime, there were cops.

"Erasmus Hall," he repeated—and he began working through the sediments of this particular crime. Swiveling back to the desk, he lit off the computer and punched in his personal code, then typed in the word "Apfulbaum" and drummed his fingers on the desk as he waited for the menu to appear on the screen. He keyed the comput-er down to "Ancillary Dossiers" and ran a search for the name "Hall, Erasmus." The computer drew a blank. Mystified, he started to read through the biographies of the secretary, Efrayim, and the three bodyguards who had been killed in the kidnapping and the one who had died later on the operating table. One of the bodyguards was named Ronni Goldman. Scrolling through the dead boy's back-ground, he came across a reference to the date 1998.

Moments later Baruch was dialing the Goldmans' home number in Brooklyn, New York, U.S.A. He got the dead boy's father on the line. "My name is Baruch," he said. "I'm calling from Jerusalem. I'm trying to catch the people who murdered your son. I'm sorry to open wounds but there's something I need to know."

"What time is it in Israel?" the father asked.

"Almost six."

"What's the weather like?"

"It's cold and crystal clear. The sun is disappearing behind a hill. Jerusalem is bathed in a golden light."

Goldman's voice crackled over the international line. "When Ronni wrote home, he always talked about Jerusalem the golden."

"According to our records, your son graduated from a Brooklyn high school in nineteen ninety-eight."

"That's right. It was in June of ninety-eight. We wanted him to go to college and study medicine. He wanted to go to Israel and study Torah."

"What was the name of the high school?"

"Erasmus, on the corner of Flatbush and Church."

"Is Erasmus the full name of the school?"

The father hesitated. "I think the full name is Erasmus Hall High School. Something like that."

"Did Ronni own a high school graduation ring?"

Baruch could hear the dead boy's father blowing his nose. After a moment Goldman came back on the line. "Thirty-five dollars he spent on the ring," he said, his voice faltering. "What's so important, you ask now about a ring?"

"What I really want to know," Baruch said softly, "is what finger he wore it on." He caught his breath so he wouldn't miss the answer.

Goldman suddenly understood why Baruch was phoning from Jerusalem to raise the painful subject of his son's mutilation. "They sold him a ring a size smaller—." The dead boy's father held his hand over the phone and collected himself and started again. "A size smaller than he asked for. Rather than return it, he wore it on the finger the newspapers say the terrorists cut off. The pinky finger."

THIRTEEN

THE DIRECTOR OF THE MILITARY AFFAIRS COMMITTEE, ZALMAN Cohen, a baby-faced prodigy whom the press had dubbed the Prime Minister's Alter Ego, ambled into the conference room. In his very early thirties, he was dressed in rumpled black trousers and a white open-necked shirt with the sleeves rolled up above his fat elbows. Baruch and the *katsa*, seated at the end of a long rectangular table, climbed to their feet. An arid smile worked its way onto Cohen's beefy face as he offered a pudgy palm in a politician's handshake—a fleeting feather-weight touching of fingers—and walked over to a sideboard to pour some mineral water into a glass. He plucked two enormous pills from a vial, threw them into the back of his mouth, tilted his head back and gulped them down with a muscular throbbing of his Adam's apple. "If you're not taking vitamins, you ought to," he grunted, flopping into a chair at the far end of the conference table, a soccer field away from his visitors. "You probably know that Zachary Sawyer has been burning up the phone lines to the Prime Minister—four Jews have been murdered, two others have been kidnapped, but as usual the White House expects us to be the ones to show restraint, maturity, moderation and discretion."

"The Americans are worried sick this will spiral out of control and scuttle the Mt. Washington peace treaty," the *katsa* remarked.

"No reason for that to happen if we all keep our eyes on the prize," Cohen said.

"And what is the prize?" Baruch inquired, blinking innocently.

"The prize is peace in our time," Cohen declared. He snickered as he came up with the line Chamberlain had used to explain Britain's 1938 abandonment of the Sudetenland to appease Hitler. It was widely known that Cohen considered any concessions to the Palestinians to be appeasement; that he would have preferred a military solution to the Palestinian question over a political one; that he, like his Prime Minister, would go to Washington and sign the treaty to get the Americans off their back and buy time. In six or eight months, when the White House was distracted by another crisis, the government would test the temperature of the water. If the public outcry from the "Peace Now" crowd could be somehow muted, they would allow themselves to be "provoked" into occupying strategic arteries and areas of the West Bank. "It goes without saying," Cohen continued, "that the Palestinians must get the lion's share of the blame if we fail to achieve peace in our time."

"Neither Baruch nor I are consulted on policy matters," the *katsa* commented. "We are nuts and bolts people who deal with the situation on the ground."

"That's why you've been brought here," Cohen said. "So I can spell out the government's position with respect to the situation on the ground. Just so we're playing from the same music, the bottom line is what it's always been. We will never bow to terrorism. We will never release terrorists or pay money to free hostages. There will be no deal now or ever with the *mechabel.*"

Baruch eyed Cohen across the table; he had the impression that all those vitamins were transforming his skin into the sallow parchment of a Dead Sea scroll. "You're not responding to the written question we submitted to the Prime Minister."

"The formal answer to your formal question is, yes, you can nibble at the edge of any deal you care to invent in order to buy time. I am authorized to release appropriately vague pronouncements in the Prime Minister's name. When the press asks if we are willing to negotiate, we will say we're not ruling anything out. We will say that all options are being explored, with the emphasis on the word *all.*"

"The Working Group appreciates the Prime Minister's willingness to play along with our efforts to buy time," Elihu informed the director. The *katsa*'s eyes narrowed, his voice turned cautious. "Given the circumstances, we didn't want to climb out on a limb and have it cut off behind us."

The PM's Alter Ego rolled his head from side to side as if he was trying to work out a stiff neck; for Cohen, cutting off limbs was indoor sport. "The Prime Minister and his cabinet appreciate your tactfulness in putting the question," he said in a patronizing tone, and Baruch was reminded, once again, of why he loathed Zalman Cohen. He was one of those wily political creatures who thought that peace was a continuation of war by other means; that the manipulation of the peace in preparation for the next war was too important to be left to people who hadn't mastered Machiavelli.

Cohen absently wound the stem of the oversized watch on his soft wrist. "If you find out where Apfulbaum is being held, organize a raid—I'm told you do that sort of thing nicely. If you get him out alive, we'll take the credit. If not . . ." The director flaunted his mirthless smile, which had been caricatured in a thousand newspaper cartoons. "We all understand that raids of this nature imply risks. Rest assured that no one will second guess you if the Rabbi is murdered before you can liberate him."

Baruch avoided looking at Elihu. "Why are you afraid of Apfulbaum?" he inquired, his eyes fixed on Cohen. "In terms of numbers, in terms of political influence, Islamic fundamentalists are a cloud of locusts. Ours are an occasional horsefly."

Cohen's smile evaporated, leaving behind the faint trace of a tired smirk. "You swat horseflies," he said quietly. "If we had a choice, we'd naturally prefer the autopsy to show the shot that killed this particular horsefly came from Abu Bakr's .22-caliber handgun."

"Are you telling us you prefer Apfulbaum dead?" Elihu asked blandly.

A trumpet-call bleated through Cohen's soft lips; Baruch realized the Prime Minister's flunky was sounding retreat. "I most certainly am not telling you we prefer him dead, for God's sake. I am telling you we prefer him alive. But we will *understand* if he becomes an unavoidable casualty. We will rend our clothing and mourn publicly, we will send the minister of public cesspools to attend the funeral of this Jewish shit."

Baruch glanced at the *katsa*. Like Elihu, he knew how to read between the lines, and he didn't like what he found there. "Moments before my father died he asked me to pinch his skin," he told Cohen. "Harder, he said. Pain is what makes you know you're alive, he said." Baruch cocked his thumb and forefinger as if they were a pistol and sighted on the Prime Minister's Alter Ego. "Meeting people like you reminds me that I'm alive."

Elihu scraped back his chair. "We appreciate your sharing the Prime Minister's views with us," he informed the director of the military affairs committee. A scowl stole over the *katsa*'s face as he added in absolutely the same conversational tone, "If it is possible to get Apfulbaum out alive, we will. And you can go to hell."

Elihu was striding toward the door before the baby-faced director could utter a word. Baruch was hard on his heels. Neither of them looked back.

FOURTEEN

THE FREE CLINIC, FINANCED BY SEVERAL MUSLIM NEIGHBORHOOD associations and staffed by Doctor al-Shaath and a handful of volunteers, was running late. First two taxi drivers had carried in an epileptic man who, when he recovered consciousness, ranted on until the Doctor calmed him with an injection. "Jerusalem is the virgin promised to the Arabs," the patient cried, clinging to one of the male nurses, "but you permitted the thief to enter her room during the night. You listened behind the door to the cries of her defloration." Then two clerics had caused a commotion when they brought in a young man with a superficial knife wound in his groin; he needed to be treated without going to a hospital, where he would attract the attention of the Isra'ili police. Angling the surgical lamp so that it bathed the boy's groin in light, bending close to the raw wound, squinting through a low-power magnifying lens positioned over the wound, Doctor al-Shaath cleaned the puncture, stitched it closed and covered it with a bandage. By the time the Doctor reached the last patient in the waiting room, a woman suffering from an ear ache, the *muezzins* were already announcing evening prayers. A nurse fitted the otoscope into the woman's ear. Looking through it, she described to the nearly blind Doctor what she saw so that he could make the diagnosis. "There is a slight reddish swelling of the exostoses obstructing the external ear canal," she reported, "but no sign of fluid in the eustachian tube."

"Are you diabetic?" the Doctor asked the patient.

The woman shook her head.

"Have you had a high fever in the past few days?"

Again she said no.

"When you grit your teeth, do you feel pain in the ear? Ah, I thought so. You are suffering from dermatitis of the outer ear. It is not serious. I will give you antibiotic drops to use in the ear. You should apply a heated compress and take aspirin to alleviate the pain."

Hurrying from the clinic through the back door minutes later, his long bamboo cane tapping nervously ahead of his flying feet, the Doctor made his way through a labyrinth of back alleys off Greek Orthodox Patriarchate Road. He went up a rickety staircase and ducked through a low door with "No Entrance—Building Condemned" painted in red on it, then climbed out a window onto a slate roof. Guiding himself with a hand on a waist-high brick wall, he crossed several rooftops and descended a flight of steps and crossed another roof before coming to the abandoned bathhouse with the narrow staircase at the back leading to the safe house on the third floor. "Everything in order?" the Doctor asked Petra when she unlocked the reinforced door and let him in. "Where's Yussuf?"

A quarter of an hour before the Doctor returned from the clinic, Yussuf had climbed onto the toilet seat in the tiny lavatory to look out of the only window in the safe house that had not been bricked over. Using binoculars, he had spotted the green shirt drying on the clothesline of a roof, the signal that someone had left a letter with the lame shoemaker across from the El Khanqa Mosque. "Yussuf's off collecting the mail," Petra told the Doctor.

"Anything on the radio?"

She shook her head. "The Jews chased a stolen car on the Nablus Road. When they caught up with it they discovered it wasn't stolen after all—a reserve colonel had borrowed it to return to his unit without telling the owner."

Washing his hands and feet, sinking to his knees before the *mihrab*, the Doctor prostrated himself four times, drumming his forehead against the tiles as he lost himself in the prayer: *Allahu Akbar, Allahu Akbar*. Later, Petra set out a break-fast of tea and biscuits, and then unexpectedly poured herself a cup of tea and joined the Doctor at the low table.

With exquisite timidity, she breathed his name. "Isma'il al-Shaath."

Startled—he didn't remember Petra ever using his given name before—he turned toward her inquisitively.

"There is an old Islamic tradition which holds," she whispered, her eyes carefully avoiding his, her fingers picking lint off the front of her Bedouin robe, "that in an ideal marriage, the wife should be half the husband's age plus seven."

The Doctor knew that Petra was an orphan, and assumed she was about to ask his permission to marry. "I am familiar with this formulation," he told her.

"Do you think there is any truth to it?"

"Half the husband's age plus seven gives to each partner in the marriage contract an important element: to the man, a young and eager wife over whom he will exercise a natural authority based on age and experience; to the woman, a mature father-figure who can guide her in all things, and in whom she can have confidence."

"Yussuf showed me a magazine article about the free clinic you organized in the Old City. It stated that you were forty-six years of age. I myself am thirty years of age." Petra steeled herself with a deep breath. "Thirty is half forty-six plus seven."

The Doctor, flustered, dipped a biscuit into his tea and held it there. "I do not know how to respond," he said, for once at a loss for words.

"Say nothing. Only consider the possibility of my becoming your wife. I must tell you that I am not a virgin; I was once betrothed to an inspector of water mains who was swept into a wadi during a rain squall and drowned before we could marry. At the time I was not following the straight path ordained by the Messenger and permitted the consummation of the relationship to take place once the engagement was published. On the positive side, I am in excellent health and reasonably attractive despite the small pox scars on my face. In addition, I have been promised a dowry by my brothers." Petra's hands trembled, her voice faded in and out, then faltered. Breathing deeply through her open mouth, she pushed herself to continue. "I realize that for someone of your station it may sound insignificant, but they speak of twenty camels, half of them female, and a portion of date trees in an oasis on the Jordanian side of Wadi Araba."

"I am already married."

"The holy Qur'an permits a man to take in marriage four wives." The Doctor quoted the Qur'an on the matter of wives. "*If you fear you will not be equitable, then only one.*'" And he said, very gently, "I fear I will not be equitable, in the sense that I have neither the time nor the energy for more than the one wife I am already contracted to." Bowing his head, he whispered, "I am married to the cause of Islam. I am engaged in a war on two fronts, the first against the external enemies of Islam, the infidels; the second against the internal enemies of Islam, who seek accommodation with the Crusaders. The second struggle is the more important of the two, for the victor will be the one to define Islam for centuries to come."

Petra thought about this for a moment. "Even in the service of Islam, a man is known to have"—she racked her brain for an appropriate expression—"physical needs . . ."

"You are more than a wife to me, dear Petra. You are a holy warrior and an accomplice in the battle to bring this sacred land, and the world, into the straight path, the way of God, to whom belongs all things that are in the heavens and all that are on earth."

After a moment she murmured, "I pray that I have not offended you."

"You have honored me, not offended me."

Petra noticed that the biscuit had disintegrated in the Doctor's tea, and the tea was no longer steaming. "I will pour another cup for you," she said.

With the tips of his fingers, the Doctor touched the rope burns on the back of her wrist; the Isra'ilis had once suspended her from the branch of a tree when they caught her throwing rotten tomatoes at a jeep. "Accept my thanks," he said huskily. And he added quickly, "For the tea."

"You are welcome, Isma'il al-Shaath." A melancholy smile worked its way onto Petra's pock-marked face. "For the tea."

Yussuf came in, handed Petra a letter to decode from the Abu Bakr cell in Ghazeh and took his place before the niche in the wall indicating the direction of Mecca. He thumbed through the Qur'an to find the marker he had left in its pages. As the Doctor removed his jacket and, rolling up the sleeves of his robe, started scrubbing his hands and forearms, Yussuf began reading where he had left off the previous evening:

> *O believers, take not Jews and Christians as friends;*
> *they are friends of each other. Whoso of you makes them*
> *his friends is one of them.*

Shaking his hands dry in the air, climbing back into his suit jacket, the Doctor had Petra read him the message from Ghazeh. The Palestine Authority police were quietly spreading word that they were ready to pay fifty thousand American dollars for information leading to the arrest of those responsible for the abduction of Rabbi Apfulbaum and his secretary, and a second fifty thousand American dollars for information leading to the liberation of the prisoners. The Abu Bakr cell had also detected an increase in contacts between the Palestinian police and Isra'ili agents; dozens of homes of fundamentalist leaders had been raided by search parties believe to include Isra'ilis disguised as Palestinians. The Doctor took this in, then, as an afterthought, checked to be sure Petra had been salting the Rabbi's food with doses of caffeine and giving him cups of tea brewed from rose hips, which was rich in vitamin C and tended to keep people awake when drunk late in the day.

Entering the back room of the safe house, the Doctor discovered Azziz pulling the secretary Efrayim back to his chair. "The *Yahoud*"—Azziz spit out "*Jew*" as if the word left a bad taste in his mouth—"has diarrhea." The young Palestinian slipped the leather hood over Efrayim's head. "He has been to the toilet half a dozen times today."

"He suffers from the fear of death," the Doctor said in Arabic, settling onto the kitchen chair in front of the Rabbi, holding a match to the tip of one of his pungent Farids, sucking it into life with shallow, nervous puffs. "I will have some weak tea prepared to prevent dehydration, and rice to solidify his bowels." He pulled the leather hood off the Rabbi's head, then reached for his wrist and checked his pulse. Venturing onto the no-man's land of English, he remarked, "Your heart is beating more normally today."

The Rabbi, delivered from the stench of the hood, opened his mouth and filled his lungs with great gulps of air. "I don't sleep," he admitted. He wasn't complaining; he was merely stating a fact. "It is not the fear of death that keeps me awake. It is not even the foul-smelling hood you put over my head. The food I eat, the tea I drink is spiked; I can tell from the taste. Rose hips. Vitamin C. Enough to keep a horse from falling asleep. When I do manage to doze off, one of the two goons"—with a contemptuous toss of his head, Apfulbaum indicated Azziz and Aown, who were sitting on the cot grinning—"yells an obscenity in my ear or kicks at the legs of the chair." The Rabbi lifted both hands, still bound in cuffs, and ran his fingers through his hair, which was flying off in all directions. "Exhausting me will achieve nothing," Apfulbaum blurted out. "I can't tell you what I don't know." He took several more deep breaths and continued on a calmer note. "You have surely proposed trading us for two or twenty or two hundred Palestinian terrorists rotting in Israeli jails. We both of us know what will happen. The Israelis will offer to negotiate. To buy time, they will even ask the Egyptians or the Jordanians to mediate. But in the end they will never reward hostage taking by agreeing to a swap of prisoners. I understand how these things work—you will have given them a deadline. When it arrives, you will execute us."

Efrayim, following the conversation from his chair, moaned, "For God's sake, Rabbi, don't put crazy ideas into his head."

The Rabbi reached out and gripped the Doctor's knee. "Make no mistake, I prefer to survive; you have to be off your rocker to choose death over life. On the other hand, maybe my murder will scuttle this infernal charade of a peace treaty. Maybe." Sitting back, Apfulbaum snorted. "The choice is between no peace on, God forbid, half the land God promised Abraham, and no peace on all the land. When the Jews understand this, they will opt for no peace on all the land."

"Every time I come in here and listen to you rattle on about the

Messenger Ibrahim," the Doctor said with quiet intensity, "I have the sensation of mining a seam of madness."

"It's you who's insane," the Rabbi retorted. He raised his right hand, dragging his left hand after it at the end of the chain, and waved it above his head. "You and your Imams and Ayatollahs and fundamentalist kamikazes who blow up innocent Jews on buses, you're all *meshuga, patzo,* off your rockers; you're all stark raving maniacs."

Breathing noisily through his nostrils, Apfulbaum melted back into the chair. After a moment the Doctor cleared his throat. "Let us begin tonight's conversation, *ya'ani,* by talking about the Jewish underground movement Keshet Yonathan in the Isra'ili occupied West Bank. In the mid nineteen-eighties, your own police arrested twenty-seven members of a Jewish terrorist cell, based on the West Bank, who were plotting to blow up the Dome of the Rock Mosque. The same people were accused of murdering three Palestinian students at Hebron's Islamic College, and maiming two Palestinian West Bank mayors, Bassam Shaka and Karim Khalef, with letter bombs. Curiously, this initial burst of Jewish underground activity roughly coincided with your arrival in Isra'il and the founding of the settlement of Beit Avram. It is well known that the Isra'ili Shin Bet picked you up for questioning on half a dozen occasions. No charges were ever brought against you for lack of hard evidence, so the Jewish police claimed. But you were an outspoken advocate of—"

"— outspoken is the understatement of the year. I've shouted it from the rooftops until I was blue in the face. Jews have no choice in the matter: we are under a sacred obligation to settle in the land God gave us, what you call the occupied West Bank and the Torah calls Samaria and Judea." The Rabbi added tiredly, "All that is a matter of record."

"Your attachment to the central spine of hills in the country of Palestine, your habit of referring to these areas by their biblical names, Judea and Samaria, is nothing more than a kind of fossilized nostalgia, a theological mania bordering on hysteria. You speak of an aching for the land. Before Hitler appeared on the scene, Zionism was only able to produce a trickle of Jews willing to settle in the Holy

Land, and the great majority of those insisted on living along the coast. As painful as it may be for you to acknowledge, the conclusion is inescapable: Hitler, and not Ibrahim, must be seen as the founding father of the modern state of Israel. Without the Holocaust, *ya'ani*, the Jews would still be living in their ghettos in Eastern Europe. The psychological conclusion one must draw is that you have no core identity; you don't exist. The Frenchman Sartre hit the nail on the head when he wrote: 'The Jew is one whom other men consider a Jew . . . it is the anti-Semite who makes the Jew.'"

"If anyone doesn't exist," the Rabbi cried, leaning forward and squinting in order to better make out the shadowy figure taunting him, "it is the Palestinians. Palestinian nationalism is an artificial flavoring; it's saccharine, as opposed to sugar. In the history of the planet earth, there never was a Palestinian people; Palestine itself belonged to southern Syria. You have been seduced by your own spin doctors into thinking there is such a thing as a Palestinian nation."

"Once again you stand history on its head—"

The Rabbi was warming to his subject. "Admit it if you dare, you are lucky to have Jews for enemies. Who today gives a flying fart for the Kurds struggling against the Turks, or the Berbers against the Algerians, or the Tibetans against the Chinese? If a Russian shoots a Chechen teenager hurling stones, does the BBC interrupt its program for a special bulletin? Don't hold your breath! But you so-called Palestinians are struggling against Jews, and the world is mesmerized." The Rabbi sniffed in manic delight. "We are the world's longest running sit-tra."

"Sit-tra?"

From under his hood, Efrayim said, "Sit-tra is an Apfulbaumism. It's the opposite of sit-com. It means situation tragedy."

Apfulbaum elaborated. "Tune in tomorrow, same time, same station, to see what the chosen people, the descendants of prophets and psalmists and a light unto the nations, see what they'll do now that they're no longer the eternal victims. Will they turn out to be like the Americans ethnically cleansing native Indians? Or the French Catholics flinging Protestants into rivers with stones tied to their ankles? Oh, the columnists can barely wait to find out. If Israel uses its power to fulfill the biblical promise to Abraham, the world will wring its hands in an ecstasy of masturbatory satisfaction. You Jews have been boring us to tears for three thousand years with all this blah-blah-blah about morality, the Sartres of the world will bleat like goats, but when push comes to shove, ha! you're like everyone else. The Sartres, the others glued to the Middle East sit-tra on their TVs will feel less guilty for having done nothing to prevent the Holocaust. Absolutely nothing," the Rabbi muttered several times, as if he were reminding himself of some terrible truth. "Zilch. Zero."

Lost in meditation, the Doctor let several minutes slip by without saying a word. Finally he looked up. "It is true that we Palestinians owe you Jews a debt, though you are the last ones in the world to understand the real nature of this debt. If today we define ourselves as Palestinians, it is because you came here with your Western money and Western technology and Western music and Western art and looked at us as if we didn't exist; you looked through us. You saw Palestinians as a drop in a sea of Arabs stretching from Morocco to Iraq, without cultural or historical links to the land of Palestine."

The Doctor stood up and turned around his seat several times to stretch his legs, then sat down again. "You have a lot to unlearn, Rabbi. You need instruction."

"Instruct, instruct." He frowned at a thought. "I am what you could call a captive audience."

The Doctor's voice took on an abrasive edge; he sounded as if he were singing slightly off key. "I will instruct you, *ya'ani*. I will teach you that there is not *one* Arab, and not one way of *being* Arab. I will teach you that, more often than not, things in the Middle East are the opposite of what they seem: it isn't a question of winning or losing wars, but how you win the wars you win, which is something you Jews never—*never!*—grasped. Take the Sixty-seven war. You swept Arab planes from the skies and three Arab armies from the fields of battle. But you didn't see then, you don't see now, that this so-called victory was a great defeat for Israel."

Apfulbaum rolled his eyes in their sockets.

"Yes, I tell you it was a great defeat. Before Sixty-seven, the struggle was between the Jews who had washed up on our shores and the invisible Palestinians living in their midst. After Sixty-seven, after you conquered Jerusalem, the third holiest city in Islam, after you occupied its sacred shrines, after you humiliated Muslim pride and Muslim faith, the conflict turned into a struggle between the world's fifteen million Jews and a billion followers of Islam. How can you not see it, *ya'ani?* After Sixty-seven, our bodies were in Isra'ili-occupied territory but our heads and our hearts were in Palestine. And now, after our *intifadas* shook your confidence, you are ready to throw us a few crumbs—you are ready to give us a mini state of our own on a small part of the land that was always ours, with the big Jewish brother breathing down our necks. And you expect us to lick your hand in gratitude. The Palestinian Authority may leap at the opportunity but not me—I don't want a miserable and truncated Palestinian state on the West Bank and Ghazeh. What do I care about the West Bank or Ghazeh? Until they were expelled by the Jews, my family lived in Haifa. I want Haifa! I want Jaffa. I want *all* of Jerusalem. Every square centimeter. I want the complete elimination of the Jewish entity the West imposed on us. If we ratify the existence of the Jewish state by accepting this peace, we will have lost the hundred-year struggle against Zionism. I don't want peace for the simple reason that without peace, the Jews can't win. Time is on our side. You will drown in a sea of Arabs. With God's help, we will look back on the Jews the way we look back on the Crusaders crushed by Salah ad-Din—as a minor episode in Islamic history."

On the cot, both Azziz and Aown dozed, the head of the younger brother on the shoulder of the older. From the front room came the voice of Yussuf reciting passages from the Qur'an. Efrayim, lulled by the drone of voices, tried to follow the conversation but eventually gave up and day dreamed, with his eyes wide open, of how his mother and father would react to the news of his death He could picture his father, his face drawn but unmistakably proud, holding a press conference on the small lawn of their modest Long Island family home. The elder Mr. Blumenfeld would spell his name to be sure it appeared correctly in the newspapers and then, with Efrayim's mother standing tearfully at his side, read from a prepared statement.

Looking up from a scrap of paper, blinking into the television cameras, he would respond to questions with questions. So what makes you think that my son was a fanatic? he would ask. So what father, he would ask, his voice finally breaking, would not be proud of a son who sacrificed his life for a biblical dream?

Getting a second wind, the Doctor again and again steered the conversation back to Beit Avram and the Jewish terrorism that began with Rabbi Apfulbaum's arrival in Israel. The Rabbi shook his head wearily. Yes, he admitted, he had known several of the Jews accused of trying to blow up the Dome of the Rock; yes, he had been to meetings in which they had analyzed where Zionism had gone wrong; yes, he himself had become convinced that the Zionists had to forget about world opinion, which would condemn the Jews no matter what they did, and concentrate on finding a solution to Israel's Arab problem; yes, pushing masses of Arabs over the frontier into Syria and Jordan had been one of the options he himself had suggested; no, he had never been tempted by Communism, although he agreed with Lenin when he said that if you wanted to make an omelet you had to crack eggs, or words to that effect.

The Doctor pulled a large watch from a pocket and snapped it open, causing it to chime the hour and the fifteen minutes. "Three thirty," he announced. He could feel the stiffness in his back and neck. "We have a great deal in common," he told the Rabbi. "I also have attended endless discussion groups—as a medical student in Beirut, later in various villages and towns in the occupied West Bank—in which we analyzed where Zionism had gone wrong. I personally made a painstaking study of Zionism in order to better comprehend the movement's mania to occupy my ancestral land. In the beginning the Zionist *raison d'etre* was to rescue Jews from the anti-Semitic environment of Eastern Europe and Czarist Russia. But with each victory over the backward Arabs, the Zionists moved away from this rescue mission and toward redeeming the land they thought God had bequeathed to Ibrahim. It does not require a Freud to grasp the psychological reasons for this change of focus. For two thousand years you Jews didn't have an army. Suddenly, with the creation by the Western powers of the colonial outpost in the Middle East called

the State of Isra'il, you not only had an army, but one that swept its
illiterate and poorly armed Arab enemies from the battle field the
way a broom sweeps sand from a Bedouin carpet. This Maccabean
revival, as I call it, intoxicated you; it was almost as if you had taken
a collective dose of LSD. You glorified military service, you deified
the soldier-warrior defending the Holy Land. You failed to notice
that Zionism succeeded because it had become the surrogate for
Western colonialism, and a mouthpiece for the West's visceral anti-
Arabism. In short, if the Jews, armed with Western planes and
Western tanks and subsidized by great doses of Western financial aid,
succeeded in occupying land belonging for centuries to Palestinians,
it was because the world was on your side—"

Apfulbaum could contain himself no longer. "I suppose the
world was on our side when the British closed off immigration to
Palestine in the nineteen thirties, dooming millions of Jews to the
flames of Hitler's furnaces. Swell! I suppose the world was on our side
when Roosevelt and Churchill refused to bomb the rail lines along
which Jews were being transported to Hitler's death factories.
Naturally the world was on our side in nineteen forty-eight when it
created a Jewish state and then failed to defend it from the British-
armed and British-trained and British-led Arab Legion and four
other Arab armies that vowed to throw the Jews into the sea. Ha! We
can cope with our enemies, but God save us from our friends!"

The Rabbi ran out of steam. "My legs ache," he announced. "My
heart, too. The problem with you, you see history through the prism
of an ancestral hate for Jews. Your Prophet and Messenger,
Muhammad, disputed with the Jews in the oasis of Medina, after
which some of the Jews were exiled, others were killed. You surely
remember what happened then—Muhammad ordered Muslims,
who until that time had been facing Jerusalem to pray, to turn
instead toward Mecca. From that day to this you are still turning
away from the Jewishness of Jerusalem, and the Jews. I am practically
blind but I can see you shaking your head. Why deny it? I have read
what your fabulous Koran has to say about the Jews."

The Doctor shut his eyes and began to recite a verse from the
Holy Qur'an.

Whoso judges not,
according to what God has sent down—
                    they are the unbelievers.
And therein We prescribed for them:
"A life for a life, an eye for an eye,
a nose for a nose, an ear for an ear,
a tooth for a tooth, and for wounds
retaliation."

He opened his eyes and attempted to bring the blurred face of his prisoner into focus. "*'For wounds, retaliation,'*" he repeated. "In my case the punishment *preceded* the crime, *ya'ani*, which meant that the crime, when I finally got around to plotting it, had to fit the punishment."

"What wounds? What punishment?"

"I will tell you what wounds, what punishment. I was studying at the American University of Beirut in the Lebanon at the time, and returning to my parents' home in Hebron for Ramadan by way of the Allenby Bridge over the River Jordan. I was so ashamed of being a Palestinian in those days that I wore a Western suit and tie and replied in English if someone put a question to me. The Jews, who knew an Arab when they saw one, dragged me from the bus and locked me in a latrine until nightfall. Not realizing I could barely see, they blindfolded me and drove me around for hours to disorient me before taking me to a prison. Only later did I discover it was the Isra'ili Army base of Hanan outside of Jericho, minutes away from the Allenby Bridge. I was questioned for forty days and forty nights, during which time I was not permitted to sleep for days at a stretch. The hair on my head and my beard were shaved off—a grievous humiliation for an Arab. The Isra'ilis never called me by name, only by number; I was seven seven two three. My Isra'ili interrogator told me that I had been denounced as a terrorist belonging to the Democratic Front for the Liberation of Palestine. When I wasn't being questioned, I sat in a small room with a leather hood not unlike the one you wear fitted over my head. It reeked of sweat and vomit; it stank of fear. Once, when I dozed, the guard touched the electrodes used to heat water to my handcuffs. I woke up screaming as the heated handcuffs burned into my swelling wrists. I still bear the scars; I wear these dark bracelets around my wrists to remind me of my humiliation at the hands of the Jews. My interrogator was something of a pedagogue. He would tell me precisely what he was going to do, and then he would do it. 'You will become completely dependent on me for permission to urinate, for food, for sleep, for news of your family,' he would say. 'At first you will resist. Then, slowly, you will come to accept this dependency. Eventually you will be grateful for every crust of bread I throw you.' He was mistaken; I devoured the crusts but I was never grateful. I tell you, *ya'ani*, that I was innocent of the charge against me—the worst thing I had done was to drink Turkish coffee and talk politics at the café called Faisal's across the road from the main gate of the university. But when, after forty days, the Jews freed me, I became guilty; I joined the group they accused me of belonging to. I tracked down the collaborator who had denounced me and attempted to strangle him. The Isra'ilis rushed him to a hospital and saved his life. I was arrested for attempted murder and sentenced to twelve years in prison. It was in prison that I decided to use a more surgical technique if I ever needed to kill someone again."

"Marx says somewhere that man does not have a nature but a history," Apfulbaum said. "Our stories illustrate this point. I myself was raised Brooklyn, but once or twice a year we used to visit an aunt who lived in Jonestown, Pennsylvania. She was a fine pianist and the only Jew in town, and played the organ at church services." The Rabbi's feet, lashed to the legs of the heavy chair, were beginning to swell and he twisted this way and that to alleviate the pain. "One December I was sleigh riding down the hill in front of her house, past the barn filled with riding horses, past the Bayshores' farm, when I got into a fight with a local farm boy over who would go first. He called me a dirty Jew—so I became a dirty Jew."

The Doctor retrieved the hood from the floor and slipped it over the Rabbi's head; he could hear Apfulbaum gagging on the airless stench of the leather. "The most interesting thing about someone's history," the Doctor remarked to the hood, "is that it reveals what he has chosen to remember."

From under the hood the Rabbi's muffled response could be heard: "Amen."

In the front room of the safe house, the Doctor found Yussuf sitting on the floor, fast asleep with his back against the reinforced door and an AK-47 across his thighs. Petra lay curled on a blanket near the radio. A bulb burned in the overhead socket. Petra had pulled a folded dish towel over her eyes to keep out the light. Bending over her, the Doctor could make out the rope burn on the back of a wrist; another bracelet of humiliation, he thought. The green Isra'ili Army radio had been left on. Through the small speaker came the static-filled voices of the Hebrew Army reporting in from the various corners of occupied Palestine. It was four in the morning and all was well, or so it appeared to the Isra'ilis, with their distorted memories and their warped histories. *"A tooth for a tooth, and for wounds retaliation,"* he whispered to the voices on the radio. It was a lesson the *mujaddid* would have to teach the Palestinians, too, if he was going to succeed in creating an Islamic state on all of the land of Palestine. Rousing the Palestinians to *jihad*, to holy war, getting them to apply the formula *for wounds retaliation*, would be easier once Apfulbaum cracked; once he gave them details about the Jewish underground, its ruthless leader who went by the code name Ya'ir and the atrocities they had committed against the Holy Qur'an and the Palestinian people. When the Rabbi started talking, the Doctor would need an independent witness; someone who could be trusted to pass the story on to the world.

The Doctor listened to the babble of Jewish voices on the radio as he scrubbed his hands over the laundry sink. Then, switching off the overhead light, removing his spectacles and massaging his bloodshot eyes with his thumb and third finger, he stretched out fully clothed on the cot Petra had left for him to use in the hope that he would sleep until first light.

FIFTEEN

THE SHIN BET MANDARINS WERE SEETHING. THE PRESS ATTACHÉ at the Israeli embassy in Washington had faxed them Sweeney's latest article, in which he described how the Israeli equivalent of the FBI had tried to recruit him as an agent. No detail was left to the reader's imagination. Only first names had been used when the Shin Bet representatives introduced themselves at an early morning meeting. He himself had reported on the budget crunch in Israel, Sweeney wrote, tongue in cheek, but he hadn't realized how tight things were in the Israeli intelligence community until he discovered that no coffee or doughnuts would be served. The individual who was clearly in charge had attempted to put the meeting off the record *after* it was over; another agent who went by the name of Itamar, furious at Sweeney for refusing to cooperate, had closed the meeting with a calumnious slur that was unprintable even if it had been said on the record.

The agent whom Sweeney had dubbed J. Edgar, an Irish Jew by the name of Moses Briscoe, put in a call to the chief government censor, by coincidence an armored division deputy commander who had served under Briscoe in Lebanon. "Revoke his press accreditation," the Shin Bet department head snarled into the phone. "Send the son of a bitch back where he came from."

"Tried to when he wrote the article about the reservists and the broken arms," the censor replied. "I was overruled."

"Try again," Briscoe said. "Take it up to the Prime Minister's office if you have to."

The censor chuckled. "That's who overruled me the last time, Moses."

"Who's protecting him? And why?"

"You're the guys who bug telephones and hide microphones in padded brassieres. You tell me."

"I may just do that," Briscoe said.

SIXTEEN

SHUFFLING ALONG IN BACKLESS SLIPPERS, MAALI WAS LED INTO the unheated room padded with foam rubber so that prisoners couldn't beat their heads against the wall and later claim they had been tortured. Dressed in a sack-like sleeveless shift that irritated her skin, she hugged herself as she settled onto the wooden stool with the front legs cut shorter than the back legs. She could hear the soothing sound of Yussuf's voice whispering in her ear.

I will love you even when you have grown old, he had vowed the night he proposed marriage.

Will you take another wife? she had asked him.

Would you object?

Not if I selected her.

I will never take another wife.

Ahhhhh.

The dazzling spotlights hanging from the ceiling burned into Maali's eyes, causing them to tear. The voice of the interrogator came from the penumbra, drowning out Yussuf's music in her ear. "Are you well?" he asked in fluent Arabic. "Do you have any complaints to make about the way you are being treated?"

Maali shook her head tiredly; the first six or seven or eight times she had been questioned—she had long since lost count—she had complained bitterly about the cold cell, the lack of privacy when she performed bodily functions, the stench of the clothes she was obliged to wear, the mold on the rice she was obliged to eat, the lack of medical treatment for the rash on her stomach. Once she had been given a sheaf of paper and a felt-tipped pen—ball points were considered weapons in prison—and invited to write a letter to Amnesty International. Kneeling on the floor boards, she had bent over the paper and had written out her complaints on what looked like an Amnesty International form. The interrogator had read her letter aloud, snickering at the errors in spelling and grammar as he went along, and then torn it to shreds on the grounds that it was illiterate.

"No complaints. Good. Let's begin where we left off." Maali could hear the sound of pages being turned. "You claim to have bought the ring sometime last month from a Bedouin selling jewelry in the souk. You maintain that you cannot recall the name of the Bedouin or the location of his shop. Has time refreshed your memory?"

Maali shook her head.

"Since our last session, we have learned more about the ring."

Shielding her eyes with a forearm, Maali tried to catch a glimpse of her interrogator. "It is a ring like any other," she protested weakly.

"It is a ring unlike any other we have seen. At first we thought the words *Erasmus* and *Hall* were a man's name. But we discovered that Erasmus Hall is the name of a high school in Brooklyn, which is a borough in the city of New York. The 1998 refers to the year of graduation. The ring in question is a high school graduation ring."

Trembling on her stool from fear and cold, Maali hugged herself tightly.

"You will be interested to hear that we have even managed to identify the owner of the ring. It belonged to an American named Ronni Goldman. He was a Talmudic student at the yeshiva run by Rabbi Apfulbaum in the Jewish settlement of Beit Avram on the hills overlooking Hebron."

"Have I transgressed Isra'ili law to buy a ring from a Bedouin?" Maali fumbled. "Has the Bedouin transgressed Isra'ili law to buy the ring from a Jew?"

The interrogator's voice droned on. "The Bedouin did not buy the ring from a Jew. You did not buy the ring from a Bedouin. Ronni Goldman was one of the boys killed when an Islamic fundamentalist group calling itself the Abu Bakr Brigade kidnapped Rabbi

Apfulbaum while he was driving back to Beit Avram from Yad Mordechai. One of the terrorists cut off Goldman's little finger to get the ring, and then offered it to you. Surely it was your husband, Yussuf, who gave you the ring the night of the kidnapping. Surely it was your husband, Yussuf, whom you were waving to near the Damascus Gate the next morning."

"I have told you a thousand times," Maali declared. "I have not set eyes on my husband since the night of our wedding."

"Then who gave you the ring?"

"No one gave me the ring. I purchased it from a Bedouin."

The interrogator shuffled more papers. "If, in fact, no one gave you the ring, it raises the possibility that you yourself cut the finger from the dead boy's hand, and took the ring from the finger. I must warn you that we have enough evidence to charge you with the murder of Ronni Goldman. You are in a great deal of trouble, Maali. No judge will believe you bought the Erasmus Hall ring from a Bedouin. You could spend the rest of your life in a Negev detention camp. I will tell you that some of my superiors are convinced you took part in the ambush; we have many examples of Palestinian women playing active roles in attacks on Jews. I myself do not believe you are guilty of murder; I believe you are protecting someone. I even have a grudging admiration for your loyalty and steadfastness. But loyalty must have a limit. What kind of a man is it who cuts the finger from the hand of a dead boy to steal a ring?"

Maali's knees turned weak and she had difficulty keeping herself from sliding off the stool. "The man who is pushed to cut a ring from the hand of a dead Jew is someone who has suffered at the hands of a living Jew," she blurted out.

The interrogator said with unnerving patience, "So you admit that someone cut the finger from the hand of Ronni Goldman to get the ring, which he then gave to you?"

"I admit nothing," Maali cried. "I curse your eyes. I spit at your feet."

Shivering on the cot in her icy cell after the evening meal had been pushed through the slot in the door later that night, Maali scratched at the rash on her stomach until it bled. The warder who checked the occupants of the cells every hour on the hour noticed blood on the front of her shift and summoned two Israeli woman guards, who walked her through the labyrinthine corridors to the infirmary. The Jewish woman doctor who was on duty, appalled at Maali's condition, had her strip to the skin and shower with a special soap. The doctor, a young draftee on her first tour of duty in a prison, cleaned the rash with antiseptic and treated it with an antibiotic cream, and issued Maali new underwear and a new shift with long sleeves. Waiting for the two woman guards to return, the doctor gave Maali a small plastic comb and a plastic container filled with vitamins.

"*Shoukran*," Maali murmured in Arabic.

"*Bavakasha*," the doctor answered, avoiding the prisoner's eye. "If the rash still bothers you tomorrow, ask to be brought back to the infirmary." She became impatient when the woman guards didn't show up and summoned the Palestinian orderly who sat at a small table outside the infirmary door logging everyone in and out. "Take her back to Cell Block four," the doctor instructed the orderly.

Maali fell into step alongside the Palestinian, a young woman whose thick tresses had been hacked short in what looked like a botched prison haircut. Moving her lips like a ventriloquist, keeping her eyes trained straight ahead, the orderly murmured, "What are you arrested for?"

"They think I killed a Jew," Maali said, suddenly proud of the charge against her.

They turned a corner and passed a control point. The Israeli guard behind the window recognized the orderly and waved her on.

"How did they catch you?" the orderly asked.

"I was denounced."

"By whom?"

"By Mr. Hajji, the one who changes money at the Damascus Gate."

"How can you be sure?"

"It was Mr. Hajji who confirmed the identification when I was brought in by the Isra'ilis. I saw him with my own eyes."

"The Holy Qur'an prescribes execution, crucifixion, amputation or exile for those who wage war against Allah and his Messenger, and sow corruption on earth. Surely Mr. Hajji will not escape the judgment of God or man."

They approached a steel door guarded by a young Israeli woman soldier wearing black Reebok sneakers and holding an Uzi submachine gun. She gestured for the prisoner to raise her arms and slowly ran the palms of her hands over Maali's breasts and thighs and buttocks. She discovered the plastic comb and vitamin pills in a pocket and confiscated them before waving the prisoner through the door.

"Are you familiar with the passage in the Holy Qur'an entitled *The Woman Tested*?" the orderly breathed as they approached Maali's cell. "*Pray to Allah, who answers all prayers. Resist the infidel with your soul and your body and your brain. Remember that God sees the things you do.*"

Maali entered her foul-smelling cell; she had grown accustomed to the odors coming from the open toilet in the far corner. The orderly started to shut the door behind her. "Take heart—Mr. Hajji will rot in hell," she whispered before the door slammed closed. "Take heart—water like molten copper will scald the collaborator's face."

Turns out that my one-time Harvard colleague Henry Kissinger got it dead wrong when he observed that the absence of alternatives clears the mind marvelously. This may be true in the real world; in the Looking-Glass miasma of the Middle East, the absence of alternatives only seems to befuddle minds even more. My telephone call to the Chairman of the Palestinian authority this morning is a case in point. Before I could get a word in, he was lecturing me on how he wasn't going to make the mistake of letting himself be seen cooperating with the Israeli Shin Bet to capture Palestinians—even though they had broken the cease fire he endorsed, even though they were jeopardizing the peace treaty he was ready to sign.

I let him ramble on for a while. When he came up for air I said, very casually, "What are your alternatives?"

When he started to tick them off, one by one, I interrupted. "Mr. Chairman, let me tell you how we see your alternatives from Washington," I told him. "You have none."

I let that sink in. "Everyone always has alternatives," he finally said. "To start with, I can sit back and let the Isra'ilis solve their own problems."

"Frankly, I thought you were too shrewd to consider that an alternative. Put yourself in Israeli shoes. What happens when Abu Bakr murders the secretary and the Rabbi? What then?"

"I telephoned the Isra'ili Prime Minister when this began. I suggested that he should follow your President's advice and treat the kidnapping as an isolated incident—"

"It's an isolated incident if the perpetrators don't get away with murder. If they do, it's not an isolated incident because they will draw the inevitable conclusions and perpetrate again—and again, and again until your nerves, and those of the Israelis, crack. Don't forget that the Prime Minister has 240,000 right-wing settlers looking over his shoulder—they would welcome an excuse to scuttle the Mt. Washington peace treaty before it can be signed."

"What does it mean, scuttle?"

"Sink. Wreck. Ruin. Destroy. Kill."

There must have been others in the room with the Chairman listening in on our conversation, because I heard someone whispering to him in Arabic. I asked, with what I hoped was a reasonable amount of sarcasm in my voice, "What did he say?"

He cleared his throat, which I took to mean that he wasn't as calm as he sounded. "He asks how is it we always seem to end up with you Americans pushing us to help the Isra'ilis crack down on Palestinians."

"I'll answer his question with a question: How is it you people don't see that this Abu Bakr is as much an enemy of the Palestinian Authority as he is of Israel? Come to think of it, maybe even more of an enemy."

"How more? Why more?"

"With the Israelis, he will consider the operation a success if he kills two of them; he will consider it a triumph if the Israelis don't turn up in Washington to sign the peace treaty. With you, he'll consider it a success if the murder of the two Israelis causes you embarrassment; he'll consider it a triumph if he and the other fundamentalists can kill you and govern in your place."

I could hear him arguing with someone in Arabic. I made a mental note to have an Arab-speaker with me next time I put a call in to the Chairman of the Palestinian Authority. After a moment he came back on the line. "I tell you frankly, Mr. Sawyer, I do not disagree with your analysis. But in this part of the world there is a big difference between analyzing a situation correctly and taking a public position on it."

"Let me put another question, Mr. Chairman: What would you do if Israeli right-wingers kidnapped a crazy fundamentalist Imam and his secretary, killing four of their bodyguards in the process? Would you agree to treat the kidnapping as an isolated incident?"

He laughed under his breath; one of the things I appreciated about the Chairman was his occasional ability to stand back and see himself and the Palestinians as others might see them. Empathy is the mother of self-knowledge. "I would dial your number in Washington," the Chairman conceded, "and ask you to put pressure on the Isra'ilis to bring the culprits to justice. I would do this knowing full well the Isra'ilis would be in no great hurry—"

"Mr. Chairman, when the Mt. Washington treaty is signed, your two peoples will have to find ways to live with each other on your postage stamp of a territory."

"We have signed treaties with the Isra'ilis before and look what happened. Remember Oslo? They built additional settlements and expanded the existing ones. They constructed a network of security roads that crisscrossed Palestine, effectively cutting it into isolated enclaves. They built so-called security walls, cutting Palestinians off from access to hospitals and universities and jobs and the fields they farmed. They dragged their feet about giving back territory. We are afraid history will repeat itself." I could hear the Chairman being interrupted again by one of his aides. When he came back on the line he said, "Perhaps it would be wiser to put off any decisions in this matter until tomorrow."

I have a Pablo Picasso quotation I used from time to time to impress my students at Harvard. I came up with it now. "Only put off until tomorrow what you are willing to die having left undone." I never did get to gauge the effect of my erudition on the Chairman because the line suddenly filled with static, and then went stone dead.

I didn't ask the White House operators to reestablish the connection. I had made the points I wanted to make and decided to stand on ceremony—having initiated the first conversation, I felt it was his place to call me back.

He never did.

SEVENTEEN

ARUCH PICKED UP ELIHU AT THE MILITARY AIRPORT AND headed back to Jerusalem on the Ramallah Road, turning east on the four-lane security highway that skirted the sprawling hilltop Israeli city-settlement of Ma'aleh Adumim. As they started downhill toward Jericho, Elihu finally broke the silence. "Lousy flight," he muttered, answering the question he felt Baruch ought to have asked. "Ran into traffic getting to the airport, almost missed the helicopter. Wish I had. The way the pilot dropped through the cloud cover and hit the runway, he must have thought he was belly-landing an F-16."

An Army reservist talking into a cellular telephone waved Baruch's beat-up two-door Honda through a roadblock. Baruch joked that the soldier was probably ordering pizza from Jerusalem but Elihu didn't crack a smile. He was in a cranky mood, gnawing on the stem of his unlit pipe as if he were trying to bite it off. Glancing quickly at Elihu, Baruch took in the collar of his raincoat turned up against an imagined storm, the woolen scarf wound like a mask over his lower jaw, his eyes dark and anxious and fixed on a horizon beyond the one Baruch could see. Elihu's black moods were part of the Elihu legend—the *katsa* always turned turtle when he was running an agent who might wind up with his throat slit from ear to ear if something went wrong. Concentrating on his driving, Baruch sped past a string of camels being led along the shoulder of the road by a Bedouin boy wearing earphones plugged into a yellow Walkman. Moments later they saw the sign that read "Sea level." Rounding a curve, Baruch spotted the northern tip of the Dead Sea glistening far below them in the morning sun. "Am I'm right in thinking you've never met Sa'adat Arif before?" he asked Elihu.

The *katsa* nodded. "I ran an agent once who dangled a numbered Swiss account in front of him. Sa'adat was representing PLO interests in France at the time. All he had to do was give us the odd scrap of information—who sat next to Arafat at supper when he was wined and dined at the Elysée, how the PLO doled out the frequent flyer miles it accumulated, that sort of fool's gold. Sa'adat wasn't biting."

Baruch snorted. "I've know Sa'adat for years—I interrogated him twice during the first *intifada*, I had lunch with him in Jericho last summer when he was named deputy chief of intelligence. He's too shrewd to let anybody get a hook into him. He knows the ropes— you sell some fool's gold, who can resist? at which point the buyer threatens to take out a full-page ad thanking you unless you deliver better grade ore."

"What's he peddling today?" Elihu wanted to know.

"Beats me. He asked for a meeting. He said he wanted to discuss the Apfulbaum kidnapping. He mentioned something about mutual interests being at stake. The key to Sa'adat is to know he never says what he thinks; you have to read between the lines." Baruch remembered something else. "In case he asks what you do for a living, I told him one of the Shin Bet Arabists was coming along for the ride."

Two-thirds of the way down to the Dead Sea, Baruch veered off the main highway onto the narrow road that meandered through the Judean hills above the oasis of Jericho. He slowed down for a group of sweaty German tourists straggling back to their air-conditioned bus after hiking along the footpath to Saint George's Monastery in Wadi Kelt, then plunged past abandoned Israeli trenches and rusting barbed wire into the lush back streets of the oldest city in the world. "Sa'adat asked me to come in the back door," Baruch explained, "to avoid the Palestinian checkpoint at the main entrance."

"Why's he keeping this meeting under wraps?" Elihu, suddenly suspicious, wanted to know.

Baruch coughed up a laugh. "He doesn't trust his own mother, so he's not about to trust the PLO police manning the checkpoint at the front door."

Circling around through the wide shaded side streets to the southern end of Jericho, Baruch came to the Army base the Israelis had called Camp Hanan and the Palestinians had renamed Aksa when they took control of Jericho in 1994. Kicking up a cloud of dust, he drove down an unpaved road parallel to a high fence with razor wire strung along the top. Half way down the road they came to an open gate. A mustached man in civilian clothing, cradling a Kalashnikov, waited inside. "We go on foot from here," Baruch announced. He locked the car and followed Elihu through the gate. The mustached man chained it closed behind them and led the visitors down a sandy path between two long barracks. He opened a side door and stepped back. Sa'adat, a round man with a shaved head in his early fifties, wearing a shiny synthetic Western suit and tie, was sitting behind a vast desk under an old British mandate poster that depicted a waterfall in a Dead Sea oasis and said "Visit Palestine." When he saw the Israelis come through the door, he closed the file he was reading and added it to a pile of dossiers, and weighed them down with a loaded Russian revolver. "Baruch, my friend, I am cheerful to see you," he said in English, rising to his feet. Coming around the desk to shake hands, he beamed a gold-toothed smile in Elihu's direction. "You, sir, are unidentified to me, but it is my misfortune to be more or less identified with your employer, which arrested me more times than I count on the fingers of two hands."

Sa'adat snapped his fingers. Two aides pushed over easy chairs and offered the Israelis glasses of freshly squeezed grapefruit juice. Sa'adat settled onto the back of the desk. Elihu, still in a foul mood, jammed the end of the dead pipe into his mouth. "We have never met before," he ventured, "but you are known to me by reputation." Sa'adat accepted this with a nod. "We hear stories," Elihu continued, baiting the Arab, "about how you tie the hands of Palestinian prisoners behind their backs and string them up by the wrists until their shoulder sockets give way. We hear stories about how you lock Palestinians who criticize the Authority in tiny isolation cells for weeks on end and make them drink their own urine. It is said that four or five prisoners have died here in recent months."

The smile froze on Sa'adat's face. "Everything we know," he said softly, "we learned from you Isra'ilis. We are school children next to you. The hooks on the walls from which we hang prisoners by the wrists, the isolation cells were built by you when you occupied Jericho."

Elihu kept his eyes fixed on Sa'adat as he sipped his juice; he clearly didn't like what he saw. Baruch cleared his throat. "Your fax said that you wanted to discuss the Apfulbaum kidnapping."

Baruch held his breath. It could have gone either way. Moving with great deliberation, Sa'adat circled the desk and sat down behind it. "I will not hold the Shin Bet against him," he said, talking to Baruch but staring Elihu in the eye, "if he does not hold the Authority's Preventive Security apparatus against me—we both work for organizations which believe ends justify means."

"Depends on the ends," Elihu growled. "Depends on the means."

"Apfulbaum," Baruch repeated, hoping to get the meeting back on track.

"Apfulbaum," Sa'adat agreed, and the gold-toothed smile reappeared on his face. "Your Prime Minister has publicly announced that he is willing to consider the principle of freeing prisoners in exchange for the release of the Rabbi Apfulbaum and his secretary. He has asked the Chairman of the Palestinian Authority to negotiate with the people who kidnapped the two Jews. The Chairman has been encouraged by Mr. Zachary Taylor Sawyer of the White House to put himself in your Prime Minister's shoes. The Chairman understands that your Prime Minister is attempting to purchase time. The Chairman is willing, even eager, to be of assistance—he is against all manifestations of terrorism and for the peaceful settlement of the differences between us. Above all else he does not want to put in jeopardy the forthcoming meeting in Washington and the signing of the treaty of peace. The situation, however, is complicated by the fact that there is no one to negotiate with. And if you take the kidnappers at their word—I myself have looked many times at the film they sent you—there would appear to be nothing to negotiate about. Either you obtain the release of the people they ask for or they will kill the Jewish hostages."

Baruch said, "You have sources that we don't have—you must have some leads on the Abu Bakr Brigade."

Sa'adat scratched at a pitted nostril. "The original Abu Bakr was a pious man, an early convert to Islam, the father-in-law of the Prophet Muhammad, as well as his close friend and first successor, what we call the *khalifa* and you call *caliph*. The fact that the kidnappers adopted this name suggests they are Muslim fundamentalists."

Elihu jammed the pipe back into his mouth. "We came a long way to hear what we already know," he remarked.

"Islamic fundamentalists," Sa'adat went on, ignoring Elihu, addressing himself to Baruch, "are the common enemy of the Shin Bet and the Authority's Preventive Security apparatus. Which is why the Isra'ilis gave us a free hand on the West Bank long before the Authority took formal control of its villages and towns. Which is why an occasional Palestinian is suspended above the ground from his wrists tied behind his back. The technique is not fool proof, but nine out of ten times we succeed in getting the information we seek. When we fail it is because the Palestinian suspended by his wrists does not have the information we seek, or suffers a fatal heart attack before he can recall it."

Baruch realized Sa'adat did know something about the kidnapping after all. He was just taking his sweet time before sharing it.

Sa'adat lifted the Russian revolver from the pile of dossiers and set it down on the desk with the barrel pointing directly at Elihu. He pulled out one file folder and opened it. "Being an Arabist, you will surely be familiar with Islamic tradition that holds that God sends down to earth, at the beginning of every century, what we call a *mujaddid* and you translate as *Renewer,* to restore to Islam the greatness it possessed in the time of the Prophet and the first *khalifa*."

Elihu leaned forward. "An American journalist published an article a few days ago that mentioned this Renewer. The journalist claimed a fundamentalist cleric in Aza told him that many among them believed that this Abu Bakr is the long-awaited *mujaddid*."

A telephone rang in an adjoining room. A woman's voice, muffled, could be heard telling someone that Sa'adat was in conference. "The Authority's Preventive Security apparatus started picking up murmurs of a *mujaddid* two and a half years ago," Sa'adat continued. "It began in the city of Hebron and then seemed to spread north to Jerusalem itself, and eventually into Ghazeh. People talked about it in whispers behind closed doors. According to these rumors, the Renewer was a blind man who saw more clearly than those with sight. He was so pious that he bore like a badge on his forehead what the Holy Qur'an calls *the trace of prostration.* He taught that Islam had not failed Muslims; Muslims had failed Islam. He taught that faithfulness to the word of God and the example of the Prophet would bring victory over the Jewish infidels. He quoted from the Qur'an the passage that begins, '*If there be twenty of you, patient men, they will overcome two hundred; if there be a hundred of you, they will overcome a thousand unbelievers.*'"

"Were you able to discover the identity of this Renewer?" Baruch asked.

Sa'adat's gold teeth flashed. "Before his untimely death, one of the Palestinians hanging by his wrists from an Isra'ili hook in the wall"—the Authority's deputy intelligence chief looked directly at Elihu as he said this—"told of a nearly blind vigilante who was executing Palestinians accused of collaborating with the Jewish infidels. According to this prisoner, the vigilante and the *mujaddid* were the same person. Because he was practically blind, this vigilante had a distinctive method of carrying out the sentence of death—he probed with his finger tips behind the condemned man's ear, and then fired a single small caliber bullet with surgical precision into the base of his brain."

Elihu looked at Baruch. "Of course! Since he's blind, he is obliged to shoot at point blank range. And since he is shooting at point blank range, he uses a small caliber pistol that is so quiet it doesn't need a silencer." He turned to the Palestinian security chief. "We have a record of eighteen such murders." He stressed the word "murders."

Sa'adat said, "All told, there were twenty-three executions." He stressed the word "executions." "The difference between your count and ours is due to the fact that five of the bodies were never turned over to the Isra'ili occupation authorities."

Baruch said, "One of the Jewish bodyguards who died in the kidnapping, as well as the terrorist whose body was found in the abandoned car, were killed by .22-caliber bullets fired into the brain stem from point blank range."

"Let us agree," Sa'adat said with bland innocence, "that the kidnapping of your Rabbi bears the signature of our blind *mujaddid*. I tell you sincerely, this vigilante is as much a menace to the Palestinian Authority and its Chairman as he is to you Jews. There is no telling what ordinary Palestinians, responding to his simple call to wage holy war against the Jews, might do if they come to believe he is God's long-awaited Renewer. Every mosque in Islam will open its doors to him; every Muslim will join his army to fight against the infidel. The Authority's peace of the brave with the Isra'ilis will be swept away by a sea of fundamentalist warriors obeying edicts issued by the *mujaddid*. Palestine will become an Islamic fundamentalist bastion. I myself will be accused of collaborating with the infidel, and a small caliber bullet"—Sa'adat, still smiling, tapped the bone behind his ear with a forefinger—"will be fired into the base of my skull."

Reading between the lines, it dawned on Baruch why they had been invited down to Jericho; the Palestinian Authority Chairman and his Preventive Security apparatus were declaring war on the blind *mujaddid* who had murdered twenty-three collaborators and kidnapped Rabbi Apfulbaum. They would hang Palestinians by their wrists in an effort to discover who he was and where he was. But once they found out, they would prefer it if someone else eliminated the *mujaddid*.

That someone else would be the Israelis.

"*Lamma lo?*" Baruch said, thinking out loud. "Why not? You find him, we'll kill him."

Beaming, Sa'adat scraped back his seat and came around to the front of the desk. "This meeting never took place," he announced. "Those who say there is an understanding between us lie through their teeth. If, by some miracle, we discover where Abu Bakr is holding the Rabbi, you will be the last to hear about it. God forbid a Muslim should denounce the *mujaddid* sent by Allah to renew Islam!"

Sa'adat accompanied his guests down the sandy path to the gate in the fence. "It was cheerful to see you," he told Baruch. "Come again when the spirit moves you. My home is your home, et cetera, et cetera." The smile etched onto his face never wavered as he added, "Next time, do me a service and leave your famous Mossad *katsa* home."

EIGHTEEN

T HE BROTHERS KARAMAZOV (AS THEY WERE NICKNAMED IN police circles) barged without knocking into Baruch's office. Azazel, wearing a heavy gold chain around his tanned neck and a white-on-white shirt unbuttoned down to a tanned navel, sank with an exasperated sigh onto a couch. Absalom, dressed in a custom-made pale mauve sports jacket and black trousers with knife-edge creases, planted himself in front of the desk and began reading the work order that Baruch had deposited in their in-basket.

"'From: Baruch.'" Absalom lifted his moist eyes from the paper clutched in his carefully manicured fingers. "That's you."

"That's him," Azazel agreed coyly.

"'To: The brothers Karamazov.' That's us."

Baruch started to say something but Azazel, from the couch, whipped both hands over his head as if they were helicopter rotors. "Listen to Absalom," he insisted shrilly. "Hear what he has to say."

"'Subject: Needle in a haystack.'" Absalom pouted. "Well, at least you got that part right." He glanced down at the work order and continued reading in a voice dripping with irony: "'Cancel all leaves, all hands on deck.' Oh, my, Baruch, aren't we being *nautical* today. 'I want you and Azazel and your people to comb through the records of former Palestinian prisoners. The list is obviously long—'"

"He's telling *us* that the list is long," Azazel bitched from the couch. He rolled his eyes. "Oh, dear."

Absalom plunged on. "'—obviously long, and much of it is still not available on the Shin Bet's main frame, which means you'll have to wade through hundreds of dusty file cabinets in the basements— but when has that fazed the brothers Karamazov?'"

"Flattery," Azazel sniffed from the couch, "would normally get you everywhere, but not today."

"'Here's what we're looking for.'" Absalom flashed a vinegary smirk in Azazel's direction. "Here's what he's looking for."

"He's already said what he's looking for," Azazel fretted. "He's looking for a needle in his haystack."

Absalom cleared his throat. "'A male Palestinian, age unknown but I'm guessing he is in his forties or fifties, who (1) is short and heavy set, (2) may have been arrested after being betrayed by one of the Shin Bet's Palestinian assets, (3) probably served major time in Israeli prisons as a result of this denunciation, (4) was in all likelihood a devout Muslim with (5) seriously enough impaired eyesight so that someone could describe him as being nearly blind.'"

"Forty or fifty," Azazel blurted out. "Possibly betrayed. Maybe jailed. Probably devout. Nearly blind. Well, at least he's sure we're looking for the *male* of the species!"

The two former Russian rabbis, who had emigrated to Israel two decades earlier and now directed a small army of researchers working for the national police, batted their eyes in Baruch's direction. Absalom and Azazel were the butt of countless office jokes, but Baruch took the position that what consenting adults did in their free time was their affair. All he cared about was that they were capable of tracking a Palestinian through the voluminous national police–Shin Bet archives on the skimpiest of leads. Only months before they had managed to identify a Nablus Arab who had thrown a Molotov cocktail at an Israeli patrol on the basis of a description limited to two details; the bomber had asthma and gnawed on his finger nails as he was waiting for the Israelis to pass.

Baruch settled back in his chair. "Look, I'm not stupid. I know there will be dozens of short, heavy male Palestinians who were devout and suffered from bad eyesight and wound up behind bars after being denounced by a collaborator."

"Dozens!" Absalom corrected him. "Hundreds is more likely."

"If there are hundreds," Baruch said in his crisp no-room-for-argument tone, "bring me their names. By the time you've narrowed it down to hundreds, I hope we'll have another detail or two so you can narrow the list down even further."

NINETEEN

OMETIME AFTER MIDNIGHT, MAALI, SLEEPING RESTLESSLY ON
a folding cot with an arm flung over her eyes to shield them
from the two-hundred-watt overhead bulb, was awakened by
the long, deep sobs of a woman. For a moment she thought she had
been crying in her sleep. Then, through the grille, she saw Isra'ili soldiers dragging someone under the armpits along the passageway. The
group came to a stop in front of Maali's door. A key turned in the
lock, the door swung open and a woman was thrown into the small
cell. She collapsed onto the cement floor as the door slammed closed
behind her with the brutal gnash of metal striking metal.

Crouching next to the prisoner, Maali turned her face up and
cradled her head in her lap. The woman's dark hair was matted with
sticky blood. There was a cut under an eye that was swollen shut, and
an ugly purple bruise on one shoulder. Her prison shift was ripped
under the armpits. Both of her knees and one ankle were scraped and
bleeding. The woman, who appeared to be in her late twenties or
early thirties, opened her good eye and peered up at Maali in fright.
"They think they can throw me into a cell with a collaborator and I'll
tell you what I wouldn't tell them," she whispered in Arabic. "It will
not happen."

"I am no collaborator," Maali said.

"Go to hell." The words were spit out from between sore lips.

Maali dragged the prisoner over to the cot and wrestled her onto
it. She pulled off the underwear the Jewish doctor had given her,
moistened a corner with saliva and began to clean the woman's cuts

and bruises. "What is your name?" she asked after a while. "Mine is Maali. I am the wife of Yussuf Abu Saleh."

The young woman tilted her head to get a better look at Maali. "There is a Yussuf Abu Saleh who is said to be a disciple of the *mujaddid.*"

Maali smiled proudly.

The woman said, "How can I be sure you are the wife of Yussuf Abu Saleh?"

"Because I say it. Because I am here. Because I have suffered as you have suffered."

Air rattled in the woman's throat as she spoke. "I am Delilah, the sister-in-law of Abu Bakr, the *mujaddid.* My husband and I were pulled from our automobile as we passed through an Isra'ili road-block on the edge of Jerusalem three days ago. I have not seen my husband since then, though I have heard his cries of pain coming from another room when they were torturing me."

The two woman embraced. Delilah put her mouth next to Maali's ear and whispered, "Have you told them what they want to know?"

"Not a word has crossed my lips," Maali shot back. "I will die before I betray my husband."

The woman managed a twisted smile. "Whatever you do, tell me nothing. What I do not know I cannot pass on to the Jews if the torture becomes too much for me to bear."

Exhausted, Delilah sank into a fitful sleep with her head propped on Maali's lap. At dawn the Isra'ilis came back for her. "*Hatha baladna, il yahud kilabna,*" the woman cried defiantly as they pulled her from the cell. "*This is our country, the Jews are our dogs.*"

An hour later the door of the cell was thrown open and Delilah, bleeding from one nostril of what looked like a broken nose, stumbled in. Sobbing convulsively like a baby, she collapsed into Maali's arms. "They are convinced I know where Abu Bakr is holding the Jewish Rabbi," she gasped when she was finally able to talk.

"Do you?" Maali whispered.

Staring deeply into Maali's eyes, Delilah nodded imperceptibly. Then she curled up on the cot and, her body jerking spastically from time to time, dozed. Every two hours or so the Isra'ilis hauled Delilah off, and dragged her back to the cell looking more beat up than before. Maali guessed the Jews were killing two birds with one stone —they were trying to beat information out of Delilah, and using Delilah to demonstrate to Maali that they weren't fainthearted when it came to making a woman talk. Delilah was sleeping fitfully some-time in the early afternoon when Maali heard a door opening at the far end of the passageway. She shook Delilah awake. They could make out the sound of footsteps approaching. Delilah looked around wildly. "Can't take any more," she moaned. "I need metal, it does not have to be sharp, with which to cut my wrists." Seeing nothing she could use, she pulled Maali roughly toward her until their foreheads were touching. "I ask you—knot a length of cloth around my neck and strangle me."

Maali shrank back in horror. "It is out of the realm of possibility."

The cell door opened. Two young Isra'ili woman soldiers, both wearing khaki miniskirts and khaki sweaters, came in. One carried a plastic basin filled with warm water. The other set a bar of soap, a towel, a pair of low-heeled shoes and a folded Arab dress on the cot. "Count your blessings," one of the soldiers sneered in Arabic. "Palestinian lawyers have brought your case before an Israeli judge and he has ordered your release. You are free to go as soon as you clean up."

"And my husband?"

"Your husband is in the hospital—he suffered a concussion when he beat his head against a wall to make it appear as if he had been tortured."

"You lie!"

The young soldier shrugged. "Your lawyers are waiting outside to take you to him. Call out when you are ready to leave."

Maali helped Delilah wash away the dried blood and fit her aching limbs into the clean dress. The two women stood in front of the cell door and embraced. "We have only known each other for a few hours, but I think of you as a sister," Delilah said.

"I will never forget you," Maali declared emotionally.

"Do you want to send word to your husband?"

Maali leaped at the chance. "Address a note to Tayzir the florist," she whispered into Delilah's ear. "Leave it with the lame shoemaker across from the El Khanqa Mosque in the Christian Quarter. Say I have been arrested but am holding up. Say that the Isra'ilis discovered the ring and know it belonged to the dead Jew."

"The Isra'ilis discovered the ring and know it belonged to the dead Jew."

"Say I have not told them who gave it to me. Yussuf will understand."

Delilah turned away before Maali could embrace her again and called for the two women soldiers to open the cell door. She stepped through it and started striding down the passageway ahead of them almost as if her limbs were not in pain. A moment later she disappeared through the door at the end of the passageway.

Around six in the evening, Maali caught the squeak of the food cart being pushed by a Palestinian orderly down the corridor. It came to a stop in front of the door of her cell and a plastic tray was slipped through the slot. Maali carried it back to her bunk and looked at the food. There was a plastic bowl half filled with cold rice and pieces of chicken, a single slice of white bread, a bowl of jello. She knew that she had to force herself to eat to keep up her strength. Using the plastic spoon, she started in on the rice, then picked up the bread. Hidden under it was a rolled up cigarette paper. Maali glanced at the door, then turning her back to it, unrolled the paper and flattened it on the plastic tray. "Beware," it said in minuscule Arabic writing. "The Jews are using a beat-up Arabic-looking woman to get prisoners to talk."

Her skin crawling, her blood running cold, Maali sank to the ground. "What have I done?" she moaned, and she leaned forward and began to slowly pound her forehead against the cement floor, each stroke incrementally harder than the one before.

TWENTY

IN THE ROOM ABOVE THE SEAFOOD RESTAURANT, THE RETIRED general named Uri poured Lagavulin whiskey neat into the six tumblers lined up on the oval table, adding a splash or two until he was satisfied all the glasses held the same amount. He passed out five of the tumblers to the members of the inter-agency Working Group, gripped the sixth in his paw and sank dejectedly onto the overstuffed couch against one wall. From his seat at the oval table, Baruch started reading out loud the police report on the Palestinian woman Maali. Prison guards had discovered her unconscious on the floor of the cell. The prison doctor had been summoned. He had noted massive injury to the forehead and dilation of the pupils of the eyes, which indicated the brain itself had been bruised by impacting against the inside of the skull; he had observed convulsions of the extremities of the limbs, which suggested the brain may have swelled, putting pressure on the cerebrum. The chief interrogator had given the doctor permission to move Maali to a nearby hospital, but had instructed him to make sure the records showed that she had been brought in to the hospital's emergency room unconscious after a motor scooter accident and had been in a coma ever since. A surgical procedure to drain the skull cavity and relieve pressure on the brain had been performed, but the pressure had built up again rapidly. A brain scan had indicated irreversible cerebral trauma. The woman Maali had died in the intensive care unit shortly after midnight.

Nursing his Scotch, Elihu stared out the window at the sea lapping against the Jaffa shore. For several minutes nobody said a word. Then the squall broke.

"Somebody screwed up," Baruch said angrily, tossing the police report onto the table. "The woman shouldn't have been left alone in the cell after our agent succeeded in duping her."

"How could we know she'd figure out she was duped?" Altmann snapped.

"It's our business to know," Baruch retorted.

"Why are we getting worked up over the suicide of a Palestinian girl?" Uri called from the couch. "She was wearing a ring her husband cut off the finger of a murdered Jewish kid."

"Uri's right," said Dror. "Let's put this into perspective. I don't see any Palestinians beating their breasts over the four Jews killed in the attack on the Rabbi's convoy."

"I don't see them beating their breasts over the kidnapping of the Rabbi and his secretary," Altmann agreed.

"The problem," announced Wozzeck, "isn't the girl Maali. She's spilt milk. The problem is the lame shoemaker across from the El Khanqa Mosque. The problem is Yussuf Abu Saleh."

Elihu turned away from the window. "Let's begin with the shoemaker," he said. "He's obviously a *mishlasim*—a mail drop and not an operational agent. He won't have the vaguest idea who sent a letter, or who received it, so there's no purpose in interrogating him. Mossad cells operating in Europe have been using this technique for years—you have mail delivered to a post box, the proprietor of the box runs a flag of some sort up a pole, the addressee watches for the flag and picks up his letter."

Altmann helped himself to another two fingers of Lagavulin. "If we have a letter addressed to Tayzir delivered to the shoemaker, he'll run a flag up the pole and Yussuf will come out of the woodwork. We could try to follow Yussuf, but that would be tricky in the narrow streets of the Old City. Even if we succeeded, chances are he'll only lead us back to the bedroom where he hangs his hat."

"Yussuf should be picked up and made to talk," Dror said. "The question is, do we do it or do we leave him to the tender mercies of Sa'adat Arif?"

"Yussuf's our problem," Baruch said flatly. "We deal with it. We don't farm the problem out to the Palestinian Authority's people in Jericho."

"Whoever deals with it will have to move fast," Altmann warned. "The clock is ticking. The deadline for the Rabbi's secretary expires the day after tomorrow. If the *katsa* can't come up with something between now and then, Yussuf—assuming he knows where the Rabbi is being held, assuming someone can make him talk—will be our last best hope."

Dror said, "There won't be time to worm information out of Yussuf, the way we did with Maali. Whoever pinches him will have to beat it out of him."

Altmann shook his head. "We'll have Amnesty International breathing down our necks. We'll have the bleeding heart lawyers filing *habeas corpus* affidavits."

"The bleeding hearts won't get the time of day out of Sa'adat Arif," the general grunted from the couch. "The bleeding hearts never heard of Jericho."

"There's another advantage to using Sa'adat's people," Dror said. "It'll be easier to make it look as if Yussuf was the victim of Arab factional rivalry, which is important if we don't want to frighten off Abu Bakr's boys."

"That's a point," Altmann said. "There's less chance of Abu Bakr ducking for cover, and taking the Rabbi and Efrayim with him—or killing them outright—if he can be made to think that Hamas's jilted jihadists cornered Yussuf."

"I don't like it," Baruch said. "I don't like owing favors to Sa'adat Arif. I don't like letting someone else do our dirty work. It looks like Yussuf killed Jews. I think Jews should deal with him."

"Let's put it to a vote," the *katsa* suggested from the window. "Who's in favor of sub-contracting this out to Sa'adat Arif?"

Dror and Altmann each raised a finger.

"Who's in favor of handling this ourselves?"

Baruch raised a hand. Wozzeck hesitated, then raised his glass of Scotch.

Everyone looked at the general on the couch. "Part of me is with

Baruch—we got into a lot of hot water in Beirut letting Arabs do our dirty work for us. On the other hand—" Uri shrugged. "I just don't know."

Baruch looked across the room at the *katsa*. "That more or less leaves it up to you, Elihu."

"It does, doesn't it."

TWENTY-ONE

THE SKINNY BEDOUIN BOY WHO DELIVERED TRAYS FILLED WITH almond biscuits and tiny cups of Turkish coffee for the café on Christian Quarter Road brought the sealed envelope to Abdullah, the lame shoemaker across from the El Khanqa Mosque, minutes after the second prayer of the day. Abdullah was an old Christian Arab and wise in the ways of the *souk*. He glanced around to be sure no one was watching, then fitted on his reading glasses and examined the envelope. He deciphered written Arabic only with difficulty, but managed to make out the words "Tayzir" and "florist" printed in ink on the coarse paper.

"Who gave this to you?" Abdullah asked the boy.

"A woman."

"What woman?"

"Her head was covered with a *chador*. I could see that her hair under the *chador* was long and black. She spoke our language. She gave me a shekel, she promised you would give me another when I delivered the envelope."

"You lie like a rug," Abdullah said with a guttural laugh. "She gave you half a shekel and said I would give you half a shekel."

The boy tossed his thin shoulders sullenly.

Abdullah reached into the deep pocket of his apron, retrieved a coin and dropped it into the boy's palm. The boy pocketed the money and darted off down the street past the four Palestinian laborers prying up flagstones to lay telephone cables.

Abdullah made his way to the back of his shop and tugged the rope of the dumbwaiter on which his wife lowered fruit juice and his medicine, and his midday meal. Two flights up a small bell attached to the rope sounded. "Is that you who rings, Abdullah?" his wife called down the shaft.

"You may hang out my green shirt to dry," Abdullah shouted up.

The shoemaker's wife climbed to the roof and fastened with clothespins the bright green shirt to the line stretched between the television antenna and the old chimney that had been sealed off since the Turkish occupation. If she wondered why she was hanging a shirt that was not wet to dry in the sun, she never posed the question. For forty-two years, she had been following her husband's instructions without asking questions; she was not going to start now.

An hour went by, then a second. Customers came and went. Several Armenian priests wandered past the shop talking among themselves in a language that struck Abdullah as exceedingly strange. A group of Italian tourists followed a short Christian Arab, wearing a fez and holding high a large red umbrella, toward Christian Quarter Road and the Church of the Holy Sepulcher. When several of the woman lagged behind to window shop in front of a jewelry store across from Abdullah's, the guide came scurrying back to get them. Snapping at their heels like a sheep dog, he herded them away from the window, raised aloft his emblem of authority and started off again in the direction of the church. Curiously, the four Palestinians laying telephone cables did not break for the mid-day meal, a fact that registered in Abdullah's consciousness at roughly the same moment the young Palestinian Abdullah knew only as Tayzir came sauntering down from Christian Quarter Road to pick up the message that had been left at the shoemaker's shop.

Pushing himself off the work bench, the old shoemaker reached for his wooden crutch and limped to the doorway. "No! No!" he called, pointing with his crutch toward the Palestinian laborers just as two of them leaped from the trench they were digging to fling Yussuf violently against a wall. In an instant they had slipped handcuffs on his wrists and taped shut his mouth. The other Palestinians drew pistols from their overalls and blocked off each end of the narrow street. A group of Japanese tourists gaped in astonishment as one of the laborers whipped out a small radio and barked into it. Seconds later an Arab taxi careened around the corner and screeched to a stop next to where the two Palestinians were pinning Yussuf to the side of a building. The taxi's rear doors were flung open, Yussuf was bundled onto the floor in the back of the car and covered with a Bedouin rug. The two Palestinians with drawn pistols backed toward the taxi. One of them pulled a piece of chalk from his pocket and scrawled something on a wall, then leaped into the taxi as it sped off through the narrow streets of the Old City in the direction of Herod's Gate and the Arab quarter of Jerusalem.

TWENTY-TWO

IN THE SAFE HOUSE PERCHED ABOVE THE MAZE OF STREETS IN THE Christian Quarter, the Doctor was pacing behind Efrayim who, relieved to be free of his hood, was trying to make his interrogation drag on as long as possible. "I don't know anything about encoding or decoding," he replied, "so how could I have encoded or decoded the Rabbi's messages?"

"Don't believe a word he says," Apfulbaum quipped, his voice muffled by his hood. "Already he writes the king's English in a kind of code—only people who spell as badly as he does can decipher it."

"What were your duties as Rabbi Apfulbaum's secretary?" the Doctor asked.

"I typed his letters on a computer that thanks to God had a spell checker. I screened his phone calls and made sure the answering machine was on for Shabbat. I reminded him of appointments. I deposited honorariums in his bank account when he gave speeches or sold Op-Ed pieces, and balanced his checkbook and warned him when he was overdrawn, which was almost always. I arranged logistics when he went on trips—I called ahead to tell them what he wouldn't eat, which was anything fried, and tasted everything first to make sure it wasn't too salty."

The Rabbi piped up, "He tasted everything first, but it was to make sure some lunatic Israeli peacenik didn't poison my food."

"You never told me that before, Rabbi."

"I didn't want you to stop tasting."

The Doctor said, "If you typed his letters, you will know whom he wrote to."

"Our Rabbi wrote to anyone, which is to say, he wrote to everyone—he wrote to every Letters to the Editor editor in America, he wrote to our Prime Minister practically once a week, he wrote to the White House and Ten Downing Street and the Elysée Palace and the Bundestag and the Kremlin—"

The Doctor tried to cut him off. "I think I get the idea."

But Efrayim couldn't be stopped. "He wrote to the heads of state in Saudi Arabia and Syria and Iraq and Iran and Egypt and Jordan and Monaco—"

"Why Monaco?" the Doctor demanded, intrigued.

The Rabbi snickered under his hood. "I sent Prince Charming a list of Palestinian terrorist groups that were laundering money in his banks and advised him to clean up his act or I'd get the American Jews to boycott his Lilliputian principality. Or words to that effect."

"Did he ever write a letter to anyone named Ya'ir?" the Doctor asked Efrayim.

The Rabbi's secretary thought about this. "There was someone named Ya'ir at the Ministry of—"

"I am talking about the Ya'ir who is the leader of the Jewish settlers' terrorist organization," the Doctor said impatiently.

"Mister, I don't know anything about that Ya'ir and I know less about Jewish settlers' terrorist organizations. Listen, I'm not even sure I'm going to stay in Israel after what's happened to me. I mean, it's one thing to be kidnapped if you can be positive you're going to be released. It's another thing to be kidnapped by people who don't know from happy endings."

"Palestinian prisoners in Israeli detention camps are also entitled to happy endings," snapped the Doctor.

"If it was up to me," Efrayim said, hoping to ingratiate himself with his captor, "I'd let them all go free. I swear to God I would."

"It is unfortunate for us that it is not up to you."

"Besides which," said the Rabbi, "only God can decide who will and who won't have a happy ending."

"It's not me who is going to say differently, Rabbi," Efrayim declared.

The Doctor looked down at the Rabbi's head bobbing under his hood. "Nor would I say differently," he remarked softly.

In the other room, Yussuf's failure to return from the mail drop alarmed Petra. She kept her ears glued to the Isra'ili wavelengths. She could hear paratroop units stationed around the Old City reporting in. Suddenly an officer spoke of an abduction near the Church of the Holy Sepulcher. Soldiers were being sent to investigate. Petra went to the door between the two rooms and summoned the Doctor with an urgent wave of her hand. "Yussuf has not returned from the shoe-maker's shop," she told him. "The Isra'ilis are reporting a kidnap-ping." On Petra's radio, there were bursts of static, then a cryptic report with the details of the abduction. Four Palestinian laborers had pounced on a young Palestinian and taken him away in an Arab taxi. One of the gunmen had scratched the words, in Arabic, "Hamas has a long memory and a long arm" in chalk on a wall.

Aown and Azziz panicked. They were all for killing the prisoners out of hand and fleeing, but the Doctor overruled them. If, in fact, Yussuf had been picked up by Hamas gunmen, it would appear to be a settling of old scores; Yussuf was known to have incensed the Hamas organization when he crossed over to join the Doctor's Abu Bakr group and took members of his Nablus cell, along with their cache of bombs and weapons, with him. Yussuf could have been betrayed by Abdullah; if he sold letters, he might also sell people. Or Hamas could have spotted Yussuf picking up mail at the shoemaker's shop, and decided to snatch him the next time he came into the streets. They would have no way of knowing Yussuf was involved in the kidnapping of the Rabbi and his secretary. And it would be out of character for Yussuf to offer this information.

Straining to make out the Isra'ili voices crackling over the wave-lengths, Petra agreed with the Doctor's analysis. "There is no men-tion of us, no indication that the Isra'ilis suspect we are hiding in the Old City. We would be foolish to lose our nerve now."

"If Hamas picked up Yussuf," Azziz said, "they must know about the shoemaker."

"The shoemaker is a dead end street," the Doctor pointed out. "As far as he is concerned, someone named Tayzir was hiding in the Old City and arranged the drop, at twenty shekels a letter, in order to receive mail."

The Doctor nevertheless took the precaution of distributing the AK-47s and hand grenades. Leaving Petra and the el-Tel brothers in the front room, he retreated into the back room with the hostages, closing and locking the second armored door behind him.

"Is the Israeli Army coming to free us?" Efrayim asked excitedly.

"It does not look that way," the Doctor said.

"*El hamdouli-lah,*" the Rabbi muttered in Arabic. "Thanks to God." In his heart of hearts, he dreaded a rescue operation as much as he hoped for it; even if the Israelis managed to fight their way into the safe house, the Doctor would surely shoot his hostages before the soldiers could blow the door to the back room off its hinges.

"In times of crisis, you invoke the Arabic name of God," the Doctor noted. "There is hope for you yet."

TWENTY-THREE

AOWN UNTIED THE LEGS OF THE RABBI AND LED HIM TO THE lidless toilet and watched him urinate into it, then brought him back to his seat and lashed his legs. Then he led Efrayim to the toilet. When the secretary was back in his seat Aown removed their hoods and gave them each a cup of tea and several biscuits, and settled onto the cot to watch them eat.

Efrayim whispered to the Rabbi, "I read somewhere that if kidnappers get to know you personally, they can't bring themselves to hurt you." The secretary turned to Aown. "So do you have a name?" When the young Palestinian didn't respond, he said, "My name's Efrayim. Efrayim Blumenfeld. Actually, I'm glad to meet you. I'm not just saying that. I really am. I never talked to a live Palestinian before. Don't get me wrong—I haven't talked to dead ones either." Efrayim indicated the Rabbi with his chin. "His name is Rabbi Apfulbaum. Rabbi isn't his Christian name. His Christian name is Isaac. So how old are you? Me, I'm going to be twenty-seven next month." Confronted with Aown's obstinate silence, Efrayim cast about desperately for something to say to break the ice. "I'm not actually Israeli," he hurried on. "I'm American. I suppose from your point of view that's just as bad. I was thinking of emigrating to Israel but I haven't made up my mind yet. I have a mother and a father and a teenage sister living on Long Island. They're not so excited about me moving to Israel. They think it's too dangerous. You've probably heard of Long Island? It's the largest island on the continental United States. I suppose they call it Long Island because of how it sticks out

like a sore thumb into the Atlantic Ocean. You've probably heard of
the Atlantic Ocean?"

The Rabbi said, "Enough already, Efrayim. Chances are he's not
going to Long Island anytime soon. If he does go there it'll be to
plant a bomb in a Walbaums."

"I only thought—"

"You should stop thinking and give your brain a rest."

"Rabbi, it's impossible to stop thinking."

"You can stop thinking if you pray."

"What should I pray for?"

"Pray to God to let you live long enough to celebrate your twenty-
seventh birthday."

"Rabbi, you terrify me when you say things like that."

"You terrify *me* when you say I have a Christian name."

TWENTY-FOUR

"**W**hich brings us back full circle to Ya'ir."

"To Ya'ir." The Rabbi tilted his head and lifted his manacled hands in a mock toast. "Long life," he tittered, his vocal cords sore from the endless interrogation. "Good health. Financial success. Fifteen minutes of fame. Whatever."

They had been at it for three and a half hours, the Doctor's precise questions and the Rabbi's demented replies grazing each other as they sailed back and forth between them. The el-Tel brothers had drifted in to listen for a while, then, bored, had returned to the front room, Azziz to strip and oil the AK-47s while his brother read aloud the nightly portion of the holy Qur'an, after which the two settled down to a game of backgammon. The sound of the dice rattling and their muffled cries of excitement could be heard through the partly open door. His eyes red with fatigue, the Doctor puffed intently on a Palestinian Farid; cigarette ashes flecked the lapels of his suit jacket, butts littered the floor around the hem of his long white robe. "The leader of Jewish underground," he droned on, lighting a new cigarette on the dying embers of an old one, "is known by the code name Ya'ir, after Eliezer ben Ya'ir, the hero of Masada who held out against the Roman Tenth Legion and talked his men into committing mass suicide when it looked as if they were going to be taken prisoner. More recently, Ya'ir was the underground name of Abraham Stern, the Jewish-Polish terrorist who led the Stern Gang against British rule until he was cornered and killed by British soldiers in a Tel Aviv apartment."

The Rabbi's feet tap-danced on the floor of their own accord. "You'd be better armed for your holy war against Israel if you understood Jewish character as well as you understand Jewish history."

"Tell me about Jewish character, *ya'ani*."

Apfulbaum pulled a face. He sensed that his interrogator had planted a land mine in his path; whatever answer he gave was likely to be turned against him. A muscle in his thin neck twitched as he leaned forward, eager to outfox the fox. "Twenty-four hours a day, seven days a week, the Jew fights an inner battle. The Torah tells us we are warriors and lions. The Holocaust tells us we are victims and lambs. Modern day Jews carry the Torah in their heads and the Holocaust in their guts; it is the tightening of an artery, the tensing of a muscle, an ear-splitting murmur of the heart. The two traditions, the two halves of this split personality, war with each other within the gizzard of every Jew."

"The predicament of the Jew is not unlike the predicament of the devout Muslim," the Doctor said. "We also have two traditions that war with each other in our gizzards, as you put it. When a Muslim no longer lives on Islamic territory and under Islamic rule, he must decide which of the two traditions to follow: armed struggle, which we call *jihad*, or emigration to a territory governed by Islamic law, which we call *hejira*. In his lifetime, the Prophet Mohammed did both. In my case, I have chosen *Al jihad fi sabil Allah*—Warring in the path of God, which must be interpreted as armed struggle to spread Muslim power and the word of the Prophet. I prefer to fight rather than emigrate."

Despite himself, Apfulbaum was beginning to feel a grudging respect for his captor. "In your shoes I would certainly do the same. In my case, in the case of the Jewish hero who has taken the name of Ya'ir, the warrior Jew has triumphed over the victim Jew."

"And your warrior Jew, by extension, has divine dispensation to steal the land from Palestinians and slaughter those who resist."

Apfulbaum wagged a trembling finger at his inquisitor. "We are not stealing the land from Palestinians, but nurturing a Jewish entity in the Promised Land."

"Personally, I have nothing against a Jewish entity in, say, Uganda."

The Rabbi snorted in satisfaction; all things considered, he was enjoying these bouts of verbal sparring, if only because he got to spend several hours without the sickening hood over his head. If he ever managed to get out of this alive, he would attempt to reproduce the dialogue in a lengthy article. He already had a title in mind; he would call it "The Children of Abraham: a Dialogue of the Deaf between Two Blind Mice." "For centuries," Apfulbaum said, rambling on in lilting imitation of his old Rabbi in Crown Heights instructing *yeshiva* bookworms, I. Apfulbaum among them, "we were dispersed like seeds across the planet, taking root where we could, moving on when the local czar acquired a taste for ethnic cleansing. We lived by the Torah, but what happened to us? Pogroms, ghettos, expulsions, inquisitions, death camps, crematoriums are what happened to us. The moral of the story would be as plain as the nose on your face if I had eyeglasses and could see your face: To live by the Torah isn't enough; we must follow God's commandment to the Jewish people and settle all of the land of the Torah. The majority of the six hundred and thirteen commandments in the Torah can't be carried out in Uganda—they can only be carried out in Israel. I'm talking all of the land of the Torah, not just half. Living the life of a Torah Jew in the land of Israel is the ultimate religious experience; it's a spiritual orgy. Here we are in direct contact with God, on the soil God gave us. We are not weekend warriors, dipping in and out of Jewishness in some Diaspora synagogue where singles and divorced circle each other looking for non-smoking soul mates; we are not New York Jews who associate Jewishness with the ritual eating of bagels and lox every Sunday morning."

Across the room the Rabbi's secretary, dozing restlessly under his leather hood, shuddered so violently that he almost tipped over his chair. "I can't swim," he cried in the high pitched voice of a frightened child caught up in a vivid nightmare. He stretched his neck like a swan and gulped for air. "For the love of God, throw me a buoy before I drown."

"You're supposed to be a consenting adult," the Rabbi, irritated by the interruption, taunted his secretary. "Sink or swim, but for God's sake, Efrayim, do it discreetly." Scratching a nostril on his slit sleeve, Apfulbaum turned back to his interrogator. "Excuse the interruption. Where was I? Ah, I remember. As for slaughtering the Palestinians who resist, Moses ben Maimon, a twelfth century *mensch* if there ever was one, taught that an individual may be killed—*must be killed!*—if killing him will prevent Jews from being harmed. This principle is known as *din rodef,* the judgment of the pursuer; the *rodef* or pursuer with a knapsack stuffed with plastic explosives can be killed by a righteous Jew before the pursuer uses the explosives to kill a Jew. In the inimitable words of Maimonides, his blood is permitted. You are too shrewd not to see what I'm driving at—someone like Ya'ir is justified in attacking Palestinians to prevent the Palestinians from attacking Jews."

The Doctor dispelled the smoke with the back of his hand. "Do you believe *din rodef* justifies preemptive strikes against Palestinians wearing knapsacks, or Palestinians in general?"

"The delicious Koran of yours authorizes Muslims to take what they think is theirs by force. Our Torah authorizes us to protect what is ours by force." Apfulbaum tittered again. "Push has long since come to shove, but which text will triumph—your Koran or my Torah?"

"You have not answered my question."

In his eagerness to reply, the Rabbi ignored the saliva dribbling from the corner of his mouth. "Given the directives of the Koran and the spin *meshugana* Muslim fundamentalists like you put on them, all Palestinians must be treated as potential carriers of knapsacks." He cocked his head and added, "Read Genesis two, fifteen: God placed Adam in the Garden of Eden '*to work and guard it.*' Israel is my Eden, and I am simply obeying God's injunction to guard it."

Unfazed, the Doctor sucked at his cigarette. "You are repeating word for word deranged passages from your book, *One Torah, One Land.*"

The Rabbi's mouth gaped open in satisfaction. "You have read my book!"

"I have had it read to me, *ya'ani.*"

"Aieeeee. Efrayim told me you had a problem with your eyes."

The Doctor laughed harshly. "You might call it a problem. Tear ducts normally drain into the nose through the nasolacrimal ducts, but in my case the membranes were clogged at birth, which caused my eyes to tear permanently. I was born crying and never stopped, and it affected my vision. By the time my parents noticed that my sight had deteriorated and took me to a doctor, who opened the nasolacrimal ducts, it was too late—I was reduced to a kind of tunnel vision, which gradually worsened as I grew older. Each time I woke up I found I could see less than the day before—but, curiously, I understood more. I tell you: people who knew me as a child say they weren't aware my vision had been impaired. I developed little tricks—I knew where every object in the house was. I used the tips of my fingers as if they were antennas. I would pour fruit juice into tumblers and offer them to visitors. My father had a horse, which I rode. When I was twelve I was dying to go to a riding academy run by a Syrian cavalry officer. I knew that if he discovered I couldn't see he wouldn't let me enter the academy. So I devised a system of taking bearings like a sailor and navigating my way around dry land. The Syrian instructor never realized I was functionally blind." The Doctor laughed under his breath. "I am still taking bearings, and still navigating."

"On what do you take bearings?"

"On the Creator, the Maker, the Shaper, the All-merciful, the All-compassionate, the All-sublime, the All-mighty. On the one true God. There is yet another name for God, the Greatest Name, concealed from all but the holiest of men. It is my dream to one day pronounce it."

"Me, too, I believe in one God," the Rabbi said with quiet ardor. "'*Shema yisro'eyl, adoynoy eloheynu, adoynoy ekh-o-o-o-dddd . . .*'" he said, drawing out the last syllable of the word "one." '*Hear O Israel, the Lord is God, the Lord is one.*' Me, too, I hope to enter the holy of holies in a reconstructed Temple of Solomon and pronounce the unpronounceable name of God before I kick the bucket."

"*La ilaha illa 'llah,*" the Doctor whispered huskily. "'*No god exists but God.*'" He felt himself being sucked onto a common ground beyond the no-man's land of English, and scraped back his chair to create more space between him and his prisoner. Changing the subject abruptly, he said, "According to my notes you are married."

The Rabbi responded reluctantly. "I have a wife. In America she was called Janet. In Israel she has taken the Hebrew name Devora."

"At what age did you fall in love with her?"

"I never fell in love with her. I married in order to procreate. She was . . . suitable." He leaned forward. "God created the female of the species on the sixth day but He neglected to say, as He did when He was contemplating His handiwork on days one to five, that it was good." The Rabbi nodded to convey that he was making an important point.

The Doctor appeared interested. "Have you ever been in love?"

His ankles straining against the lengths of cloth binding them to the legs of the chairs, Apfulbaum lowered his voice to a hoarse whisper. The last thing in the world he wanted was for Efrayim to hear what he was going to say. "Once, when I was studying to become a Rabbi, I danced with a girl at the St. George Hotel in Brooklyn. It was summer. There was no back to her dress. I remember feeling the vertebrae of her naked spine under my finger tips. I got . . . excited. The girl laughed and pressed herself into my . . . excitement." Apfulbaum was suddenly defensive. "So what about you—have you ever been smitten? Come clean: Have you ever ached to caress the female body with all its perfections and imperfections? Are you blind or indifferent to all those young ladies with brassiere straps slipping off their bronzed shoulders or bare navels with earrings in their belly buttons? I'm not talking platonic friendship, I'm talking permanent erection, I'm talking coitus un-interruptus. You are obviously a control freak. What I'm really getting at is, have you ever lost control?"

The Doctor cleared his throat. "My answer will surprise you. As a matter of fact, yes. I am not ashamed to admit it was love at first sight. Only remembering it now takes my breath away. The touch of her vertebrae left the tips of my fingers tingling. I wanted to drink her in, penetrate to her most secret parts, surrender myself to her, become one with her. It was my profoundest wish to die in her bare arms."

"What became of her?"

"She is still alive and well and aging nicely, thank you." The Doctor actually smiled. "The name of my beloved is Jerusalem. You must understand the difference between the secular Muslims who direct the Palestinian Authority and Islamists like me. The secular Muslims are only interested in a nation-state; the Authority's functionaries, little men from refugee camps in Tunis, sit behind large desks and drink Turkish coffee and accept envelopes stuffed with cash in return for favors. Me, I am crazy about the *land*. I tell you frankly, *ya'ani*, when I walk in the hills above Jerusalem, I wear sandals and never wash the dust off my feet until I go to the mosque to pray."

The Rabbi lowered his eyes, acknowledging that he was in the presence of a pious man. "I know, I know. With me it's exactly the same." He buffed his lips with his knuckles as he recited words he had memorized as a young man and never forgotten. "When a man plasters his house, let him leave a small area unplastered to remind him of Jerusalem. Let a man prepare everything for a meal; then let him leave a small thing undone to remind him of Jerusalem. For it is said: '*If I forget thee O Jerusalem, may my right hand forget its cunning.*'"

The Doctor said emotionally, "I never dreamed I would come across another human being, let alone a Jew, who loved this city as I do."

"The first time I set foot in Jerusalem," the Rabbi, almost giddy with bliss, ranted on, "oy, I must have been sixteen at the time, I wound up, like every Jew visiting the Holy Land, praying at the Wailing Wall. And suddenly it hit me that I wasn't praying, I was actually talking to God! I beat my head against what was left of the Second Temple until I had bruised my forehead. When I pressed my ear to the cold stone, I swear to you I heard voices and the clash of swords and shields. I heard Canaanites and Hyksos and Egyptians and Philistines, I heard Hebrews and Babylonians and Persians and Syrians and Greeks and Romans, I heard the Muslim warriors from Arabia and the Christian crusaders from Anjou, I heard the Turks and the British. Oh, I tell you I had taken a mountain climber's grip on the Wailing Wall, working my fingers into its crevices as if I intended to scale it; they had to pry my hands loose from the stones, they had to drag me away. I was in a trance, I was in another world. I was home."

"You are a fossilized Jew," the Doctor said, not without sympathy. "Your spiritual home is the Isra'il of Kings and Judges and burning bushes and rams' horns bringing down the walls of cities."

"You are a fossilized Muslim," Apfulbaum retorted with an agitated laugh. "You would be more comfortable if a time capsule whisked you back thirteen centuries to the golden age of Islam, if you could eavesdrop on the angel Gabriel whispering verses of the Koran into the ear of the Messenger."

"I would go back further," the Doctor admitted. "I would return to the dawn of time when Ibrahim left the land of Ur; when his Egyptian bondwoman, Hagar, bore him a first-born son named Isma'il; when Isma'il helped his father build the Kaaba at Mecca, the first shrine to the one true God, with the nail in the floor the ancients believed to be the navel of the world; I would watch Ibrahim raise the sacrificial knife to the throat of his son Isma'il on the black stone at its heart only to have God stay his arm at the last instant. When Ibrahim came out of Ur, *ya'ani*, the religion of Islam already existed. It is written: *Ibrahim was not a Jew, nor was he a Christian. He was a Muslim, a man of pure faith.* This pure faith, this *Islam* of Ibrahim, this submission to God, is the straight path. It tells us all we need to know about human affairs—it tells us how to run a government, how to wash when there is no water available, how to pray and fast, how to dress, how to buy and sell, how to make love to our wives, how to eat and drink and defecate. In the Messenger's scheme of things there is no place for *bid'a*, for innovation. Thus said the Prophet: '*The most truthful communication is the Book of God, the best guidance is that of Muhammad, and the worst of all things are innovations: every innovation is heresy, every heresy is error, and every error leads to hell.*'"

"Amen again," muttered the Rabbi. "I invite you to lecture on the subject of innovation to my Torah students in Beit Avram."

Petra came up behind the Doctor. "If we are going to be there and back before first light, we must leave now."

"Is everything prepared?" the Doctor asked her.

"It is."

The Doctor rose stiffly to his feet and slipped the leather hood over the Rabbi's head with unaccustomed gentleness. Then he pulled something from the pocket of his robe and dropped it into Apfulbaum's palm. "During the twelve years I was imprisoned by the Isra'ilis, these helped me to keep my sanity."

The Rabbi's fingers closed around a set of worn silver worry beads. A feeling of gratefulness, of affinity even, surged in his breast as he began to work them through his fingers. "You're coming back, right?"

"*Inshallah*," the Doctor said. "God willing."

TWENTY-FIVE

THE BEAT-UP SILVER SUZUKI WITH ISRAELI LICENSE PLATES crawled along the dirt road and drew to a stop next to the back door of a fruit and vegetable warehouse on the outskirts of Ramallah, eight miles north of Jerusalem. A cat in heat, patrolling the tin roof of the warehouse, screeched with an almost human voice as Petra pulled the scarf from her head and used it to unscrew the naked electric bulb in the socket over the door. In the darkness, the Doctor got out of the car and slipped into the warehouse. He kept the tips of his fingers on Petra's shoulder and followed her through the maze of aisles formed by shoulder-high stacks of crates. Overhead, shafts of silvery moonlight pierced the rain-streaked panes of the skylights, strewing the cement floor with slippery shadows. From every side came the fragrant scents of oranges and apples and carrots and parsley. A fat woman materialized in the aisle. She sank with difficulty to her knees, caught the hem of the Doctor's robe in her thick fingers and brought it to her lips. "I ask you, I beg you, in the name of Allah, the Merciful, the Compassionate," she whimpered. "Spare the life of my husband for his family's sake." A young man loomed behind the fat woman. "For my father's life," he said, his voice a muffled moan of dread, "in accordance with Islamic law, we offer *diyah*—"

"It is not a question of blood money, but justice," the Doctor snapped. He stepped around the two and continued on behind Petra. Under a large skylight in the heart of the warehouse they came upon Mr. Hajji, bound hand and feet to a stanchion. "A monumental error has been made," Mr. Hajji whispered when the two figures came up to him. He spoke as if he were letting them in on a secret. "There is absolutely no grain of truth—"

The Doctor cut him short. "I know everything. If one word of deceit crosses your lips, I will execute the sentence that has been ordered for all Palestinians who collaborate with the Isra'ilis. Your only hope is to tell the truth and trust me to exercise the compassion ordained by the Qur'an for those who repent. Do you comprehend what I am telling you?"

Mr. Hajji, his eyes fixed on the bruise disfiguring the Doctor's forehead, nodded weakly. "Are you the *mujaddid* of whom they speak in the *souk*?"

Petra murmured a verse from the Qur'an. "'*Their mark is on their faces, the trace of prostration.*'"

"There are those who say I am the Renewer," the Doctor said. "Only time will tell."

"It is true I worked for the Jews," Mr. Hajji cried. "They forced me."

"When did they recruit you?"

"In the summer of 1997."

"How?"

The story gushed out. "My son Ahmed was in prison near Tel Aviv. They threatened to charge him with the murder of a Jewish settler. They said only I could save him from a long prison sentence. They threatened to revoke the authorization of my son Sufian to cross the green line and work in Isra'il. Sufian's wages supported him and his wife and his four children and his wife's parents and the crippled brother of his wife's father. The Jews threatened to spread rumors that I had already collaborated if I did not agree to collaborate." Mr. Hajji groaned softly. "What was I to do? I have three daughters who require dowry. I have eleven mouths under my roof to feed. I had no choice."

The Doctor moved to one side of Mr. Hajji. "We shall feed them for you," he said. "Do you believe in God?"

"I do. I do. With all my soul."

"Turn your head toward the Kaaba at the heart of the holy city of Mecca, built by Ibrahim, the father of us all, and pray with me."

"I will. I will."

The Doctor reached out and touched Mr. Hajji lightly behind his left ear as if he were bestowing a blessing. "In the name of God, the Merciful and Compassionate. Praise be to God, Lord of the Universe. You do we worship and call upon for help—"

"Worship," Mr. Hajji repeated, his dentures rattling in his jaw. "Help . . ."

"Guide us along the Straight Path."

"Guide us—" Mr. Hajji faltered. Tears streamed down his weathered cheeks.

"I assume from your name that you have made pilgrimage to Mecca."

Mr. Hajji managed a miserable nod.

"Now you will make *hajj* to a better place than Mecca," the Doctor said, feeling for the distinctive knob of bone behind the ear with the tips of the fingers of one hand, drawing the small pearl-handled pistol from the inside breast pocket of his jacket with the other. "As you approach, remember to shout, as the pilgrims to Mecca shout, *I am here, O Lord, I am here!*"

"What place is better than Mecca?" Mr. Hajji almost choked on the question; he was terrified of the answer.

"Paradise is better than Mecca. You have confessed yourself to me. Your confession is written in the Book of Deeds. On the Day of Reckoning, when the earth is ground to powder and those who have deviated become firewood for Gehenna, it will be recorded in your favor." He raised the barrel of the pistol to the knob of bone. "If God knows of any good in your heart, He will give you better than what has been taken from you; surely God is All-forgiving, All-compassionate."

"Surely God—"

The Doctor pulled the trigger. Mr. Hajji's body jerked as if it had been struck by a bolt of lightning, then sagged into the ropes binding him to the stanchion.

From the other end of the warehouse, the shrill *yous-yous* of a widow mourning the death of a husband echoed over the crates filled with oranges and apples and carrots and parsley.

An Excerpt from the Harvard "Running History" Project:

I'm running late. Couldn't be avoided. The Defense Department's National Security Agency hawks came over to play at the White House this morning, after which I had to take an important conference call.

The folks from NSA, as usual, brought along their favorite toy: dominoes.

You heard right. Dominoes, as in the famous "domino theory" that provided Lyndon Johnson with the intellectual justification for upping the ante in his calamitous war in Vietnam. The National Security Agency trots them out when it wants to scare the trousers off everyone in the White House. I'm here to tell you, ten times out of ten it works.

Who? Tell him to send me a memorandum. I'll speak to him when I've had a chance to read it.

Where was I?

Dominoes.

This morning's session was held in the cabinet room. The President presided and the Administration's top guns were present—the Vice President, the Secretaries of State and Defense, the Chairman of the Joint Chiefs, the National Security Advisor and yours truly, Zachary Taylor Sawyer, the President's Special Assistant for Middle Eastern Affairs. The NSA Director, a holdover from when Secretary Rumsfeld ran the Defense Department, set up his dominoes and began to knock them down, which is to say he explained what he thought would happen if the shooting started again in the Middle East. I stole a look at the President from time to time—she seemed to turn various shades of mauve. Who can blame her?

Her desk is where the last domino stops. She doesn't particularly like the idea of presiding over the end of the world as we know it.

I admit it, I am exaggerating. But not as much as you might think.

The week's domino theory, according to the National Security Agency, starts with that Rabbi—I can never remember his name. Apfulbaum. That's it. It starts with this Apfulbaum fellow being execut- ed by his kidnappers. Then the ultra right-wing Israelis exact some sort of vengeance, at which point one of the crazy Palestinian fundamental- ist cells that has gone to ground exacts vengeance for the vengeance. After which both sides cancel their plans to come to Washington and the Mt. Washington peace treaty goes down the drain.

That was only the appetizer.

The NSA analysts estimate there is a ninety percent chance that if the Middle East explodes again, the Saudi monarchy will not survive and Saudi Arabia will be taken over by Wahhabi fundamentalists, some of whom tend to be slightly to the right of that fellow who brought down the Twin Towers in 2001, Osama bin Laden. (Yes, I do remember his name, don't I?) One quarter of the world's oil reserves, the NSA Director reminded us—as if we needed reminding—are buried under Saudi sand. If Saudi Arabia went, we were told, the rest of the countries in the area would topple like the proverbial dominoes. Jordan, where the Hashemite Bedouins and their king rule the seventy percent of the pop- ulation that is Palestinian, would be the first to go. Kuwait, Qatar, Yemen, Oman, the United Arab Emirates, eventually even Algeria and Morocco, could follow. Do you realize what it would mean for the free world—for Europe and for us—if these vast reserves of oil and natural gas were controlled by Islamic fundamentalists? Imagine the resources they could commit to furthering Islamic revolution in countries with Islamic majorities. On any given day they could decide to pump a cou- ple of million barrels less and the price would jump higher than it already has, leading to hyper inflation, leading to whole industries going bankrupt, leading to the collapse of stock markets, leading to panic in the streets.

There was worse to come. It appears the Kremlin's Americanologists are telling their counterparts in Washington that all of Muslim Central Asia would be destabilized if the Middle East question isn't resolved.

And the Muslim states in Central Asia—some of which still have nuclear-tipped Soviet missiles on their territory—in turn would destabilize the entire Russian land mass. Think of the possibilities— Uzbekistan or Kazakhstan selling nuclear warheads to Gulf fundamentalists who are swimming in oil money. My god, September 11th would look like a fender-bender by comparison.

You don't have to be an NSA analyst to imagine how this might play out in the rest of the world. Pakistan, Indonesia, Malaysia, even Turkey, could go fundamentalist. China, which has a large Muslim minority, especially the Uighurs in Central Asia, could wind up fighting a civil war with breakaway Islamic provinces. It wouldn't take long for the Japanese, who import every drop of oil they use, to know which side their bread was buttered on. Oil producers like Russia and Venezuela and, eventually, even England, under enormous pressure to increase production to prevent the industrialized nations from becoming prisoners of the Gulf's imams, would do so on condition they could hike their prices.

Bleak? I'd say the picture was more black than bleak.

All the while the President sat there, her high heels tapping on the floor, fiddling with a paperclip, contorting it into different shapes until it broke, at which point she started in on a new one. When the NSA Director finished, there was one of those thick silences that you can cut with a knife. Everyone in the cabinet room was staring at their finger nails. I became aware of the President's eye on me. "You're our in-house Middle East guru, Zack," she said very quietly. "What do you make of all this?"

I shrugged and said as far as I could see there was nothing new in it. I reminded them of the old proverb that existed long before the Washington whiz kids invented the domino theory. For the want of a nail the shoe was lost, for the want of a shoe the horse was lost, for the want of a horse the rider was lost, and so on.

"So you're saying that the NSA scenario is on the money," the President remarked.

I raised my brows and murmured something (paraphrasing Will Rogers) about how an NSA analyst's guess was as likely to be as good any anybody else's.

That was too much for the NSA Director's boss, the Secretary of Defense, who leaped to defend his turf. "I assume the Special Assistant for Middle Eastern Affairs has a better take on the ticklish situation we find ourselves in," he said.

The President was gazing at me intently, as if to say: Do you?

"Figuring out history before it happens," I said tiredly, "is like trying to predict what route lava will take when it flows down the side of an erupting volcano."

The Secretary of State, true to form, attempted to identify the common ground in the discussion; once again the policy makers were eager to convey the impression that the highest level of government speaks with one voice. "If I'm reading Zack right," he said carefully, "he's telling us that the execution of I. Apfulbaum will bring on the equivalent of a volcanic eruption in the region. Which way the lava will flow—which is to say, how it will play out—is anybody's guess."

I noticed the President's chief of staff in the doorway tapping the crystal on his wristwatch, so I nodded in vague agreement and let it go at that.

I was back in my office visualizing rivulets of lava coursing down the side of an erupting volcano when the urgent conference call from my counterparts at 10 Downing Street and the Elysée came through. Both of them were extremely agitated. (The timing of the call led me to suppose their respective intelligence services had circulated the NSA's domino briefing.) They didn't waste time on small talk. Their principals, they explained, which is to say the British Prime Minister and the French President, both held the view that the peace treaty must be salvaged, whatever the cost. I asked if they had any new ideas to offer on how this might be accomplished. A reasonably long silence followed, as if each was waiting for his vis-à-vis to deliver the bad news. The Middle East specialist from 10 Downing finally cleared his throat. "We are of the opinion that the Israelis should be made to cede to the logic of yielding to the demands of the kidnappers," he announced. "Paris stands shoulder to shoulder with London on this analysis," the Elysée specialist added. "Give them the goddamn prisoners in exchange for that Rabbi and his secretary, and let us get on with the signing ceremony and the creation of a sovereign Palestinian state."

"Why are you telling me this?" I asked—as if I didn't know, but I thought I would get them to spell it out for the record. "Why don't you guys phone up the Israeli Prime Minister and tell him yourselves?"

"We are of the opinion that it must be the American President who personally delivers the message," the 10 Downing Street man said. "Only Washington has enough clout with the Israelis to make them heed the voice of sweet reason."

The Frenchman started to say something but I cut him off. "Don't even go there, my friends. First off, the American President has climbed as far out on this limb as she plans to; another inch and she risks having popular opinion turn against her, which would mean an end to her hopes for a second term. More importantly, you can only push the Israelis so far; there are things they can't be forced to do and exchange Palestinian prisoners for Jewish hostages is one of them. For the obvious reason that such exchanges only invite more kidnappings."

The Frenchman, whom I knew slightly from NATO brainstorming sessions, said, "You could raise the stakes, Zack. You said as much in your book Breaking Vicious Circles. *You could threaten the Israelis—"*

I interrupted again. "Threaten them with what? Another Security Council resolution condemning Israel?"

"The French would be ready to join an international move to isolate Israel—I'm talking about cutting off their commercial airline landing rights, I'm talking about freezing their overseas bank accounts, I'm talking about organizing a trade embargo the way we did years ago with South Africa."

"Escalate, that's the ticket," the man from 10 Downing, an old Foreign Office Janus known to be viscerally pro-Arab, heartily agreed.

"And when the Israelis refuse to buckle, what do we do then? Mine Haifa harbor? Bomb Tel Aviv? Listen, gentlemen, this is not an idea I will raise in the Oval Office. Before you raise the stakes, it's essential to have a sense of how far someone can be pushed. If you cross this line, you invite defiance."

They argued on for the better part of three quarters of an hour. I stood my ground. I knew it would be impossible to push the Israelis past where their finely honed national instinct for survival told them they could safely go. To try would be to lose whatever credibility you had when you threatened to raise the stakes. My counterparts in London and Paris were still functioning with an imperfect grasp of Middle East reality. One way or another, what was happening on the ground would educate them.

You bet your socks, I'm still detached. But to tell the god-awful truth, I'm also scared. I understand why the Europeans are panicking. If we lose control of events, where oh where do we go from here?

TWENTY-SIX

SWEENEY WAS MIGHTILY PLEASED WITH HIMSELF. HALF A DOZEN colleagues from the international press corps had phoned over the past few days to congratulate him on the Shin Bet article; two of them had even interviewed him for the articles they were writing about his article. After all, it wasn't every day that someone gave the world a glimpse of what went on behind the closed doors of the super-secret and super insolent Shin Bet. Dropping his cellular telephone into the pocket of his sheepskin jacket, wrapping an old college scarf around his neck, Sweeney pulled on a pair of ski sunglasses and climbed up to the roof-top terrace over his apartment. He had filed three hundred and fifty words on what appeared to be a Hamas-organized kidnapping of a member of a rival fundamentalist group in the Old City right under the noses of the Israelis and was going to unwind with the first dry martini of the day. The air was crystal clear and wintry. Light from the setting sun glinted off the gold leaf of the Dome of the Rock mosque on the Temple Mount—the dome that sheltered the great boulder on which Abraham, according to Jewish tradition, came a hair's breadth away from sacrificing his son, Isaac; from which Muhammad, according to Muslim tradition, ascended to heaven on his steed el-Burek for his rendezvous with Allah. To the southeast, beyond the Church of the Dormition, Sweeney could make out the pale shroud of mist hovering over the Dead Sea, the lowest geographical point on the surface of the planet, and, behind it, the dark ashen hills of Moab. It was not surprising, he thought, that *homo sapiens* had been battling over

Jerusalem for three thousand years. Some scholars attributed the city's greatness to the lay of the land; the earliest settlement had been astride a caravan crossing and eventually grown into an important trading center. Others attributed the city's strategic importance to the discovery of an underground spring, which guaranteed its garrison an endless reserve of drinking water. But gazing out now past the walls of the Old City, Sweeney knew where the greatness came from. The power of Jerusalem, the magic it worked on people, was first and foremost aesthetic; every time you saw it, it took your breath away.

The cellular phone in Sweeney's pocket bleated. He assumed it would be another reporter calling to compliment him on his Shin Bet article; to ask, facetiously, which plane he would be taking once the Israelis relieved him of his press pass.

"Yeah," Sweeney said into the phone.

"Mr. journalist Sweeney?" a melodious voice asked.

"Speaking."

"Do you recognize my voice?"

"You bet I recognize your voice," Sweeney said; he could picture the Vestal Virgin, with his round blue-tinted sunglasses and pointed beard and white *galabiya*, feeding Israeli coins into the slot of a Gaza public phone.

"The last time we met you raised the possibility of an exclusive interview. Are you still interested?"

"Interested is an understatement."

"The individual in question has read your article—the one describing how some of your Israeli friends who only use first names offered you part-time employment. He was impressed by your independence, not to mention your integrity. To make a short story shorter, he has agreed to meet with you."

Sweeney was all business. "How do I find him?"

"Do not make any calls from your house phone or your mobile after you hang up. Depart from Jerusalem by car in precisely seven minutes, which is the time is will take you to lock your house and walk up to the parking lot. Travel alone. Take the Beit Shemesh-Kiryat Gat road down to the Ghazeh. Leave your car in the parking lot and walk across the Erez crossing. A car will be waiting for you on our side."

"How will I recognize the driver?"

The Vestal Virgin laughed quietly into his end of the line. "The driver will recognize you."

The phone went dead in Sweeney's ear. "Bingo," he said aloud. A faint smile of satisfaction disfigured his lips as he slipped the phone back into his pocket.

TWENTY-SEVEN

ABSALOM HAD ONE OF HIS PATENTED "I-TOLD-YOU-SO" SMIRKS pasted on his hide-tanned face when he ran into Baruch at the water cooler. "Azazel's boys and girls are working through the last file cabinets in the last aisle of the last basement," he informed him. "There is so much dust down there, two of them began sneezing and had to be let off on sick leave. You realize this is no piece of cake. Roughly half of the male Arabs betrayed by collaborators wound up serving time. Half of the ones who served time were short and heavy. Half of the short heavy males who were betrayed and served time were rabid Islamists."

"Which leaves the suspect's bad eyes," Baruch noted.

"Bad eyes narrowed it down to one hundred and eighty-three, not counting the forty-eight who are known to be out of the Middle East, not counting the thirty-six who are known to be deceased, not counting two who are known to be in a Jordanian insane asylum, not counting whatever Azazel comes up with in the last batch of file cabinets." Absalom seemed very pleased with himself. "The list is being typed up now."

TWENTY-EIGHT

CUTTING THROUGH THE HILLS BEHIND EIN KAREM TO AVOID THE inevitable rush hour gridlock at the entrance to Jerusalem, Sweeney rejoined the main Jerusalem–Tel Aviv highway near Motza and headed west at a fast crawl. Fiddling with the dial of the radio, he came across an English-language talk show. "I don't agree at all," a man speaking English with a thick German accent was saying, "From the Jewish point of view, it's more accurate to speak of a Judeo-Islamic tradition than a Judeo-Christian tradition."

"Why's that, professor?" a woman inquired.

"One could make the case that Christianity, with its baffling doctrine of the Trinity, has betrayed Old Testament monotheism. Islam, with its uncompromising belief in one God, has preserved its monotheistic purity. There is a passage in the Koran, if I can find it—ah, here it is." The professor cleared his throat. "'They are unbelievers who say, *God is the Third of Three. No god is there but One God.*'"

"There's also that anti-Christian Koranic inscription on the Dome of the Rock Mosque," someone else pointed out. "'*Praise be to God, who begets no son.*'"

"For Jews, there is also the problem of the visual iconography of Christianity," still another person observed. "Which is why Maimonides, in his 'Epistle on Martyrdom,' asserts that Jews can convert to Islam if it's a question of saving their lives, but they cannot convert to Christianity under any circumstance, since by doing so they become idolaters, which for Jews is a fate worse than death."

"If the Jews and Arabs are kissing cousins," Sweeney asked the radio, "why have they been at each other's throats for a hundred years?" For answer, he got a station break and a commercial advertising an Israeli toothpaste that left your teeth whiter than white and your breath fresher than fresh. He provided his own response to the question. "It doesn't take a genius to figure it out," he mumbled. "They've been fighting over land."

At the Beit Shemesh turnoff, Sweeney passed a group of soldiers trying to thumb rides back to their bases in the Negev. He would have stopped to see if anyone was going to Gaza, but he remembered the Vestal Virgin's admonition: Travel alone.

Traffic was light and Sweeney made good time. Just south of Tel Azeka, his headlights illuminated an orange road-work warning up ahead. A hundred meters further along, plastic markers were strung across his side of the highway, closing it to traffic. A bearded man wearing a *yarmulke* and orange coveralls flagged him onto the Agur road detour. As he turned off, Sweeney could see the bearded man talking into a small walkie-talkie. Half a kilometer down the Agur road, within sight of a traffic circle, two men standing alongside a van with the logo "Fine Bedouin Robes and Carpets" printed in English on its side waved frantically as he approached. Sweeney recognized one of them; there was no mistaking his round blue sunglasses or the beard that seemed to have been sharpened to a fine point. It was the Vestal Virgin himself, dressed this time in blue jeans and a tee-shirt with "Hard Rock Café" printed across the chest. Sweeney slammed on the brakes and rolled down the window on the passenger's side of the car. "And here I thought you were a pious Muslim," he called teasingly.

The Vestal Virgin stuck his head in the window. "Do not judge what is in a man's heart by the clothing covering his breast," he said with great seriousness. "If you still want to interview Abu Bakr, you must continue the journey in a different vehicle."

"I can't abandon my car in the middle of nowhere."

"I will drive it to Ghazeh and leave it in the parking lot on the Israeli side. My friend here will take you to Abu Bakr."

Sweeney grabbed the satchel with his camera and tape recorder

and got out of the car. A pock-marked Bedouin smoking a thick cigarette opened the back doors of the van and lifted the lid of a large
straw hamper.

"You expect me to get into that?" Sweeney asked.

"Trust me," said the Vestal Virgin with a disarming smile. "Be
quick."

Sweeney looked from the Vestal Virgin to the Bedouin, then with
a shrug climbed into the hamper. The Bedouin covered him with
some carpets and closed the lid. Sweeney heard him hefting another
hamper on top of the one he was in, and rearranging other hampers
in front of it. The back doors slammed shut. The driver must have
inserted a cassette into the van's tape deck, because Sweeney heard the
muffled sound of a popular Egyptian song. With a jerk, the van
pulled onto the road. It reached the traffic circle and turned around
it six or seven times to befuddle Sweeney's sense of direction. Then
the van started down the road at a brisk clip. Forty minutes later—
the hands on Sweeney's wristwatch glowed in the dark—the vehicle
slowed down and Sweeney, snug in his hamper of Bedouin rugs,
thought he could make out young men speaking Hebrew. Were they
passing through an Israeli checkpoint into the West Bank? Half an
hour later they slowed down for what could have been another
checkpoint. Soon after that the van must have been caught in a traffic jam; Sweeney heard horns blaring, and someone complaining,
though he couldn't make out if the complaint was in Hebrew or
Arabic. Eventually the van turned onto cobblestones and bumped
its way through a labyrinth of streets before pulling to a stop. The
driver's door slammed shut. Seconds later the door of a building
closed and there was absolute silence.

Stifling in his hamper, Sweeney pushed the rugs away from his
face and waited. He must have dozed, because the next time he
glanced at his watch, twenty-five minutes had gone by. Moments
later footsteps approached the van and the back doors were flung
open. The hampers were shoved aside, the lid of his straw trunk was
lifted and Sweeney was confronted with the unsmiling smallpox-
scarred face of a young Arab woman. She gestured for him to climb
out of the hamper and follow her. Vaulting nimbly from the back of

the van, she tugged the scarf over her short hair and set off at a brisk pace through a maze of narrow alleyways. Sweeney, who didn't have the vaguest idea what city he was in, jogged along behind her. At one point she hiked the hem of her Bedouin robe—Sweeney noticed that she was wearing blue jeans and running shoes—and darted up a rickety staircase, then ducked through a low door with some Arabic words painted in red on it. A young Palestinian was waiting inside what appeared to be an abandoned building. As the young Bedouin woman turned her back, he gestured for Sweeney to strip off his garments. "You're kidding," Sweeney said. Then: "You're not kidding." He began to peel off his clothing, tossing them to the Palestinian, and finally stood stark naked on the cold floor while the young man searched every item meticulously, clearly looking for some sort of radio transmitting device. He confiscated Sweeney's shoes and gave him a pair of sandals in their place. While Sweeney was climbing back into his clothing, the young Palestinian opened the journalist's satchel and removed the camera and the cellular telephone and the four spare rolls of film. He opened the camera and the battery compartment of the telephone, removed the film and the battery, then smashed the camera and telephone, along with Sweeney's quartz wrist watch, against a wall and carefully inspected the broken fragments. As an afterthought, he crushed the rolls of film and the battery with a brick and examined them, too.

"Jesus," Sweeney moaned. "What people put up with to get an exclusive interview." The Palestinian, who obviously didn't speak a word of English, motioned for Sweeney to turn around and fitted a blindfold over his eyes. The Bedouin woman and the Palestinian exchanged some words, after which she took Sweeney's hand and led him out a window onto a slate roof. From somewhere below came the indistinct sound of voices speaking Arabic, and the delectable odor of lamb being grilled on a barbecue. With one hand on the woman's shoulder and the other on a waist-high brick wall, Sweeney felt himself being led across several roofs and pushed through a door into another building that, judging from the hollow ring the door made when it closed behind them, must have also been abandoned. The woman led him to the far end of the building, up a narrow staircase and along a corridor. She knocked three times on a metal door, then twice and then once. Bolts were thrown, the door was flung open and then closed and locked behind them.

As the blindfold was pulled away from his face, Sweeney found himself gazing into the bloodshot eyes of a short, heavy-set Arab wearing a shiny gray double-breasted suit jacket over a long white robe with a soiled hem. On his forehead was the purple bruise that Sweeney had seen once before in a Gaza mosque—on an ultra-religious Muslim who beat his head against the floor when he prostrated himself in prayer. The Arab squinted at the visitor through round, windowpane-thick, wire-rimmed spectacles. "I am Abu Bakr," he announced, holding out a hand. "You must excuse all these precautions—my people are paranoid about my safety. Please, please, sit. My house is your house."

Abu Bakr settled cross-legged onto a Bedouin cushion at a low round table and invited Sweeney, with a wave of the hand, to sit across from him. Petra, modestly avoiding eye contact with the two men, set a plate of sweet biscuits, two glasses and a pitcher of fruit juice on the table, then returned to the Army radio and pulled on the earphones. The Doctor, who could make out shadowy shapes and enjoyed fooling people into thinking his vision was perfectly normal, poured juice into both glasses—he could tell from the sound when it was time to stop—and pushed one glass toward his guest. Hefting a paperweight filled with snow flakes falling on a pastoral landscape, Sweeney took in the armored door with the bars across it, the Kalashnikovs stacked in a corner, the young woman monitoring the Army radio, the large map of Palestine on the wall. He took in the second door, reinforced with steel plating, which led to . . . where? "I don't suppose you'll tell me what city I am in," he remarked.

The Doctor grunted. "We went to a lot of trouble so you would not know."

"Turning around the traffic circle was very effective."

The Doctor sipped his juice. "I tell you frankly, *ya'ani*, this is the first time in my life I have granted an interview to a representative of the press. I have long been intrigued by the rapport between a journalist and his subject, with each one, in effect, trying to use the other for his own ends. You, for instance, will try to seduce me into thinking you are extremely sympathetic to my point of view in order to lure me into making revelations that may, in the end, undermine my point of view and embarrass my side. I, for my part, will try to convince you that I am being extremely open and candid in order to get you to write admiringly about my point of view and my side. From both our perspectives, it is an extremely dishonest relationship, yet even as I point this out, you will surely suspect that I am trying to beguile you into thinking I am different."

Sweeney smiled. "There is no danger of your beguiling me. I am an experienced journalist."

The Doctor squinted at Sweeney, trying to imagine what he looked like from the sound of his voice. "I am aware that you are an experienced journalist. You wear a memento of one of your experiences in your left ear."

Sweeney brought a finger up to the hearing aid. "I got too close to an incoming round in Beirut."

The Doctor seemed interested. "From a medical point of view, what happened to you?"

"I suffered a concussion and damage to the middle ear of my left ear—there was some kind of injury to a membrane, the name of which escapes me."

"Was it the tympanic membrane?"

"That rings a bell."

"What were your symptoms at the time?"

"Dizziness, bleeding, a slight and temporary facial paralysis, not to mention the loss of hearing in my left ear."

"What type of hearing device do you wear?"

"Analogue."

"Do you have more difficulty hearing high-pitched or low-pitched sounds?"

"It's the low intensity, high-pitched sounds—the *s* or *sh* or *ch*—that give me trouble." Sweeney laughed uncomfortably. "Did you think I invented the explosion in Beirut? Do you suspect my hearing aid is a secret transmitter broadcasting this conversation to the Israelis?"

"The thought crossed our minds. The young woman who brought you here is a genius with radios. After you were blindfolded, she used a meter to see if your hearing aid was transmitting a signal." The Doctor spread his hands in embarrassment. "Someone in my position must be prudent. Let us move on. Why did you become a journalist?"

"What is this, a psychoanalytic session? How much do you charge an hour?"

"I am trying, in my clumsy way, to figure out who you are."

"In college I had my heart set on becoming an actor. My first big role was Vanya in Chekhov's *Uncle Vanya*. I stumbled over the love scenes and was heckled. The review in the college newspaper didn't mince words. Do you understand the expression, mince words? I decided it was safer to review plays than act in them, and went to work for the newspaper. One thing led to another. Which is how I became Mr. journalist Sweeney."

The Doctor puffed thoughtfully on his cigarette. "Let us move on to the world of politics. What do you understand to be the essence of the conflict between Arabs and Jews?"

"Are you interviewing me or am I interviewing you?"

"Bear with me, Mr. Sweeney. There is a method to my madness."

Sweeney pulled his copybook and a pencil from a pocket. "Do you mind if I copy down your questions and my answers?"

The Doctor nodded. "Please.

"To answer your question: the essence of the conflict, Mr. Abu Bakr, in a word, is land."

"Many people would offer the same response. But not me. Let me begin our conversation by telling you a story. Once I was driven up to the occupied Golan for a consultation with an important Druze. Coming back, I ordered the driver to pull up at the side of the road and got out to urinate as the sun was setting in the west. From where I was standing I could make out the shadows of Lebanon off to my right. Behind me, the snow at the summit of Mount Hermon appeared to glisten with the last rays from the sun sinking into the sea. Below me, the electric lights in the Jewish *kibbutzim* in the Hula Valley began to come on. Pfffft-pffffft. Pfffft-pffffft. Can you picture the scene, Mr. Sweeney? There I was, standing in the cold, dark electricity-less Golan as the lights of the Jews flashed on. Pffffft-pffffft. With each flash, I could hear the West saying 'Fuck-you, fuck-you' to the Arabs. Please excuse my language. I use the term for the sake of accuracy. Those are the words I heard. The *kibbutz* lights, billboard advertisements for a secular and material and superficial Western culture, drive home to us our seeming backwardness and humiliate Islam. Land, of course, is an important element of the problem. But the essence of the conflict between Arabs and Jews, Mr. Sweeney, is dignity."

"When you refer to Western culture as secular and material and superficial, I assume you are comparing it to Islamic culture. But you fall into the trap that many of your co-religionists fall into—you are comparing Western realities like poverty and crime and sexual promiscuity and drugs and racism with Islamic ideals, as opposed to Islamic reality."

"Western reality—your culture of drugs and sexual promiscuity—*is* the Western ideal; you live this way, Mr. Sweeney, because you think this is the best way to live. Islamic ideals at least show that there is a better way. Given the chance to function in an Islamic state guided by the Holy Qur'an, Islamic reality will move in the direction of Islamic ideals."

"I know Jews—religious Jews, that is—who would say pretty much the same thing about the Torah." Sweeney looked at his notes to get Rabbi Apfulbaum's words right. "*We must follow God's commandment to the Jewish people and settle every square inch of the land of the Torah. Without the lava of the land burning through the soles of our shoes, we are spiritual cripples.*"

The words slipped out before the Doctor realized what he was saying. "I also know such a Jew."

Sweeney looked sharply at his host. "If you're not careful, Mr. Bakr, you'll have me thinking that the person who kidnapped Rabbi Apfulbaum and his secretary is a pro-Semite."

"I am more than a pro-Semite—I am a Semite, in as much as I am a descendant of Shem, the oldest son of Noah. If you are using Semite in its narrower sense to refer to Jews, you would not be wrong. I am, in my own way, an admirer of Jewish culture and Jewish creativeness and Jewish energy. But somewhere along the way these past three thousand years the Jews went wrong. I think I know where. It was when they rejected the word of God brought to them by God's Prophets and Messengers, and discovered in its place *chutzpah*; when they became convinced that this *chutzpah* was a virtue and not a vice. You surely will be familiar with the classical definition of *chutzpah*, Mr. Sweeney. It is when a boy kills his parents and then asks the judge for leniency because he is an orphan. I will offer you another definition of the word: to claim all the land God promised to the patriarch Ibrahim when someone else is living on it is *chutzpah*."

Sweeney scratched away on his pad. "Can you tell me something of your background, Mr. Bakr."

"My background is unremarkable. My father was a *fedayeen* fighter, a guerrilla in the war against the Jews. He was killed while trying to cross into Isra'il when I was still a boy. I remember little about my father's appearance but I can summon his voice in my ear at will. I can hear him talking quietly with his sons before the evening meal. Where Muslims do not live under Islamic rule, and on Islamic territory, he would tell us, they are in what the Qur'an calls the *Dar al-Harb*—the Realm of War; they must follow the example of the Messenger Muhammad and wage *jihad*, or armed struggle against unbelief. Ever since Muhammad led raids on Meccan caravans, Islam has been waging war against unbelief. I see myself as part of this ancient tradition. In its most recent phase, this war involved the kidnapping of Rabbi Apfulbaum, himself a fundamentalist associated with the Beit Avram settlement and the Jewish underground known to have its roots there."

"Which brings us to the kidnapping of Rabbi Apfulbaum. What do you hope to achieve?"

"You must understand, *ya'ani*, that my reasoning begins with the presumption that there exists a post-colonial plot against Islam. The world's secularists and Zionists are all out to destroy us. Salman Rushdie is part of the plot orchestrated by World Jewry and backed by American imperialism. Over the decades, Mr. Sweeney, we Muslims have tried everything under the sun to thwart that plot—

we have tried Nasserism, Baathism, Ghadhafi-ism, Khomeini-ism, Saddam Hussein-ism, and more recently, Arafat-ism. Nothing turned the clock back; the Hamas suicide bombings, like the British and American terror bombings of German cities during the Second World War, only serve to unify the people who are the targets of these attacks. In short, nothing brought us closer to *Dar al-Islam*, the Realm of Islam, where the pure faith of the Prophet prevails. Clearly it was time for a fresh approach."

Sweeney snapped his copybook shut. "You didn't bring me here to listen to your ideas on how *chutzpah* ruined the Jewish people, or how Salman Rushdie is part of a Zionist plot to bring down Islam." He leaned forward. "What do you want, Mr. Abu Bakr?"

"A witness."

One of the el-Tel brothers emerged from the back room carrying a tray filled with empty plates. Sweeney watched as he stacked them in the laundry sink. "A witness to what?" he asked.

"I am convinced that Rabbi Apfulbaum will divulge details of the ruthless anti-Arab campaign waged by the Jewish underground movement, as well as the identity of its ruthless leader, Ya'ir. If I publish this information, no one will believe it; the Jews will claim the Rabbi's confession was coerced, and everyone will accept their word. If a respected American journalist publishes it, the world, which up to now associates all terrorism with Muslim fundamentalists, will understand, for the first time, what the Jewish fundamentalists are doing to us. That understanding will undermine international support for Isra'il and strengthen the hand of Muslim fundamentalists like me."

At the Army radio, Petra removed her earphones and studied the American. She didn't speak English but she sensed that the discussion had reached a turning point; she wasn't sure what the Doctor wanted from the American but she knew that if he didn't get it, the American would never leave here alive.

Sweeney felt his lips go dry. He sipped some fruit juice, then set his glass down and nodded carefully. "You're handing me the story of my life on a silver platter. I'd be a fool to turn it down. You wanted a witness, you've got a witness."

TWENTY-NINE

IN THE EARLY HOURS OF THE MORNING, PETRA SAT UP WITH A start. At first she thought she had been awakened by the sound of Hebrew being spoken on the landing outside the door. Slowly it dawned on her that she had been dreaming; in her dream, Isra'ili soldiers were taping sticks of dynamite to the outside of the armor-plated door. Over her field radio, an occasional voice burst through the background static to report, in Hebrew, that nothing could be seen moving on the roads in the West Bank. Splashing cold water on her face, Petra looked around for Aown, then remembered that he had tucked an ancient but serviceable British Webley into his belt and had taken Sweeney up to the attic crawl space over the safe house for the night. She glanced at her wrist watch, then got up to boil water in the electric kettle. Minutes later she was tiptoeing into the inner sanctum with a cup of steaming tea. Azziz was folded into a fetal position, sound asleep on the cot. The Doctor was deep in whispered conversation with the prisoner; Petra didn't understand a word they were saying, but she could see that the two men were talking almost as if they were old friends. They sat with their knees touching, their foreheads bent to within centimeters of each other. She tapped the Doctor on the shoulder. When he turned around, he looked annoyed at the interruption. "What is it?" he asked sharply.

Petra said, "I have brought you tea."

The Doctor gripped the cup with both hands and let the tea warm his fingers for a moment. Then he did something that struck Petra as extremely bizarre—he called the prisoner by his given name.

"Isaac."

Whispering, the Doctor said something to him in English. The prisoner raised his eyes; the Doctor had said that, without his eyeglasses, the Jew could only make out shapes and shadows. The prisoner shook his head no. The Doctor spoke to him again more firmly and pressed the cup of tea into his manacled hands. The prisoner shrugged and muttered something in English. In the middle of a sentence he pronounced the Doctor's given name.

". . . Ishmael . . ."

The Rabbi brought the cup to his lips and blew loudly across the surface of the tea, and then began to sip noisily at it. The Doctor stood up and came around behind the Rabbi and started to massage his bony neck with the tips of his fingers. Looking over the head of the Rabbi, he nodded toward the door. As she backed out of the room, Petra could hear the two of them resuming their whispered conversation.

"Ah, Ishmael . . ."

". . . Isaac . . ."

This must be a new technique of interrogation, she told herself, one designed to gain the trust of the prisoner and lull him into thinking of his interrogator as a friend, someone in whom he could confide. Once the Jew's guard was down, the Doctor would extract from him the information he wanted. Surely this was the meaning of the strange bond that appeared to be growing between the two men.

How else could a reasonable person explain the Doctor's permitting the Jew to call him by his given name?

THIRTY

ALARGE OVERHEAD FAN STIRRED THE PUTRID AIR IN THE interrogation chamber as the prisoner shrieked in agony. Sinking back, he mumbled through his swollen lips a verse from the Qur'an. "'*Whoso rebels against God . . . His Messenger . . . for him . . . the Fire of Gehenna.*'"

From the small Sony portable radio on the shelf came the sound of frying fat. Precisely on the hour, the Voice of Palestine, a popular call-in talk show, burst through the static. "Goooood Morning, Palestine," a young woman brayed breathlessly into the microphone. "To everybody, everywhere, inside and outside the homeland, a morning of love and well-being. Palestine, have a happy morning. Okay, I'll take the first call."

The strains of a well known Palestinian folk song filled the room, then faded as a listener from Hebron phoned in to the Jericho station to complain about the shortage of specialists in the local Palestinian hospitals. "My wife was diagnosed with cancer of the breast," he said. "My doctor was obliged to get in touch with one of the Jewish specialists in Jerusalem to find out about the latest chemotherapy techniques."

"What's your question?"

"My question is, why aren't our medical schools and hospitals sending more young doctors abroad for specialist training?"

"We are sending young doctors abroad for training," the woman running the Voice of Palestine responded. "The problem is luring them back to the homeland once they get accustomed to those Western salaries."

"Turn up the volume," ordered Sa'adat Arif, the Palestine Authority's deputy chief of intelligence, "and give him another jolt."

In the heart of the Palestinian Army base of Aksa, on the southern edge of Jericho, Yussuf Abu Saleh, stark naked, with electrodes clipped to his testicles, sagged limply from his wrists fastened behind his back to a hook embedded high in the wall. His left shoulder had come out of its socket, causing excruciating pain every time Sa'adat tugged playfully at one of his ankles.

Sa'adat nodded at a young Palestinian policeman, who tripped the switch, closing the electric circuit. Gagging in pain, Yussuf's body stiffened and twitched. A chalky saliva seeped from the corners of his mouth. When the current was cut he sank back and then howled as the weight of his body wrenched his dislocated shoulder. On the radio, a listener was putting a question about police brutality. "I'm not saying it exists," a taxi driver from Nablus said over the phone. "But we've all heard rumors of what happens to some who openly criticize the Palestinian Authority."

"There is no place for police brutality in the new Palestinian state we are constructing," the woman declared into her microphone. "If you know of any instances of actual police brutality, it is your sacred duty to come forward and expose it. Those responsible will be severely punished, this I promise you."

Sa'adat strolled across the room and looked up at Yussuf. "You are a courageous young man, I will give that to you," he said. "Few have managed to hold out as long as you have. You are also an intelligent man. You must know that you will break eventually. Without exception, everyone does. Why don't you save yourself more suffering. Tell us the identity of the blind *mujaddid*. Tell us where he is hiding the Rabbi Apfulbaum. Is he in Ghazeh? Hebron? Nablus? Only nod and your suffering will be over."

"Case of mistaken identity," Yussuf moaned, half delirious. "You have the wrong man. I am Bosnian—Koskovic, Asaf."

Sa'adat signaled to the doctor standing by in a corner. He came over and climbed up on a chair and monitored Yussuf's heartbeat through a stethoscope. "To be on the safe side," he said, "I would advise an hour's repose."

Sa'adat nodded to the policemen, who removed the electrodes, then climbed onto chairs and lowered Yussuf, his head rolling from side to side, to the cement floor. "I don't want to lose him," Sa'adat warned the doctor, who was kneeling next to Yussuf and waving a cracked vial of smelling salts under his nose. Yussuf's eyes flicked open and he fixed them on the Authority's deputy chief of intelligence with a gleam of dark hatred.

Sa'adat leaned over the prisoner. "You have an hour to reflect on the hopelessness of your situation," he whispered. "Are you able to hear me, Yussuf Ben Saleh? Be reasonable—Abu Bakr is not worth suffering for. Granted, a certain amount of terrorism is useful—the threat of fundamentalists waiting to pick up the pieces strengthens the Authority's image as a moderate alternative. But terrorism is a matter of timing and dosage. Your *mujaddid* risks to ruin everything for us if he succeeds in rallying the Palestinian masses to holy war against the Jews. If we are careful not to scare the Jews off with terrorist bombs and kidnappings and threats of holy war, we will get our Palestinian state along the Sixty-seven frontiers in a week's time. When a year or two have passed, it goes without saying we will remind the Jews that we have not gotten what was in the original United Nations partition plan of 1948; that Acre and large parts of the Hula Valley and the Negev rightly belong to our new Palestinian state. Then, alternating doses of terrorism with doses of plausible reasonableness, we will push the Jews back to the original Forty-eight partition borders. In fifty years Isra'il will be reduced to a coastal strip that is without economic viability. The Jewish state will wither away. The Jews who are still there will emigrate to America. Remember the old joke about the sign at Lod Airport: *Will the last Jew to leave the country please turn out the lights.* Reflect on what I say. Cast your lot with the Palestinian Authority. Only tell us where the Rabbi is being held captive. Ghazeh? Hebron? Nablus? It would cause me great distress to have to hang you back up on the wall."

On the radio, a Palestinian school teacher from Tulkarm was saying, "With the *intifada*, the younger generation set an example for us. Now, with an independent Palestinian state almost in our grasp, it is important for us to set an example for the *intifada* generation."

"I agree," said the talk show hostess. "With God's help, we will create the first really democratic Arab nation in the region and live side by side with the Jews."

Returning to his office, Sa'adat discovered Baruch slouched in an easy chair reading the matrimonial advertisements in a Palestinian newspaper. "Ah, I am cheerful you could come down from Jerusalem," Sa'adat said, sliding in behind his desk. "Fruit juice for my friend Baruch," he called to an aide. "Don't tell me you are think-ing of taking a second wife," he remarked to his visitor with a wink.

"I am very happy with the one I have, thank you," Baruch replied.

Sa'adat snickered. "There are some who think the four wives per-mitted to a Muslim by the Qur'an are not enough. There are others who think one is a wife too many."

"How are things going with Yussuf Abu Saleh?" Baruch asked.

"He is what your interrogation specialists would call a tough bis-cuit. He will eventually tell us what we want to know, for sure. It is only a question of time."

"Time is what we don't have on our hands," Baruch mumbled. He could visualize Sa'adat's method of questioning Yussuf and it turned his stomach. He had seen Shin Bet reports on what went on behind the closed doors of Aksa; there had even been some discus-sion of leaking the details to the foreign press, but the idea had been abandoned when it was decided that Sa'adat and Company could strengthen the Authority's hand against the Islamic fundamentalists. Baruch gazed out a window so Sa'adat wouldn't notice the look on his face and focused on the fact that this same Yussuf had participated in the kidnapping of the Rabbi and his secretary, and the murder of four Jewish boys; had cut the finger off one of them to get a souvenir for his wife. "Is there anything in Yussuf's file that might give us a lead while we're waiting for him to talk?"

Sa'adat sipped some grapefruit and lime juice as he opened Yussuf's dossier. "Abu Saleh was born and raised in the Kalandia refugee camp north of Jerusalem. When he was fourteen he worked as a plasterer building houses for Jews in the West Bank by day, by night he raided the settlements to demolish the houses he had helped build. He was first arrested at the age of fifteen for distributing anti-Israeli leaflets. It is the usual story, my friend—during the first *intifada* he threw stones at your tanks and wound up joining a Hamas cell in Nablus." Sa'adat looked up at Baruch, the usual smile fixed on his round face. "You Jews created the monster—"

Baruch, who had been up most of the night, bridled. "Don't tell me, let me guess—we should have lost the Sixty-seven war and let you push us into the sea and avoided all these problems."

Sa'adat shrugged. "At one point in the Nineties Abu Saleh's two brothers were killed and he was wounded in a shootout with Isra'ili soldiers. Abu Saleh was sentenced to preventive detention in the Negev camp Ketziot, but he soon managed to escape in a garbage truck. He went to Ghazeh and then snuck into Egypt, and from there made his way to Afghanistan, where he joined a contingent of al Qaida *mujahidin* and wound up fighting against the Americans. When the Taliban lost the war, Abu Saleh escaped to Pakistan and later surfaced in Nablus holding a Bosnian passport identifying him as Asaf Koskovic from Mostar. He had this passport in his pocket when we picked him up in Jerusalem. We think it was during this Nablus period that he fell under the spell of the blind vigilante and came to believe that he was the long-awaited Islamic Renewer. The rest of the story I think you are familiar with. Hamas turned out not to be fundamentalist enough for Abu Saleh, so he defected, along with half his Nablus Hamas comrades, to form a cell loyal to the blind vigilante. It was about then that we raided his bomb factory in Nablus. I can tell you—where is the harm?—that we were tipped off by the local Hamas people, who were furious with Abu Saleh."

"You nailed two of his pals but Yussuf slipped through your fingers," Baruch said.

"Ah, Baruch, you do keep your ear to the soil."

"In this corner of the Levant people who don't keep their ear to the soil, as you put it, wind up being buried under it."

Sa'adat sank back in his chair and eyed his guest. "We are strange bedfellows, you and me, Baruch."

"How so?"

"Neither of us would collaborate with the other if we had a

choice." Sa'adat glanced at a very large wrist watch. "On the other hand we harbor no illusions, which makes for a successful collaboration."

"It's true I harbor no illusions about you," Baruch agreed. "I would have less qualms about a Palestinian state if people like you weren't going to run it."

"You Jews always prefer to think you sold your souls to the devil than consider the alternative—that you *are* the devil."

Baruch tossed his head in disgust; Sa'adat couldn't have known it but the person he was disgusted with was himself. "Our struggle to keep our heads above water in this sea of Arabs has changed us—some would say corrupted us. We are not the same people we would have been if we had accepted the British suggestion to make the Jewish state in Uganda."

Sa'adat decided to change the subject. "Abu Bakr's deadline for the Rabbi's secretary approaches."

"We can count as well as you." Pushing himself out of the chair, Baruch leaned over Sa'adat's desk and scratched a phone number on a pad. "That's a direct line. I'm sleeping in the office these days. Call me if Abu Saleh talks."

Sa'adat closed his eyes. "I will call you *when* Abu Saleh talks," he said softly.

At the door Sa'adat took Baruch's elbow and said, "By the way, I have a gift for you. It is in Arabic. Do you read Arabic?"

"Only matrimonial advertisements."

Sa'adat handed Baruch a slip of paper. "We found it folded into Abu Saleh's wallet. It is a curious document. It even bears a number—seven. My people are unable to figure out what he was doing with it, unless of course it is a coded message." As Baruch scanned the paper Sa'adat started back toward his desk, then turned on his heel. "Incidentally, there has been a twenty-fourth execution of a collaborator—a Mr. Hajji, who used to change money and guard valises for tourists at the Damascus Gate. He was killed with a .22-caliber bullet fired at point blank range into the base of his skull behind the ear. The family claimed Mr. Hajji died of heart failure and tried to bury him quietly to avoid disgrace. We got wind of it and had an autopsy performed." A shrewd smirk spread across

Sa'adat's fat face. "You are not the only one to keep your ear to the soil, my friend."

"It was Mr. Hajji who spotted Yussuf Abu Saleh's wife waving to her husband at the Damascus Gate," Baruch said quietly. "Where did his murder take place?"

"Somewhere in the state of Palestine."

Baruch sniffed at the warm dry air outside the door. "There is no state of Palestine."

Sa'adat lifted his eyebrows. "In less than a week there will be."

When Abu Saleh's hour of respite was up, Sa'adat returned to the interrogation chamber. "Have you seen the light?" he asked the prisoner.

Abu Saleh, who was on his knees and urinating into a plastic bucket, looked up. "My name is Koskovic, Asaf," he groaned, his swollen lips barely moving. "You have arrested the wrong man."

Sa'adat tossed his bald head in the direction of the hook on the wall. "String him up," he ordered the policemen.

As the story won't become public for another twenty-five years, I suppose there's no harm in my telling you what happened. This turned out to be the fist time in my life I was ever involved in one of those cloak-and-dagger meetings that you read about in spy novels. The Air Force, listing me on the manifest (someone in operations has a nice sense of humor) as Commander Philip Francis Queeg, flew me to Paris in one of their transports. The CIA whisked me through a gate at Le Bourget and the two armed policemen on duty, instead of asking for a passport, actually saluted. In the early hours before dawn, an embassy car drove me through the deserted boulevards to 37 Rue de la Ferme in Neuilly. Two young men with crew cuts and tiny plastic contraptions in their ears were waiting to take me to a fourth-floor safehouse. The apartment was furnished in CIA modern: cameras were hidden behind two-way mirrors, microphones were concealed in bouquets of plastic flowers. The metal shutters looked as if they had been welded closed. Finger sandwiches and a pitcher of apple juice had been set out on the table.

At the stroke of five a fiery woman named Lamia Ghuri appeared at the door. We settled down around the small table and I poured out two glasses of apple juice and handed her one.

"To your health," I said, raising my glass.

Madame Ghuri was a stocky women with a gorgeous face. I knew from my briefing paper that she was forty-two, the only daughter of a Palestinian father and a Jordanian mother; that as a young woman she had studied Russian history and Marxism at the Sorbonne; that she was married to a mysterious Lebanese who had supplied Russian surplus arms *and explosives to laic Palestinian splinter groups until the Authority, under American pressure, cracked down on them and him; that she was considered by left wing Palestinian radicals to be their Passionaria.*

She raised her glass and clanked it against mine. "L'chaim," she replied, a mischievous glint in her dark eyes.

I was somewhat taken aback and said so. "The last thing I expected was for a Palestinian like you to come out with a toast in Hebrew."

"Our argument is not with the Hebrew language or the Jews who use it, Mr. Sawyer," she retorted. "It is with the Zionist colonialists who have taken our land from us, who have humiliated our people; who now, aided and abetted by the Palestinian Authority, which has been backed into a corner by the American President, expect us to be thankful for the crumbs they throw us."

"You will finally get your state," I said. "You will get back roughly ninety-four percent of the land that Israel seized in the 1967 Six-day War. Most of the settlements on the West Bank will either be dismantled or, if the Jews choose to remain, come under Palestinian rule. That doesn't sound like crumbs to me."

Lamia Ghuri flashed a very thin smile that, to my astonishment, was filled with mirth, almost as if she were reacting to a joke. "Perspective is everything," is what she told me. "We are being given sovereignty over something like twenty-five percent of the pre-1948 Palestine. We are being given control of but not sovereignty over the Temple Mount, with its holy mosques. We are getting far less than half the water even though the water table runs under our cities and towns on the West Bank. We have had to tell the three and a half million Palestinian refugees that they will not be permitted to return to their homes in Israel. We have been obliged to agree to limit the weapons that we import into our state and cede control of the air space over the state to the Isra'ilis. All this sounds suspiciously like crumbs to me."

"The Palestinians you speak for have agreed to accept these terms—"

"I speak for no one but myself and my husband."

"If I thought that were true I wouldn't have come all this way to see you."

"Believe that it is true because I tell you that it is true."

I must have taken a very deep breath because that's what I usually do when I'm confronted by a boldface lie delivered with utter sincerity. "Okay. You speak for yourself and for your husband. Still, the position you and your husband have taken on the matter of the peace treaty— despite your reservations—has had an enormous influence with certain elements among the Palestinians."

"Some have suggested that this is the case. I myself have no way of confirming it."

"Let's move past the question of the Mt. Washington peace treaty, which has been settled. Let's talk about this Abu Bakr fellow. Let's talk about his abduction of that Rabbi—"

She supplied the name when she saw I couldn't remember it. "I. Apfulbaum."

"I. Apfulbaum. It's my understanding that you and your husband might not be averse to using what little influence you have—" I managed to keep a straight face when I pronounced the words "little influence"—"under the right conditions."

She deployed that thin smile of hers and waited for me to continue.

"Abu Bakr, whoever he is, does not have the profile of a Palestinian patriot, which is to say he couldn't care less if there is a secular Palestinian state run by elected representatives who answer to the people. What he wants is an Islamic state in an Islamic Middle East run by mullahs who answer only to God. I have been led to believe"—I was quoting here from the top-secret CIA report that had sent me on my quest to meet Lamia Ghuri—"that you and your husband, along with many of your husband's former clients, would feel out of place in an Islamic state; would, in fact, be the first to be jailed, perhaps even executed, by the leaders of an Islamic state who wanted to set an example by punishing prominent laic personalities. This is what the ayatollahs did when they took over Iran. This is what the Taliban did in Afghanistan."

"Your analysis of the situation is self-serving," she remarked. And she added a quote she said came from the Koran: "'Justifying yourself will not bring you camels in reward.'"

"Because it is self-serving doesn't make it any less true."

All through my (I have to admit) well rehearsed presentation, Lamia Ghuri had been looking me straight in the eye. Now, for the first time, her gaze drifted away and the thin smile that seemed to be a permanent fixture on her lips faded. She suddenly looked a good deal older than her forty-two years and I caught a glimpse of the strain that people like her lived under. When she finally spoke, she seemed a lot less sure of herself.

"If we knew who he was we would make sure the information reached you. If it was within our power to stop him before he kills Rabbi Apfulbaum, we would do it."

I nodded fatalistically. Lamia Ghuri had been a long shot. But the stakes were high and we couldn't afford to leave a stone unturned. I pushed the plate of finger sandwiches across the table, but she ignored them. "Thank you for agreeing to this meeting," I said, but her mind was obviously elsewhere. She sat there breathing very quietly for what seemed like an eternity. I don't know why but I got the impression that she was arguing with herself, which is—here I speak from personal experience— always a no-win situation. Finally she nodded and scraped the chair away from the table and stood up, very straight, her shoulders squared, her head high and angled slightly to one side. (I remember all these details because I watched the scene on film after she'd left.)

"He's a medical doctor," she said softly.

I'm have to admit that I didn't have the foggiest idea what she was talking about. "Who's a medical doctor?" I asked stupidly.

"Abu Bakr. In the territories, it is said that he with the mark of prostration on his forehead is a medical doctor."

I climbed to my feet. "Why didn't you tell me this straight away?"

There was a hint of tears in her eyes as she said, "It is not easy to betray a Palestinian, even one whose vision of a Palestinian state would set it back centuries. Creating a Palestinian state is only the beginning of the struggle for many of us. Pulling it out of the fundamentalist swamp and into the twenty-first century is our ultimate goal. Goodbye, Mr. Sawyer. I do not like Americans. I do not like your President. I do not like you. I hope we never meet again."

THIRTY-ONE

MOSES BRISCOE, THE IRISH JEW WHO RAN ONE OF THE SHIN Bet's flagship divisions, was fuming. Baruch, who had a passing acquaintance with Briscoe—they had crossed swords before when both were assigned to investigate back-to-back Hamas suicide bombings—could hear him biting off his words over the phone. "Let's scramble this conversation," Briscoe, nominally higher in the security apparatus pecking order than a cop from Jerusalem, snapped. The Irishman came back on the line breathing fire. "I'm calling about the American journalist Sweeney—"

"What's Sweeney have to do with—"

"I had his phone tapped—"

"You had author—"

"I have a blanket authorization to tap the phone of anyone who might lead us to terrorists."

"Last I heard, Sweeney was a journalist."

"This guy is an Arab lover."

"That doesn't make him a Jew hater."

"He got a phone call from an Arab speaking in English—"

"How'd you know it was an Arab if he was speaking English?"

"An Arab can speak Mandarin Chinese, I still know he's an Arab. He told Sweeney to come down to Aza for a scoop—we figure he was being invited to interview the man himself."

For once Baruch didn't respond.

"Did you hear me? The man himself is *Abu Bakr*, the *mechabel* who kidnapped I. Apfulbaum! According to the article Sweeney wrote after his trip to Aza, *Abu Bakr* may also be the celebrated Renewer."

"I don't see—"

"Sweeney was supposed to find a welcoming committee on the Palestinian side of the Erez crossing point into Aza. I had some assets spotted around waiting to tail him once he made contact with his Palestinian driver. Sweeney must have parked his car in the lot on the Israeli side of the Erez crossing because we found it there. But he never showed up on the Arab side. He vanished into thin air."

Baruch's pulse was pounding in his temple. "Listen carefully, Moses," he murmured icily into the phone. "Whatever you do, don't interrupt me. When I finish saying what I'm going to say, I'm going to hang up. Then I'm going to put in a call to the *katsa*. Elihu will phone up the director of the Prime Minister's military affairs committee, a son-of-a-bitch named Zalman Cohen. Within fifteen minutes, you will receive a personal phone call from the Prime Minister. He is going to tell you exactly what I am telling you now, only less politely. Get off Sweeney's case. Don't tap his phone, don't waste assets keeping track of him, don't ask questions, don't argue. You're walking on the *katsa*'s toes. Back-pedal before you get pulverized in the *katsa*'s grinder. You mention the name Sweeney once more, you'll be out on the street hunting for a job. In another country."

Briscoe could be heard breathing hard, as if he had run across a back lawn to take the call. When he spoke he seemed to be wrestling with his rage. "I resent your tone, not to mention—"

Baruch cut the connection with his forefinger, waited for a dial tone, then punched in a Jaffa number. The barefoot contessa in the miniskirt who forgot to buy diet cream put him through to the *katsa*. They scrambled and Baruch quickly explained the situation. "I'll get through to the Prime Minister's office right away," Elihu said.

Baruch said, "We had assets spotted around the Palestinian end of Erez too—they didn't notice Briscoe's assets, they didn't notice Sweeney, either."

"There were twelve thousand Palestinian workers returning to Aza when Sweeney came through. The Abu Bakr people timed it so he would be lost in the shuffle."

Baruch knew the *katsa* well enough to understand that he was trying to convince himself, and not succeeding. "It's been almost twenty-four hours," Baruch said. "Our antennas should have picked something up by now."

"Aza is a big place," Elihu said softly, and he hung up.

Baruch ordered in a sandwich and a beer, and reread the most recent letter from his son, who was hiking with friends through the Himalayas to celebrate the completion of his three-year stint in the Army. "If we can buy bottles of oxygen from the sherpas," Ami had written, "we're going to try to get up to six thousand meters. Otherwise we'll stay at four thousand and enjoy the view, which is almost as good as the one from our Mt. Hermon. For god's sake don't worry. I won't do anything you wouldn't have done at my age. (That leaves me a lot of leeway!)"

Baruch had to smile. At Ami's age, he'd taken part in one war and half a dozen raids across the Jordan, then had worked his way around the Horn on a tramp steamer to spend six months hiking through Thailand and Laos. He had left Israel vaguely thinking he might never return. (Almost every Israeli who went abroad toyed with the idea of staying abroad, though very few actually did.) Who needed to spend his life in a pressure cooker? Foreigners, Baruch told himself, not for the first time, didn't understand the strain that's put on Israelis from the day of their birth. Israelis are born old and age fast. They feel the weight on their shoulders while they're still crawling around a crib. Baruch swiveled a hundred and eighty degrees and gazed out the window at Jewish Jerusalem; from his office, which was on the fourteenth floor, he could make out the black scar on the pavement where a suicide bomber had blown up a number eighteen bus, killing twenty-six Jews and wounding half a hundred others. We live on the edge, Baruch thought, surrounded by dozens of millions of people who would exterminate us if they could. It is this aspect of the conflict that the world doesn't grasp, but we understand in our gut; it is drummed into us from the moment we are taught, in kindergarten, to duck under our desks and cover our heads when the siren sounds. My daughter understood it when she was waiting for her bus at Beit Lid; my son understands it when he climbs higher and higher in the Himalayas and tries, for a day or two, to leave the world behind him. Our enemies don't want to conquer us. They want to obliterate us. Which leaves us no margin for errors: in the wars, in the fight against terrorism, in weapons procurement, in budget allocation, in the endless diplomatic haggling. Every day we make thousands of choices, and they must be the right choices if we don't want to wind up victims of a second Holocaust. By the time a young Israeli finishes his Army service, he is fed up with making choices that absolutely have to be correct; he wants the luxury of making a mistake now and then, and then doubling back on his tracks and casually correcting it.

This is the weight on our shoulders that we cannot shrug off.

Baruch took a deep breath, and a second. Then he shook his head and laughed under his breath and opened the slip of paper that Sa'adat had found in Yussuf Abu Saleh's wallet. He was completely mystified by the small number seven inked in on the top right. Was this page seven? Or the seventh copy of the same page? One of the bright young Arabists down the hall had given Baruch a rough translation of the document, which appeared to be a textbook description of a cell in the human nervous system. There is the body of the cell, where all the cell's activity originates. Then come the *dendrites*, which branch out from the cell body. Then the *axon*, the long single fiber that snakes out toward other nerve cells and along which instructions to the other cells are carried. There is no actual contact with the other cells: the messages from one cell to another are transmitted at a gap called the *synapse*, where the cells approach each other but do not touch.

If Sa'adat's guess was correct, if the document was a coded message, there was little the Israelis could do to decipher it; the Islamic fundamentalists had mastered the use of the primitive but unbreakable one-time pad system, which involved enciphering and deciphering from a random substitution key, of which only two copies existed, one in the hands of the person who originated the message, the other in the hands of the person who received it. To make the code even more unbreakable, the key was used only once and destroyed.

Baruch read the document again. It suddenly struck him that

this paragraph out of a biology textbook offered an uncannily accurate description of a fundamentalist terrorist cell. Orders originated in the heart of the cell. *Dendrites* or activists branched out from the cell to carry out these orders. Instructions to other cells were passed along the *axon*, which snaked out in the direction of other cells but, for security purposes, never actually made contact with them. The messages were passed across a gap called the *synapse*. If Yussuf Abu Saleh could be described as a *dendrite*—perhaps he was dendrite number seven!—then the lame shoemaker across from the El Khanqa Mosque in the Christian Quarter of the Old City was clearly the *synapse*, the gap across which messages between cells were transmitted without the cells touching. If I'm right, Baruch thought, if this document is really an Abu Bakr Brigade organizational chart, it certainly wasn't the handiwork of Yussuf Abu Saleh, who had been a plasterer before becoming a Muslim activist. Which left the man himself, as Briscoe put it: Abu Bakr! Abu Bakr, the almost blind fundamentalist with the mark of prostration on his forehead. Abu Bakr, the vigilante who had personally executed twenty-four collaborators with .22-caliber bullets fired, so Elihu had reported at the first session of the Working Group, *with surgical accuracy* into their medullas, the lowest part of the brain stem, which controls the heart beat and breathing and brings instantaneous death. *What you're describing*, Baruch had remarked when Elihu reported how a short, heavy-set man with short cropped hair, listening for signs of life, had pressed his ear to the mouth of the wounded Jew lying on the road during the kidnapping, *could be the professional gestures of a medic or a male nurse.*

The telephone on Baruch's desk rang shrilly. He resented the interruption and considered not answering it. With a fatalistic shrug, he lifted the receiver.

"That you, Baruch?" a man asked.

Baruch recognized the voice and sat up straighter. "It is, Prime Minister."

"Scramble this conversation."

Baruch hit the scramble button, then said, "Go ahead."

"I don't know if what I am about to say can help you. I just received a secret cable from Sawyer, the President's Special Assistant for—"

"Sir, I know who Sawyer is."

"Yes, well, his note was short and to the point. He said he has reason to believe that Abu Bakr is a medical doctor." When Baruch didn't say anything, the Prime Minister asked, "Did you hear me, Baruch?"

"I did, Prime Minister."

"Is this detail useful?"

"I think it may be. Thank you for calling."

The line went dead. Baruch leaned back in his chair. *Of course! Not a medic or a male nurse but a doctor!* "Why didn't I think of it sooner?" Baruch said out loud. The sound of his own voice startled him. *Who else but a doctor would be familiar enough with anatomy to execute people with a low-caliber bullet fired into the medulla? And familiar enough with biology to model his terrorist cells along the lines of human cells?*

Baruch snatched a sheaf of eighty-weight bond and scrawled "From, To, Subj:" on the top left. Then he addressed it to the brothers Karamazov in the research department, and wrote: "The short, heavy-set nearly blind religious Muslim who spent time in Israeli prisons after being denounced by a collaborator at some point in his life had formal medical training. Does that narrow it down for you?"

Baruch signed the work order and set it on Absalom's desk under a plastic flower pot filled with a plastic geranium. Wandering back into his office, he felt physically and mentally drained—he was so exhausted he doubted he would be able to fall asleep. He filled the small crystal glass, which his late father-in-law had brought with him from Vilnius when he immigrated to Israel, with three-star brandy from the Golan Heights and, setting the phone on the floor within arm's reach, stretched out on the couch. If his wife had been there she would have made a sardonic remark about his shoes. "Just because terrorists are kidnapping Israelis is no reason to put your dirty soles up on a clean couch," she would have groaned, as if one thing had anything to do with the other. She would have untied his laces and slipped the shoes off his feet, and covered his feet with a blanket. She would have put one of the late Beethoven string quartets on the new compact player his daughter had bought him for his last birthday, and settled into the rocking chair to stand guard against evil spirits while he lay there, his eyes wide open, trying to close the gap between possibilities and probabilities.

THIRTY-TWO

MOSES BRISCOE SNATCHED THE PHONE OFF THE HOOK WHILE the first ring was still echoing in his ear. The Prime Minister must have dialed the number himself because Briscoe could hear his cranky growl coming down the tube. "That you, Moses?"

"Sir."

"As far as the Shin Bet is concerned, the journalist Sweeney does not exist. No phone taps, no surveillance, electronic or otherwise. Nothing. Period. Am I coming across loud and clear?"

"You certainly are."

"A messenger will deliver a formal written finding to this effect within the hour. If your division disregards any part of it, don't waste time with explanations—draft a letter of resignation and send it to my office. It will be accepted before it arrives. Questions?"

"I have an endless list of questions, but I know better than to ask them."

The Prime Minister relaxed for the first time. "How's your family?"

"Fine."

"Your son still in that sapper unit?"

"Yes."

"You must be worried."

"You bet I'm worried—I'm worried sick about my son, I'm worried sick about Rabbi Apfulbaum, I'm worried sick about his secretary, Efrayim."

"Me, too, Moses. Me, too."

THIRTY-THREE

TIME HAD RUN OUT ON THE RABBI'S SECRETARY. "WHERE ARE you taking me?" Efrayim sobbed under his hood as Azziz untied his feet and prodded him toward the door. "I don't have to urinate. For God's sake, Rabbi, don't just sit there, say something. Ask them where they're taking me."

The hood-muffled voice of the Rabbi could be heard. "So where are you taking him?"

"There is no reason for him to be alarmed," the Doctor said soothingly. From somewhere over the rooftops came the recorded wail of the *muezzin* summoning the faithful to evening prayers at the El Khanqa Mosque. "He stinks," the Doctor explained. "There is an old Arab public bathhouse under us. We're taking him downstairs for a shower."

"Oy, oy," Efrayim groaned. "The Nazis told the Jews at Auschwitz they were being taken to the shower." His fingers found the knob on the door. He dug his Reeboks in on the floor and clung to it for dear life. "For God's sake do something, Rabbi!" he pleaded.

Behind him, the Rabbi's curiously detached lament drifted across the room. "'*There is a time for being born and a time for dying . . .*'"

Azziz pried Efrayim's fingers from the knob and half dragged, half pushed the prisoner into the outer room. Azziz's brother, Aown, armed with the Webley, had taken Sweeney up to the attic crawl space over the safe house to cat nap until the Ramadan break-fast and the session with Apfulbaum. Azziz kicked the door to the inner room closed behind him, then shoved Efrayim roughly against the wall so that his cheek was glued to it. The Doctor came up behind Efrayim. He grasped his pearl-handled revolver in his right hand, with his left he probed under the hood for the distinctive knob of bone behind the ear. "'*In the Name of God, the Merciful, the Compassionate,*'" he intoned in a brittle voice. When his fingers discovered the knob he felt a surge of elation. "'*O unbelievers, I serve not what you serve and you are not serving what I serve.*'"

Stony faced, Petra stood by with a large towel to blot up any blood before it stained the floor.

Efrayim's shoulders shuddered uncontrollably. From under the leather hood came a long, muffled moan of terror. Then he gasped and began reciting the only words of the Torah he could recollect. Each word emerged from his throat as a whimper of despair. "'*Shema . . . yisro'el . . . adoynoy . . . eloheynu . . . adoynoy—*'"

The Doctor cut him off with one of his favorite verses from the Qur'an. "'*To you your religion, to me my religion!*'" He brought the pistol up and jammed the barrel against the hood behind Efrayim's ear and, sliding his left hand free, squeezed the trigger. The phffffft was barely audible. Then the executioner did something he had never done before at one of his executions: as Azziz caught the dead Jew under the armpits and lowered him to the floor, the Doctor giggled uncontrollably.

Leaning over the corpse, Petra pressed the towel to Efrayim's neck to soak up the trickle of blood oozing from under the hood. Working quickly, she and Azziz rolled the corpse in an old carpet. Without a word, Azziz hefted the carpet over one sturdy shoulder and started down the flight of steps and across the roofs toward the alleyway and the van with "Fine Bedouin Robes and Carpets" printed in English on its sides.

THIRTY-FOUR

KEEPING A HAND ON THE BUTT OF THE WEBLEY IN HIS BELT, Aown pushed open the door to the inner sanctum with a toe and stepped aside to let the American journalist past. Sweeney discovered the Rabbi swaying back and forth in his chair in the windowless room illuminated by the naked bulb hanging from the braided electric cord. Puffing on one of his thick Farids, the Doctor hauled the leather hood off of Apfulbaum's head. The Fiddler on the Roof looked as if he had aged twenty years since Sweeney had last set eyes on him; his hair had thinned and started to turn gray, his eyes had enormous bags under them, on the back of his hands the wrinkled skin seemed to hang in folds off the bones. His voice rising and falling like a tired tide, Apfulbaum prayed under his breath as he worked a set of silver worry beads through his skeletal fingers.

The Doctor tugged gently on the slit sleeve of the Rabbi's rumpled suit jacket. "You have a visitor, Isaac," he announced, settling onto a chair facing the prisoner, motioning Sweeney to the stool that Aown was dragging in from the other room.

The Rabbi's prayer trailed off. "Are we night or are we day?"

"You know very well, *ya'ani*, that I always come to you at night."

Apfulbaum opened one eye and squinted at Sweeney without bringing him into focus. "So who is this visitor?" he asked huskily.

"It's me, Rabbi. Max Sweeney. I interviewed you the day you went to Yad Mordechai, just before—"

The Rabbi's other eye flicked open. "Say it, say it. Just before my convoy stopped to lend benzene to some stinking *haredim*. You prob-

ably think the episode slipped my mind but it hasn't. It's still fresh in
my memory—I can hear the tall Jew speaking Hebrew with a funny
accent, I can feel the hypodermic needle pricking my arm."
Apfulbaum angled his head in the direction of his secretary's chair.
"Damn it, Efrayim, I specifically told you I wasn't going to grant him
a second interview until I saw what he'd written about me in the
first." The Rabbi snorted in displeasure. "You're going to have to
shape up or ship out, Efrayim."

The Doctor cleared his throat. "I'm afraid Efrayim has . . .
shipped out."

"Efrayim's shipped out," the Rabbi repeated dully. He ran the
fingers of both hands through his hair. "So where has my amanuen-
sis shipped out to?"

"With any luck, heaven."

Sweeney scratched the Doctor's answer in his copy book before
glancing at the empty chair. The sight of the strips of cloth that had
bound the secretary's ankles to its thick wooden legs turned his stomach. For a moment he thought he was going to throw up. He swallowed hard and breathed deeply through his mouth.

Apfulbaum wrestled with the meaning of the Doctor's words.
"Efrayim's gone to heaven?"

"There is a time for dying, ya'ani," the Doctor reminded him.

The Rabbi's brow filled with creases, his eyes bulged in their
sockets. "Ah, I see. Why didn't come right out and say it without
beating around the burning bush? You *excarnated* Efrayim!" When
the Doctor remained silent, Apfulbaum, shaking his head in agitation, began forcing the worry beads through his fingers. "I'm not surprised. A deadline's a deadline. Question of maintaining one's credibility. So poor Efrayim has shipped out. Which means I'm next in
line for excarnation. Ha! I'm ready when you are! Contrary to the
conventional wisdom on the subject, people who are dying want to
talk about their deaths. Everyone avoids the subject out of embarrassment. But you and I, we're way past mundane things like embarrassment. Talk to me about my death, Ishmael. Tell me how you're
going to excarnate me."

"Let's not cross bridges—"

Sweeney was amazed to see that the prisoner seemed to have turned the tables on his kidnapper. It was the prisoner who was eager, and Abu Bakr who hung back, obviously ill at ease.

"Knock off the clichés about crossing bridges," the Rabbi burst out angrily. Then he shouted, "I want you to describe my excarnation." He calmed down and elevated a quivering chin and spit whispered words through clenched teeth. "Give me details, for God's sake!"

The Doctor scraped his chair closer to the Rabbi. "I do it myself," he confided.

The Rabbi sighed. "I'm relieved it will be you and not some dirty Palestinian."

"I can say, speaking from a medical point of view, that if it comes to that—I hope with all my heart it will not, but if it does—the end will be utterly painless. I insert a small caliber bullet into the lowest part of the brain stem, which regulates the beating of the heart and the breathing. Death is instantaneous."

"You're not trying to comfort me? You're not saying that so I won't lose my nerve?"

"Allah is my witness, Isaac. I give you my word as a Muslim."

Apfulbaum accepted this with a nod. Turning to Sweeney, he said impatiently, "I'm going to tell you something. Hang on my every word. You can take notes but remember to spell Apfulbaum with an f after the p. As long as you spell my name correctly, resurrection is guaranteed or I get my money back. Here it is: in another incarnation I could have liked this guy. He's one of the chosen; he's one of us."

Sweeney looked up, bewildered. "I don't follow—"

"What Isaac is trying to tell you," the Doctor picked up where the Rabbi had left off, "is that a sort of affinity has developed between us during the long and difficult hours we have spent together."

"It's not the usual bull shit of the kidnappee falling head over heels in love with the kidnapper," the Rabbi explained quickly. "Nothing as banal as that."

"It is simpler," the Doctor said, "and at the same time more complex."

"On this disputed land," Apfulbaum continued, "we have discovered a common ground besides the no-man's land of English."

"Common ground?" Sweeney asked, totally mystified.

"Looking back," the Rabbi rambled on, "I can see it was more or less inevitable. I mean, there is an abundance of superficial affinities. We're both circumcised. We both write from right to left—"

"Without vowels," the Doctor interjected.

"Without vowels," Apfulbaum repeated. "We both refuse to eat pork. We both pray to the same God at frequent intervals during the day, me three times, Ishmael here, five. We both believe that holy scripture is the word of God. But that only scratches the surface."

"There is much more to this affinity than meets the eye," the Doctor agreed. "The quintessence of the Jewish faith is Deuteronomy 6, the *shema*, which is recited in the morning and evening liturgy." He removed his spectacles and massaged his eyes with his thumb and third finger as he murmured, "'*Hear, O Israel, the Lord our God, the Lord is One.*' Did I get that right, Isaac?"

"The essence of Islamic faith," explained the Rabbi, his tongue tripping over the words as they spilled through his dry lips, "is the recitation of the *shahada*, the witnessing; the testimony that begins with '*la ilaha illa 'llah, no god exists but God.*'" Apfulbaum would have come flailing out of his chair if his ankles had not been lashed to it. "For God's sake, do I have to write it on the wall in capital letters? You have to be blind to not see it. *We're both children of Abraham.*"

"This being the case," Sweeney said, "how can you bring yourself to kill him? And how can you, Rabbi, bring yourself to be *excarnated* without hating the person who *excarnates* you?"

Rolling his head from side to side, the Rabbi snickered. The Doctor chuckled. Soon they were both shaking with quiet laughter.

The Doctor was the first to catch his breath. "He does not comprehend," he told the Rabbi, "what you and I comprehend, Isaac— that killing people is not that far removed from curing them. Death and life are two sides of the same coin." He turned back to Sweeney. "To be absolutely frank, I hope with all my heart that the Jews will give me something—anything!—so that I will not be obliged to go through with my threat and excarnate Isaac here who, like Ibrahim, is a man of pure faith, and no idolater."

"Thank you for that," Apfulbaum said with great modesty. "For my part, I hope with all my heart that the Israeli government will refuse to negotiate and oblige Ishmael to excarnate me. Thanks to Ishmael, I have come to see myself as the modern incarnation of what our biblical Isaiah referred to as the Suffering Servant, someone who is fated to suffer for the sins of his people and thereby expiate these sins. If the Jews are destined to be a light unto the nations, I am destined to be a light unto the Jews. Dead, I will become a symbol for those who are against abandoning the land God promised to Abraham and his seed. My tomb will become a place of pilgrimage, a rallying point in the struggle against the Arabs. After my death— because of my death!—our Jewish settlements will continue to grow, the way the fingernails of a corpse grow after death."

"Fingernails do not grow after death, *ya'ani*. The skin recedes, giving the impression that fingernails grow."

"Oh. Still, you see what I mean?"

"I do. I do."

"You're both off your rockers," Sweeney moaned.

The Rabbi's feet danced in their bonds. "They said I was off my rocker when I talked fourteen families into leaving Brooklyn and setting up shop in some derelict trailers on a craggy hill overlooking Hebron. *For two years we had to shit in a portable toilet!* They said I was off my rocker when I figured out we could grow lettuce in flower pots during the seventh sabbatical year when the land, according to the Torah, is supposed to lie fallow. I caused the lettuce to be sprayed with insecticides, which excarnated the worms—we sold the lettuce in the Jerusalem *shouk* for a fortune to religious Jews who didn't want to run the risk of eating non-kosher meat. The windfall from this put Beit Avram on the map, financially speaking."

"Calm yourself, Isaac," the Doctor pleaded. He reached for the Rabbi's wrist and checked his pulse, which was racing. "I think we will cut this session short and give Isaac a rest. I do not like it when he gets too worked up."

"No, no, Ishmael, I'll simmer down, I swear it."

The Doctor slipped the hood back over the Rabbi's head. "Rest your eyes, *ya'ani*. Take a nap. We will come back in a while." He shooed Sweeney out of the inner sanctum, but left the door ajar in case the Rabbi should call out to him. "He is quite a number, is he not?" he said. "Salt of the earth."

"Can I quote you?" Sweeney asked sarcastically.

"Of course you can quote me." The static-filled voices of Israeli soldiers reporting in from various corners of the West Bank burst over Petra's radio. "For the sake of God, turn that down," the Doctor barked at her. "Rabbi Apfulbaum is trying to sleep."

THIRTY-FIVE

THE DOCTOR LIFTED THE HOOD OFF OF THE RABBI'S HEAD AND shook him gently. "Are you up to another session, Isaac?" he asked. "I promise to keep it as brief as possible."

As Sweeney looked on, the Fiddler on the Roof stretched his manacled wrists over his head and yawned several times to clear out the cobwebs, then exercised his jaw, elongating it first to one side, then the other.

"Why don't you undo his feet and let him walk around the room?" Sweeney asked.

"Kindly don't lose sight of the fact that I am a prisoner," the Rabbi answered for him. "At any instant the Israeli Army could come bursting through the door. For security reasons, it is essential that I remain tied to my chair." He stood up in his bonds and hiked his trousers and arranged his testicles and settled down again. "We're not children playing cops and robbers here," he went on. "This is the real McCoy. Isn't that correct, Ishmael?"

"This is a death and life business," the Doctor agreed soberly.

"Death and life," the Rabbi echoed, rolling his head from side to side to exercise his neck muscles. "In that order."

"You have not had an easy day, Isaac, but if you are not too fatigued, I would appreciate it if you would elaborate on the theme of the Jewish underground that we have been talking about. You told me during one recent session that you were its spiritual leader—"

"And proud to be," Apfulbaum interjected. "I interpret Torah for them. Even *thou shalt not excarnate* has exceptions." He corkscrewed his body in his chair and spoke directly to the Doctor, who was standing with his back against the bricked-in window. "Each of us contributes what he can to the struggle."

Sweeney suddenly had the impression that he was interviewing two inmates of an insane asylum. "Are you saying your settlement of Beit Avram is the home of *Keshet Yonatan*, the Jewish underground movement?"

The Rabbi managed an angelic smile. "So where else would they hang their hats?"

"How many members of your settlement belong to *Keshet Yonatan?*"

"Let's see. Beit Avram has a population of three hundred souls. Of these, one hundred and eighty are adults. I define as an adult any-one who has reached the age of Bar Mitzvah. Of these hundred and eighty, one hundred and seventy-eight identify with the program of *Keshet Yonatan*, which can be summed up by the title of my small book, *One Torah, One Land*. The other two adults are laborers imported from Rumania and don't speak Hebrew. Of the hundred and seventy-eight sympathizers, twenty-eight or thirty are in the trenches at any given moment."

"Tell him what you mean by in the trenches, *ya'ani*."

"Our front-line soldiers are divided into three squads," Apful-baum explained patiently. "One squad actively gathers intelligence on our Palestinian enemies in Judea and Samaria—where they live, who they live with, where they work, what routes they generally take when they go to work, what make of car they drive, that sort of thing. The second squad is in charge of weapons and explosives—providing the right equipment for the job. The third squad is the arrow in *Keshet Yonathan*, the bow of Jonathan. Its members are the ones who actually go out and do the dirty work."

"You want to spell out what you mean by dirty work?" Sweeney asked.

The Doctor answered for the Rabbi. "All you have to do is take a look at the *Jerusalem Post* headlines over the past dozen years. There were letter bombs exploding in the hands of Palestinian mayors, there were attacks on important individuals, there were excarnations, there were raids on homes or schools to intimidate Palestinians."

Apfulbaum stifled a giggle with his fist. "Ha! We would set off bombs in trash bins at night in the middle of an Arab village, which invariably sent everyone within earshot diving under their beds."

Sweeney asked, "Did your dirty work accomplish anything?"

"He has to be pulling my leg!" the Rabbi exclaimed. "You have to be pulling my leg. It demonstrated to the Palestinians that the Jews were in Judea and Samaria to stay, for one thing. And it pushed the more radical movements among the Palestinians to retaliate. They would retaliate, then we would retaliate for the retaliation. For every Jewish settler knifed while shopping in an Arab store, more money and more recruits would flow into *Keshet Yonathan*. And more Israelis would turn against the so-called peace movement that wants us to abandon holy land to the Arabs."

"What he is describing," the Doctor said, "is a vicious circle."

"Not only a vicious circle," the Rabbi said, "but a *vicious* vicious circle."

"You cannot have a vicious circle," the Doctor pointed out, "if both sides do not hold up their end."

"As usual, Ishmael has disambiguated a complex situation," the Rabbi declared vehemently. "I didn't really see that part until he pointed it out to me. Long before our paths crossed, long before this affinity between us developed, we were *collaborating*. Now Ishmael and I are breaking new ground by articulating this complicity for the first time."

The Doctor came over and sat down facing Apfulbaum. "Let us move on. Do you know the identity of the leader of *Keshet Yonathan*, the famous—or should I say infamous?—Ya'ir?"

Apfulbaum arched his neck; when he spoke, his Adam's apple throbbed against the soft folds of skin on his throat. "Did Moses know the identity of the voice coming from the burning bush? Did Pharaoh know the identity of God's anointed who led the Israelites out of Egypt?"

"And who is he?"

The Rabbi's mouth shut with an audible click. His jaw trembled. He squirmed in the chair, but remained silent.

The Doctor addressed Sweeney. "There are puzzles Isaac is not ready to solve. He removes his shoes and tip-toes to the edge of the Rubicon—but he will not wet his feet, he will not cross over. He is not yet sure enough of me—he is not sure what I will do with the information."

"It's not *that*," whined Apfulbaum. "Of course I know what you'll do with the information. You'll excarnate Ya'ir. You'll discredit *Keshet Yonathan* in the eyes of the world. So what? That's the least of it. There will be others ready to step into Ya'ir's shoes and form a new underground movement."

Sweeney looked from one to the other. "Why won't you tell him, then?"

The Rabbi seemed to grow smaller in his chair. When he finally got around to answering Sweeney's question, his voice sounded as if it came from a little boy. "Please, *please* understand—if I give Ishmael all my secrets, he won't have any reason to come back every night and milk me." A pained expression stole over Apfulbaum's face. "You're absolutely positive it's heaven that Efrayim's shipped out to? The reason I'm asking is that the clock is ticking, and with each tick we're getting closer to the second deadline, the Feast of the Breaking of the Fast. With any luck, I'll be shipping out next . . ."

An eyelid twitched, a vein in his neck throbbed as he waited for the answer.

THIRTY-SIX

TWO TEENAGE BOYS, VETERANS OF THE *intifada*, ONE WITH HIS wrist in a cast covered with Islamic slogans, were rummaging on a mountain of rubbish at the edge of the sprawling Jabaliya refugee camp outside Gaza City before morning prayers when they spotted a black Reebok jutting from the trunk compartment of a burnt-out taxi. Coming closer, they saw that the sneaker was practically new and still attached to a human foot. They exchanged greedy glances as they pried open the warped door of the trunk. Inside, the rigid body of a religious Jew—he was wearing rumpled black trousers and a filthy white shirt, and still had the ritual fringed *tzitzit* protruding from under his black suit jacket—was folded into the small space. A leather hood covered the corpse's head. One of the boys reached into the trunk and stuck his pinky through the small hole in the leather hood roughly behind where the dead man's ear should have been. He jerked out his finger as if he had been burned and held it up for the other boy to see. His finger nail was covered with a sticky reddish-brown substance. Quickly, the boys unlaced the Reebok sneakers and worked them off the dead man's feet. Scrambling over broken furniture and burnt tires, they raced off with their prize just as half a dozen Palestinian police cars, their sirens screaming, their lights flashing, came tearing down the unpaved road and screeched to a stop at the foot of the mountain of rubbish.

An Excerpt from the Harvard "Running History" Project:

Where did we leave off? Ah, yes, my tête-à-tête with the Israeli Prime Minister.

Five minutes into our conversation I was ready to believe something I recently read in the newspapers, namely that a homo sapiens only has twice as many genes as a fly or a worm. Nobody denies that the Prime Minister has good reason to be outraged; the murder of the Rabbi's secretary, the discovery of his body on a heap of garbage in Gaza, would test the patience, not to mention the mettle, of any political leader. (Between you, me and the wall, I still wonder how much of his notorious anger is genuine and how much is put on, like theatrical makeup before the curtain rises, in order to give him greater freedom of action or, in this case, reaction.)

"How many Jews must be murdered before you Americans decide that reprisals are justified?" he asked rhetorically. (I've come to realize, over the months I've been dealing with the Prime Minister, that most of his questions didn't require answers; they only require listening to.) "On your advice, Zachary, I sat on my hands when we buried the four bodyguards. And now we will bury a Rabbinical student whose only crime was to serve as a secretary to Rabbi Apfulbaum. And in a few days we will surely bury the Rabbi. And you will come on the long distance telephone line—my God, your phone bill alone would probably pay our Mossad's annual budget—and tell me the American President and the American people expect us to show restraint. Show restraint! You remind me of the diplomat who advised the Jews being shipped to Auschwitz not to do anything that might make the Germans angry."

I've noticed that conversations with Israelis almost always come back, at some point, to the Holocaust; you don't understand anything about the Jews if you don't grasp that, under stress, it is the psychological point of departure for their emotions. It's no coincidence that every foreign visitor to Israel—here I am speaking from personal experience—is hauled off to visit Yad Vashem, their Holocaust museum, before they get to spend quality time with the political leaders. You put on a skull cap and stand with your eyes closed in the building where a voice is reading out the names, one by one, of the million and a half Jewish children who perished during the war. Sarah Goldstein, aged six, Vilnius, 1941. Israel Katz, aged four, Prague, 1944. They soften you up with guilt before they talk to you. And it always works. How can you be hard on a people who have suffered the way the Jews have?

The answer is detachment: I can be hard on them when it's necessary because I force myself to be detached—from their history, their fears, the plight, their problems.

Not that I'd do things differently if I were in their shoes. Even when there is no shooting, the Israelis are at war: with the Arabs, with themselves. And all is fair in love and war. Everyone plays the cards that are dealt to them.

Including me.

Which is why I told the Prime Minister not to worry about our phone bill. Which is why I told him the retaliation he proposed wouldn't be against the criminals who had abducted and murdered the secretary, but against innocent civilians. Which is why I added that arbitrarily killing a reasonable number of Palestinians wouldn't save the life of the Rabbi. The only way to save the life of the Rabbi was to give in to the kidnapper's demands or find the kidnappee before they killed him.

I must have touched a nerve because the Prime Minister didn't say anything for so long I thought I'd lost the secure connection. "Are you still there?" I finally asked.

"Never," he said.

"Never, what?" I asked, though I had a pretty good idea what he was talking about.

"We will never give in to their demands. Even you don't have enough leverage on Israel to make us do that."

"I wouldn't make the mistake of asking you to do that."

The Prime Minister only grunted.

"Which narrows the choices available to you down to one: find the Rabbi before they kill him."

"Believe me, we're trying."

I'd reached the heart of the matter. "If you don't find him, if they kill him, if his body turns up in a garbage dump the day before the Mt. Washington peace treaty is due to be signed—"

I could hear the Prime Minister breathing heavily into the phone. "What does the President of the United States expect us to do?" he inquired, and I could detect, as I was meant to, the sarcasm in his voice.

"Roll with the punch, Mr. Prime Minister. Take the heat. Fly to Washington. Sign the treaty. Shake the hand of Arafat's successor the way Rabin shook the hand of Arafat. You can hesitate to show how reluctant you are, but then reach out and grasp his hand and shake it. And together we will try to get him and the Palestinian Authority and the Palestinian police to bring this Abu Bakr to justice. Maybe you can save your people, not to mention the Palestinians, from another Intifada. And maybe, just maybe, you can find, amid all this religious clutter and territorial confusion, a small island of common ground. And on it you and the Palestinians can together construct an edifice of peace. On it you can make history—"

"History," the Prime Minister shot back, "is fiction. Robespierre said that before the blade of the guillotine cut into his neck." He cleared his throat in precisely the same way the Palestinian Authority Chairman cleared his throat and for an instant I lost track of whom I was talking to. Then the Prime Minister sighed and I could hear the pain in his voice—real pain, as opposed to staged anger—as he said, "Alright. We will stand down and stick our necks out once again."

"I owe you an apology," I said.

"For what?"

"For thinking you had only twice as many genes as a fly or a worm."

THIRTY-SEVEN

I N THE APARTMENT ABOVE THE SEAFOOD RESTAURANT ON THE
Jaffa shore, the *katza*, leaner and hungrier and crabbier than
usual, haunted the communications alcove, hovering over the
barefoot contessa as she pecked away with two fingers on the computer keyboard, deciphering the coded reports pouring in from Aza.
Some two dozen Israeli technicians, armed with small black boxes
crystal-tuned to a single ultra high frequency, were systematically
crisscrossing the Strip in unmarked cars driven by Palestinian
Authority detectives. At precisely eighteen minutes to and eighteen
minutes past the hour, they listened—after which the reports began
to filter in. Mobile units 17 through 20 in Khan Yunis, Aza's second
largest city, reported in first: no joy. Mobile units 21 through 24 in
Rafa came through next: no joy. Mobile units 1 through 10 in Aza
City: no joy. Mobile units 11 through 15 on the coast road: no joy.

"What's that?" Elihu demanded as the barefoot contessa typed
out the random five-letter groups coming in from mobile unit 16.
The deciphered message appeared on the screen: "C-o-n-t-a-c-t
o-b-t-a-i-n-e-d" it read, "c-o-o-r-d-i-n-a-t-e-s a-l-e-f d-a-l-e-t." The
message broke off.

Elihu, his nerves raw, snapped, "What's going on?"

"How would I know?" the barefoot contessa asked defensively.

Gnawing on the stem of his unlit pipe, Elihu prowled back and
forth behind her as she filed away at a hang nail. The screen lit up
again with random five-letter groups beamed down to the antennas
on the Jaffa roof, via an American communications satellite, from

mobile unit 16. A moment later, as the barefoot contessa copied the random groups of letters onto the software program, the plain language text appeared below.

"F-a-l-s-e c-o-n-t-a-c-t d-u-e v-e-h-i-c-l-e p-a-s-s-i-n-g P-a-l-i-s-t-i-n-e A-u-t-h-o-r-i-t-y r-a-d-i-o t-o-w-e-r n-o j-o-y r-e-p-e-a-t n-o j-o-y."

The *katza* was on the phone moments later. "You've heard about the Rabbi's secretary?" he asked Baruch over the scrambled line.

"I caught it on CNN. They said something about an anonymous phone call to the Palestinian police leading to the discovery of the body. Hang on—the autopsy report is coming through." Baruch came back on the line. "The murder has Abu Bakr's signature—the cause of death was a .22-caliber bullet fired directly into the base of the skull."

"The mobile units reported in eighteen minutes before the hour. No joy. Not a peep. Something has gone very wrong."

"Sweeney's not in Aza," Baruch said flatly.

The *katza* wasn't ready to let go yet. "The person who phoned Sweeney instructed him to come to Aza. Then we found his car parked at the entrance to Aza."

"I played our tape of the conversation on Sweeney's cell phone again. The Arab who phoned told him to take the Beit Shemesh-Kiryat Gat road down to Aza. I could kick myself for not seeing it before. What did they care how he went to Aza as long as he got there?"

"You think they flagged him down somewhere along the way and whisked him off in another direction, and then drove his car down to Erez for us to find."

"It's possible." Baruch corrected himself with a bitter laugh. "It's *probable*."

The *katza* let this sink in. "If you're right, if Sweeney's not in Aza, that means the Rabbi's not in Aza."

"Abu Bakr's been planting clues with Aza written all over them since the kidnapping," Baruch said. "The Aza bank calendar we discovered on the wall, the kidnapper dressed in a short sleeved shirt, the Mercedes with the dead *mechabel* in the back, the cassette mailed from an Aza post office—everything pointed to Aza. Then Sweeney is invited to Aza—they took it for granted we'd be tapping his phones—and conveniently parks his car at the Erez crossing where we can find it. Now Efrayim's body turns up on a garbage dump outside Aza City."

"If they could smuggle the Mercedes with the *mechabel* back into Aza after the kidnapping, I suppose they could smuggle Efrayim— alive and drugged, or dead and stuffed into a sack—into Aza."

"All roads were meant to lead to Aza," Baruch plunged on. The more he talked, the more he became convinced he was right. "Which meant we'd jump to the logical conclusion that the Rabbi wasn't in Aza. Then we'd smile our superior smiles and assume we were supposed to *jump* to this conclusion, and decide he was in Aza after all. But Abu Bakr was always one jump ahead of us."

"If the Rabbi isn't in Aza, it would explain the no-joy from the mobile units. My God, the Rabbi could be anywhere in Judea or Samaria," Baruch reminded himself. "Where do we start? Nablus? Hebron? Jenin? Tulkarm? Or one of the four hundred and sixty Palestinian villages between them? We don't have enough mobile units to check out an area that size."

"There's still Yussuf Abu Saleh," Baruch reminded Elihu from his Jerusalem office.

"I hate Sa'adat's guts," the *katsa* growled from Jaffa. "It makes me sick to my stomach to think he's on our side. But let's hope he gets Abu Saleh to talk. It may be our last shot at finding Apfulbaum before the Feast of the Breaking of the Fast."

THIRTY-EIGHT

For several days Sa'adat's "technicians" had been avoiding the deputy chief's eye when he wandered into the interrogation chamber, a scented handkerchief delicately pressed to his mouth and nose as the overhead fan stirred the stench that emanated from festering wounds and loose bowels. The doctor who monitored Yussuf's pulse and heartbeat was recommending longer and longer periods of repose and allowing the technicians shorter and shorter working sessions, as they were called. As a result Sa'adat's specialists felt obliged to crowd a lot of "questioning" into the little time they were permitted with the prisoner. "Abu Bakr has abandoned you," one of them would whisper in Yussuf's ear. "Why do you go through hell for him?"

"You have everything to gain, nothing to lose, by giving us the information we seek."

"The Palestinian Authority punishes enemies and rewards friends."

"Wise up. Don't ruin your life for a scoundrel like Abu Bakr."

"I am Koskovic, Asaf . . . a Bosnian . . . mistaken iden—"

The interrogator nodded at the man nearest the door, who tripped the switch, closing the electric circuit. The electrodes attached to Yussuf's testicles hummed. He gagged on the pain as his bruised body danced grotesquely in the air, then, as the current was cut, sagged back and down onto the manacled wrists attached to the hook in the wall. Yussuf shrieked as the weight of his body pulled on his dislocated shoulder. The doctor, his face a mask of professional disinterest, checked the pulse and heart and, with a gesture, ordered the prisoner to be taken down from the wall. When Sa'adat came by a quarter of an hour later he found Yussuf stretched out on the cement of the floor, his eyes fixed on the overhead fan as he sucked short noisy doses of air through his tightly clenched teeth. Sa'adat kept the handkerchief pressed to his mouth and nose as he leaned over the prisoner.

"I have a photograph to show you," he said. "Can you hear me, Yussuf Abu Saleh?"

"Koskovic, Asaf," Yussuf muttered.

Sa'adat produced a color photograph from the breast pocket of his shiny synthetic suit jacket and held it up directly in front of the prisoner's eyes. It took a while for Yussuf to focus on the photograph. Then it took half a minute more for what he saw to register in his brain. He swallowed hard and exhaled and rocked his head from side to side as if he were trying to obliterate an image; undo an event.

"You recognize the corpse?" Sa'adat demanded. "There is no mistake. It is your wife, Maali, dead as a stuffed camel. The photograph was taken as she was being dressed by her father's servants for the funeral."

"How?" Tears filled Yussuf's eyes. "Why?"

"Abu Bakr discovered that she had betrayed you to the Jews and sentenced her to death as punishment," Sa'adat lied. "Open your eyes. Look again. You can see the bruise on her forehead where she was bludgeoned with a blunt instrument. Her death was excruciatingly painful and extremely slow." A moan of pure despair seeped from the back of the prisoner's throat. "Abu Bakr punished your bride," Sa'adat continued. "He is Satan masquerading as the *mujaddid*. He is a false prophet who mocks Islam with his pretensions. You owe him nothing." Sa'adat snapped his fingers at a guard. "A glass of water."

The doctor lifted Yussuf's head and raised a tumbler to his lips. Yussuf felt the water trickle down his throat.

Sa'adat slipped the photograph of Maali into Yussuf's good hand and stood up. "Bring him a mattress, a robe. Wash him. Feed him some broth. I will return in half an hour. When he has had time to study the photograph, he will realize this has all been a terrible mistake and tell us what we want to know, won't you, Yussuf?"

When Sa'adat had gone, the doctor and another technician lifted Yussuf onto his knees so that he could urinate into the plastic bucket. Before scurrying off to look for a mattress and a robe, they helped him settle into a twisted sitting position, his right shoulder against the wall, his left shoulder, swollen and deformed, hunched in front of his chest.

At noon the recorded voice of the *muezzin* summoning the nation of Islam to prayer reached Yussuf's ears. The single guard remaining in the interrogation chamber, a bearded man with a broken nose who happened to be pious, turned to face Mecca and prostrated himself on the floor. Yussuf, his eyes swollen to slits, raised the photograph and studied it. It was Maali, there was no doubt about it. She was laid out on the narrow table on which her father's servants worked dough into loaves. Her face and half-naked body were the color of chalk, her long jet-black hair was combed out behind her. He could make out the dark smudge of a bruise on her forehead. Her lids were closed; the fire smoldering in the eyes he loved more than life and almost as much as the Qur'an had been extinguished. Yussuf crushed the photograph against his chest. In a haze of despair, he could make out a woman shrugging the thin straps of a night dress off her shoulders, drawing the turtleneck over a man's head, pressing herself against his body. "My heart, my husband, welcome home to your bridal chamber, welcome to your marriage bed," the woman murmured.

The memory produced more pain than the electric shocks to his testicles.

Sa'adat had been lying through his teeth, of course. Yussuf had been betrayed into the hands of the Authority's secret police by someone—it could have been the lame shoemaker across from the El Khanqa Mosque, it could have been the Hamas people from Nablus, who were still bitter at him for defecting to the *mujaddid* with half the members of his cell. It could *not* have been Maali, of that he was positive. She would have died before betraying him. And he would die before he betrayed the *mujaddid*.

Yussuf raised his bruised eyes. The remaining guard was still praying, his back to the prisoner. The two electrodes were arranged on a piece of canvas between Yussuf and the guard. The electric wires ran off from the electrodes to a crude, jury-rigged interrupter, and from there to a socket in the wall near the door. Gripping a leather strap hanging from a hook in the wall, Yussuf struggled onto his knees. Then, easing the plastic bucket with urine along with his right hand, dragging his left shoulder and left arm behind him, he crawled soundlessly across the concrete toward the electrodes. He could hear the guard muttering verses from the Qur'an as he reached the electrodes. Muslims believed that it was a sin to commit suicide, but you were perfectly justified in taking the life of someone who was going to betray Islam. If the torture continued, he would end up betraying the *mujaddid*. Yussuf had been wrestling with the moral dilemma for days. Now, for the first time, he could see the straight path stretching before him. In the Book of Deeds it would be recorded by the angel Jibril that Yussuf Abu Saleh had killed someone to prevent him from betraying the nation of Islam. Tonight he would rest in Gardens of Eden at the side of Maali, he would quench his thirst from the pure rivers flowing under them. Tonight he would sit at the right hand of God. Moving warily, he worked the electrodes onto his chest, one pinched to each nipple. He maneuvered the bucket so that it was next to his useless hand, and lowered his fingers into the cool urine.

Yussuf looked up just as the bearded guard turned his head to check on the prisoner. The guard's eyes gaped and he groaned "Noooooooo!" He leaped for the prisoner as Yussuf, mustering the last of his strength and all of his will power, lunged for the interrupter.

THIRTY-NINE

ELIHU FINISHED THE STORY AND THEN FELL QUIET. FOR BARUCH, at the other end of the line in his Jerusalem office, the silence came across as the distant whine of a jet engine idling; this was the constant background sound of the telephone signal being scrambled by an electronic device. Finally the *katsa* came back on the line, drowning out the distinctive whine. "Can you tell me what live electric wires were doing in the same room as the prisoner, for God's sake?"

Baruch said huskily, "You don't want to go there."

"Shit."

"Shit," Baruch agreed. "Elihu, I'd better get something off my chest. As long as I live, don't ever ask me to do business with Sa'adat or anyone like him again."

The *katsa* thought about this. "The Russians have a proverb," he finally said. "*To dine with the devil use a long spoon.* You'll notice the proverb doesn't suggest you shouldn't dine with the devil. On the contrary, it assumes you will one day be obliged to and merely advises you to take a sensible precaution. If you sleep with the devil, use a condom; if you dine with him, use a long spoon. When you decide that it's in the interests of the State of Israel, you'll do business with Sa'adat. So will I. What that day comes, let's be sure to use a long spoon." Elihu could be heard chewing on the stem of his pipe. "Well, I suppose that's that, then. You have to hand it to Abu Saleh—electrocuting yourself under the noses of your jailers takes a certain amount of courage, not to mention courage. So there's nothing left to do now except wait for the Feast of the Breaking of the Fast, after which the Rabbi's body will turn up on some rubbish heap and Abu Bakr will reveal to the world what Apfulbaum told him about the Jewish terrorists in Beit Avram. I hope to God Sweeney surfaces to file his interview with Abu Bakr."

In Jerusalem, Baruch let his eye run down the neatly typed list of names that the brothers Karamazov had left on his desk, along with letters of resignation from the two researchers who were allergic to dust. Next to each name on the typed list was a number; next to the last name was the number one hundred eighty-three. A yellow Post-it had been stuck to the bottom of the page. "Azazel has only now emerged from the basement's dusty bins (in as grumpy a mood as I've ever seen him) with the names of twelve more potential Abu Bakrs, herein attached." Twelve more names were printed on the Post-it immediately over the signature: "Yours 'til the stars cease to shine, Absalom."

Baruch toyed with the idea of filling the *katsa* in on the brothers Karamazov: they were combing the list to see how many of the one hundred and ninety-five short, heavy males on it had had formal medical training. But he let it go. They might come up with forty. Or none. And the Working Group would be right back where it was now, with the director of the Prime Minister's military affairs committee phoning the unlisted number in Jaffa every hour on the hour to pass on the latest pithy comment from the Prime Minister; with surrogates from the Shin Bet and the Mossad quarreling in public over who was responsible for the fiasco; with the leader of the opposition boasting on television talk shows that if he were running things, Islamic fundamentalists would not get away with killing Jews; with a prominent Rabbi from the settlements openly asking how the government could go to Washington and sign a peace treaty with Palestinians who had the blood of Jews on their hands.

"Hang in there," Elihu told Baruch, though he might have been talking to himself. And the distant whine of the electronic device scrambling the conversation was replaced by the banal purr an Israeli phone makes when it offers up a dial tone.

FORTY

ABSALOM STUCK HIS HEAD IN BARUCH'S DOOR. "HERE'S THE latest bulletin from the dust bins," he drawled, slipping into a good imitation of BBC Hebrew. "Azazel came up with a short, heavy ex-convict who had an eye shot out in the Sixty-seven war and sports an eye-patch that makes him look like one of those old advertisements for Hathaway shirts. The Palestinian in question flunked out of a Cairo medical school after two years and wound up opening a pharmacy, which he still operates, in the village of Jalazun near Ramallah. How's that for formal medical training? At one point in his life he was denounced and arrested, but released for lack of evidence. Watch this space for more bulletins."

Baruch raised his wrist so Absalom could see his watch. "Tomorrow is the last day of Ramadan."

"I'm dancing as fast as I can," mewled Absalom. Grimacing as if he had been stung by a bee, he vanished down the corridor.

FORTY-ONE

THE VOLUNTEER NURSES HAD FINISHED DISINFECTING THE WAITING room and were about to lock up for the morning when the woman, in her early twenties and very pregnant, appeared at the door of the clinic. There was an air of desperation about her. She was immediately taken in to see Doctor al-Shaath.

"What is the problem?" he asked.

The young woman, who kept the veil over the lower part of her face as she spoke, stared intently at the bruise on the Doctor's forehead. "My child reaches term in ten days," she said in a low voice.

"Do you have a husband?"

"He is being held in an Isra'ili detention camp in the Negev." She glanced over her shoulder to make sure they were not being overheard. "I came to you because I cannot go to a hospital for the delivery—I am on the Isra'ili wanted list."

"What did you do to merit this honor?"

"I smuggled explosives into Tel Aviv for my cousin Daoud, who blew himself to heaven and twenty Jewish infidels to hell in a shopping mall. It was child's play for me to cross the green line—when the Isra'ili girl soldiers on duty confirmed I was pregnant, they did not search me further. But a man from my village spoke of my role on a portable telephone. He was overheard by the Isra'ilis and I had to flee to avoid arrest." The woman absently kneaded the taut surface of her bulging stomach with the palms of her hands as she squirmed to alleviate the pain in the small of her back. "You cannot refuse me.

I do not wish my baby to be born in a Jewish prison hospital. I ask you to perform a cesarean delivery. Now."

The nurses administered a spinal anesthetic, and the Doctor performed the operation on the stainless-steel table in the clinic's examination room. With his head bent directly over the scalpel and the fingers of his left hand guiding him, he cut through the skin and fatty tissue with a vertical incision that began under the navel and ended above the pubic bone. As the two nurses sponged blood away from the open wound, he cut through the fascia and the lining of the abdominal cavity, exposing the uterus. Working swiftly, he made a crosswise incision in the lower part of the uterus above the bladder. Reaching in, he pressed the bladder downward before enlarging the opening in the muscular wall of the uterus to expose the placenta and the fetus. As the nurse ruptured the sac filled with amniotic fluid she told the mother, "Rejoice—you are bringing into the world a man child." Reaching in with both hands, the Doctor grasped the fetus, worked it free of the uterus and handed it to one of the nurses while the other nurse cut the umbilical cord. The first nurse gripped the baby by its ankles and slapped it lightly on the buttocks. A rich pinkness seeped through the child's etiolated body and he uttered his first tentative gasps, and then bawled at the top of his tiny lungs. On the table, the young woman laughed and cried at the same time. The Doctor removed the placenta, and with the deft gestures of a seamstress, stitched up the layers of wounds. "There is a cot in the small room off the toilet," he told the young woman as he worked. "You will have to remain hidden there for four, perhaps five days. The nurses will take turns staying with you. They will give you medication for the pain you will experience when the anesthesia wears off. You are young and strong and pious—put your trust in God and you will not have any difficulty in coping."

The young woman clutched the newborn baby to her breast. "I know who you are," she blurted to the Doctor. "That our first-born has been brought into this imperfect world by the *mujaddid* brings great honor to my husband, to my family, to my clan. I will call the boy Daoud, after my martyred cousin."

"Raise him to follow the straight path of the Messenger," the Doctor whispered.

"It will be so, I vow this." She held the baby at arm's length to look at it. "Do you think God sees the birth of this child?"

The Doctor said, "The holy book tells us, '*Not a leaf falls, but He knows it.*'"

Moved by the experience of delivering a baby—because of the problem with his eyes he had not performed a cesarean section since his internship years—the Doctor felt the need to give thanks to God before returning to the safe house above the maze of streets in the Christian Quarter. Tapping his bamboo cane on the cobbled pavement, he wandered through alleyways and narrow side streets he had known as a youngster to the Moslem Quarter and the long street known as Bab El-Silsileh, the Street of the Chain. The scent of spices and herbs and dried plants reached his nostrils as he made his way down Bab El-Silsileh to the great doors at the end of it that led onto the Haram-esh-Sharif, the mount where Solomon's temple stood until the Babylonians destroyed it. Looking up, the Doctor could make out brilliant spears of sunlight ricocheting off the golden dome of the Qubbat es Sakhra, the Dome of the Rock. Removing his shoes, walking in his white silk stockings, he climbed the steps into the mosque and circled around on the worn oriental carpets to the other side of the massive boulder from which the Messenger Muhammad had leapt to heaven on his steed el-Burek. It was said that the horse had left the imprint of a hoof on the stone, but the Doctor, with his impaired vision, had never actually seen it.

Prostrating himself on the carpet in front of the boulder, he pounded his bruised forehead against the floor as he recited a verse from the Qur'an. "Nearer to thee and nearer," he intoned. He savored the dull ache in his head and marveled, once again, at the degree to which pain and pleasure, one the handmaiden of death, the other of life, were indistinguishable from each other. In his imagination, he could feel the massive weight of the boulder pressing on the surface of the planet; feel, too, the feather-weight of the baby in his hands as he plucked God's creature from the uterus. What destiny awaited this child? Would he one day fill a knapsack with explosives and, like his martyred namesake, the woman's cousin Daoud, blow himself to bits in order to kill Jews? Did the boy have a choice in the matter or was his fate preordained? Suddenly the Doctor was startled to hear a verse from the Qur'an in his ear; it was as if he were listening to the voice of God. *Does man reckon he shall be left to roam at will? Was he not a sperm-drop spilled?* The Doctor moaned and beat his forehead against the carpet again until he heard a ringing in his ears. The ringing gradually subsided, only to be replaced by another voice; where the first voice had been melodious, with a trace of an echo, this one was bilious and scratchy, and reminded the Doctor of one of those seventy-eight rpm records his father used to play on the family's American Victrola. *It hit me that I wasn't praying,* the voice rasped. *I was actually talking to God! I beat my head against what was left of the retaining wall of the Second Temple until I had bruised my forehead. Oh, I tell you they had to pry my fingers loose from the stones, they had to drag me away.*

It was Isaac, of course, the Doctor's Ibrahimic cousin whom he would sacrifice tomorrow night after the Feast of the Breaking of the Fast—unless God stopped his hand at the last instant the way He had stopped the hand of Ibrahim when he was about to sacrifice Isma'il. The Jews, as usual, had twisted the story; they believed that the patriarch Abraham had been prepared to sacrifice his second born, Isaac, on this very boulder when, as every Muslim knew, it was Ibrahim who had almost sacrificed his first born, Isma'il, at the Kaaba in Mecca. Shuddering, the Doctor climbed onto his knees and, with the help of his cane, pushed himself erect. He reached out in his near blindness and grazed the great cool boulder with the tips of the fingers of his left hand, the ones that guided him when he performed the cesarean section, the ones that searched out the telltale knob of bone behind the ear when he fired a .22-caliber bullet into the brain stem. It dawned on the Doctor, in a sudden flash of lucidity, that the two Ibrahimic tales did not really contradict each other; in subtle ways the two versions of the same story, recounted by cousins, *complemented* each other; breathed life into each other.

The meaning of the story was not to be found in where it took place or who was to be sacrificed; it was that the Messenger Ibrahim was prepared to slay a beloved son with his own hand to demonstrate his perfect love of God.

Could a sightless doctor do less and still claim to be the *mujaddid*?

He had never before looked into the heart of the heart of the person he would sacrifice; never felt an affinity with his victim; never been confronted by someone who was so cocksure he was serving God's will that he encouraged the person who would kill him to take his life.

For heaven's sake, and Islam's, the Doctor would have to steel himself in order not to lose his nerve.

I taught at Harvard for fourteen years before coming to Washington. During all that time I never heard of a society called the Harvard Jewish Faculty Lunch Circle. Which is why I thought the invitation to be their guest speaker was someone's idea of a joke. When they followed up the invitation with a telephone call from the professor emeritus who organized the lunches, I realized the Harvard Jewish Faculty Lunch Circle was not a figment of some prankster's imagination. And in short order I found myself standing before a microphone waiting for a decidedly chilly round of applause to dissipate. I didn't have to wait long. Everyone had stopped eating. Peering out at the faces that stared back at me with open hostility, I took this as a bad, even ominous, sign.

Clearly, the members of the Harvard Jewish Faculty Lunch Circle didn't appreciate an administration that leaned on Israel. Clearly, they didn't think the signing of a peace treaty would lead to peace.

I delivered my usual talk about how American Jews ought to think twice before criticizing the first American president to nudge the Israelis and the Palestinians into a permanent peace arrangement. This arrangement might not be one hundred percent to the liking of the Jewish lobby, I conceded, but it was the best deal Israel was going to get. I recounted how I once asked my 92-year-old father if he enjoyed life. "When you consider the alternatives," he'd answered, "yes." Before you disparage the Mt. Washington peace treaty, I told my audience, consider the alternatives. I was willing to concede that the peace plan was imperfect. But the alternatives to an imperfect peace, I suggested, were eternal hostility, chronic terrorism and occasional war. I reminded my audience of Abba

Eban's famous dictum about how the Arabs never missed an opportunity to miss an opportunity. I invited them to search their memories, not to mention their souls, to see if this didn't characterize Israeli attitudes also.

They searched their memories and their souls and found nothing to support my thesis.

With barely disguised relief I reached the end of my presentation and thanked the members of the Jewish Faculty Lunch Circle for hearing me out. Two younger faculty members at the back of the room started to applaud politely, then stopped when they realized nobody else was joining in.

If looks could kill I would have had, at the very least, indigestion. The moderator called for questions. The first one came from my single ally in the audience, a former student of mine who had served a stint working for the National Security Advisor before returning to Harvard. Could I explain, he asked, knowing full well (because we had once discussed the matter) that I could, what had motivated Arafat to spurn the generous offer that Prime Minister Barak had put on the table during the 1999 Camp David negotiations.

I could and I did; I had been thinking about this for some years and eventually planned to write an essay on the subject. The secret to understanding Arafat, I began, was to realize that the Arab world has been waiting with baited breath for another Saladin, the twelfth century warrior who conquered Richard the Lion Hearted and his Christian army during the Third Crusade. In my view, Arafat saw himself as the reincarnation of Saladin, the paladin who not only expelled the infidels from Jerusalem and Arab lands, but would achieve this liberation through force of arms. The Christians of the first Crusade had conquered Jerusalem and drenched its holy places—the Temple Mount, the Mosque of Omar, even the Church of the Holy Sepulcher—in blood; before the battle was over some 40,000 Muslims—men, women and children— were said to have been slaughtered. Now Saladin, after decades of Arab humiliation, wanted revenge. So when the Crusader knights emerged from the walls of the surrounded city of Jerusalem to negotiate the terms of surrender, Saladin turned his back on the offer. Jerusalem was rightfully his, and he didn't want it to appear that he'd won the city as a result of a negotiated treaty; he wanted to win it by force. Only then would

Arab honor and Arab arms be cleansed of decades of humiliation imposed on them by infidels.

Like Saladin, Arafat wanted what he considered to be rightfully his—in Arafat's case, a Palestinian state on Palestinian land. But after years of humiliation at the hands of the Jews, he wanted to win it by force of arms. And so he used the first excuse that came to hand to launch the second Intifada. The rest, as they say, is history.

The next question came from a brilliant young essayist whose anti-administration diatribes had filled the New York Times *Op-Ed page since the peace treaty had been initialed. It turned out to be more of a tirade than a question. The administration's tilt toward the Arabs, he argued, was driven by hand-me-down State Department prejudices inherited from the British when they were obliged to abandon Mandate Palestine. The Jewish state, surrounded by a sea of Muslims, was engaged in a life-and-death struggle for survival. The peace treaty we'd rammed down Israel's throat obliged the Jews to live side by side with an Islamic people who, in their heart of hearts, wanted nothing less than the destruction of the Jewish state. If things didn't work out along the lines that the Special Assistant to the President for Middle Eastern Affairs expected, the Special Assistant to the President, currently on an extended leave of absence from Harvard, would sign his six-figure book contract and return to the relative safety of the university; the Jews in Israel, on the other hand, would have to fight for their lives.*

Long about then the moderator interrupted to remind the speaker that the ground rules required him to pose a question.

"Sure, I'll pose a question," the young professor shot back. "Who had the bright idea of inviting this eristic apologist for Arab revanchism to speak at our lunch?"

Though I doubted they knew what "eristic" meant, a number of professors nodded in agreement.

The subsequent questions were only slightly less belligerent. Not surprisingly, this collection of faculty was starting to rub me the wrong way. I have a long-standing aversion to people who are more sure of themselves than I pretend to be; this is particularly true when it comes to discussing the Middle East. I'm sorry to report that the rough and ready side of my personality surfaced. I don't really remember the next question; what I do

ROBERT LITTELL

remember is that I launched into a passionate defense of the administration's Middle East approach which, I explained, my voice rising into the edgy octaves reserved for intellectual confrontations, was constructed on a self-evident premise, namely that the United States had promoted a peace process for years and nothing had come of it. So we became convinced that what we needed to promote was a plan, as opposed to a process. The advantage of proposing a plan and not a process is that it denied a veto to the handful of extremists on both sides who didn't want peace; who could, until recently, undermine the process by keeping the caldron aboil with acts of violence.

Contrary to what the members of the Harvard Jewish Faculty Lunch Circle might think, the plan in question didn't simply surface on the President's desk one fine morning; it was meticulously worked out in coordination with our allies in Europe and the moderate Arab states in the Gulf, and most especially with Saudi Arabia, which had demonstrated its moderation and its vision when it called, several years back, for a "just and equitable" solution to the Palestinian refugee problem (as opposed to the infamous "right of return") as part of an overall peace package that included recognition of Israel by the Arab world.

It must have been long about here that the Q and A session started to get out of hand. Tempers flared. Professors were shouting abuse from their tables. It wouldn't have come as a surprise to me if someone had thrown an uneaten dessert in my direction. I may or may not have raised my voice as I batted away their insults. I honestly don't remember. What I do remember is getting in the last word before the microphone was turned off. "You ought to all go out into the real world and put your reputations on the line by influencing policy, and eventually history, instead of wrestling with the really big problems, such as whether James Joyce ever used a semicolon after 1919. Henry Kissinger once summed it up very well: The reason academic infighting is so bitter is that the stakes are so small.*"*

Needless to say, I don't expect to be offered grub by the Harvard Jewish Faculty Lunch Circle anytime soon.

FORTY-TWO

ABSALOM SLUMPED IN THE OTTOMAN THAT THE HOUSEKEEPER'S inventory listed as Victorian and Azazel, with his rabbinical mindset, described as antediluvian.

The heavy lids on his eyes were shut tight but twitching, evidence of a dreadful dream or an inability to doze off while he waited for his sidekick to emerge from the dungeons with the residuum. Damn Azazel and his phobia about elevators—he was no doubt *walking* up the six flights and stopping on each landing to catch his breath, no matter that Absalom, not to mention the entire Israeli intelligence community, was anxiously (and sleeplessly) waiting to see the results of the search that had been based on the tip from the American Sawyer. Absalom had heard on the grapevine where Sawyer had unearthed the detail that the blind Redeemer with the mark of prostration on his forehead was a bona fide medical doctor. Sawyer's "secret" trip to Paris had not gone unnoticed. Israeli Mosad operatives had been watching the Palestinian agents who were watching the woman Lamia Ghuri. Not that it mattered—one *passionaria* less wouldn't seriously distress the Palestinian diaspora—but Absalom wondered how long she would remain among the living now that Sawyer had attracted attention to her.

Wheezing, Azazel pushed through the fire door and shambled across the room to stand over Absalom. "How you can catnap at a time like this is beyond me," he said breathlessly.

Absalom permitted his lids to open lazily as he sat up. "Question of the purity of one's heart," he murmured. "And what pray tell have we here?" he demanded, blinking at the wad of brown index cards clutched in Azazel's soft fist.

"Five."

"Five?"

"Correct. What we have here is five."

"Five what?"

"Easy to see you've been getting forty winks. Wake up, Absalom. Focus. We have narrowed the list down to five, count them, five prime suspects who were all short, heavy, ardently Islamic *medical doctors.*"

"You might have said so in the first place."

"I thought I did."

Absalom sniffed at the index cards. "Baruch, bless his copper's soul, will be tickled fuchsia."

FORTY-THREE

THE *KATSA* DIDN'T PUT MUCH STOCK IN BARUCH'S LEAP OF IMAG-
ination. Even if you managed to swallow the notion of a doctor
who was *blind*, to assume that a blind man could direct a terrorist cell and organize an elaborate kidnapping operation defied reason. Still, with Ramadan drawing to a close, Elihu was ready to
clutch at straws. He picked up Dror in front of the Israeli "Pentagon"
in Tel Aviv and made it to Baruch's Jerusalem office in forty minutes
flat. "His tires never touched the ground," quipped Dror, who was
dressed in faded Army fatigues with tarnished lieutenant colonel bars
and had an Uzi with a folding metal stock slung under his shoulder
and several spare clips tucked into the pouch pockets on his legs.
Baruch, slouched over a desk heaped with the dross from a dozen
ordered-up meals, was leafing through a sheaf of sightings. Working
from the Brothers Karamazov's latest list, he had set in motion—with
the *katsa*'s reluctant accord—surveillance of the targets: the one-eyed
pharmacist in Jalazun; an Israeli Arab urologist with cataract-scarred
eyes who had moved to Nazareth after serving out his sentence in one
of Israel's Negev prisons and now lectured in Nablus when the border was open and his son-in-law was available to drive him; a nearly
blind American of Palestinian extraction who had retired after a
career as an anaesthetist in a Chicago hospital, returning to live off
his pension and American social security checks at his family home
in Ramallah, not far from where he'd been denounced and arrested
as a teenager; a Hebron-based general practitioner who had been
released from an Israeli prison halfway through an eight year sen-

tence after being diagnosed with retinal degeneration; a nearly blind
doctor who had served twelve years in Israeli prisons for the attempted murder of a collaborator and now ran a free clinic in the Old City
of Jerusalem; an extremely near-sighted American-trained Palestinian
psychiatrist who had made use of his own time in Israeli prisons to
publish a seminal study on the effects of incarceration on teenage
Palestinians.

Squads of Israelis, specially chosen because they had been born
and raised in Arab countries and could speak Arabic fluently, had
been dispatched to shadow the targets, all of whom were short,
heavy-set Islamic fundamentalists who had seen the inside of Israeli
prisons. At the same time Elihu's technical teams, equipped with
small black receivers crystal-tuned to a single ultra high frequency
and accompanied by members of the Palestinian Authority police,
had begun crisscrossing the neighborhoods where the six lived and
worked.

So far the only thing they had picked up was what Baruch, in less
frenzied times, would have called the music of the spheres: static.

"Two of the six doctors," Baruch told Elihu and Dror, "went to
prison on my watch. I remember them both. The first one was the
Hebron general practitioner—his name is Ali Abdel Issa. He was the
ringleader of a Hamas *intifada* cell in Hebron which specialized in
booby traps. After several of our soldiers were wounded, Abdel Issa
went underground, abandoning his medical practice, altering his
appearance, never spending two nights under the same roof. We
finally nabbed him when a collaborator told us which of his wives he
would be sleeping with that night. He served four years in prison
before being released in the general amnesty that accompanied the
signing of the Oslo accords with Arafat. Israeli doctors at Hadassah
Hospital, using the latest laser techniques, managed to arrest the retinal degeneration, but they weren't able to restore the lost vision.
Abdel Issa resumed his medical practice in Hebron, where he con-
sults at a local hospital."

Dror, lounging against the window sill, said, "You said you
remembered two."

"The second one is Ishmael al-Shaath. He was picked up in the late seventies at the Allenby Bridge while returning home for Ramadan from his medical studies in Beirut. The Shin Bet had a collaborator who claimed al-Shaath belonged to a Lebanese-based terrorist organization. I was doing reserve duty at the time and happened to be a junior member of the team that questioned him; it was more or less my initiation into the mysteries of interrogation. I remember the chief interrogator, a reserve captain who was a psychoanalyst in civilian life, feeding al-Shaath the usual line about becoming completely dependent on his captors for creature comforts, for news of the outside world. The captain tried everything to break al-Shaath—he told him that he might resist this dependency at first, but that, with time, he would become grateful for every favor, for every kind word, for every smile, for every hour of sleep, for every crust of bread. We were interrogating two dozen Palestinians at any given moment back then. Al-Shaath stood out in the crowd. He had . . . something the others didn't. It took me a while to put my finger on it." Baruch swiveled in his chair to stare out the window. "I remember he was composed, serene, grave, even formal, but that wasn't it. He had a sense of who he was; he had this fire curtain of dignity that protected him from all of our threats and all of our psychological blandishments. If there was a way to ruffle his feathers, we didn't discover it. His eyesight was severely impaired, the result of a childhood malady, if I remember correctly, but you would never have known it talking to him—he conducted himself with unflinching tactfulness, almost as if he didn't want to hurt *our* feelings by pointing our what brutes we were. He calmly denied the charge against him, he nibbled delicately on the crumbs we threw him, but he never allowed a trace of gratefulness to appear on his face or in his comportment."

Dror wanted to know what had happened to al-Shaath.

"We had to let him go for lack of evidence, at which point he apparently discovered the identity of the collaborator who had fingered him and tried to strangle the poor bastard."

Elihu raised his haunted eyes. "Seems as if you ruffled his feathers after all," he said. "He just didn't let you catch a glimpse of the psychological wound."

Baruch nodded tiredly. "I suppose that's so," he said. "Al-Shaath spent twelve years in prison for attempted murder. I sometimes wondered what would have happened to him if we hadn't picked him up, if we hadn't violated his sense of who he was by imposing on him our sense of who we thought he could be."

"It's par for the course in this neck of the woods," Elihu observed. "We all wind up becoming the persona the enemy thinks we are. It's almost as if we don't want to disappoint him." He snorted and shook his large head and lowered his eyes and finished reading one of the sighting reports, then rolled the piece of paper into a ball and lobbed it into Baruch's waste basket, which was overflowing with paper plates and cups. "You really think one of these six blind medical people could be Abu Bakr?"

Baruch's patience was wearing thin. "You have a better idea?"

The two men eyed each other. Dror appealed to Elihu. "I don't see what we have to lose."

"We have limited resources," muttered Elihu. "They could be deployed elsewhere."

"Where?" Baruch demanded.

"Sweeney's not in Aza," Dror reminded the *katsa*.

"Sweeney's body could be in Aza," Elihu said, finally putting into words his darkest fears. His teeth ground in anguish on the stem of the mangled pipe.

A middle-aged woman peering through eyeglasses with bright red frames turned up with a handful of sightings she had torn off the teletype. She added them to the pile on Baruch's desk. "Can I get anyone coffee?" she asked.

Baruch raised a finger in acceptance as he started reading through the new batch of sightings. Elihu nodded, too.

"With or without?" the woman said.

Elihu, staring out the window at the Jewish neighborhoods of Jerusalem, said absently, "With or without what?"

"Sugar. Milk."

"He takes his coffee black, like his mood," Dror told her.

Baruch skimmed another of the sightings. "Damn it! We drew a blank in Ramallah." He looked up, his face frozen in a scowl. "We found out the pharmacist from Jalazun had been sneaking off to Ramallah for lunch every day, so we thought, what the hell, Ramallah is a hot bed of fundamentalism, this could be it. Twenty minutes ago one of our people spotted him talking to a woman in a restaurant who turned out to be his third wife. So much for his daily visits to Ramallah."

The *katsa*, who kept in touch with the barefoot contessa in the communications alcove in Jaffa by satellite phone, said, "In any case, there was no joy from the black boxes deployed this morning in Jalazun or in Ramallah, so that more or less eliminates your one-eyed pharmacist and your anaesthetist from Chicago."

Baruch glanced at the clock on the wall—he had the sinking sensation of watching sand flowing through the waist of an hour glass, with no way of slowing it down. He snatched another sighting off the pile. Maybe his hunch about formal medical training had led them up a dead end street; maybe Abu Bakr was still one jump ahead of them. "Ah—here's my old friend al-Shaath. A pregnant woman turned up at his clinic in the Old City as it was closing. A nurse let her in and then locked the door. The doctor and one of the two nurses emerged an hour and a quarter later. The pregnant woman and the second nurse never came out. Tapping the ground ahead of him with a long bamboo cane, Doctor al-Shaath walked down the Street of the Chain, Bab El-Silsileh, and through the doors at the foot of the street onto the temple mount. He disappeared into the Dome of the Rock for seventeen minutes, then made his way back along Bab El-Silsileh to the Christian Quarter. Near the Church of the Holy Sepulcher, the streets filled with pilgrims and the doctor, mingling with them, vanished down a maze of alleyways. Our people nosed around—none of the shop owners near the clinic seemed to know where al-Shaath lived or how to get in touch with him in an emergency. The head of the surveillance team sent word to your boys with the black boxes, Elihu. He suggested they scrub the area between Christian Quarter Road and the New Gate, which is where the good doctor was last seen."

Dror ducked out of the room to use the secretary's phone; if Baruch was on to something, there would be precious little time to organize a raid. To cut corners, Dror had decided to bring forty-five members of the elite General Staff commando unit into Jerusalem, but he wanted to do it without attracting attention. The last thing they needed was for some smart-ass journalist to realize a raid was in the offing. It wouldn't take a genius to figure out why. The men from the commando unit were stashing their weapons and uniforms and bullet-proof vests and night vision goggles in the trunks of private automobiles and filtering into the city in twos and threes, assembling at a movie theater in the German Quarter owned by the unit's one-time executive officer. Dror rang through to his adjutant, who had set up a command post in the theater manager's office. All but seven members of the putative raiding party had already turned up; the men were oiling their weapons, sharpening their knives, calling their wives or girl friends on mobile phones, playing gin, dozing. One had brought along a laptop computer and was working on his thesis for a master's degree in art history. "We have a complete set of atlas slides of Samaria and Judea ready at hand," the adjutant told Dror. "Any word on where we might strike?"

"It could be anywhere—or nowhere," Dror said.

The secretary with the red-framed eyeglasses returned with a new batch of sightings, along with a tray filled with Cokes in paper cups and tuna sandwiches on dark rye bread. Baruch pored over the sightings before slipping them across the desk to Elihu. Two more of the six Abu Bakr candidates seemed to have been eliminated: the Israeli-Arab urologist with cataract-scarred eyes who lived in Nazareth had been tracked down to a sanatorium in Akko, where he was recuperating from a hip operation; the American-trained psychiatrist had been abroad since early January, giving a seminar on Palestinian teenagers at Alfred University in upstate New York. His lecture series was entitled: "Growing Up With a Chip on Your Shoulder."

The satellite phone in the *katsa*'s pocket purred from time to time as the barefoot contessa checked in with more no-joy reports. Hebron had been swept from one end to the other at eighteen minutes to and eighteen minutes past the hour. All told, four transmission cycles had been covered without detecting a squeak on the appropriate ultra high frequency.

The atmosphere of cranky irritability in Baruch's office must have been contagious. Staffers strolling past in the corridor talked in the muted undertones reserved for hospitals and cemeteries. Somewhere on the floor a telephone shrilled and a voice could be heard bellowing, in English with a heavy Israeli accent, "This is *not* the Jewish gay rights league, this is *Mishteret Yisra'el,* the national police." A woman cried out in Hebrew: "*Sheket*—quiet." Oblivious to everything, Baruch read and reread the most recent batch of sightings. He talked on a scrambled phone line with a field coordinator in Hebron, then swiveled to stare out the window. The sky had turned raw and a cold rain squall had begun to pelt the city. He watched the buses and cars crawling soundlessly through the downtown streets. Focusing on the drops trickling like tears across the dirty window pane, he decided that the weather fitted the mood in Israel perfectly: everyone he knew was depressed. With or without a peace treaty, Israelis had grave doubts about the Palestinian Authority's ability to police its own fundamentalists, and were ready to settle for something as simple and as invigorating as spring, though even that seemed a world away. The memory of the acacias bursting golden, the wild anemones bleeding red seemed to belong to a Jerusalem on another planet, and not the city in which they waited out the waning of winter and the advent of the ominous Ramadan deadline.

Just before midnight, the night-shift secretary came in with a single sighting hot off the teletype. Baruch actually groaned as he read it. "Ali Abdel Issa, the Hamas organizer from Hebron who specialized in booby traps, was rounded up by the Authority's cops after the bus bombings last year—he's been in one of Sa'adat's Jericho cells for the past eight months. That eliminates him."

Dror said, "There's still that blind doctor—"

"Al-Shaath."

"—who disappeared in the back streets of the Old City early this afternoon."

Elihu waved his pipe. "The last place they'd stash a hostage is under our noses in the Old City."

"The last place is often the best place," Baruch noted, but he wasn't able to muster much conviction in his voice.

Dror shrugged. Technically speaking, the prospect of launching a surprise raid on short notice in the narrow labyrinthine streets of the Old City didn't appeal to him; getting the troops into position without attracting the attention of the kidnappers seemed almost impossible.

At twenty-two minutes after two, the satellite phone in Elihu's pocket purred. The *katsa* lifted the receiver to his ear. Dror was dozing on a couch. Baruch raised his head off the desk. He could hear the sharp buzz of the barefoot contessa's nasal whine coming through the telephone, but he couldn't make out what she was saying. Suddenly Elihu's lidded eyes flicked open. He plucked the stem of the dead pipe out of his mouth. "Tell them to triangulate," he ordered very quietly. Then he killed the connection. "I owe you one," he told Baruch. "They picked up the signal at eighteen past the hour—a single two-hundred-meter vector. It was coming from the maze of buildings north of the Greek Orthodox Patriarchate Road and east of the Hospice on Casa Nova."

"It fits!" Baruch exclaimed. "From the top floor of one of those buildings, Yussuf Abu Saleh could have seen the green shirt hoisted by the lame shoemaker across from the El Khanqa Mosque." He melted back into his chair, drained of everything except hope, and let his eyes roam over a map of the Old City. "Finding the Rabbi was the easy part," he muttered.

FORTY-FOUR

A T THE MOVIE THEATER IN THE GERMAN QUARTER, DROR conferred once again with his second in command and the officer in charge of planning, then hefted himself onto the stage and gazed out at the intent faces of the young soldiers who would soon be going into combat. They had stacked their array of assault rifles and sniper rifles and submachine guns, along with the cartons filled with all manner of grenades and plastic explosives, against a wall, and settled onto the old folding wooden seats in the front rows. The officers among them had pistols fitted with silencers tucked into webbed shoulder holsters. All forty-five members of the General Staff commando unit were battle-hardened veterans, and had undergone paratrooper and special forces training. Within the Israeli Army, they were the elite of the elite.

The commando unit's former XO, who owned the theater, sat beside Elihu and Baruch in the first row of the balcony, his large hands folded pensively on the low brass rail in front of him, his unshaven chin on his hands. He was still fit from daily stints of bicycle riding and would have traded the deed to the theater, not to mention his soul, for a chance to take part in the raid, but he knew better than to ask. Behind him and to the left sat two lean lieutenant generals from the General Staff and the paunchy civilian in charge of Shin Bet field operations. Peering down from the last row in the balcony was Zalman Cohen, the director of the Prime Minister's military affairs committee, with his famous arid smile draped across his round lecherous face.

Dror tapped a finger nail on a microphone to make sure it was alive. "Gentlemen," he said. The word "gentlemen" echoed back from two enormous wall speakers. Dror fiddled with the gain knob, then tried again. "We'll be going into the Old City as soon as it is dark, so we have twelve hours to prepare this raid down to the last minute detail." He cleared his throat; public speaking was not his cup of tea. "We'll begin with an overview of the operation. Then we will take it apart and examine it piece by piece and put it back together again. We'll take it apart a second time, and a third. We'll keep taking it apart until the components are as familiar to us as the thirty-seven bits of metal in an assault rifle. Then we'll load our weapons and go out and get the job done."

Dror nodded at a corporal sitting behind the slide projector set up on a table. The first slide, an aerial view of the Old City, appeared on the overhead screen. "We have reason to believe that Abu Bakr, almost certainly accompanied by several terrorists, we'd be asses to think otherwise, is holed up in a safe house here," Dror said, tapping the screen with a long pointer. "We have no way of knowing for sure, but we expect—we hope to God—that the hostage, I. Apfulbaum, will be there, too. We know for sure that the American journalist Sweeney is in this building. Okay. The target building, which is forty meters off Greek Orthodox Patriarchate Road, is situated in a maze of alleyways and courtyards and passages, some of them on ground level, some of them over rooftops."

The livid shrapnel scar across Dror's cheek burned like a neon sign. The soldiers hung on his words. Many of them had been on raids with him before; along the Litani River, to the Bekaa valley, to Iqlim el Tuffah in southern Lebanon. The others knew him by reputation; it was said he'd been the second in command on the *katsa's* fabled swansong raid into Nablus at the time of the second *intifada*. "Abu Bakr and the people with him are hardcore fundamentalists and terrorists," Dror continued. "They slaughtered four Jews when they ambushed the Rabbi's convoy, they murdered the Rabbi's secretary in cold blood when the first deadline expired. So I don't need to tell you this will be bloody. The purpose of this briefing is to make sure any blood shed comes from their bodies, and not ours. If you'll give me

the second slide . . . the target is the large building in the center of
this cluster of buildings. It is an Arab bathhouse that was abandoned
when we occupied the Old City after the Sixty-seven war. In this old
photograph, you can make out the back door and the loading port.
I'll take the next slide. Okay. What we have here is a rough sketch of
the building based on a description of it in a nineteen-fifties guide
book, as well as the recollection of one of the officers whose unit
secured the area in Sixty-seven. As you can see, there are four floors.
The ground floor is a warren of corridors and changing rooms, along
with the reception room and an inner office. These spaces are likely
to be deserted. There are two staircases—I should say there were two
staircases the last time anybody looked—leading to the tiled baths on
the second floor. In the back of the building, there used to be a narrow flight of stairs leading to the third floor and several furnished
two-room apartments which were used by important Arabs visiting
Jerusalem. We're going on guesswork now, but we believe that Abu
Bakr will have barricaded himself into one of the apartments on the
third floor, mainly because the only toilets, aside from the ones in the
changing rooms on the ground floor, are there, and he will have to
use a toilet from time to time." This drew a nervous laugh. "There is
a crawl space above these offices and apartments which can be
reached only by a ladder leading to a trap door. We have no idea
what's up there, but we will assign two men to cover the trap door,
and three others to secure the crawl space once the raid has gone public, not a moment before."

Signaling for the next slide, Dror took a sip of water as it was
being focused on the screen. "You will all be issued briefing books
containing printouts of these slides when we get around to discussing
actual squad assignments. For the moment we want to give you the
structure of the raid. We propose to set up blocking squads on the
alleyways here, here, here and here. Also at the three doors and the
loading ramp of the bathhouse. Also on the roofs here, here and here.
We'll post the sniper unit here on the roof of the Hospice Casa Nova,
where they'll have a good line of sight on the target building. Once
the escape routes have been blocked off and the snipers are in position, the assault party will come in over the roofs from the northwest.

To avoid friendly fire casualties, everyone participating in the raid will be issued a arm band, to be worn above the elbow on the left arm. These red arrows on the slide mark the route the assault party will take up from the street level and over the roofs. There will be sixteen troopers in the assault party, which I will lead. My second will bring up the rear and instantly take over command if I am put out of action. My third will follow twenty meters behind, with the medical unit, and take over if the second is put out of action. The first squad in will be equipped with night vision glasses and secure the stairway. In operations of this nature, everything—*everything*—depends on achieving surprise. Our only chance to attain surprise, which is essential if we are to free the Rabbi, is to break into the safe house without firing a shot. If the first squad encounters anybody, and by that I mean *any body*"—this elicited another titter—"you will eliminate him or her with silenced pistols or knives, depending on your distance from the body in question. We will not, I repeat, *not* take prisoners at this stage—or any stage—of the operation. The second squad coming up behind will be armed with explosives. In all of our past raids on terrorists hideaways, there have been doors, often reinforced with steel plating, to break through. The explosive experts will tape their plastic, fitted with radio-detonated fuses, to the door—an operation that should take no longer than two minutes—at which point they will fall back and let the actual assault squad though. They'll blow away the door and storm into the hideaway. Okay. Any questions so far?"

"Will there be any windows in the apartment through which light can enter or terrorists can escape?"

"The original cassette the terrorists mailed to us after the kidnapping showed the Rabbi and his secretary sitting in front of a bricked-in window. Again, we're guessing, but we think they will have bricked in the windows so that nobody outside would notice signs of life in the apartment, such as an electric light at night." Dror made a tick on a file card, and looked up. "That brings us to whom we can expect to find in this safe house." A full-face and profile of Rabbi Apfulbaum filled the screen. "Study these faces closely. You'll each get copies. Look at them all day. Memorize them. Get to know them better than you know the faces of your father or brother. Make allowances for the fact that Apfulbaum will have been subjected to a lengthy inquisition. He is fifty-three years of age, five foot nine, extremely thin—around one hundred and thirty pounds—stoop shouldered, with oversized ears and a prominent nose. He will probably be unshaven and disheveled. Without his eyeglasses, which were found at the scene of the kidnapping, he is practically blind, so there's a good chance he will be squinting. He speaks English and Yiddish and Hebrew and Arabic."

Sweeney's image materialized on the screen, full-face and profile. "This is the American journalist. His name is Max Sweeney. He is forty-three years of age, tall, lean, with curly hair and a high forehead and prominent cheek bones. He has a way of listening with his head tilted to one side because he is deaf in his left ear. He speaks English and understands a few words of Hebrew, but not enough to carry on a conversation. The assault squad will accordingly consist entirely of soldiers fluent in English. In the confusion of combat you may want to order the Rabbi and Sweeney to hit the deck. All such instructions will be given in English."

"Is the American being held hostage along with the Rabbi? Will the terrorists kill him if they get the chance?"

Dror avoided looking at Baruch and Elihu in the balcony. "We don't know the answer to that one." He nodded for the next slide. "This is the only known photograph of Abu Bakr, the leader of the so-called Islamic Abu Bakr Brigade. His real name is Ishmael al-Shaath. The police mug shot was taken when he was arrested for attempted murder twenty-three years ago. He was twenty-three years of age at the time, which makes him forty-six today. He is a medical doctor who runs a free clinic in the Old City. He is short and heavy-set. He may be dressed in a western style suit jacket over a long Arab robe. He wears thick eyeglasses, but even with them he is said to suffer from acute tunnel vision that renders him functionally blind. Don't be deceived by the fact that he is nearly blind—he spent twelve years in prison for attempted murder. We now know that after his release he executed, with his own hand, twenty-four collaborators by shooting them at point-blank range in the brain. He personally exe-

cuted the driver of the Rabbi's automobile following the kidnapping,
as well as the Rabbi's secretary. He will in all likelihood be armed
with a .22-caliber pistol, but he can only use it accurately at very
close ranges." Dror paused. "Abu Bakr is to be shot on sight, along
with any Palestinians found in the hideaway."

"Does that include females?"

"That includes females, yes."

"Does that include children?"

Dror drew a deep breath. "What does it mean, children? Any
person found in the hideaway will be an active member of the Islamic
Abu Bakr Brigade, and as such, armed. If you don't shoot them they
will surely shoot you."

"You said that Abu Bakr operates a clinic. Why don't we capture
him when he goes to work?"

"It will be too late. The deadline for murdering the Rabbi is the
Feast of the Breaking of the Fast, which marks the end of Ramadan.
Ramadan ends and the feast begins at sundown tonight, which will
occur at exactly eighteen hundred zero six. We will start to move into
position when darkness settles over the Old City, which will be at
approximately nineteen hundred hours. The full moon will rise at
nineteen forty-eight. That gives us forty-eight minutes of total darkness to get in and get out again."

"If the deadline for killing the Rabbi is set for the end of
Ramadan, what makes you think the terrorists will hold off another
two hours?"

Dror glanced at Zalman Cohen in the back of the balcony. "The
Prime Minister has scheduled a press conference for fifteen hundred
hours today—he will announce that the government, bowing to
pressure from the United States, has agreed to meet the demands of
the Abu Bakr Brigade; El Sayyid Nosair, the Palestinian serving a life
sentence for killing Rabbi Meir Kahane, along with the Palestinian
prisoners, will be released at the Lebanese border at twenty-hundred
hours tonight. We expect the terrorists to hold off killing the Rabbi
until then, by which time the raid will be over."

A short soldier in the back row stood up. "You mentioned that
the apartments on the third floor of the bathhouse had two rooms.

What if we break through the first door and find a second door?"

"That's a good question," Dror said. "If Abu Bakr and his hostage, or hostages, are barricaded behind a second door, they will obviously know we are there after we blow open the first door. At that point we will try to talk the terrorists into surrendering—we will offer them their lives in exchange for the lives of the two men in the room. The explosive team will tape charges to the second door while we engage Abu Bakr in a dialogue. Depending on his reaction, the terrorists will either open the door and walk out with their hands over their heads, or we will blow our way into the second room and hope for the best."

"In the unlikely event that Abu Bakr and the others surrender, do we at this point take prisoners?"

"No. If we take prisoners, the fundamentalists will only take new hostages and offer to exchange them for these prisoners. Don't lose sight of the fact that Abu Bakr is a serial murderer. Those who live by the sword die by the sword. As far as the world will know, they were killed when we stormed the hideaway to free the Rabbi and the American journalist."

"Will the Rabbi and the American journalist have any way of knowing we are coming in? I'm asking this because if they had some way of knowing, they might attack the terrorists, or somehow divert them long enough for us to get through the door. At the very least they might hide under a table when the shooting starts . . ."

"The answer to your question is: hopefully, yes. Without going into details, we have a method of warning them that a raid will take place. On the other hand, we cannot count on them assisting us in any way whatsoever. We have to go in and do the job ourselves."

"How will the different squads communicate with each other during the raid?"

"They won't. Squads will know their roles so well they will not have to communicate with each other. Under no circumstance will anyone break radio silence until the operation is completed." Dror looked around. "If there are no further—"

In the back of the balcony, Zalman Cohen waved a pudgy hand. "You mentioned at the start of the briefing that everything depended on achieving surprise. How are you planning to slip forty-five men—forty-seven including you and Baruch, who, as I understand it, will be going in with the medical team—into the Old City without someone phoning up CNN to tell them a raid is in progress?"

At that moment, as if on signal, two soldiers pushing dollies with large cartons on them came through the swinging doors at the back of the theater. Dror flashed a grim smile. "We will get into the Old City without CNN, or the Arabs, knowing about it . . . by converting to Christianity."

FORTY-FIVE

d al-Fitr, THE FEAST OF THE BREAKING OF THE FAST, GOT UNDER way as the cry of the *muezzin*, broadcast from the minaret of the El Khanqa Mosque, drifted over the roofs of the Old City. "*Allahu Akbar, Allah Akbar.*" Shuffling along unsteadily on his numb legs, Rabbi Apfulbaum kept his right hand glued to the Doctor's left shoulder as he followed him into the outer room of Abu Bakr's safe house. "The blind leading the blind," quipped the Doctor as he steered his guest toward the low round table in the corner.

"Oh, God, I feel like a fish out of water," the Rabbi groaned, massaging a wrist where the manacle had rubbed off the hair and chafed his pasty skin. He ironed creases out of his rumpled jacket with his palms, then threaded the fingers of one hand through his unkempt hair as he allowed Ishmael to gently push him down onto a cushion next to the table.

"It is perfectly normal for you to feel disoriented," the Doctor said, hiking his long robe and settling onto the cushion next to him. He waved Sweeney toward a cushion across the table. The el-Tel brothers, looking ill at ease (neither of them had ever broken bread with a Jew), took their places opposite the Rabbi. Aown removed the ancient British Webley from his belt and placed it on the floor near his thigh. Petra, who was cooking rice and zucchini and lamb chops on a small portable stove heated by a canister of camping gas, hummed to herself. She seemed very light-hearted. "The feast will be ready in five minutes, please," she called shyly.

The Rabbi squinted in confusion. "What feast will be ready in five minutes? Who's got an appetite at a time like this? For God's sake, Ishmael, let's not drag this out."

Leaning toward the Rabbi, the Doctor patted the back of his thin wrist. "Isaac, I have magnificent news for you."

Apfulbaum's lips produced a lopsided smirk. "I know, I know. Tonight I will sit at the right hand of God."

"It is not that at all," the Doctor burst out. "The Isra'ilis have given in to our demands. Your Prime Minister himself made the announcement during a public press conference at three this afternoon."

Sweeney cocked his good ear. "You're sure of what you say?"

"I would have told you sooner," the Doctor plunged on, "but I wanted to avoid torturing you with false hopes. I waited for the international press to confirm it. The radio has been filled with the news all afternoon. The Jews talk about nothing else, *ya'ani*. The opposition party denounces the Prime Minister for ceding to terrorism. The mother of a soldier excarnated by a suicide bomber says the life of every Jew is sacred and sides with the Prime Minister. Petra even heard someone grumbling over the Army wavelengths about the government's shameful capitulation to Islamic terrorists. In any case, I thought it would be a marvelous surprise for you when you sat down to our Feast of the Breaking of the Fast."

The Rabbi, swaying slightly from side to side, appeared dazed. He opened his mouth and rolled his eyes and started giggling. Soon he was laughing uncontrollably. He laughed until his chest heaved and sobs emerged from the back of his throat and tears streamed down his sunken cheeks. "Ishmael, *Ishmael*," he moaned, and he shook his head and laughed some more. Across the table, the el Tel brothers exchanged puzzled looks. The Rabbi breathed deeply and blotted his eyes on the back of his slit sleeve. When he was able to find his voice, he said, "Being blind is no excuse for not seeing the handwriting on the wall. The Israelis are trying to trick you—"

"Perhaps I did not explain myself well, Isaac. They're not saying they are *going* to negotiate, they're not stalling for time. They are saying, in front of foreign journalists, in front of television cameras, in front of the world, that El Sayyid Nosair and the Palestinian prisoners will be released at the Lebanese frontier at eight o'clock tonight—that is less than two hours from now." The Doctor jammed one of his Palestinian Farids into his mouth, lit it with a match and took several shallow puffs. "How could they lie about that, *ya'ani?* The whole world will be watching! When the prisoners reach the Lebanese side of the frontier, the Arab journalists will interview them. As soon as we hear their voices, we will begin making arrangements for your release." The Doctor reached over and curled his fingers around the Rabbi's gaunt neck and pulled him closer so that the bruises on their foreheads were almost touching. "You will surely sit at the right hand of God, my friend," he said quietly. "But thanks to God, it will not happen tonight. Tonight you will celebrate with us the end of the holy month of Ramadan and the beginning of the rest of your long life."

Sweeney remarked, "You actually look disappointed, Rabbi. Anyone else would jump for joy—"

An eyelid twitched in the Rabbi's face. Veins stood out in his neck. "Who is this joker, Ishmael?" Before the Doctor could respond, Apfulbaum's claw-like fingers snaked out and clamped onto his wrist. "You are being naive, *ya'ani*. Never trust a Jew, *ya'ani*." He cackled wildly at his own little joke, then caught himself with a gasp. "You set a deadline, *ya'ani*. Ramadan has come and gone, *ya'ani*. It's the moment of truth. Put up or shut up. I'm betting into four spades, so what. I'll see your twenty and raise you twenty."

From Petra's Army radio came the static-charged voice of an Israeli reporting, in the shorthand phrases of military Hebrew, from somewhere in the occupied zone. "Arabs . . . celebrating . . . fireworks," the soldier said. "Teenagers . . . hundreds . . . dancing . . . barn fire . . . chanting Abu Bakr, *mujaddid*, Abu Bakr, *mujaddid*. We can hear them up here . . . hills above the town."

The Rabbi's eyes, bulging and dark, darted in the direction of the green radio on the table near the door. "So what's that supposed to be?" he wanted to know.

"We monitor the Army's wavelengths," the Doctor explained, flicking ashes onto the floor.

Apfulbaum snorted in derision. "Oh, for God's sake, Ishmael, they *know* you monitor their wavelengths. The last thing they're going to do is tell you what they're up to *on the radio*."

Petra added the lamb chops, along with the zucchini and olives, to the steaming pot of couscous. Tugging the scarf over her head down around her neck, using the end of it to grip the handles of the pot, she came over to the table and began spooning food into each bowl.

The nostrils in the Rabbi's hawk-like nose flared as he sniffed at his bowl. Very pleased with himself, the Doctor announced, "In your honor, Isaac, the Feast of the Breaking of the Fast is kosher." He peered across the table in Sweeney's direction. "Be sure to include that detail in your story, Mr. Sweeney. 'Arab terrorists serve kosher supper to Jewish hostage.'" He edged the bowl closer to Apfulbaum. "I instructed Petra to purchase the lamb from a kosher butcher in the Jewish Quarter of the Old City. I thought that combining your ritual with mine would give pleasure to you."

Petra, who had caught the word *kosher*, said in Hebrew, "Even the olives are kosher, Mr. Rabbi. They must be because I bought them in the Jewish shop next to the butcher."

It took a moment for all this to sink in. Then it dawned on Apfulbaum where he was being held prisoner. "I assumed I was in Aza . . ."

"In the eighth century, *ya'ani*, Imam Ali said, '*If you want to see a corner of paradise, regard Jerusalem.*'"

The Rabbi said emotionally, "The Babylonian Talmud tells us: '*Of the ten measures of beauty that came down to the world, Jerusalem took nine.*'"

"If the windows were not bricked in," the Doctor said, "you could look out on the holy city of your King David."

"I bless God, I thank you, Ishmael. If I am to die, let me die in Jerusalem."

"Let us talk no more of dying, *ya'ani*." Raising a glass of grape juice, the Doctor proposed a toast in Hebrew. "*Ad meya v-esream*— may you live to a hundred and twenty."

The Rabbi tossed a single bony shoulder. "You'll see, Ishmael," he said sulkily. "Eight o'clock will come and go, and nine, and ten, and there will be no Palestinian prisoners talking to reporters on the Lebanese side of the border. Ha! This will turn out to be the last supper after all."

Sweeney picked up a lamb chop with his fingers and began to nibble on it. He wondered if he would be able to reconstruct the conversation from memory. It was surreal. The blind leading the blind, the Doctor had said. The mad leading the mad would have been closer to the truth. He decided to needle the Rabbi. "If this is the last supper," he ventured, "that makes you the Messiah. From a journalistic point of view, this has to be the scoop of the century. The Islamic Renewer and the Jewish Messiah in the same room! At the same table!"

Apfulbaum inched his cushion closer to the Doctor and the two men gazed into each other's unseeing eyes. "Ishmael," he declared with fervor as saliva seeped from the corner of his mouth, "is surely the long-awaited Renewer for whom the Islamic world is waiting with baited breath. As for me being Messiah . . ." The Rabbi's jaw trembled. He hauled the silver worry beads from his pocket and began working them through his bony fingers. "I have never told this to anyone before, Ishmael. When I was a Talmudic student in a Brooklyn yeshiva, there were some who whispered I was Messiah. When the others around me were still learning to read, I gave interpretations of Torah that flabbergasted my teachers. It was said of me that if I started out in a storm, to the left of me was rain, to the right of me was rain, but where I was there was only sunshine. It was said of me that if I started out on Friday and the sun set while I was on the road, to the left of me was *Shabbat*, to the right of me was *Shabbat*, but where I was it was still Friday. My father, Apfulbaum the grocer at the A & P on Albany Avenue, God rest his soul, had a nickname for me as a child. *So ask the Eastern Parkway Messiah*, he'd say when he didn't know the answer to something." The Rabbi swatted a large tear from the corner of an eye with the back of his hand. "I'm not saying I am Messiah, I'm not saying I'm not, I'm only saying—what am I saying?—*that it is within the realm of possibility*. Ha! The Renewer and the Messiah, side by side! Think of the *puissance* of it! Together we could set the world back on the straight path. It goes without saying but I'll say it, what do I have to lose? Jesus of Nazareth was a false Messiah, the Koran tells us that, all Muslims are convinced, all Jews, too."

The Doctor ground out his cigarette on the sole of a shoe and dropped the filter tip into an ashtray on the table. "There is no place in Islam for a god who permits his enemies to execute him on a cross," he exclaimed, caught up in Apfulbaum's fantasy.

"No place in Judaism, either," the Rabbi agreed eagerly. "The putative son of God, the King of the Yids, oy, oy, he maybe never walked on water but he got one part of the myth right: *Messiah has to die for his people!*"

"What does he babble about?" Aown asked his brother in Arabic.

"It can only be the odor of kosher food that has unsettled him," Azziz replied.

Sweeney looked from the Rabbi to the Doctor and back again. Clearly, the constant menace of a bullet in the brain had pushed Apfulbaum over the edge. It was common, in situations like this, for the victim to fall in love with his captor as a way of protecting himself. But the Rabbi seemed to have fallen in love with death. The Renewer! The Messiah! They were both mad as hatters.

The Rabbi, his voice pitched half an octave higher, rambled on. "I'm not perfect, who is? But you don't have to be perfect to be Messiah. King David wasn't perfect. When he coveted Bathsheba, he excarnated the competition by rerouting her husband, Uriah, to certain death in the forefront of the battle."

"Even the holy Messenger Muhammad was not perfect," the Doctor observed. "The Qur'an, 93:7 if my memory serves, records that God found the Prophet *erring* and gave him guidance."

"Perfection," the Rabbi noted, smacking his lips in satisfaction at the end of each phrase, "is like the horizon. You race in a motor boat towards it from morning till night . . . at the end of the day it's still beyond reach."

"That is beautifully put, *ya'ani*."

The Rabbi turned on the journalist. "You are not in the same league as Ishmael and me, Mr. whatever your name is. You and I don't talk the same language. The so-called Western liberalism about which you're so smug is *man*-oriented. Its pride and glory are Hollywood films and slick magazines with naked ladies on the cover and upwardly mobile Wall Street yuppies clambering over each other to get to the top of the garbage heap known as Western civilization. And at the top of the heap is what? Oy, I'll tell you what. At the top of the heap are penthouse apartments with wrap-around stereo speakers playing dirty rap music, and dope and divorce and abortion on demand, not to mention extra-marital monkey business and same sex marriages. *Same sex marriages!* My God, what will they invent next?" The words were spilling out so fast the Rabbi had difficulty catching his breath. "So what, in your opinion," he said, gasping for air, "is America's greatest contribution to the Middle East, Mr. whatever your name is? I'll tell you what. Air-conditioned supermarkets with junk food on one side of the aisles and health food on the other." Apfulbaum lowered his voice. "For God's sake, don't print this in your newspaper but an Israeli, when he wants good food, eats in an Arab restaurant."

The Doctor rocked back and forth in agreement. "An Arab who wants good medical care goes to a Jewish doctor. This is well known."

"And what today stands against your man-oriented Western liberalism?" Apfulbaum demanded, cocking his head. "I'll tell you what." He hissed like a snake. "Torah Judaism, and its kissing cousin, Koranic Islamism, stand against it. Torah Judaism and Koranic Islamism are *Allah*-oriented. Their pride, their glory are God and God's word. At the top of the heap is Paradise—"

"*'Gardens of Eden,'*" the Doctor breathed, "*'underneath which rivers flow.'*" He peered through the haze of his impaired vision, trying to perceive the Rabbi's saintly features as he added, "*'God is well-pleased with them who fear the Lord.'*"

Apfulbaum's head bobbed deliriously as he batted the compliment back. "*'Blessed is he who blesses you,'*" he whispered huskily.

"You are talking too much and not eating," the Doctor chided his neighbor. "Here—you will need your strength. Think of the press conferences you will hold after your release. Think of the talk shows you will be invited to. You will have the entire world at your feet."

He edged the bowl closer to the Rabbi. Apfulbaum picked up a fork and toyed with his food. He filled his mouth with couscous and a morsel of zucchini, then spit it back into the bowl. He was too excited to swallow. Glancing in the direction of Petra, he mumbled an apology with a well-turned Arabic phrase. She pulled the scarf up around her face as her eyes wrinkled at the corners in a pleased grin.

At a nod from the Doctor, Petra cleared away the bowls and set out kitchen tumblers and a pewter pot filled with steaming sweetened tea. She sank cross legged onto the floor behind the Doctor as he filled the tumblers. He began pouring with the spout touching the glass and deftly swooped up the pot until the tea was cascading through the air into the tumbler. He could tell from the sound when the glass was full. From somewhere in the streets below came the electric whine of a loudspeaker. Gradually the clamor grew louder and more distinct. Everyone around the table heard it. Conversation stopped. Sweeney angled his head, straining to make out the words. "It's Hebrew," he said. "What's she saying?"

"It's one of those Israeli state lottery sound trucks," the Rabbi said. "The voice of Western liberalism is telling people they can win twelve million shekels if they pick the right number."

Petra said in Hebrew, "This is the first time I have heard them advertise the lottery in the Old City."

"At least they had the decency to wait until Ramadan was over," the Rabbi noted.

Sweeney took hold of Aown's wrist and pushed up the shirt sleeve to see his wristwatch. Aown, annoyed, jerked his arm free.

The Doctor slid a glass filled with tea across the table to the American journalist. Sweeney, his brow creased, seemed lost in thought. "What? Oh. None for me. I'm not a tea drinker."

"Well, we won't oblige you, will we, Isaac?"

But the Rabbi, his eyes glazed over, was in another world. "If I am to survive after all, there is no hope for me," he whispered. Then he remembered Hertzl's famous dictum and brightened. "To succeed in a great enterprise," he murmured, "it is necessary to be without hope."

His lips kept forming words long after sounds ceased to emerge from his throat.

FORTY-SIX

A VELVETY DUSK SETTLED LIKE SOOT ON THE ROOFS OF THE OLD City. High on the Temple Mount, the golden dome of the great mosque seemed to tarnish in the deepening shadows. Along the narrow cobblestone streets, shop owners winched metal shutters down over store windows as the last tourists started back toward their hotels. Arab men in Western clothing crowded into coffee shops and plucked the backgammon boards off the shelves and talked in excited undertones of Abu Bakr's stunning triumph over the Jews. At seven, they interrupted their games to crowd around giant color television sets and catch the latest news bulletin: two buses with blackened windows, preceded and followed by a flotilla of police cars, had been spotted heading north from Haifa toward the Lebanese border; the Isra'ili Prime Minister, under heavy fire from the opposition, which was calling for a vote of no-confidence in the Knesset, had scheduled another press conference for an hour from now; in the great mosque of Al Aksa on the Temple Mount, the faithful had already begun offering thanks to Allah for the release of the imprisoned Palestinian warriors.

Outside the Jaffa Gate, a large bus crawled up the ramp and into the Old City. In the bus window, a cardboard sign read, in English: "Maccabean Friars of the Holy Order of the True Cross." Hardly anyone paid attention as the bus pulled to a stop in front of the steps leading to David's Tower. Priests and friars and monks of every religious order were a common sight in the streets of the Old City. With a hiss, the doors of the bus swung open and forty-seven friars—all dressed in identical coarse brown robes tied with rope belts, the hoods drawn low over their heads, their heads bowed, their hands folded across their chests—filed off. Walking in twos, they started down Latin Patriarchate Road. The hems of their robes dusted the ground, concealing the fact that the friars were all wearing black Reebok sneakers. The occasional clank of metal drew a sharp look from one of the friars at the head of the column. Several Christian Arabs, locking up their shops for the night, stepped back and crossed themselves as the procession filed past. One pious old woman bowed from the waist to the lead friar, who bowed back to her. At Saint Peter Road, the procession jigged right and then left again through the now deserted streets, coming upon the Casa Nova Hospice from the rear.

As the friars filed past the little used back door of the Hospice, eight figures detached themselves and ducked inside. The others continued on through an alleyway that ran along the side of the Hospice to Casa Nova Road. The friars sank to their knees, as if in prayer, at the foot of the hospice wall, all but vanishing in the murky shadow at the side of the building. The friar at the head of the procession surveyed the road, then pumped his arm once. Instantly six of the friars dashed across and disappeared into the side streets on the other side. In three minutes, the last of the friars had sprinted across the road and started into the maze of alleyways and passageways that cut through the neighborhood, at the heart of which was an abandoned bathhouse.

FORTY-SEVEN

AN THE DARKENED WAR ROOM OFF THE PRIME MINISTER'S office, Zalman Cohen paced back and forth in front of the bank of telephones, fanning his puffy face with a sheaf of papers. Elihu stood motionless in front of a window staring at his reflection without seeing it. He envied Baruch, who was younger and fitter and had talked his way onto the raid as a representative of the interagency Working Group. Waiting, for the *katsa*, was sheer agony; it was psychologically easier to be on a raiding party than in a command center dreading each ring of the telephone. The chief of the general staff, a barrel-chested general with a crimson beret jammed under an epaulet, growled orders into a satellite phone fitted with a scrambler; troops were being deployed in anticipation of Arab protests if and when the so-called *mujaddid* was shot to death by Israeli soldiers. The Shin Bet people, along with the Minister of Defense and two other members of the inner cabinet, helped themselves to fruit juice at a sideboard and talked in undertones. The Prime Minister, the only tranquil person in the room thanks to his legendary self control, sat alone at the oval conference table smoking one of the rare cigarettes he permitted himself. Every now and then he would grip it between his thumb and three fingers, a habit he had picked up from a Polish uncle, and pluck it from his mouth to watch the end burn down, as if there was a message waiting to be deciphered in the glow of the embers. On the blotter in front of him were the two versions of the communiqué that Cohen had prepared for the eight o'clock press conference. Both versions started out by explaining that the release of the Palestinian prisoners had been announced to give the General Staff commando unit time to raid the hideaway where Abu Bakr was believed to be holding Rabbi Apfulbaum; that all the prisoners demanded by the hostage takers were still in Israeli custody, where they would remain for the foreseeable future. The first version of the communiqué went on to disclose that the raiders had succeeded in freeing the Rabbi. The second version announced that Apfulbaum had been killed by his abductors before the Israeli soldiers could reach him. Both versions ended with a solemn declaration of the government's intention to never give in to terrorist blackmail. "There is no rear area in the war against Islamic fundamentalist terrorism," Cohen had the Prime Minister saying. "There are no non-combatants. All of our citizens—the private patrolling West Bank roads, the mother crossing Jerusalem on a number eighteen bus, the Rabbi returning from Yad Mordechai—are on the front lines."

A red telephone on the table purred. The men drinking fruit juice around the sideboard broke off their conversations and wheeled toward the sound. The *katsa* took two steps in Cohen's direction as the director of the Prime Minister's military affairs committee reached out and snatched the phone off its hook.

"Cohen," he mumbled. He listened, nodded once, nodded a second time and dropped the phone back on its cradle. "They're inside the Old City," he announced. "Operation *Simon Bar-Kokhba* is underway."

FORTY-EIGHT

KNEELING ON THE FLOOR, AZZIZ AND AOWN HOVERED OVER THE backgammon set, flinging the dice out of small leather cups, bleating like sheep as they slapped the plastic pieces down on the board. At the field radio, Petra toyed with a dial, tuning in the voice of an Israeli officer broadcasting from a command car leading the convoy up the coast road north of Acre. She plugged in a headset and handed it to Doctor al-Shaath. He pressed one of the earphones to an ear and listened intently. "They're passing the Misrafot Junction," he announced, "five kilometers south of the Lebanese border and ten kilometers south of the United Nations post in the Lebanese town of Nakura. What time do you have?"

"Seven twenty-five."

"Another twenty minutes and the prisoners should be free."

At the table, the Rabbi slurped his second glass of sweetened tea. Some of the liquid trickled from the corner of his mouth into the stubble on his chin, but he didn't appear to notice. Sweeney took a quick look at the front door of the hideaway—both steel bars had been driven home, bolting the steel-plated door shut. He stretched his lanky body and got up and came around the table and squatted down next to Apfulbaum.

"Rabbi."

Smacking his lips gleefully, Apfulbaum closed one eye and scrutinized the blurred figure of Sweeney with the other. "Well, if it isn't the *goy* journalist with the chip on his shoulder! I was, believe it or not, planning to make a formal statement about my incarceration.

Do you have a pencil? Are you all ears?" Apfulbaum giggled into his glass of tea. "Be careful to spell my name correctly—it's I. Ap*ful*-baum, with an f after the p—and quote me accurately, that way my solid arguments will resist your efforts to liquefy them."

Sweeney threw a quick glance over his shoulder. The Doctor was still glued to the earphone. On the floor, Azziz knocked off one of Aown's pieces. His brother chopped the air with an open palm in exasperation. "Rabbi," Sweeney whispered, gripping Apfulbaum's arm, "there's something extremely import—"

"I don't deny I said Torah Judaism and Koranic Islamism are *Allah*-oriented, but I want to explicate, I want to put it in context. Up to now I've been too busy studying Torah to go to a dentist, which is why I had difficulty sinking my teeth into the Koran."

Sweeney tightened his grip on the Rabbi's arm. "The Israelis know where you are—"

"I am absolutely convinced the creation in 1948 of the Garden of Eden, underneath which rivers are thought to flow, was a religious event. Are you copying this down word for word, Sweeney? Get a single comma wrong and your name will be forever engraved on my feces list. Gehenna will freeze over before I give you another interview. Here's the deal: I would shoot my enemies instead of my friends if I had a weapon smart enough to distinguish between the two."

"For god's sake, Rabbi, *listen* to me," Sweeney pleaded. "Any moment now the Israeli Army is going to come bursting in—"

Apfulbaum set his glass down on the table and ran a finger around its rim, producing a soft moan. "For me, Genesis 17:8—that's where Allah gives Ibrahim and his seed *all* of the land of Canaan—is the heart of the heart of the Koran . . ." The Rabbi's closed eye opened wide. He swayed drunkenly toward Sweeney. "*What did you just say?*" he sputtered.

"Rabbi, I want you to stand up and walk with me, very casually, back to the back room. If the Doctor asks where we're going, I'll say you have to urinate."

The Rabbi shuddered like a wet dog coming out of the rain. "For too long we Arabs were a people without a Renewer . . ." His voice trailed off. He screwed up his face and asked slyly, "So how do you know they're going to come bursting in?"

Sweeney checked over his shoulder again. "The sound-truck advertising the state lottery," he whispered. "It's a signal. It means the raid is underway." He tugged at the Rabbi's elbow. "They could be taping explosives to the door right now. We have to get to the back—"

"Taping explosives," Apfulbaum repeated. He tilted his head and chewed on the inside of a cheek. "To the door." He thought he detected a flaw in the story. "How could they have found me?"

"They found *me!*"

Apfulbaum's mouth sagged open, baring a set of rotting teeth. A mournful yowl emerged from the back of his throat. "*Ish-ma-el!*"

Startled, the el-Tel brothers looked up from their game. The Doctor turned away from the radio. The Rabbi's arm swept out, knocking over his glass and the pewter pot, splashing tea on the table. "The *goy* journalist," he cried, his voice a raspy shriek, "is a Jewish spy. The lottery truck was a signal." Spittle flew from his mouth as the words spilled out. He punched at Sweeney but the journalist brushed off the feeble blows. Tears began to stream down the Rabbi's face. "Ohhhhhh, I told you this would be the last supper but you wouldn't listen, would you? The Isra-ilis aren't delivering any Arabs to any border. They're on the other side of our *door.*"

Sweeney swallowed hard. "He's ranting—"

The Doctor gestured with a forefinger. Aown pitched his ancient Webley to Petra as he and Azziz dove for the AK-47s. The Doctor barked at them in Arabic, "He says the journalist is a Jewish spy. Azziz, Petra, be quick, get them into the back room. If you hear shooting, execute them both immediately."

The Rabbi and Sweeney were hustled at gun point into the inner sanctum. The Doctor pressed his ear against the door and closed his eyes and listened. He motioned to Aown. "Slip out and take a look around. If the Jews are really outside, get off at least one burst to warn us. If nobody is there, sit outside with your back to the door. I'll let you in when we're sure the first group of prisoners has been released."

Stuffing two extra clips and two grenades into his pants pockets, Aown put the AK-47 on automatic, cocked it and snapped in the folding stock so he could use the weapon it as if it were a hand gun. "If I should be killed—"

The Doctor touched Aown lightly on the forehead. "Those who fall in battle are rewarded with eternal life."

Aown slid back one of the bars. "Life is beautiful but the death of a martyr is more beautiful," he whispered in a quivering voice.

The Doctor hauled the pearl handled Beretta from his breast pocket and worked back the slide on the top of the barrel, chambering the first round. Behind him, Petra was carrying the carton filled with spare clips and grenades and gas masks into the inner sanctum. He put his ear to the door again, then nodded at Aown, who dragged back the other bar, opened the door a crack and ducked out of the hideaway. The Doctor slammed the door and drove home the bars. Hurrying into the back room, he pulled the door closed behind him and drove home the bars on that door, too. Azziz had lashed Sweeney's feet to the legs of the heavy chair the Rabbi's secretary had been bound in, and was fastening his wrists behind the chair with a length of wire. His head bobbing in agitation, Apfulbaum collapsed into his chair and held out his wrists. "I must have my manacles," he groaned like a child deprived of a plaything. Petra looked at the Doctor. When he nodded, she snatched the manacles off the floor and snapped them onto his bony wrists. The Rabbi croaked in relief. Azziz dragged over the other chair. The Doctor sat down on it facing the door and laid the Beretta across his knees. Azziz, worried sick about his brother, cocked his AK-47 and settled back against the Gaza Central Import-Export Bank calendar. Petra spun the cylinder on the Webley, checking to make sure it was loaded, then cocked the pistol and, gripping it with both hands, sank onto the floor with her spine against the wall.

"Gar-dens of Eee-den," the Rabbi sang under his breath in the ethereal voice of a choir boy, "un-der-neath which ri-vers flow."

FORTY-NINE

HIS FINGER CARESSING THE COLD TRIGGER OF THE AK-47, AOWN drropped to one knee at the top of the narrow staircase. He had been through every nook and cranny of the building, in the pitch darkness, many times, and knew it as he knew the alleyways of Abu Dis, the Palestinian suburb of East Jerusalem in which he'd been raised. He bent forward and listened to the hollow emptiness of the bathhouse below. In his mind's eye, he tried to imagine what paradise would be like. Would the beautiful gardens, where the tears of his mother were transformed into roses and jasmine, have different flowers at different seasons? Would the flowing rivers dry up like wadis in the summer? Would there be different seasons? Would the sky cloud over? Would there be thunderstorms or never ending sunshine? If never ending sunshine, would the heavenly mansion of perpetual bliss have a roof? Would his skin turn black like an African's? He himself loved the way dogs curled their tails between their hind legs and cringed under beds at each bolt of lightning, and the damp breath of the cool air on his cheek after a summer thunderstorm. The eternal life that awaited him, so promised the *mujaddid*, Abu Bakr, would clearly not disappoint him. The more so if he were to die a martyr. But if there were no bone-dry summers, and no thunderstorms . . .

Aown's eyes had grown accustomed to the darkness. Hugging the wall he started down the narrow flight of stairs. Several of them creaked under his feet. He stopped half way down to listen again. Somewhere in the labyrinth of cubicles a rat scuffed over the cracked tiles of the floors. A shutter slapped lightly against an inside wall.

Could it be that the American journalist had somehow led the Jews to the bathhouse? The fact that the Doctor, whom Aown considered infallible, had sent him to scout meant that it was a genuine possibility. He must be careful not to jump at shadows, lest he alarm the people in the neighborhood and give away the location of the safehouse. But he would fire off all thirty rounds in the clip at the first human body that stirred. Stealing down the steps, crouched low, swinging his AK-47 in a wide arc at each doorway, Aown began working his way through the maze of tiled baths. He lingered at the top of one of the two wide staircases leading to the ground floor and listened. He could almost make out the evening breeze whispering through the warren of corridors and changing rooms under his feet.

Peering into the dark emptiness, Aown started down the stairs. One by one he explored the changing rooms, with their doors hanging half off their hinges, their ceramic hooks long since pried from the walls by souvenir hunters scavenging through the abandoned building. Turning down one corridor, he could make out the high double door of the enormous reception room looming ahead. Sinking onto one knee with his back to the wall on the corridor-side of the double door, he peered into the darkness and listened again, then wheeled around the corner and lunged across the threshold into the room, landing on a small mountain of soft coarse fabric that had not been there the last time he had passed. Climbing to his feet, he kicked at the fabric with his shoe and groped for a shred of logic to explain its presence. Who would have stored cloth in the bathhouse, where anyone could sneak in and steal it? As his thoughts raced, a ghost-like luminous streak floated out of the darkness in front of him. In the blink of an eye the shadow transformed itself into a goggled human figure and a long soot-blackened grooved commando blade slipped between Aown's scapula and rib, severing the pulmonary artery of his heart. There was no pain, only a sudden and total loss of muscle strength as hands reached out of the blackness to lower him noiselessly to the ground. Aown actually felt his spirit floating free of his body as many feet raced past him. As the blackness turned into blinding brilliance, the answer came to him. Of course! Why hadn't he seen it before? Not a phrase, not a word in the holy Qur'an was there by chance. The angel Jibril had not whispered into the Messenger's ear the words *Garden* of Eden, but *Gardens*. Which surely meant there was one Garden with never ending sunshine, and another for those, like Aown, who loved the crack of summer lightning and the damp breath of the cool air on their cheeks after a thunderstorm.

FIFTY

IN THE INNER SANCTUM, THE MINUTES CREPT BY WITH THE SPEED of measuring worms. When he wasn't staring at the reinforced door as if he could see through it, Azziz would glance at his watch. He imagined his brother stealing through the tangle of corridors and rooms on the first two floors of the building. If there were Jews hiding down there in the darkness, Aown would smell them; he would skid a grenade into one of the changing rooms and leap through a back window and escape through the maze of dark alleyways.

And still no sound came from the bowels of the bathhouse. "He is gone eight minutes," Azziz finally announced.

Petra lowered her pistol. "If there are Isra'ilis in the building," she said in a low voice, "Aown would have come across them by now."

"I tell you he was ranting," Sweeney insisted from the heavy chair.

"Takes two to tango," the Rabbi fretted, kneading the silver worry beads. "I have it on good authority that you can't have a vicious circle unless both parties hold up their end."

"Isaac, precisely what exactly did the journalist tell you?" the Doctor demanded.

His bulging eyes fixed on the single bulb dangling from the ceiling, the Rabbi sucked on one of the worry beads. After a moment he replied, "We met on the no-man's land of English. He said the sound-truck was a signal. He said the raid was underway. I asked him how the Isra'ilis had found me. He said they had found him. Un-der-neath which ri-vers flow, lah di dah."

Sweeney fidgeted in the chair. "Can't you see he's deranged?"

"How is it possible for Sweeney to have led the Isra'ilis to us?" the Doctor asked in Arabic. He addressed Petra. "You are sure you were not followed when you brought him here?"

"We took the usual precautions," she said. "That is out of the realm of possibility."

"I destroyed his camera and his cellular phone and his wrist watch," Azziz said. "I destroyed even the spare rolls of film."

"The only thing we did not destroy was the device in his ear," Petra said.

The Doctor remembered Sweeney's description of his hearing disability. *I suffered a concussion and damage to the middle ear of my left ear—there was some kind of injury to a membrane.*

Was it the tympanic membrane?

That rings a bell.

The Doctor moved to the door and rubbed his bruised forehead against the steel plating. The coolness calmed the migraine lurking behind his eyes. "Break open the hearing aid," he ordered with a sigh, "and tell me what you see."

Petra leaped to her feet and snatched the small plastic button out of Sweeney's ear. She set it on the floor and smashed it with the butt of her Webley and sifted through the pieces. "There is micro-circuitry with what looks like minute transistors. There is a tiny speaker, a round wafer-thin battery."

Sweeney's wrists strained at the wires behind his back.

The Doctor frowned. "The circuitry could be transmitting a signal—"

"I checked the hearing aid with my meter," Petra reminded him.

"It could be programmed to transmit in short bursts at intervals. If you failed to test it when it was actually transmitting . . ." The Doctor had another idea. "Petra, fetch the otoscope from my medical valise in the corner. You can't miss it, it's an instrument for looking into ears. You flick the switch in the handle to turn on the light. I want you to look in his bad ear and tell me precisely what you see."

As Petra approached Sweeney, he angled his head away. Azziz came over and jammed the muzzle of his AK-47 into Sweeney's good ear. Kneeling next to Sweeney, Petra fitted the end of the otoscope into his left ear and switched on the light. Leaning forward, she closed one eye and peered into the instrument with the other. "I see three jagged-shaped holes in what looks like a membrane. Two are big enough to pass a pencil through. They are rimmed with white scar tissue. The membrane itself is grayish-brown and covered with crusts. There is a tiny pearl—white and glistening and hard—near one of the perforations."

"That will be a subepithelial pearl of cholesteatoma. Continue."

"Through one of the holes in the membrane I can see a small white bulb-shaped object—it looks not unlike the eatable end of a spring onion. It seems to be floating—"

"That will be the head of the stapes," the Doctor announced triumphantly in English. "It will have been detached in the Beirut explosion you talk about, Mr. Sweeney. Which means your left ear is permanently dead—the hearing aid you wear is not there to augment your hearing because, with a floating stapes, there is no possibility of sound being transmitted to the inner ear." The Doctor switched back to Arabic. "I blame myself—I should have thought of it before. His hearing device must be programmed to send a signal." He spoke again in English. "How often does it broadcast?" he asked Sweeney.

Sweeney drew a quivering breath. The Israelis would break through the outer door at any instant; his only chance was to respond to the Doctor's questions and hope he asked more of them. "I was told there would be five signals, each lasting a tenth of a second, at eighteen minutes to the hour and eighteen minutes past."

"What is the range of the signal?"

"Depending on whether it's broadcasting from inside or outside, somewhere between two hundred and two hundred and fifty meters."

"Excarnate him, excarnate him, for God's sake," the Rabbi whimpered, his feet dancing in agitation. "Betrayed us, deserves death. Don't spell his name right in the Book of Deeds. Ship him out to the burning fiery furnace, DOA in Gehenna."

Sweeney, faint with terror, closed his eyes. His breath, suddenly sour, came in shallow gasps. Bile rose to the back of his throat. He was bone-weary and drained of energy. It had been a long hard road from Seattle to Beirut to Israel. His luck, which had been running for him when the mortar shell landed next to his car in Beirut, had run out in a shabby bricked-in room on the third floor of an abandoned Jerusalem bathhouse. The only thing really surprising was that it had lasted as long as it did.

"Shoot him," the Doctor instructed Azziz.

Grabbing a pillow off the cot to dampen the noise, Azziz angled the AK-47 and flicked it onto single shot and motioned with his chin for Petra to step away. As she backed toward the cot, the Rabbi repeated the order. "What are you waiting for? Excarnate the son of a—"

He was interrupted by a series of muted dry explosions—it sounded as if a string of Chinese New Year's firecrackers had gone off in a distant room. The reinforced front door to the hideaway, blown neatly off its hinges and bolts, slammed inward onto the tiled floor. Men grunted as they flooded in. Azziz sank to one knee behind Sweeney and sucked in his breath and flicked his weapon back onto automatic and aimed it at the door. Petra plucked the Webley off the cot and flattened herself against the back wall. The acrid stench of nitroglycerine seeped under the door. The Doctor, shaken, crouched next to the Rabbi.

"Do what you have sworn to do, *ya'ani*," Apfulbaum goaded him. "Think of my death as my modest contribution to our vicious circle."

Through the reinforced thickness of the door, a hard voice speaking through a bullhorn declared in English, "We know you are in there, Doctor al-Shaath. If you want to save your life, as well as the lives of your comrades, do not kill the Rabbi, do not kill the journalist. We will exchange their lives for yours and those of your compatriots who are with you."

"The light bulb," the Doctor whispered.

Azziz came around under the dangling bulb and, gripping it with a handkerchief, unscrewed it. The room was plunged into a tunnel-like blackness.

"I know you can hear me, Doctor al-Shaath. We are all soldiers here. Let us talk soldier to soldier. We can respect a soldier who fights on the opposing side as long as he doesn't execute defenseless people."

"They are putting explosives on the door," Apfulbaum warned. "For God's sake, Ishmael, shoot me before we both lose our nerve."

In the perfect darkness, the Doctor started to feel for the knob of bone behind his prisoner's ear. "I have lost my way," he breathed. "I can no longer distinguish the straight path."

"I will lead you down it," the Rabbi told him.

"Rabbi Apfulbaum, Mister Sweeney," the voice of the bullhorn called. "Call out if you are still able to." Someone else shouted over the bullhorn in Arabic, "If you want to live, do not harm the Rabbi and the American journalist. If you kill them, make no mistake about it, we will kill you."

"What did you do to my brother?" Azziz screamed.

"The one who came down the stairs surrendered without a struggle," the voice answered in Arabic. "He is alive and well and has been taken prisoner."

"You lie through your teeth!" Azziz screamed through tears of rage.

"Ishmael, I can tell you now," the Rabbi confided urgently. "I'm not the spiritual leader of the Jewish underground group *Keshet Yonathan.* I am *the* leader. It's me who tried to blow up the Dome of the Rock Mosque. It's me who sent those letter bombs to Arab mayors. It's me who excarnated those Arabs at Hebron's Islamic College. It's me, Ya'ir!"

"I do not believe you, *ya'ani.* You are saying this in order to provoke me into shooting you."

"I swear it, as God is my witness." Apfulbaum's voice broke with emotion. "Only bring me a stack of bibles, I will swear it in a way that will convince you."

Sweeney's brittle words echoed through the dark room. "I believe him."

The Rabbi's fingers wrapped themselves around the Doctor's wrist. "Ishmael, kinsman, cousin, brother, let us collaborate on my death," he pleaded, his mouth bone dry, his voice taut. "Let us, you and me together, shipwreck this stinking peace treaty before the crazy politicians can sign it." He had difficulty finding the right words, difficulty spitting them out once he found them. "Don't you see it? The Messiah alone, the Renewer alone are less than blades of grass in a pasture. But together we can generate a windstorm that will destroy the peace process. My God, the *khamsin* from the furnace of hell will be nothing compared. Think vicious circle, Ishmael—kill me and my people will take revenge for my death, then your people will take revenge for the revenge." Apfulbaum bared his teeth as a giggle made its way up from his gut. He could feel the Doctor wavering. "You abducted me, you brought the goy journalist here in order to back yourself into a corner. You invited a witness so that your identity would be known; so that the story would end in martyrdom. For me. For you. It's the ultimate *hejira*, the ultimate retreat from unbelief. Ishmael, Ishmael, even with tunnel vision you ought to be able to see the straight path. If you can't live in an Islamic state governed by Islamic law and the example of the Prophet, if I can't live in a Jewish state governed by the Torah and the example of our prophets, let's seek religious asylum together in Paradise and sit with the Prophets and Kings and Caliphs. Let's join the martyrs at the right hand of God. You and me, Ishmael, the Islamic Renewer and the Jewish Messiah, side by side. A real *simcha*, a real joy."

And still the Doctor could not bring himself to shoot his friend. "I cannot take your life, Isaac. You are a *kafir*, an infidel who rejects the message of Islam. You will be condemned to everlasting hell, where the bodies of the damned are doused in sheets of fire, where their faces are scalded with molten copper. *How can I do this to you?*"

"Doctor al-Shaath, your time is running out. Open the door and step out with your hands over your head and we will treat you as prisoners of war. No harm will come to you."

When another voice repeated the message in Arabic, Azziz said in a savage whisper, "My only wish is to kill many Jews before I die."

"Ishmael, I have the solution to our little problem," the Rabbi said quickly. "Because of our common belief in one God, the *Epistle on Martyrdom* of the Rebbe Moses ben Maimon permits Jews to save their lives by converting to Islam. How could it have escaped me! If a Jew can convert to Islam to avoid death, he can convert to avoid life!"

"You would actually convert—"

The Rabbi began rocking back and forth in his chair in the traditional Jewish posture of prayer as he recited the *shahada*, the Muslim confession of faith that is said when converting to Islam and at the moment of death: "*Ash'hadu an la illahu ila Allah wa'ash'hadu anna Muhammadan rasulu Allah*"—"*I bear witness that there is no God besides Allah, I bear witness that Mohammed is the messenger of Allah.*" Apfulbaum bent his head as if bowing to God. Tears of ecstasy flooded his eyes. "My Lord has guided me to a straight path, a right religion, the creed of Ibrahim . . . my living, my dying belong to God."

Sweeney whispered, "You are both loony."

"Doctor al-Shaath, this is your last warning—"

The Doctor's fingers, working furiously, located the knob of bone behind the Rabbi's ear. He brought the Beretta up and breathed twice on the tip of the barrel to warm it, then touched it to the spot under the bone. "If you had been born into the Qur'an," he murmured in Hebrew into the Rabbi's ear, "you would have been my brother."

The Rabbi, his sightless eyes burning with fever, responded in Arabic. "If we had read Torah together in Brooklyn," he moaned in a child's voice, "you would have been family."

The Beretta coughed up its bullet. The Rabbi, instantly brain dead, collapsed into Abu Bakr's arm. The Doctor accepted the weight as if it were a gift from God. "Before the day is done," he whispered, "you will be in the holy of holies of the Third Temple, you will pronounce the unpronounceable name of God that only the most pious are permitted to—"

FIFTY-ONE

IN THE WAR ROOM OFF THE PRIME MINISTER'S OFFICE, THE WELL of conversation had long since run dry. The clock on the wall read twelve minutes to the hour; two floors below, half a hundred journalists were gathered for the press conference due to start on the hour. The Prime Minister, a cigarette bobbing on his thick lower lip, was rereading the two versions of his remarks for the dozenth time when the red telephone purred. Zalman Cohen had the receiver pressed to his ear before the ring faded.

"Cohen." He listened. "Hold on," he said testily. He held the phone out to the *katsa*. "It's Baruch. He says he'll only speak to you."

The *katsa* walked over and accepted the phone. "Elihu here."

He listened intently, nodding slightly once, twice, a third time. Then he said, "Thank you, Baruch." Then he set the phone back on its cradle and stared at it for a long moment.

Cohen bleated, "Well?"

"How did it go, Elihu?" the Prime Minister asked gently.

"My man Sweeney is alive. He was tied to a chair, in the darkness he tipped it over when they blew open the door. He's got a splitting headache from his head hitting the deck, and two bullets in the fleshy part of his shoulder, but he's going to be all right. The vests saved the boys who came through the door. Two of them were wounded, one in the neck, one in the hand, but neither seriously."

"And Apfulbaum?"

"Dead."

"Dead how?" Cohen demanded. "How dead?"

"He was killed by a small caliber bullet fired at point blank range into his brain while he was tied to a chair."

Cohen beamed. "Abu Bakr killed him!"

"What about Abu Bakr and the others?" asked the chief of the general staff.

"Abu Bakr fired at the flashes with his pop gun. The first man in was Dror. As all revolvers pull to the right, he had the good sense to plunge to *his* right, which may have saved his life. He put a bullet through Abu Bakr's eye."

"The bastard was already blind," cracked Cohen, but nobody smiled.

"The night vision glasses gave our boys the edge," Elihu continued. "A second terrorist was almost decapitated by a burst of soft-nosed bullets from an Uzi. When the smoke from the explosion cleared, they discovered a young woman cowering against a wall with the barrel of a pistol in her mouth. Before they could shoot her, she pulled the trigger."

"Everything came up roses," exalted Cohen. "The Renewer shot to death a helpless Rabbi tied to a chair. Our people shot the Renewer. Tit for tat. Who could ask for a better denouement?" Several of the Shin Bet people murmured in agreement.

"I can think of a better denouement," Elihu said with quiet intensity. The room fell still; he could feel the eyes of the Prime Minister and the generals and the Shin Bet mandarins on him. "We're back to square one," he said. "We're back to where we were when I was running raids into occupied Palestine and shooting terrorists in their beds." He remembered quoting a passage from the Torah to his commandos on his swansong raid into Nablus and dredged up the words now. "'*Life shall go for life, eye for eye, tooth for tooth, hand for hand.*' The Abu Bakr Brigades live by the same creed. One of them will exact vengeance, then we'll exact vengeance for the vengeance."

"*Occupied Palestine!*" Cohen could not contain himself. "The *katsa* forgets who he is and where he is."

"Correct me if I'm wrong," the Prime Minister said, addressing Elihu with evident sadness. "I don't recall ever hearing those words cross your lips before."

Elihu, never one to be intimidated by rank, shot back, "It's high time we called things by their real name. The late demented Rabbi Apfulbaum and his cronies called Judea and Samaria *liberated* Palestine. The entire world thinks of it as *occupied* Palestine. The occupation has corrupted our souls. Our citizen army, created to defend this sliver of a Jewish state from the sea of Arabs around us, has become an army of occupation."

With a visible effort, the Prime Minister pushed himself to his feet. "I am relieved that your man Sweeney came out of this in one piece," he informed the *katsa*. "Please convey my personal thanks when you see him." He crumpled one of the two typed speeches and tossed it into a waste basket. "I will with great reluctance accept your resignation when you deliver it in writing, Elihu. You've been in the forefront of our never-ending battle for survival too long. You're burned out—you need a change of scenery; you need a rest." Striding toward the door, the Prime Minister motioned for Cohen to follow him. "Time for us to go down and tell the world what heroes we all are," he said.

An Excerpt from the Harvard "Running History" Project:

As usual I had one eye glued to CNN and caught the news bulletin as it flashed on the screen—the Prime Minister appeared relieved but grim as he read his prepared statement. When he refused to take questions, CNN cut to the Palestinian Authority Chairman—he looked as if he had weathered a bad case of intestinal flu. My first reaction? The death of Abu Bakr was balanced by the death of the Rabbi. I don't mean to be crude about it but for us, for the Mt. Washington treaty, that's the best thing that could have happened. It lets everyone off the hook.

The call from Zalman Cohen came through while the Chairman was still being interviewed. "The bullet that killed the Rabbi came from the terrorist's pistol," he said gleefully. I could tell from his voice that he was celebrating the denouement. "Are you watching the Chairman on CNN?" he asked. "The son of a bitch didn't give us much help—our people found Abu Bakr on their own. Which is par for the course. You need to understand, Zachary, they can't be trusted. They condemn terrorism in public but in their heart of hearts they are very happy to keep the pot boiling. Well, now that nobody has started shooting we can come to Washington and sign your treaty. But the Palestinians are going to have to crack down on these Abu Bakr jokers if they expect us to hold up our end of the bargain."

I know why nobody likes this guy Cohen. He is a worst-case Cassandra. He believes that if something can go wrong, it will. The trouble with this attitude is that too often it becomes a self-fulfilling prophecy.

Hang on a minute. Yes, I'll take the call.

. . .

Jesus! You're sure?

. . .

How did you find out?

. . .

Thank you for letting me know.

Excuse me—I need a moment to collect my thoughts.

Yes, terrible news. That Palestinian woman I met in Paris—Lamia Ghuri—they found her body under one of the bridges early this morning.

How did she die? She'd been tied to a stanchion and executed with a single small caliber bullet fired with surgical accuracy into the brain behind her ear. Someone's trying to send us a message—the Abu Bakr brigade has a long arm.

Oh my God, it must have been me! I led them to her . . . I'm responsible for her death!

FIFTY-TWO

A QUICKSILVER DAWN SPREAD ACROSS THE JUDEAN WILDERNESS, then slipped under a low ceiling of sullen clouds to stain, in washed-out blood, the stone houses and twisting alleyways of the ancient city of Hebron, which trickled like a lava flow through a north-south *wadi* between the hills. A short walk into the *wadi*, at the entrance to the old *Kasbah*, stood the imposing fortress-like Herodian walls around the Cave of the Patriarchs, the tomb of the progenitor the Jews know as the Prophet Abraham and the Arabs call the Messenger Ibrahim. On the lower terraces of the hills surrounding the city, women collecting firewood on the backs of donkeys moved between century-old waist-high stone walls through orchards and vineyards and gardens. Above the stone walls, goats clung to the flanks of the hills, grazing with sure-footed laziness between the silvery-green leaves of the olive trees.

On one of the windswept hills dominating Hebron, a procession of mourners snaked out of Beit Avram and started down the dirt path toward the small Jewish cemetery inside the chain-link fence marking the settlement's limits. At the head of the procession, religious Jews dressed in black skull caps and black suits, their lapels slit in sign of mourning, carried a body wrapped in a white shroud on an Army stretcher. Television cameramen scurried along on either side, filming the funeral.

Far below, a cortège of religious Muslims appeared on one of the walled paths angling off from the Hebron *wadi*. They wore white skull caps and white robes and carried on their shoulders a body wrapped in a white shroud. As cameramen sprinted ahead to film them, they began the steep climb toward the Muslim cemetery a stone's throw downhill from the chain-link fence.

Israeli soldiers in khaki and Palestinian police in blue, armed with long riot batons and plastic shields, stood around in small groups on either side of the fence. Occasionally a metallic voice would blare from a walkie-talkie, then cut off in mid sentence. The Israeli colonel in charge of security chatted with his Palestinian counterpart through the links of the fence. Off to one side of the Jewish cemetery, near a white television relay truck with a dish antenna on its roof, Baruch was deep in conversation with Max Sweeney.

"Elihu never did tell me how you got into the business of spying for Israel," Baruch said.

"It's a short story," Sweeney, his right shoulder taped in bandages, his arm tucked into a sling, replied with a caustic smile. "My father was Irish Catholic, a whiskey-drinking County Cork Sweeney right down to the laces on his working class boots. He left Ireland for the proverbial streets paved with gold and wound up, God knows how, in Seattle, where he fell in love with my mother, who was Jewish. Her mother was a survivor of Bergen-Belsen. Two months shy of my seventeenth birthday, my father ran away with his boss's secretary. To get me out of the line of fire, my mother packed me off to a kibbutz in the Galilee for the summer, at which point I discovered my Jewishness and fell in love with the country. I wanted to settle here and would have, except the kibbutz secretary turned out to be a Mossad talent scout. The next thing I knew I was being interviewed by Elihu, who convinced me that if I really wanted to serve the state of Israel, I should return to Seattle and become a journalist. All that seems like a lifetime ago. I enrolled in journalism school and put in time on a bunch of small town newspapers before landing my present job. I spent four years reporting from Rome, which is where I had my first contacts with the Palestinian Authority people. The stories I wrote about them were invariably sympathetic —given my paper's reputation, my editors were delighted to publish anything critical of Israel. I portrayed the Palestinians as Davids bravely struggling against the Israeli Goliath. Because my

Arab connections were hot, I was shipped off to Beirut for four years. Gradually the Palestinians there came to trust me, too. I used to buy whiskey at eighty dollars a bottle at the St. George Hotel and wind up drinking into the early hours of the morning with the Palestinian leaders in their apartments. Later I would pass on their addresses, and the floor plans of their apartments, as well as the license plates of their cars, to the *katsa*."

"So you were the source for those commando incursions into the Lebanon and the helicopter raids that singled out automobiles on the roads and destroyed them with missiles."

"I was one of the sources, yes. When the shell exploded near my car at the height of the Lebanese civil war, I went back to Seattle for a series of ear operations, after which I was posted to Jerusalem. It was Elihu who got the bright idea of putting a hearing aid in my dead ear so the Mossad could keep track of me. When I was taken to meet the would-be suicide bomber in Gaza right after the Rabbi's kidnapping, Elihu's people homed in on the signal and knew exactly where the interview took place."

"You were taking a big risk."

Sweeney shrugged his unbandaged shoulder. "Since the hearing aid actually amplified the sounds it picked up, and since it only transmitted a signal in bursts eighteen minutes before and eighteen minutes after the hour, we figured it was pretty safe."

"When I came on the scene, Elihu had you writing stories that got you in hot water with the Israeli censors," Baruch remembered.

"My anti-Israeli, pro-Arab slant pretty much cemented my reputation with the Palestinians."

The *katsa*, watching the funeral from the edge of the Jewish cemetery, was breaking in the Mossad officer who'd been named as his replacement. The agents Elihu was running, the safehouses and ciphers he was using, had been passed on at the Mossad hideaway in Jaffa. Now he was bringing him up to date on the Apfulbaum affair. Spotting Sweeney and Baruch below him on the hill, Elihu scrambled over from the cemetery to join them. Above him, under the watchful eye of the new *katsa*, the religious Jews were lowering the body of their Rabbi into a freshly dug grave in the rust-colored earth.

"'*Ashes to ashes, dust to dust,*'" Elihu remarked. "Let's hope this miserable episode ends here."

"Did you catch Sa'adat on CNN last night?" Sweeney asked the *katsa.*

Baruch grimaced. "The rat accused us of murdering the blind *mujaddid* and demanded an international inquiry into the raid. Coming from him the accusation has a special irony."

"We had no intention of taking prisoners," Elihu reminded Baruch.

Baruch studied the ground in discomfort. "You have a short memory, Elihu."

"What am I forgetting?"

"You're forgetting that Abu Bakr had no intention of taking prisoners when he gunned down the four young Jews guarding I. Apfulbaum. You're forgetting Efrayim, whose body turned up on a garbage dump in Aza. You're forgetting the Rabbi—he may have been a crazy Jew, but he was a Jew all the same. You're forgetting the twenty-four Palestinians who were executed because they cooperated with us." Baruch studied the katsa's face; he appeared to have aged a decade in the last week. "So what's eating you, Elihu?"

The *katsa* kicked at a rusting tear gas canister. "These funerals are what's eating me. They're burying two killers on this hill as if they were national heroes."

Sweeney said, "Does that mean Apfulbaum really was the head of the Jewish underground?"

Baruch flashed a dark look in Elihu's direction. "Apfulbaum was a deranged Rabbi even before Abu Bakr terrorized him," he declared. "Speaking as a cop, I can tell you we have no reason to take anything he may have said in that room literally."

Sweeney said softly, "When he admitted he was Ya'ir, I knew it was true."

"Whether he was or wasn't Ya'ir is beside the point," Elihu said. "Look at those characters—there are a dozen Ya'irs, a dozen Abu Bakrs waiting to step into their shoes."

The Jews from Beit Avram began filing by the Rabbi's open grave. As they passed, each one dropped a handful of dirt onto the

shroud. At the foot of the grave, a tall rangy Jew with a long scraggly
beard and a singularly intense gaze rocked back and forth on the soles
of his scuffed black shoes. His side curls dancing in the wind, the
hem of his ankle-length black overcoat caressing the freshly turned
earth, he began intoning the *Kaddish*, the Jewish prayer for the dead.
"*Yisgaddal v'yiskaddash shmay rabboh b'olmoh dee v'roh chirusay . . .*"

Below, in the Muslim cemetery, the body of Doctor al-Shaath was
being lowered on ropes into a crude crypt as an austere young Imam
with a neatly trimmed beard recited verses from the Koran. Sunlight
glinted off his thick spectacles as his words drifted up the hill.

> *God has bought from the believers their selves*
> *and their possessions against the gift of Paradise;*
> *they fight in the way of God; they kill, and are*
> *killed; that is a promise binding upon God*
> *in the Torah, and the Gospel, and the Qur'an;*
> *and who fulfills his covenant truer than God?*
> *So rejoice in the bargain you have made with Him.*

Elihu raised a hand to shade his eyes and peered toward the east.
The swollen sun was slicing upward into the underbelly of a cloud.
In the fault behind the ridge of mountains, the Jordan River gushed
down from the Galilee to empty into the Dead Sea. Beyond the sea,
the hills of Edom, which burned a fiery red when the sun set into the
Mediterranean, perched like a smudge of smoke on the horizon.
From where Elihu was standing, he could make out narrow *wadis*
cutting eastward toward the Dead Sea. He had patrolled them scores
of times during the long years of military service; in the rainy season
the soldiers would strip and bathe in the icy needle-like falls spilling
down the sides of the *wadis*. Secret ravines filled with wild peach and
plum trees branched off from the *wadis*. It was in a cave in one of
these ravines that the young giant-killer David had hidden from the
mad king Saul a thousand years before Jesus. From the spine of the
central Judean hills, on which Elihu was standing, to the Dead Sea
surely had to be one of the wildest and most glorious places on the
surface of the planet.

What was it about this land, these *wadis*, these blood-tinted stone walls, that stirred, in the people who trod the Judean hills, the brutality lurking immediately beneath the beauty?

On the fringes of the funerals, mourners drifted away from the graves toward the chain-link fence. No one could say who shouted the first insult, who hurled the first stone, but within seconds the battle was raging. A group of young religious Jews leaped onto the fence and tried to scale it to get at the Palestinians, who filled the air with flying stones and beat at the fence with sticks. Two Jews fell back, bleeding from head wounds. An Arab boy was knocked unconscious, a second clutched a broken wrist. Cameramen on both sides knelt on the hill and filmed the brawl for the evening news, which only spurred the rioters on. In an age-old gesture, the young Arabs drew their *kiffiyehs* across their faces, obscuring everything but their eyes, which burned with fierce loathing. Palestinian police and Israeli soldiers came running up on both sides of the fence to separate the combatants. The wail of sirens filled the air as ambulances pulled over the slopes to pick up the wounded. Tear gas canisters rolled downhill and exploded. Voices blasted over bullhorns in Hebrew and Arabic, warning the rioters to disperse.

With the *katsa* and Baruch trailing after him, Sweeney ducked behind one of the television relay trucks. As the tear gas spread like morning mist over the hill, the Rabbi's demented cackle echoed in Sweeney's good ear. "*Let us seek religious asylum together in Paradise,*" he had said. "*You and me, Ishmael, the Renewer and the Messiah, side by side. A real simcha, a real joy.*"

"Do you know Chekhov's *Uncle Vanya?*" Sweeney called to Elihu as he reached the relay truck. "I acted in it once in a previous incarnation. There's a scene where someone asks Vanya what's new. Nothing's new, he says. Everything's old." Sweeney smothered a raw laugh. "Everything—these hills, these *wadis*, this blood feud between tribes that worship the same God—is old." He shook his head in an agony of despair. "If they really are up there," he said, "two mad hatters hanging out at the right hand of God, they've got to be laughing their deranged heads off watching their funerals."

A whiff of tear gas stung Sweeney's nostrils. Backpedaling to get away from it, he spotted something that caused him to catch his breath. On the flank of the hill, the austere young Imam in the white robe, the tall lean Jew in the black overcoat could be seen standing on small knolls behind the melee. Oblivious to the whorls of tear gas scouring the rock-pitted ground around their feet, they appeared to be taking the measure of each other over the heads of their disciples. Around them the air filled with the whetted lisp of cicadae and the sky began to grow dark, almost as if a plague of locusts had blotted out the sun.

And then the dry crack of a rifle shot reverberated through the Judean hills.